CW00926223

A Man of No Country

i

A Man of No Country

by

Philip K. Allan

A Man of No Country by Philip K Allan
Copyright © 2018 Philip K Allan

All rights reserved. No part of this book may be used or reproduced by any means without the written permission of the publisher except in the case of brief quotation embodied in critical articles and reviews.

ISBN-13: 978-1-946409-60-7(Paperback)
ISBN :13: 978-1-946409-61-4(e-book)
BISAC Subject Headings:

FIC014000FICTION / Historical
FIC032000FICTION / War & Military
FIC047000FICTION / Sea Stories

Editing: Chris Wozney
Cover Illustration by Christine Horner

Address all correspondence to:
Penmore Press LLC
920 N Javelina Pl
Tucson, AZ 85748

Dedication

To my Father, with thanks

Acknowledgements

The creation of a work such as *A Man of No Country* relies on the support and help of many around me to help bring my vision to the page. The books of the Alexander Clay series start with a passion for the Age of Sail. Mine first began to stir when I read the works of C S Forester as a child. Then, in my twenties, I graduated to the novels of Patrick O'Brian. That interest was given some academic rigor when I studied the 18th century navy under Pat Crimmin as part of my history degree at London University.

Many years later, when I decided to leave my career in the motor industry to see if I could make it as a novelist; I received the unconditional support and cheerful encouragement of my darling wife and two wonderful daughters. I strive to make sure that my work is accessible for those without a detailed knowledge of the period, or a particular interest in the sea, and it is with them that I first test my work to see if I have hit the mark. I have also been helped, yet again, by the input of my dear friend Peter Northen.

One of the most unexpected pleasures of my new career path is to find that I have been drawn into a community of fellow authors, who offer generous support and encouragement to each other. When I needed help, advice and support the most, I received it from David Donachie, Bernard Cornwell, Marc Liebman, Jeffrey K Walker and in particular Alaric Bond, creator of the Fighting Sail series of books. Finally my thanks go to the team at Penmore Press, Michael, Chris, Christine, Terri and Midori who work so hard to turn the world I have created into the book you hold in your hand.

Contents

A Man of No Country

Prologue

Beneath the cobalt blue of a Mediterranean sky, the crew of the little trading brig were sailing for their lives. She was an old ship, with timbers that had been battered by too many storms and bleached by too many summers. Her paintwork was flaking and her patched sails had been worn so thin that they were now translucent scoops in the fierce light of the sun. Her captain could feel her ancient frames creaking in protest at the exertion now expected of them and his face grew grim.

'That's the last of them, sir,' said his first mate as he came across to join him by the wheel. 'Every sail we possess has been set and drawing. I even found an old flying jib that's not seen the light of day since Michaelmas last. Do we gain on them at all?' The captain looked over the stern rail and sheltered his eyes beneath a hand. Their wake was a long streak of white drawn across the dark blue of the sea. Halfway to the horizon he could see the other ship. She was a much sleeker craft, long, low and fast. The triangular shape of her lateen sails reached skywards like the fins of a shark. Even at this distance he could tell that they were losing the race.

'We are still too slow, Silas,' the captain replied. 'We must endeavour to lighten the load and see if that will answer. Start what fresh water we still have over the side, and then get the hands to

1

work pitching the cargo into the sea.' He watched as his crew worked, their haste desperate, sparing only the occasional glance backwards towards their pursuer. They were a motley collection of men. Greeks, Bulgars, Sicilians, Lebanese, even an Egyptian. Only Silas and I are left from the original English crew that came out here all those years ago, he thought to himself. He felt a tug on one arm of his shirt, and he looked down at a curly haired boy of twelve.

'Father, why is the deck heeled over at such an angle?'

'Well, Jack, the heel of the deck is caused by the wind on our quarter,' he explained. 'It is more pronounced than is normal because we have set every sail we own, see? For once we stand in great need of haste, and I am putting at hazard our rigging that we may go all the swifter.'

'Oh, I see,' said the boy. He looked up at the profusion of sail above his head, and then back down to the busy deck. The main hatch was open now, and bundles were being swayed up from the hold. 'Is that why the men are casting our trade goods overboard?'

'Yes, Jack,' said his father. 'I would sooner save the ship than spare the cargo.'

'Mother would have been very angry if she could have seen the men doing that.'

His father smiled at the recollection of his wife. He felt under his shirt for the locket he kept around his neck and glanced at the little portrait. The boy was right. She looked tranquil enough in the miniature, but would have been furious at him for losing as much as a farthing, let alone an entire cargo. He glanced towards the ship that pursued them and his smile vanished. They were a mile closer than when he'd last looked. He could see the huge green banner that streamed out from her masthead, and the twinkle of sunlight on polished steel from her deck. For the first time since he had lost his wife he was glad she was gone. He thought about what Barbary pirates might do if they chanced to find a woman onboard. Then he glanced down at his son, and shuddered.

He returned his attention to the crew, and realised that what they were doing was hopeless.

'Silas!' he bellowed. 'Belay throwing the cargo by the board. The damned Turks are much too fast. Even if we made the old girl as empty as a beggar's pocket, they would still overhaul us.' The first mate looked over the stern rail and lifted his arms in a gesture of despair.

'What shall we do, sir?' he asked. The captain drew him to one side.

'Issue the men with weapons and make shift to defend ourselves as best we may. I shall return shortly.' He went over to his son. 'Jack, I need you to come with me,' he said. He took the boy's hand and walked across to the main ladder way that led to the deck below.

Down in his cabin he looked around for somewhere that the boy might hide. He considered the row of lockers built into the bench that ran below the window lights at the back of the space, but rejected them. That would be the first place any boarders would search. The sides of the cabin were lined with more storage lockers. He started to open doors at random but he drew a blank at every turn. Through the cabin windows the churning wake of the brig led back towards the pirate ship. It was growing closer all the time, pounding across the sea and throwing white spray up from its bow. The captain stooped down so that his head was level with that of his son.

'Jack, can you recall how you used to play hide and go seek about the ship with Uncle Silas when you were small?' The boy nodded at this. 'Good lad. Now try and think of the best place that you ever found to hide, where he never could track you down, and he was left to curse and holler for you.' The boy smiled at a recollection and pointed towards the aftermost locker.

'Over in that corner,' he said. 'There's a little hole in the floor. I got through it once, and hid amongst some dusty sacks.' The boy led his father across the cabin and opened a door. He pulled aside the clothes that hung there and pointed to a little wooden hatch in the deck.

'Of course!' exclaimed the ship's master. 'The scuttle down to the bread room. You are a clever lad!' He pulled the hatch aside and peered down. Below him was a layer of large, knobbly sacks, full of ship's biscuit. He craned his head to peer into the dark. He was trying to find the door to the room on the deck below, but all he could see was more sacks. A child who lay quite still on top of them might well pass unnoticed by a searcher who glanced through that door. He dropped to his knees and drew the boy to him. 'Now Jack, I need you to be very brave for me. I want you to hide in here once more, and whatever you hear, you must be quiet as a church mouse. Do you understand?'

'Yes, father,' said Jack. 'But what shall I do when I am found? Will it be my turn to seek?'

'No, lad, not this time,' said his father. He drew the little locket over his head and slipped it around the neck of his son. 'The men on the other ship are wicked as the devil, but they may very well miss you in here. You must lie still and silent. But should that not answer, and they chance to find you, you must tell their captain that you wish to join with them. You are young enough that they may accept you into their crew. Agreed? Good lad. Now give your old father a kiss, and in you go.'

Once the cover was fitted back in place over his head, there was no glimmer of light in the bread room. Jack held his hand up

4

in front of his face and tried to see what difference opening and closing his eyes made. The blank dark was the same. He decided to keep his eyes closed and settled back on the sacks. He could feel the discs of hard ship's biscuit through the cloth. The sharp edges jabbed through the material as he shifted around in an attempt to get comfortable. The sacks under him rustled and biscuit pieces snapped as he moved, making him freeze once more. Quiet as a church mouse, his father had said.

As he lay there his ears became accustomed to slight noises in the dark. The wash of the sea dominated, as it rushed past the oak wall of the room a few feet from where he lay. Beneath this sound he could hear other noises in the room. As he listened he became aware of a slight rustle that seemed to come from all around him. He wondered what else might be in here with him. Could there be rats? He felt his heart start to pound with rising panic at the prospect, but then he remembered the close fitting door and the lead sheets that lined the bread room to armour the precious biscuit from vermin. But the tiny sound persisted, filling the space all around him. He thought back to the last meal he had had. It had been breakfast with his father at the cabin table above his head. He could see his father's strong brown hand as he held one of the pale discs of biscuit in his long fingers and tapped it on the top of the table. One by one little white weevils had spilt out to squirm on the polished wood. He shifted around on the sacks once more and wondered if, on the whole, he might have preferred to share his hiding space with rats.

After a while he began to hear other, sharper, noises. First came the sound of his father as he barked orders on deck. Then there was the loud bang of a musket from somewhere above him. Finally he heard more distant shots, followed by the judder and crash of hulls coming together. He felt the room around him slew to one side from the collision and he almost toppled down from his hiding place. The rush of water past the outside of the hull slowed and died. Then he heard a roar of noise as of a distant crowd, a ragged volley of shots and the stamp of feet on the main deck. Quiet as a church mouse, he urged himself, but this proved harder than he had expected. He could feel the gritty dust of old ship's biscuit all over his skin and clothes. It itched around his neck and face, and penetrated far up his sleeves and breaches. He scratched at his neck and stifled a cough and then forced himself to lie still once more. In the quiet he heard more distant sounds, a scream of pain, a voice that pleaded and then a splintering crash. Now the noises were very close. A shouted order followed by the sound of furniture being overturned in his father's cabin. Suddenly a guttural voice, impossibly loud, just above where he lay, followed by the sound of laughter. Jack squeezed himself close into the sacks and held his breath.

The bread room door crashed open and flickering orange light flooded in from a lantern. The pile of sacks shifted as a few were pulled out. Jack heard the rasp of steel on scabbard followed by the rip of cloth. Ship's biscuit pattered down onto the floor, accompanied by a growl of disappointment. He tried not to breathe, but then he could hold his breath no longer. He drew in a lung full of air, felt dust catch in his raw throat and coughed. A moment later the sacks around him were pulled away, and a dark bearded face appeared in their place. It peered at him for a moment, grinned, and then a large arm shot forward and gripped the collar of his coat.

Up on deck was a scene of utter chaos. Jack saw strange men everywhere, searching through boxes, dragging up bundles of cargo from the hold while others slashed them open to root through the contents. He looked about him for any familiar faces. Most of the crew were huddled in a group in the bow being covered by three of the pirates armed with muskets. Silas, the first mate, lay near the top of the ladder way and clutched at a bloody wound in his leg. Their eyes met, and he read terror in the other man's gaze. Then two of the corsairs came over and dragged the old sailor towards the side of the brig. He cried out in pain as his wounded leg bounced across the planking. They lifted him up and with a couple of swings pitched him overboard. His cry of protest was choked off by a loud splash.

'Father!' shouted Jack. He twisted free from the hold the bearded man had on his upper arm and ran across the deck to where the ship's captain knelt with his hands tied behind his back. Two guards stood over him. 'Your head is all bloody. Are you hurt?'

'I am fine, lad,' he said, and he bent his face close to his son. 'Remember what I said,' he hissed. 'You must join them, or they will make a slave of you. Go and see their leader, over by the wheel. The tall one who wears a blue turban. He speaks fair English—' Any chance of further conversation was cut off by a kick from one of the guards that doubled his father up in pain and drove the breath from his chest. Jack avoided a lunge from the man who had found him, and dodged his way over to the wheel.

Ali Hamadu, captain of Barbary pirates, laughed aloud when Jack made his request. 'What need do I have for a little white Kafir boy?' he scoffed. 'I have plenty of corsairs to fight for me already. You will fetch a very good price back in Tunis, with your pale skin and curly hair.'

'I am worth much more to you than that!' exclaimed Jack. 'My father has shown me how to shoot and use the short sword. And he has taught me how to navigate. I know the stars, and can use a sextant to take sightings of the sun. I can plot a ship's position as well as any man.'

Ali Hamadu looked towards the ship's side, where the body of one of the pirates lay. That fool Selim, he thought, always he has to be the first to board an infidel ship. Well, he has paid for his folly this time with a pistol ball in the stomach. But his stupidity does leave me without a navigator. 'Which star gives you true north?' he demanded.

'Polaris, sir, the brightest star in the lesser bear,' replied the boy.

'We call it Aljadi, the goat,' said the captain. 'So you say you can fight, boy? But can you follow orders? Can you be ruthless, as one of my corsairs must be?'

'Yes, sir,' replied Jack. Ali Hamadu drew out his razor sharp knife, hefted the curved blade for a moment and then passed it across.

'Very well, little man, prove yourself to me. Go and cut the throat of your father.'

Chapter 1
Plymouth

Captain Alexander Clay settled back into the leather seat of the phaeton and watched with admiration the way his coxswain, Able Sedgwick, handled the carriage's two horses. They were on the final descent of the journey, down Crown Hill and into Plymouth, and sheets of autumn rain had swept out of the west to polish the cobbles till the road was slick and treacherous. Sedgwick was crouched forward in the rain and was talking to the horses in his quiet bass voice. The words were incomprehensible to the listening Clay. They must be in his native tongue, he concluded. He knew that his coxswain was a physically strong man, but what surprised Clay was the different side of him he was now seeing. In his left hand he held the wet reins with a loose but sure grip. His big arm moved, backwards and forwards, with each surge of the horses, making sure there was just the right amount of tension in the leather. Enough pressure to give the horses confidence on the wet road, yet slack enough to give them the freedom to pick their way down the slope. His other hand was wrapped around the top of the brake lever, which he dabbed on and off whenever the carriage threatened to run away from him.

9

'Might I pay you a farthing for them?' said Lydia, his new wife of four months from the seat beside him. Clay turned towards her and realised she must have been watching him for some time. He matched her smile and once again wondered how he could have won the love of such a beautiful woman. The waves of thick dark hair he had run through his fingers in bed that morning were tucked away inside her bonnet now, but that only served to emphasise the classic beauty of her oval-shaped face, with its pale skin and high cheek bones. From beneath the brim of her hat two clear blue eyes looked into his calm grey ones.

'Your pardon, my dear,' he replied. 'I hope I have not become dull. I was just wondering to myself when I shall find the limits of Sedgwick's abilities.' He waved towards the driver's seat. 'Where the deuce does a run field slave learn how to drive a carriage?'

'Do you remember after the wedding we went on our bridal tour and spent a month on my uncle's estate in Herefordshire?'

'How could I forget?' said Clay, sliding closer across the leather of the seat.

'Yes, I suppose you may hold my hand inside the carriage,' she said. 'Well, while we were so pleasantly diverted, your coxswain took the opportunity to get Chatham, my uncle's coachman, to teach him. Chatham says he has quite a gift with horses.'

'Goodness,' he marveled. 'And this in a man who has learnt to hand, reef and steer as well as any sailor, in two scant years.'

'He has also accomplished a tolerable fluency with his letters,' added Lydia. 'His writing still leaves a little to be desired, but he reads very well indeed.'

'Unlike all of his shipmates,' grumbled Clay.

'Not all of them, dear,' corrected his wife. 'He told me of a seaman who has been teaching him. I believe he said his name was Rosie, although why a sailor should have a girl's name was never made clear.'

'Rosie is what the men call Joshua Rosso. He used to be a merchant's clerk in Bristol. The two of them are messmates.'

'Might more not be made of Sedgwick, if so few of his peers are literate?' asked Lydia.

'It might indeed,' said Clay. 'I did ask him if he would like an acting warrant to be a master's mate, or even try his hand as a midshipman. He has a very easy but natural authority with the men, you know.'

'Does his race not stand against him? There cannot be many negro officers in the navy.'

'Not many, I grant you,' he replied. 'But there are a few. There is even a captain now. John Perkins is his name. He was promoted to master and commander earlier this year, and like Sedgwick, he joined the service as a run slave.'

'So how did he respond to your suggestion to advance him?' she asked.

'He thanked me for my offer, and said that he was quite content as he was. It does seem a sad waste of his talents.' The couple looked again at the broad shoulders of the coxswain, and in the moment of quiet Lydia felt the dread of her husband's impending departure steal over her like a chill mist.

'Oh, why are you not ordered to rejoin the Channel Fleet?' she lamented. 'At least I would be able to see you when the *Titan* came into port. The Mediterranean seems so very far away.'

'I expect that they have need of a frigate there, and mine was the next available,' he said. He saw the moisture in her eyes and drew her into his arms. 'Oh, Lydia, my darling. I have long since learnt that a sea officer must accept his duty without question and go to whichever corner of the world he is bidden. If being a naval officer's wife is not to drive you quite out of your senses, I fear you must learn to do the same.' She smiled through her tears and stroked his head of chestnut curls. Then she kissed him and pushed him away.

'You are quite correct, Alex,' she said. 'I have so enjoyed our last few months together it has made me selfish. I just might have wished that the corner of the world to which you were being sent was nearer at hand. Fear not, I will soon regain my composure.'

'I shall not be quite as distant from you as you fear,' said Clay. 'Hanging Jack's command may be named the Mediterranean Fleet, but they retreated from that sea almost a year ago. In the meantime the French have made much of our absence to spread their power.'

'Where will you operate then?' she asked, a little hope showing in her face.

'The fleet is principally based in the Atlantic blockading the Dons in Cadiz. An occasional resupply in Gibraltar is as close to the Mediterranean as I am likely to actually go.'

'Hanging Jack?' she queried. 'Is that what they call Admiral Lord St Vincent? It seems a little disrespectful for such an august leader.'

'The hands began to call him that after the rather firm way he suppressed an attempted mutiny aboard some of his ships earlier this year,' he explained. 'He had all the ringleaders hanged and made their messmates perform the execution. But sailors are no respecters of rank or reputation. Before he was Hanging Jack they used to call him Sour Kraut because he is reputed to never smile.'

'There is no danger that you shall ever warrant such a given name,' she said.

'Too true,' he said and favoured her with his most dazzling example. 'No, instead they call me Pipe.'

'Pipe?' she exclaimed, a twinkle in her eye. 'Why do they call you that?'

A Man of No Country

'Oh, I imagine it to be a simple play on my name – a clay pipe that you might smoke, or possibly the pipe clay that the marines use to whiten the leather of their cross belts. None of the men are impertinent enough to use it in front of me, so I have never had occasion to ask about the origins.'

Lydia laughed aloud at this, causing Sedgwick to glance around.

'We shall be coming into this 'ere town soon, sir,' he said, indicating the approaching buildings. 'Shall I go to the Crown Inn or directly to the *Titan*?' Clay looked at Lydia and raised his eye brows in inquiry. She longed to spend some more time with him, but she could tell he was eager to get onboard his ship again. His tall body leant forward in the seat and one gloved hand tapped against his knee. She felt a brief flicker of annoyance at how much less distressed he was, before she remembered his words. A sea officer must accept his duty without question.

'The *Titan* please, Sedgwick,' she ordered.

'Are you sure, my dear?' he asked. 'I am not expected before noon.'

'You have your duty to attend to,' she said, and then leant forward to whisper in his ear. 'But when you have completed that, come and find me at the inn tonight, Captain Pipe.'

*****

'Home at bleeding last,' exclaimed Sam Evans. He expanded his arms out on either side like a large bird about to take flight and sniffed at the air with a smile of appreciation. 'And for once the barky smells moderately sweet.' At six-foot-six he was the tallest member of the *Titan*'s crew. His legs spread far under the mess table and his massive frame occupied much of one side.

'That be the smell of new-hewn oak and fresh paint,' said Adam Trevan in his thick Cornish accent. 'I grant you, the dockyard have done a fair job at putting the ship to rights. You would barely know it had been through a battle not four months ago. But don't you go getting too content with that fresh smell, Sam lad. After a week at sea with us packed in her she'll reek like a charnel house privy. Be just like that London town of yours.'

The two sailors taking their ease at the mess table could not have been more of a contrast. Where Evans was huge and dark, his companion was lean and athletic. Trevan's long blond hair was tied in a neat pig tail that hung down his back. In one ear he wore a hoop of gold, while his seaman's clothes hung easily on his wiry frame. He had frank blue eyes set in a handsome face, burnt brown by his many years at sea.

'So where's Able, then?' he asked the big Londoner. 'I thought you said as how he was onboard already?' In response Evans pointed over his friend's shoulder. Trevan looked around to find a familiar figure approaching the table.

'Good evening, shipmates,' said Able Sedgwick, his smile broad in the dim light of the lower deck.

'Able!' exclaimed Trevan and Evans together, and the friends slapped backs and embraced.

'How you been getting on with our Pipe?' asked the Cornishman. 'I hear he got spliced to a right comely wench, by all accounts.'

'She is certainly a beauty, and right kindly too,' said Sedgwick. 'But truth to tell the wedding was a strange, cold affair. They are sweet enough on each other, but her family are a proud lot. Peacocks ain't in it. I reckon they look down on our Pipe as not being good enough for them.'

'That's nobs for you, all over,' growled Evans. 'Always turning up their noses at the likes of us. Still, you would have thought Pipe would be a fair catch. A post captain like him with piles of bleeding prize money to flash, what more does they want?'

'I am not sure that it is a matter of money, Sam,' explained the coxswain. 'They are noble through and through. You should have seen Lady Ashton's place.'

'Bah! That's all so much bleeding gammon,' said Evans. 'Go back awhile, and most of these grand lords will have a maid for a grandma as couldn't keep the King out of her petticoats. I used to see no end of them as a lad back in London. Dukes and Earls and the like, with noses all pointed up to the sky, but happy enough to come a scuttling out east to Whitechapel when they felt randy for a whore, or wanted to see one of my prize fights.'

'Any news as to where we might be bound then, Able?' asked Trevan. 'I heard we may not be going back to join the Channel Fleet.'

'You heard right then, Adam,' said Sedgwick. 'It's to be the Mediterranean Fleet for us, which suits me just fine. I was dreading a winter off the Brittany coast.'

'Compared with Barbados even the Med will seem devilish cold,' said Evans. 'Not as I'm complaining, mind. Don't mind a jug of bishop in the sun. Remember Madeira back in ninety five, Adam, when that bleeder Rosie tricked me into eating them revolting bean things?'

'Olives, weren't it?' chuckled the Cornishman. 'And Sean got so pissed he took on all them Yankee sailors in a mill, and you had to come and rescue him!'

While the laughter subsided, Sedgwick looked around the lower deck. More and more of the crew were now arriving on board. They poured down the ladder ways and out onto the lower deck of the frigate. Friends greeted each other with smiles and back-slaps, while old rivals met with glares or patrician disregard. The noise level had been climbing steadily as the number of seamen increased. The predominant buzz of English was threaded through with other languages – Welsh, Gaelic, Cornish, the sing-song tones of Scandinavia, the guttural growl of German. Through all this babble and swirl he could see the occasional newcomer to the ship as they picked their uncertain way through the crowd.

'Speaking of Rosie, there he is,' he exclaimed. 'Talking with that new hand. Hoy, Rosie!'

Joshua Rosso looked round at his name, and waved a friendly hand in the direction of his messmates. He had a swarthy, Mediterranean look about him with his dark curly hair, olive skin and deep brown eyes, but when he spoke his accent was pure Bristol. Once he had finished his conversation with the new volunteer he came over to join them.

'Who's your new mate, then?' growled Evans. 'Skinny little bleeder, ain't he?'

'Just one of them new volunteers who wouldn't know a back stay from his back side,' said Rosso, as he thumped down on one of the mess stools. 'Said his name was Oates, I think. He's another Bristol boy, so maybe there is some hope for him yet. Bugger me, I'm knackered.'

'Knackered!' exclaimed Trevan. 'You're fresh back from a run ashore!'

'Aye, but I just spent the last two days searching every grog shop in Plymouth for our Sean,' he said. 'And I have not found any trace of the daft bugger.'

'Have you tried the brothels?' asked Sedgwick.

'That I have, every last one.'

'No wonder you're knackered,' said Evans to general laughter.

'Why do you suppose he ain't come back from leave, then?'

asked Trevan.

'Wasn't he going to head back to his village in Ireland?' said Sedgwick. 'He got all melancholy and sick for home last commission when he clapped eyes on the Munster coast.'

'That's right,' agreed Evans. 'He kept rattling on about the green of the hills like he'd never seen bleeding grass before. You don't suppose he will have run, do you?'

'Not a chance.' said Trevan. 'With all that prize money we have yet to touch? The Sean O'Malley I know wouldn't want to leave that behind, not while there's still a mug of gin to be bought or a willing whore to be found.'

'He was talking about some girl he said he was sweet on back home,' said Sedgwick. 'He got you to write to her, didn't he, Rosie? Maybe she was warm on him too?'

'What, do you reckon he might have settled down with her?' asked Rosso

'Ha!' exclaimed Evans. 'Sean O'Malley, getting settled all regular with a girl! That'll be the bleeding day!'

*****

'So here is the choice, like,' said Liam Dougherty. 'Either you can be after marrying my daughter, or me and the lads are going to beat the shite out of your miserable fecking hide.' The farmer patted the club he held in one hand in the open palm of the other, to emphasise each word. There was a growl of approval from the group of his male relations who were assembled behind him in the barn.

'Now hush there, Liam,' urged Father O'Connell. 'There will be no need for such violence. I am sure Sean is after doing the right thing by your girl.'

17

'That's right, Father,' said Sean O'Malley. 'If there is any cause for such a demand, of course I'll oblige. But the fact is, on my honour, I never lay with the colleen.'

'Will you give me the lie to my face, and before a priest an' all?' roared the indignant parent. He pointed his club towards the upper floor of the barn. 'Didn't I catch you in that hay up there with her?'

'Sure you did, but I was only after giving her a kiss, like,' protested the sailor.

'She was as naked as Eve from the waist up!'

'Ah, now, Mr Dougherty, be fair. I didn't say as I was kissing her on the face.'

Liam Dougherty made a lunge for O'Malley, who slipped behind the large figure of the clergyman.

'Liam!' warned the priest. 'Lay no hands on this man. Away with you now, and take your family outside. Let me see if with a little calm, I can't reason with him.'

'Very well, Father,' grumbled the farmer. 'But you watch this ruffian's blarney. I thought that St Patrick cast all the serpents out of Ireland, but I'm after thinking he might have missed one.' He looked O'Malley up and down. His hostile gaze travelled from the dark hair on top of O'Malley's head, via his twinkling brown eyes, down past his short sailor's jacket, to his high waisted trousers. 'Five foot six?' he asked.

'Five seven and a fecking half,' corrected the sailor. He drew himself upright. 'Every inch of it trained top man.'

'Did you hear that, fellers?' said the farmer as he left the barn. 'Your man says he's five seven and a half. We're going to need to make that grave we dug earlier a little longer.'

'Now Sean, I have known you since you were no more than a baby,' began Father O'Connell. 'I need to hear the truth from you about all of this. You can think of it as your confession to me as a priest. Tell me straight, did you perform an act of fornication with Dougherty's daughter?'

'She's a comely enough wench to be sure, but as God is my witness I did no more than kissing and cuddling with her.'

'Are you quite sure now?' asked the priest. 'Sailor's have a reputation, you know, even this far from the sea.'

'Am I fecking sure?' exclaimed O'Malley. 'Pardon my language, Father, but I have done a fair bit of whoring in my time. I think I know when I've had my fill.'

'Very well, I believe you, Sean. And do you have any proper feelings for this girl at all?'

'That I do, Father. Did you not see the letters I wrote to her from my ship? I know she's not a reader, so I thought she might have brought them to you, so you could tell her what was in them, like?'

'She certainly didn't bring them to me, if she ever got them, Sean,' said the priest. 'And since when did you learn your letters? You were a very indifferent scholar when I tried to teach you as a boy.'

'Ah, well now, Father, when I say I wrote them it was more like dictation. It was my shipmate Rosie, Joshua Rosso that is, who did the actual setting of the words down like,' said O'Malley. 'Goodness, what a lot of this confessing I'm after doing today.'

'Sean, this is serious,' warned Father O'Connell. 'Liam Dougherty is not a man to be trifled with. I don't think as he was jesting about that grave. If you truly have feelings for this girl, why not come before me in the church and let's have you two wed properly? You may not have left her with child, but after this ruckus she will still be as good as ruined.'

'Father, I do care for the colleen, but I can't be marrying her now,' said the sailor. 'Like I said, since I joined the navy I have done a deal of whoring. I can't lie with a nice girl before I am certain I'm clean like. That's why I never took advantage of her in the hay. She was game enough, I can tell you, unbuttoning her frock like and showing me the goods. Things might have got properly out of hand if Dougherty hadn't shown up when he did. But do you see? I can't, in all honesty, marry her just yet.'

'But are you saying you will make an honest women of her in time?' asked the clergyman.

'Sure I will,' he said. 'I promise, just as soon as I can do it proper like. I'll stop my whoring, save up some of my pay and prize money and come back and do it right. But for now I have to get back to my ship in England, or they'll take me as a deserter.'

'And how exactly do you propose to get out past this mob of angry Dougherties?'

'Might you have a word with them for me, at all?' said O'Malley.

'Matters have gone a long way past the point when words will answer, Sean,' said the priest. He looked around the barn in the hope of inspiration. The only other occupant was Dougherty's mare Kerry, in her stall by the door. Father O'Connell got up from his upturned tub, and went to inspect the horse. Kerry stopped chewing hay as he entered her stall.

'Hush there, my beauty,' he said, as he ran a hand along her back. Her skin flinched a little under the contact, but she seemed otherwise content. Hanging on a rail at the back of the stall was a bridle and reins, but no saddle. Father O'Connell listened to the sound of the family out in the farmyard for a moment, before he left the horse and made his way to the back of the barn. There was a second, smaller door here. He peered out between the slats, and saw a path that led across an area of rough grazing, bordered on its far side by a farm track. He opened the door with care and peeped both ways, but could see no sign of life. Once he was satisfied the coast was clear he turned back to the sailor.

'Sean, my boy,' he said. 'Would you be knowing how to ride a horse, at all?'

'In truth I never had occasion to try, Father, but I can run along the top of a wet yard when it's blowing a fecking gale. How much harder than that can it be?'

Chapter 2
Privateer

For the first time in over four months, His Majesty's frigate *Titan* was at sea again. She had slipped out of Plymouth at high water, and as she cleared the lee of Rame Head, the full force of the westerly wind heeled her over. It was almost winter now, and the air that swept across the ship had a chill sting to it. Green waves flecked with spume battered against her bow and tossed up cascades of white water that spilt across her forecastle and streamed out of her scuppers.

Had anyone been out to enjoy a blustery walk along the cliff tops, they would have been treated to a magnificent sight. The *Titan* was a fast ship and her lofty masts bore a profusion of sail to drive her out into the Channel. Her long, freshly painted hull was a hundred-and-seventy feet from where her name was picked out in gold letters across her stern to the muscular figurehead of a titan glowering out at the world from beneath her bowsprit. As she drove on, across the strengthening wind, a thin strip of her shiny new copper flashed like the skin of a fish as it broke clear of the waves. On her quarterdeck her captain breathed a lungful of the keen air deep into his chest and smiled at his first lieutenant.

A Man of No Country

'Ah, this is more like it, Mr Taylor,' he said. 'There is nothing to compare with a good topsail gale to make one feel alive once more.'

'Or indeed to find out any faults in this new rigging that the inattention of the dockyard may have left us,' said his first lieutenant, looking aloft. George Taylor was a shorter man than his captain. He was fifteen years his senior, and had short, iron-grey hair and anxious brown eyes.

'I am sure Mr Hutchinson has it all in hand,' said Clay. 'He is an excellent boatswain, and quite as suspicious of the dockyard hands as you are. But look how well they have repaired her. See the gunwale over there? Not a trace of that ugly hole the *Immortalite* left us with.'

'No, that has been well done, sir,' admitted Taylor. 'The carpenter is less impressed with some of the repairs to the frames, but overall I am pleased.'

'A newly restored ship, almost a full complement of hands, and adventure ahead, perhaps just over the horizon,' said Clay. 'What could be better?'

'We are fortunate to have as many men as we do, sir,' said the first lieutenant. 'With so long spent on leave, I was very apprehensive that some of the Irish hands might desert. But we have them all back, although Sean O'Malley only rejoined the ship an hour before we weighed anchor, in a very indifferent state.'

'Ah, the dissipation and vice of a sailor ashore,' said Clay. 'Was he drunk?'

'Not on this occasion, sir. He was so badly battered that he had to be helped aboard. Mr Corbett reports him to have a broken clavicle and several cracked ribs. He has him bound up like a Christmas goose and confined to the sick bay till he should recover.'

'Had he been fighting again?'

'He claims to have fallen from a horse, sir,' replied Taylor. Captain and first lieutenant exchanged glances and both men burst out laughing.

'Oh, the deceptions that the people come up with to explain their misdemeanours,' said Clay. 'Pray tell, was he riding to hounds or racing in the St Leger?'

The men were still chuckling together when the *Titan*'s young third lieutenant came up the ladder way and staggered over to them across the steep pitch of the deck. Edward Preston was a pleasant looking, gangly young man of nineteen with dark hair and eyes. He saluted his two senior offices by touching a hand to the hat that he struggled to keep in place in the wind.

'I see that your mother has been feeding you up over the autumn, Mr Preston,' said Clay. 'You are in danger of filling that coat of yours at long last. Yorkshire fare must agree with you.'

'Aye, she does try her best when I am home, sir,' he replied. 'She also wanted me to thank you on her behalf for my promotion.' Clay waved the compliment aside.

'Thank yourself, Edward,' he said. 'You have amply earned your step. What was it that you wanted?'

'Begging your pardon, sir, but it was Mr Taylor I required to see on this occasion,' replied the young officer, turning to the first lieutenant. 'Mr Blake's compliments and the item is now in position and ready to be viewed.'

'Ah, that is good news,' enthused Taylor. 'Kindly pass the word for the others to gather in the vicinity of the, eh... item, and I will be down presently.'

'Aye aye, sir,' replied Preston. He hurried back below and Clay turned towards his first lieutenant.

'This all sounds very intriguing, Mr Taylor,' he asked. 'What manner of viewing do you have planned?'

'Just something that has been installed in your cabin, sir,' he replied. 'It is in way of a gift to you from your officers. Please do not press me for the particulars, as I would not wish to spoil its first effect on you.'

'How very mysterious you are, Mr Taylor! So be it, I shall push my interrogation no further.' Clay looked around the quarterdeck for a moment and indicated the *Titan*'s new sailing master, who was officer of the watch. 'Is Mr Armstrong to be part of your gathering?'

'No, sir,' replied the first lieutenant. 'Our surprise was arranged before he joined the ship. If you will excuse me, sir, I will go and check on progress. I will call for you directly.'

While he waited, Clay studied the ship's new master as he stood by the wheel. He rode the lively motion of the frigate with ease, with his legs spread apart and his body swaying with each new plunge the ship made. Jacob Armstrong was a large, rotund man in his late forties. His head was quite bald, and he wore a horse hair periwig which was held in place by a hat pulled so firmly down against the wind that only his hazel eyes could be seen beneath the brim.

'Have you settled in now, Mr Armstrong?' asked Clay as he came over to join him.

'Yes, thank you, sir,' drawled the new officer. 'The wardroom has been most welcoming.' Clay looked at him in surprise.

'Are you an American, Mr Armstrong?' he asked. The master shrugged his shoulders in reply.

'I guess that I might be so described, sir,' he replied. 'Back in the year fifty-one when I came into this world no such nation existed. I was born as British as you, sir. My family were prominent Tories in the New York colony during the revolution, so when the damned Yankees won the war, we had to depart in haste with the rest of the loyalists.'

'I see,' said his captain. 'I ask because when the Admiralty assigned you to the ship they informed me you were an expert on the Mediterranean. Was that correct?'

'And so I am, sir. My father made use of the compensation he received from the government to buy into a merchant ship on the Smyrna run. I served first as mate and then as master for most of the peace. Why, I am as familiar with that sea as I know the hairs on my head.' Clay glanced first at Armstrong's wig, and then at the twinkle in the officer's eye, and laughed out loud.

'We are ready for you now, sir,' said Taylor, returning to the quarterdeck. 'Would you kindly accompany me below?'

'Good day to you, Mr Armstrong,' said Clay. 'We will speak further. When I started my career in the navy as a boy, it was on the North American station during that very war.'

Outside the captain's suite the marine sentry snapped to attention at the two men's approach, and then held open the door. Clay ducked under the low frame, stepped into his day cabin and looked around him. The chart of the western approaches to the Channel was where he had left it on the table, and all else seemed the same. From the great cabin at the rear of the ship the sound of quiet voices drew him on, and he entered that space followed by Taylor, his face wreathed in smiles. Ahead of him was the broad sweep of glass that ran across the entire back of the ship, through which he could see the remains of the Cornish coast as it disappeared into the distance to be replaced with a growing plain of lumpy, green sea. He turned towards the sound of voices and saw his officers gathered around one of the bulkheads. On it hung a large gilt-framed oil painting of a lady in a blue dress. Staring out at him from the canvas, and holding his gaze, was the face of his wife Lydia.

'God bless my soul!' he exclaimed. 'How simply splendid!'

'Felicitations from the wardroom of the *Titan* on the occasion of your marriage, sir,' said Taylor, and the other officers all politely applauded.

'Gentlemen, you have me taken all aback! How has such a magnificent portrait come to be produced?'

'Would you care to meet the artist, sir?' asked Thomas Macpherson, the *Titan*'s Scottish marine officer.

'Above all things!' said Clay. 'But surely he cannot be aboard?' He looked from face to face and stopped at the ship's second lieutenant. John Blake was a thin young man with sandy hair and blue eyes. He had blushed as red as Macpherson's scarlet coat. 'I knew you to be a talented draftsman, Mr Blake, but I had no idea you were capable of this. The likeness is astounding. But Lydia has barely left my side these last several months. How on earth did you even contrive to meet with her, without my knowledge?'

'I will be the first to confess it was not easy, sir,' replied the young lieutenant. 'Your friend Captain Sutton arranged for me to conduct an initial sitting before the wedding with Miss Browning, as she then was. I principally used my sketches from that, supplemented by another portrait I borrowed that was in the possession of her aunt, Lady Ashton. I am delighted to hear that you believe that I have captured her likeness. I was most uncertain about the nose, and thought perhaps I had made her ears a little too small.'

'You have done it perfectly, Mr Blake,' Clay assured him. 'It is as if she were here with us. Thank you all so very much for my gift.'

*****

Two weeks later Clay was still enjoying the portrait of Lydia. He had repositioned his desk such that whenever he looked up from his work, his eyes would meet hers, and he would be reminded of the wife who waited for him at home. But it was a pleasure that was bitter as well as sweet. Sometimes, like now, gazing at her face only served to bring to mind the yawning gap between them that opened ever wider with each passing mile that the frigate sped on.

He looked away from the portrait in response to a knock on the cabin door. He had been expecting a visit from one of the frigate's collection of ungainly midshipmen, ever since the hail from the masthead had echoed down through the skylight above him.

'Come in!' he called, picking up a piece of paperwork from the desk and making sure he appeared to be studying it when the door should open. He looked up to see the figure of Midshipman Butler shamble into the cabin.

'Mr Blake's compliments, sir, and there is a sail in sight two points off the starboard bow,' he said. Clay looked at the youngster for a moment. He was stood to attention in front of his captain's desk with both his arms held down by his sides. A two inch wide strip of shirt sleeve protruded from each arm of the coat.

'How old are you now, Mr Butler?' Clay asked.

'I turned sixteen August last, sir,' replied the midshipman.

'And have you been growing particularly quick of late?'

'I am not sensible of having done so, sir,' the boy replied, looking puzzled. Clay indicated his sleeves. 'Well, I never did. I had thought that my coat was a little snugger than before we went on leave, sir.' In his mind's eye, Clay was transported back to his time in a crowded midshipman's birth, with all its fights and

28

rivalries, and laced through with the cruelty of the young. He wondered how the slow-witted Butler would cope with being teased over his coat.

'See that you have it altered,' he concluded. 'I will ask my steward, Hart to furnish you with broadcloth, and help you with the work. My compliments to Mr Blake, and I will be up directly.'

When Clay came on deck, Jacob Armstrong was locked in a heated discussion with the officer of the watch.

'I assure you, Mr Armstrong, she will just prove to be one of our merchantmen engaged in the wine trade,' insisted the young artist.

'I dare say she might, Mr Blake, but why then did she alter course the moment she saw our topsails?' asked the ship's new sailing master.

'Good morning, gentlemen,' said Clay. 'What an animated discourse you are having. Has all this been occasioned by one scrap of sail on the horizon?'

'We have a sailing brig on the bow ten miles distant, sir,' reported Blake. 'She was on a similar course to ourselves when sighted, but she has now changed direction and is heading directly away.'

'What is the ship's position?'

'We are thirty miles from the Portuguese coast with Oporto bearing north northeast, sir,' reported Armstrong.

'Get the topgallants on her if you please, Mr Blake, and let us close with your trading brig,' ordered Clay. 'I dare say she will be one of ours, but I am inclined to Mr Armstrong's view. If she should prove to be a British ship full of port wine, it is passing strange that she was not heading north from Oporto, back home with her cargo. If I understand you correctly this ship was on a southerly course.'

Philip K Allan

With her topgallants set, the frigate began to shoulder her way through the long Atlantic swell and quickly closed in on the ungainly little brig.

'She is flying British colours,' reported Armstrong as the distance dropped.

'Send up the private signal for merchantmen, if you please, Mr Blake,' ordered Clay.

'They seem to be having difficulty making their reply, sir,' reported the officer of the watch. Clay took his telescope and saw the figures of two sailors on board the brig as they hauled backwards and forwards on the signal halyard, as if trying to clear a blockage.

'When it comes to playing for time, that's one of the oldest of tricks, sir,' said Armstrong. 'Ah! Here we go.' A single flag climbed up the mizzen mast and broke out at the top. It was plain yellow.

'A yellow jack?' queried Blake. 'What kind of response is that?'

'It means he has an outbreak of disease on board,' said Clay. He lowered his telescope and looked thoughtful. 'Stranger and stranger. Order them to heave to if you please, Mr Blake, and have a boat crew ready to go across to them.'

'What is all this talk of fever, sir?' asked Taylor, as he joined the other officers by the rail.

'A trading brig on the wrong course, unable to make a correct reply who now claims to have disease onboard,' replied Armstrong. 'All very suspicious, if you ask me.'

'Matters will soon be clear. They have heaved to at last,' said Clay. He picked up a speaking trumpet from the becket by the wheel. 'Bring us to within hailing distance, if you please, Mr Blake.'

'But not too close,' added Taylor. 'We would not want any infectious miasma to drift across.'

'Ahoy there,' yelled Clay. 'What ship is that?'

'*Charlotte* of Bristol,' came the bellowed reply. 'One day out of Oporto with cargo of vine.'

'Even I can tell that is no Bristol accent,' muttered Armstrong. 'He sounds more like a German.'

'You are on a strange course for a ship bound for Bristol,' said the captain.

'Going to Lisbon, next home,' said the man.

'That doesn't sound right, sir,' said Blake. 'How would he propose to dock there if he has fever onboard?'

'Why are you showing a yellow jack?' asked Clay.

'We are having three cases of bilious fever,' said the man. 'Oporto full of it, so we are leaving.' Clay put his head on one side and listened with care.

'Can anyone hear the sound of banging?' he asked the others. 'Mr Blake, you have young ears.'

'I can, now you mention it, sir,' he replied. 'And perhaps some shouts too.'

'Might it be the delirious ravings of the sick?' suggested Taylor.

'They seem very animated for persons who are unwell,' snorted Armstrong. Clay thought for a moment, then raised his speaking trumpet to his lips again.'

'Are you master of this ship?' he asked.

'Yes, sir.'

'How high does the spring tide reach above low water at Bristol?' The man hesitated for a moment before replying.

'Two or three fathoms?' he offered.

'I am sending a boat over,' said Clay. 'If you move, I shall have

31

you and your ship blown out of the water.'

'But, sir,' protested Taylor. 'What of the bilious fever on board? Think how it will spread amongst the crew.'

'Balderdash, Mr Taylor!' exclaimed Clay. 'That flag is just a ruse to put us off the scent. Quite apart from his strange accent, did you ever hear tell of a Bristol trader who is unaware that his home port has the largest tidal range in Christendom? If there is so much as one man suffering from a cold aboard I'll... I'll... eat Mr Armstrong's wig. You had best have the boat crew armed, and once he has been rescued, have the master of that ship brought back here, if you please.'

*****

The true master of the trading brig proved to be a large, florid man in a pea green jacket, who grasped Clay's hand enthusiastically when he was shown into the cabin.

'Thank you most kindly for my release, sir,' he said in his strong Bristol accent. 'I am Seth Benjamin, master and owner of the *Charlotte*.'

'Good to make your acquaintance, Mr Benjamin,' said Clay. 'I am delighted to have been in a position to affect a rescue. Can I offer you some refreshment after you ordeal? Hart, a glass of wine for the captain, if you please.'

'Thank you kindly,' said the ship's owner as he accepted the drink. He drained his glass thirstily and held it back towards the steward. 'We contrived to make as much noise as we were able, but what with our being confined to the hold, and the wind set in the wrong direction, I wasn't sure as you would hear us, sir.'

'In truth we only just managed to perceive your cries, although our suspicions had already been aroused,' said Clay. 'But tell me, I had expected to find a French or Spanish prize crew onboard, but the men we have captured seem to be neither.'

'No, that's right,' said the merchant captain. 'They have all manners of strange folk amongst them, but for the most part they are Russian. I wasn't aware we were at war with Russia, which is how they managed to surprise me so easily.'

'Nor are we,' said Clay. 'God knows we are not short of enemies, but Russia is not numbered amongst them. And even if war has been declared in the two weeks since I left Plymouth, word could hardly have arrived here off the coast of Portugal any quicker than my ship. Could you explain what happened to you, Mr Benjamin?'

'We left Oporto yesterday morning with the tide, sir,' he began. 'Soon as we was clear of land and was heading for home, up comes this ship-rigged sloop flying Russian colours. She must have been waiting in the offing for just such an opportunity. Well, we reckoned as how she was just heading into the port herself, so we thought nothing of it. Before you could blink, she had fired a six-pounder across our bow and ranged up alongside. Full of men she was, all armed to the teeth. The whole attack was over as soon as it began.'

'This was yesterday you say, just off Oporto?' asked Clay. 'Could you describe this ship?'

'She was ship rigged, as I said. Not big at all, probably no more than three or four hundred ton, I should say,' said Benjamin. 'Her hull was painted dark blue, but had seen better days, and her sails were right heavily patched. No more than six guns per side, so she would be no match for a proper man-of-war like this.'

'What do you think, Mr Taylor?' said Clay, to his lieutenant.

'The Russians had a good deal of privateers operating a few years back when they were at war with the Turks, sir,' he replied. 'I would imagine that this ship may have been one of them. It could be the usual story. The crew get such a taste for the buccaneering way of life that when the war ended, they continued.'

'A privateer that has turned into a pirate?' said Clay. 'They would not be the first. But now they have tried their hand upon British commerce, they have become our responsibility. Can you show us where you were captured on the chart, Mr Benjamin? If they struck lucky there only yesterday, there is a fair chance they will continue to cruise the same waters in the hope of further prey.'

*****

'Wake up, sir,' urged Samuel Yates. He rocked his captain's cot with one hand while he held aloft a horn lantern in the other. Clay opened his eyes and focused with difficulty on the face of his young servant. Then he frowned.

'What is that deuced noise?' he asked. He could hear a steady thunder on the deck over his head.

'That'll be the rain, sir,' said Yates. 'Fair pelting down, it is. Noah's forty days ain't in it. Five bells in the morning watch has just struck. There is hot water fresh up from the galley in your washstand, and I will go and get your clothes ready. You'll need your oil skins, unless this downpour blows over, sir.'

The ship was still in the centre of the rain squall when Clay came on deck. The planking beneath his sea boots was slick with water, and it filled the night with its hissing roar. He glanced over the side onto the surface of a black sea that seethed and foamed like the yeasty brew of a witch. He struggled across to join the other sou'wester-clad figures, grouped around the glow of light coming from the binnacle.

'Good morning, gentlemen,' he shouted, as he attempted to

make himself heard. 'Although good may be over egging our pudding. We shall have little hope of finding anything in this. What is our position?'

'We have circled around north in the night as you ordered, sir,' yelled Armstrong. 'We shall cross the spot where the *Charlotte* was captured around dawn. You may find it difficult to credit, but this rain is actually a little less intense than earlier.'

'It will still serve to cloak that Russian ship, sir,' grumbled Preston, who was officer of the watch.

By tiny increments the light of dawn crept upon the ship. The black world around them divided between dark sea and slate-grey sky. The web of ropes and shrouds inked themselves in, and the shape of the frigate resolved itself from out of the gloom. Then the squall of rain swept away to one side and the ship emerged into clear sea at last. On the eastern horizon Clay could see a faint sliver of coral pink, as the first light of dawn stole into the world. He tilted his head up towards the foremast to watch the lookout perched high up on the royal yard, just as the sailor turned his face down towards his captain, cupped a hand next to his mouth and hailed.

'Deck there! Sail ho! Sail on the starboard beam!'

'Mr Russell,' said Clay to the midshipman of the watch. 'Get yourself aloft with a glass and tell me what you make of her.'

'Aye aye, sir,' replied the youth running to the main chains and scampering aloft.

'I do hope it may prove to be our quarry,' said Taylor.

'Deck there!' yelled Russell from the top of the main mast. 'She's ship rigged alright, sir. Looks like a small sloop. I cannot make out any colours. She is standing towards us.'

'That sounds promising, sir,' said Armstrong. 'It would be passing strange if two such similar craft proved to be in the same vicinity.'

'It is also a good sign that she is making so bold as to come towards us, sir,' added Preston. 'A merchantman would be much shyer of a strange sail. Perhaps she thinks we might be another victim?'

'Deck there! She has hauled her wind now and is going about,' called Russell.

'She cannot like the look of us and has realised her mistake,' said Clay. 'Put the ship on the other tack and get the topgallants on her, Mr Preston. You can trial the royals too, if she will bear them. We have new copper and spars. Let us see if we cannot run her to ground.'

'All hands!' cried the boatswain's mates. 'All hands to make sail!'

Clay picked up one of the telescopes and strode forward along the starboard gangway with Taylor at his heels as the men poured up from the lower deck. The top men paused to knuckle their foreheads in respect to the captain and first lieutenant, before spinning round to fly up the shrouds. Clay paused for a moment to watch them go, higher and higher, up the masts before they spread out along the yardarms to release the furled sails.

'We have a well drilled crew Mr Taylor,' he commented. 'I thought that four months ashore would have made them slow, but they seem just as quick as before. Look at Trevan up there, running out along that yard as if it were the path to his door.'

'They are still a little more cumbersome than they were, sir,' said Taylor. 'But I live in hope that a few more weeks of sail drill will sweat the last of the drink from their hides.'

Once they reached the bow of the ship, the effect of all the extra canvas that had been set was starting to be felt. Looking down, Clay could see the frigate's sharp bow as it sliced through the water and the creamy wave that was climbing higher and higher up the ship's side as their speed increased. A polished grey shape arched out of the water before it plunged back into the sea close to the hull, followed by two more.

'We have dolphins, Mr Taylor,' said Clay, pointing. 'A good sign, I believe. I have been told that they only favour the swiftest of ships.'

'Let us see if the creatures have judged correctly, sir,' said the first lieutenant. He pulled out his telescope and focused it in the direction of the sighting. He paused for a moment and then backtracked a little. 'Ah, there she is, sir. I can see her mizzen royal lifting above the horizon. If you direct your gaze a shade to starboard of the bowsprit you should have her.'

Clay tracked his telescope to the spot that Taylor had indicated. So soon after dawn the sea was a dark pool that filled the bottom half of the image in his eye piece, but the sky in the top half was growing clearer all the time. He tracked slowly round till he found the little white square of something more solid.

'I have her, Mr Taylor,' he said. 'And is that not a little of her topgallants appearing just below? I believe we are gaining on her quickly.'

'Maybe,' said the lieutenant. 'It might also be a wave, sir.'

'Too permanent for that,' said Clay. 'No, we are certainly the swifter ship, but it will be a few hours before we are up with her. Are you hungry, George?'

'Very much so, sir.'

'Good, will you join me for breakfast?'

*****

When the two officers returned to the quarterdeck later it was full morning. The rain had gone altogether and in the clearer air they could see the distant mountains of Portugal as a purple line away to one side. The watch had been changed, and Lieutenant Blake had replaced Preston. The ship continued to race onwards through the water, sending sheets of spray that flew away downwind. Every fibre of the rigging seemed to hum in the air all around them with the strain of so much sail. Clay glanced across an expanse of green sea to the Russian sloop, now well over the horizon and getting closer all the time.

'She is trying her hardest to escape, sir, but it will not answer,' reported Blake with satisfaction. 'By the look of her she would have been a swift ship in her day, but those sails of hers are very old. I doubt if they hold the wind much better than a net would.'

Clay focussed on the little sloop ahead. Her sails were brown and streaked with age, with squares of newer canvas to mark where they had been mended. She was close enough now for him to see the detail of her hull. Blake was right; it was sleek and long, capable of a fair turn of speed once. It was also painted blue, just as Seth Benjamin had described.

'Sails so in want of repair speaks to me of a long period away from her home port, sir,' added Taylor. 'In which case her hull will be foul with weed.'

'Doubtless you are correct, but they will still do all they can to evade capture,' said Clay. 'They must realise that as pirates we shall hang them out of hand.'

'They are changing direction!' warned several of the watching officers at once. The silhouette of the ship altered as her other two masts emerged from behind her mizzen. She swung round and settled on her new course.

'Due east, sir,' said Blake, standing over the compass rose to take the bearing. 'Where can she be bound? Surely only the coast of Portugal lies in that quarter. She will be trapped between our guns and the shore.'

'She is up to something,' mused Clay, still watching her. 'Kindly follow her around, Mr Blake. And have one of the bow chasers manned. We may be able to slow her up by throwing a few shot in amongst her rigging presently.'

Clay put his telescope to his eye again. The sloop filled his disc of vision now. He could see some of the detail of her battered rigging. One of her yards had been fished together from two broken pieces. He could even make out individual crewmen, ant-like figures amongst her sails. He refocused on the land beyond the ship. With the greater magnification, the purple smear on the horizon changed into green wooded hills backed by blue mountains farther inland. Where the hills met the sea, he could just make out a faint line of cream that formed and went as successive Atlantic rollers broke on the sand of a distant beach.

'I am not entirely sure, but has she sprung a leak, sir?' asked Taylor. 'Off on her larboard side, do you see?' Clay returned his attention to the ship. From the side a pulsing line of silver shot out to cascade into the waves beside her.

'I think not, George,' said Clay. 'I believe they are starting their fresh water. They mean to pump her dry to see if that won't answer to coax a bit more speed from her.'

'A few tons of water will not achieve much, sir,' scoffed the first lieutenant. 'We are almost in range now. I wonder what they will try — Oh, sir! Did you see that huge splash?'

'I did, Mr Taylor,' said Clay. 'That was a gun being thrown by the board, for sure.' Splashes followed at regular intervals as the ship cast anything heavy over the side, and still the gap between them shrank.

'How do you suppose they mean to evade us, sir?' asked Blake. The coast of Portugal was much closer now.

'It makes no sense to me, sir,' said Armstrong. 'I have studied the chart and I can see nothing to occasion any alarm. All that lies ahead is a bay with no exit save that we shall use to enter it. The longer they proceed on this course, the more certain will be their capture.'

'And they can hardly mean to fight with us,' added Taylor. 'Even if they had the pluck for it, they have now cast all their great guns away.'

'Let us see what unfolds, gentlemen,' said Clay. 'In the meantime we must prepare for all eventualities. There is nothing to gain from clearing the ship for action, Mr Blake, but turn up the watch below and let us have the guns manned. Mr Taylor, please see that the launch crew are ready in case we have need of them, and warn Mr Hutchinson that we may wish to drop anchor.' He picked up his speaking trumpet and called towards the forecastle. 'Mr Russell! You may try a shot with the bow chaser. I am sure we must be in range.'

'Aye aye, sir,' came the distant reply. The bang of a cannon rang out, and a puff of dirty white smoke drifted away on the wind.

A buzz of anticipation ran through the ship as they prepared for action. Lieutenant Thomas Macpherson appeared on the quarterdeck accompanied by his sergeant. He pulled his scarlet jacket straight and settled his sword by his side before he approached his captain.

'What do you require of my men, sir?' he asked. 'I would normally post them as sharpshooters for a single ship action, but yonder wee sloop doesn't seem to warrant such attention.'

'No, I doubt if they intend to fight us at all,' said Clay. 'In truth, Tom, I have no notion as to what they are about. All they seem bent on is to drive themselves onto the shore.' The marine stroked one of his bristling black sideburns with a gloved hand as he looked at the Russian ship.

'With your permission, I will have the men formed up on the quarterdeck and hold them in readiness till matters become a little clearer. Ah, I believe the bow chaser may have hit them!'

Clay lifted up his telescope and focused on the Russian ship. Clear in his field of vision he could see the battered stern of the sloop. The paintwork of the hull was mottled, with squares of lighter and darker blue that showed where the woodwork had been patched and repaired. Above the hull was a run of window lights across her stern. Some of the individual panes were cracked, others replaced with squares of wood. Higher still he could see faces that stared back at him over her stern rail. The bow chaser fired again and a tall splash reared up. The shot was in line with the target but had fallen a little short. He lowered his telescope and looked around. On either side of him, long arms of land reached out to form the sides of the bay, and still their quarry rushed on.

'Mr Blake, let us reduce sail,' he ordered. 'We have her trapped now, and I have no desire to hit some sand bar not represented on Mr Armstrong's chart at this speed. Topsails only, if you please.'

'Aye aye, sir,' replied the officer of the watch. 'All hands! All hands to take in sail.' Clay returned his attention to the Russian ship as she sailed closer and closer to the shore. No sign of her taking in any sail, he thought. What are they trying to do? A puff of smoke appeared in his view from the bow chaser and this time he saw splinters fly as the ball crashed home, leaving a jagged hole in the counter.

'Surely she must turn or slow down,' said Taylor at his elbow. 'We have her beat for certain, but she will run aground on that course. Look, she is almost in the surf already.'

'I don't believe she will turn,' exclaimed Clay. 'I believe she means to beach herself and escape from us on foot! See, now she has let go her sheets.'

Even with all of her sails flapping in the wind, the sloop still had enough momentum to drive her bow deep up the beach with a crunching roar. The impact was too much for her worn out rigging. As the hull ploughed to a halt the three masts continued forward, crashing down together in a welter of destruction. Beneath a canopy of tattered sails and broken spars the hull of the ship lay over on one side, with gentle waves stirring the wreckage that lay all about her.

'Mr Blake! Bring the ship up into the wind if you please and drop anchor,' ordered Clay. 'Send the launch to take possession of what is left of that privateer.'

'Aye aye, sir!'

'There they go, sir!' shouted Taylor. Clay followed where he pointed. From the bow of the ship he could see little figures as they clambered down into the shallow water with their bundles of possessions and waded towards the beach.

'Mr Macpherson!' he called. 'I'll trouble you for a landing party of your marines to see if you can capture any of the crew. Mr Taylor, kindly get the pinnace and cutter in the water to ferry them ashore. You had best accompany the marines, too.'

Clay watched the launch as it rowed quickly towards the stricken wreck of the sloop. The boat had covered no more than half the distance before wisps of smoke began to drift up from the privateer.

'Well I'll be damned!' exclaimed Clay. 'That's our prize! They must have set her on fire!' The smoke thickened quickly into a black column, and hungry orange flames appeared beneath it. They licked and flared across the hull, and the sound of cracking timbers drifted across the surface of the water towards them. Through the growing heat haze, Clay watched the last of the crew as they disappeared into the woods. No, not all of them, he corrected himself. He could see one single figure as he stood on the beach, his possessions by his side. He raised a hand and waved towards the approaching launch, as if impatient for them to reach him.

Chapter 3
Gibraltar

'Are you telling me we only captured one of these pirates, Mr Taylor?' said Clay, a frown of annoyance on his face.

'I'm afraid so, sir,' reported the lieutenant. 'By the time the marines had disembarked, the crew had long gone. Mr Macpherson pursued them inland, but the forest proved to be very thick, with few trails for his men to follow. After an hour without result he abandoned the hunt.'

'And the ship was completely destroyed, of course,' said Clay. He turned in his chair to look through the windows at the back of his cabin. A few charred curves of timber, like the shattered rib cage of some ancient beast, stood proud of the water to mark the place where the sloop had beached herself.

'Once the fire reached the magazine she was doomed, sir,' said Taylor. 'There really was little the launch crew could do. At least she will no longer prove to be a threat to our commerce.'

'I suppose that is true,' conceded his captain. 'And the prize crew we captured will meet justice when the *Charlotte* returns home. So tell me of this one man we did apprehend then, Mr Taylor.'

A Man of No Country

'I am not sure that apprehend is quite the right word,' said the lieutenant. 'While the others fled, he waited for the marines on the beach, and welcomed them ashore as if they were his rescuers.'

'Curious behaviour for a pirate, wouldn't you say?' mused Clay. 'Do you know who he is?'

'That is where matters become unclear, sir,' said Taylor. 'He says that he is an English sailor by the name of John Grainger, but he doesn't look like any tar that I have ever seen. For a start he is dressed like a Turk, and his skin is as dark as any Arab. His English is fair, but he has an accent that I cannot place at all.'

'Where in England does he say he comes from?'

'That's just it, sir. He claims not to know. Says he was but a youngster when he left home with his parents to come out here,' said the first lieutenant. 'And they both died many years ago, according to his account.'

'How very convenient,' snorted the captain. 'So what has he been up to all these years?'

'He says that he has been serving on all manner of vessels in the Mediterranean, first as a deck hand, later as a navigator.'

'Very curious indeed,' said Clay. 'Very well, let us have him in.'

John Grainger certainly did cut a remarkable figure as he came into the cabin accompanied by his two marine guards. He was a tall, strong looking man in his thirties, with a large bushy beard and short dark hair concealed by a dirty round cap. He wore baggy white trousers drawn in at the ankles and a red sleeveless tunic over his shirt. Around his waist was tied a thick green sash. His skin was burnt so dark that only his piercing blue eyes gave any hint that he might not be a native of North Africa.

'Mr Taylor tells me you are an English sailor,' said Clay. 'But I struggle to conclude that from your general appearance. Why are you dressed in such a fashion?'

'When I was but a boy I was captured by Barbary Pirates, sir,' Grainger replied. 'They made me become a Mohammedan, and dress as one of them.'

'Did your parents do nothing to prevent it?'

'My mother had died before then, sir,' replied the man. 'My father fought against the pirates, but he was killed.'

'And where did all of this happen?' asked Clay. The man shrugged.

'Somewhere out in the eastern Mediterranean, I think, sir,' he replied. 'I was only young then. It is hard to remember clearly the substance of it.'

'Did they make you a slave?' asked Clay.

'Not once I agreed to follow Allah, peace be upon him,' he replied. He touched his forehead and face with an elegant gesture of his long fingers. 'Then I became a sailor, sir.'

'In a Barbary Pirate ship?' queried Clay. 'Surely that would make you a pirate yourself, Grainger?'

'No, no, never a pirate, sir,' he insisted. 'I served on a trading dhow out of Algiers.'

'You say it was not a pirate ship, yet I find you on board a vessel that committed an act of piracy when it attacked a British merchantman in these very waters but two days ago,' continued the captain. 'Why should I not hang you for that crime?'

'I am not with them!' exclaimed the sailor. 'They took me prisoner from my last ship, sir. I was a navigator on a Neapolitan merchantman, the *San Giovanni Battista.* We were two weeks out from Palermo with a cargo of oil and grain, bound for Lisbon. They captured my ship and took me off it as a prisoner. I am not a pirate. I did not run like those other Russian scum.'

'What were you doing on a Neapolitan ship?' asked Clay. 'A

moment ago you said you were on a trading dhow? I must say this all seems very strange.'

'My ship foundered on the coast of Sicily some years ago, when it was driven onto the rocks in a storm,' he said. 'I survived the wreck, and found work with a Naples ship owner. He took me on because I speak Arabic, so I could help him to trade with the Levant, Africa and Egypt.'

'This all appears most irregular,' said Clay. 'What do you think, Mr Taylor? Should we hang him for serving on board a pirate ship, or take him at his word that he is a British sailor and press him into the crew?'

'I believe he is a sailor, as he says, sir,' replied the lieutenant. 'He certainly seems to know his way about a ship, although I have yet to ascertain if he can hand, reef and steer. As he says, he could very well have cut and run earlier on the beach, but chose to remain, which is in his favour. Even if his past is shady, we already have a good sprinkling of convicted smugglers, poachers and former mutineers amongst the crew. I can't see one more ne'er do well causing too many problems.'

'Very well, John Grainger, the English-Algerian-Neapolitan found aboard a Russian ship, you may be of many countries or none, but as of now you are a sailor in the Royal Navy and subject to the Articles of War. If you step out of line from now, you can be flogged or hanged for the offense. Have him read in, Mr Taylor, if you please, and then let us be on our way, I beg you. We have spent too long on this coast. We should have joined the fleet off Cadiz some days ago.'

*****

George Amery wore the immaculate uniform to be expected of the flag captain of an admiral who was a byword for both discipline and ill humour. He held the door open for Clay with a

47

polite smile, and his guest stepped through into the admiral's cabin and stopped in wonder. It was the largest room he had ever seen onboard a ship. Before him was a sweep of glass that was at least thirty feet wide, through which he could see the rest of the fleet, stretched out in a line of warships, spaced a perfect cable length apart as they followed their flagship across the green waters of the Atlantic. Inside, the interior bulkheads had been painted a delicate primrose yellow, which complemented the rich reds and blues of the oriental carpet on the floor, and the warm chestnut furniture that crowded around him.

'We so often refer to the stern cabin of a ship as the great cabin, but that of the *Ville de Paris* truly merits the name, does she not?' asked the flag captain as he closed the door behind him.

'Indeed so,' said Clay. 'Why, my first command had a great cabin that might fit in this space a dozen times. The *Ville de Paris* is new built I collect, sir?'

'Only finished eight months ago,' confirmed Amery. 'They gave her to the admiral to replace the *Victory*, which had been rather roughly handled during our triumph off Cape St. Vincent last year. She has a hundred and ten guns, which makes her the biggest first rate in the navy; although I hear the French have some even bigger ships. There is one called the *L'Orient* that is being fitted out in Toulon as we speak. She carries over a hundred and twenty guns, if you will credit it.'

'And doubtless has an even greater cabin, sir,' said Clay.

'Quite so,' said Amery, with another smile. 'Do please take a seat. May I get you a glass of Madeira?'

'That would be most welcome, sir,' said Clay.

'Are you acquainted with the admiral, then?' asked the flag captain, decanter in his hand.

'I met him briefly when I was third lieutenant on the *Minerva*, long before he became Earl St Vincent. He was plain John Jervis then.'

'Or Hanging Jack, if you are one of the hands,' said Amery, passing over the glass.

'So I understand,' said Clay. 'Capital drop of wine this, sir.'

'The wine is one of the few benefits of blockading Cadiz. When supplies run perilously low, we have the island of Madeira a scant five hundred miles west southwest of here. They send us supplies of Malmsey on a regular basis. Good health to you.'

'Will the admiral be joining us soon, sir?' asked Clay

'I would imagine so, sir. If I know his lordship he will be perusing the despatches you brought from England, searching for news of the Chosen One's return,' said the flag captain.

'I am not sure I follow you, sir,' said Clay. 'To whom do you refer?'

'Why, to Sir Horatio Nelson,' he replied. 'We all call him that in the fleet. His Lordship fair dotes on him, and in consequence Sir Horatio can do little wrong in his eyes. He was invalided home last year, but that don't stop the admiral pining for his return.'

'Does calling him the Chosen One not seem a little disrespectful, sir? I was under the impression that Sir Horatio gained considerable distinction for his part in the defeat of the Dons at the Battle of Cape St Vincent?' Amery smiled at this.

'He did, but not nearly enough distinction to satisfy the Chosen One,' he replied. 'He was most displeased at only being honoured with a knighthood for his efforts. The admiral did try for more, but to no avail.' He looked over Clay's shoulder and muttered, 'Speak of the devil,' as he rose to his feet. Clay stood up, too, and turned towards the cabin door, where a large man had darkened the entrance.

Admiral John Jervis, Earl St Vincent, had a square, jowly face topped with grey curly hair that he wore long at the back and sides, perhaps to compensate for the rate at which it was thinning on top. He was not as tall as Clay, but was considerably wider than his new subordinate. Clay found his gaze locked and held by two intense, china-blue eyes for a moment. Then the admiral held out a big hand and crushed that of his visitor.

'A very warm welcome to you, captain,' he growled. Clay searched the scowling face in front of him in vain for any trace of either warmth or welcome. 'You come with a fine reputation as a fighting man.'

'Thank you, my lord,' replied Clay, resisting the urge to wring his hand when it was finally released. 'I am delighted to make your acquaintance.' The admiral advanced past Clay and settled himself into one of the larger chairs in the cabin.

'Do please be seated, captain,' he boomed. 'I see Amery has let you sample my best Madeira. I must apologise for the necessity of keeping you waiting. I needed to examine the despatches you brought from London.' The flag captain exchanged glances with Clay and allowed one eye brow to rise a little.

'If it is not impertinent, might I know if their contents were satisfactory, my lord?' asked Amery

'Highly satisfactory,' said St Vincent. 'They hold very welcome tidings. It would seem that their lordships are sending us reinforcements under the command of Rear Admiral Nelson, just as I requested. Ain't that the grandest thing?'

'Indeed, your lordship,' said the flag captain, his face impassive. 'The fleet will be pleased.'

'Are you acquainted with Sir Horatio, captain?'

'Only by reputation, my lord,' said Clay

'He is quite the naval genius, you know,' said the admiral. 'Every action he has with the enemy is attended with victory.'

A Man of No Country

'Except, perhaps, for his unfortunate attack on Santa Cruz last July, my lord,' offered Amery. The admiral waved away the comment.

'An excess of zeal on his part,' he replied. 'Combined by the most shamefully indifferent intelligence. And pray remember that he paid for his mistake with the loss of his arm.'

'Quite so, my lord,' agreed the flag captain. 'Are the Admiralty certain that Sir Horatio's health has recovered sufficiently to withstand the rigours of a return to duty?'

'Apparently so,' said St Vincent. 'He will be here in the spring, with a fresh squadron of ships.'

'How splendid,' murmured Amery. The admiral swung his attention back onto his new subordinate.

'Now, Clay, can you favour me with an explanation as to why you took so long to join us?' he asked, his eyes becoming hard. 'I have been expecting you this last four days, and if there is one matter upon which I am most firm it is that of punctuality.'

'I did make a tolerable passage down to Cape Finisterre, my lord,' explained Clay. 'But just south of Oporto I encountered a British merchantman that had been captured by a privateer. I was obliged to hunt down that ship before any more attacks could be made upon our commerce. We overhauled her the following day, and once I had seen her destroyed, I came on to join you as swiftly as I was able.'

'Hmmm,' said St Vincent, a frown still prominent on his face. 'Well, that seems to be in order, Clay, but I had wanted you to join me sooner. The fact is the deuced Admiralty have been starving me of frigates. The First Lord has too much interest in the City for my liking. He has all of our smaller vessels based in home waters protecting commerce. Frigates, like your *Titan*, are worth their weight in gold when they are permitted to serve as the eyes of the fleet. Can you conceive how provoking it is to have a great ship like this, and yet not to be able to find my enemy for want of a few vessels to do my scouting for me?'

'I'm sure the First Lord of the Admiralty knows...' began Clay.

'I'm damned sure he don't!' exclaimed St Vincent. 'Look at the deuced way he gave in to mutiny in the Channel Fleet last spring! We had a little of that nonsense out here, but do you suppose I yielded to the scoundrels? No, sir, I did not! I ordered the marines armed and stopped them from any fraternising with the men. At the first hint of trouble I strung up all of their leaders, after which the rest of the people were meek as lambs. I can take being called Hanging Jack if it serves to keep the men loyal. I suppose your ship rose when you were in the Channel Fleet?'

'It did, for a number of hours, but I was able to suppress the mutiny with the help of some loyal hands.'

'Good for you, Clay,' enthused the admiral. 'What became of the blackguards?'

'One of the ringleaders was killed during the suppression and another was hanged for the murder of an officer, my lord. There was a third instigator who benefitted from the general pardon issued by the King.'

'Pity,' rumbled St Vincent. 'Still, a brace bagged from three ain't too shabby, what?'

'Would now be an appropriate time to brief Captain Clay on the mission we have in mind for the *Titan* to perform, my lord?' asked Amery. 'I am conscious that you are due to see Sir Peter at five bells.' The admiral rolled his eyes at this, then returned his attention to the newest member of the fleet.

'Captain Amery is worse than a damned nurse maid, but he do serve to keep me punctual,' he said. 'Now, you will recall that the Admiralty stripped me bare in the spring to reinforce the Channel

A Man of No Country

Fleet, and in consequence we were compelled to pull out of the Mediterranean for want of ships? As you can well imagine, with us off the dance floor, the damned Frogs have grabbed all the ladies they can with both hands.' The admiral's own considerable hands began to count off his large sausage fingers.

'They retook Corsica. That damned young upstart Bonaparte conquered half of Italy, and not a week goes by when they don't capture another dashed Greek island. Meanwhile in Toulon they lay down new warships faster than our spies can count them.' He slammed a fist down onto the desk. 'This has to stop, and when Nelson arrives in the spring, by Jove it will!'

'I understand, my lord,' said Clay. 'What is to be the *Titan*'s role in all of this?'

'You are to enter the Mediterranean to be my eyes and ears,' said the admiral. 'Use your frigate's strengths. You should be swift enough to avoid trouble, and powerful enough to deal with any ship you cannot run from. I need to know what is happening, so that when I am reinforced I can strike at the heart of whatever mischief the damned French are planning.'

'I see, my lord. Where in particular should I focus my search?'

'Look into the enemy's naval bases and ports,' said St Vincent. 'See if there are any suspicious concentrations of ships. And see if you can find out what is afoot in Italy. In your orders Captain Amery has listed most of our existing intelligence, but it is precious thin. I need you to use your nose, Clay. If you get wind of anything, follow that trail and then come back and tell me what you have found.'

'Our ambassador in Naples, Sir William Hamilton, is a valuable contact,' added Amery. 'He is a wise old hand, with excellent connections. His wife, Lady Emma, is very close to Queen Maria Carolina of the Kingdom of the Two Sicilies, so he

53

generally knows all that is happening on the Italian peninsula.'

'Aye, but be careful of Lady Emma Hamilton,' cautioned the admiral. 'Before she wed she was plain Emma Hart, the artist's model. Apparently she used to dance on the dinner table at Uppark House without a stitch on, when she was Sir Henry's mistress.'

'Good heavens!' exclaimed Clay. 'I can't say I am acquainted with the lady, my lord.'

'And I suspect Mrs Clay would prefer you to keep it that way. She has a reputation for eating men for breakfast, and is rather partial to a naval uniform I am told.' Lord St Vincent seemed to bare his teeth at his new subordinate, and it was only with difficulty that Clay realised the admiral was smiling, for once. Five clear bell strokes rang out from up on the forecastle of the *Ville de Paris*, and the admiral pulled himself out of his chair, followed by his two subordinates.

'Amery will give you your orders on the way out,' he said to Clay, shaking his hand once more. 'Take on fresh stores at Gibraltar, but when you leave the Rock you shall be on your own. I cannot aid you if you get into difficulty. The *Titan* will be the sole Royal Navy ship in the whole damned Mediterranean. Good luck, Captain Clay. Come back in a few months and tell me what the deuce is going on.'

*****

HMS *Titan* sailed into the bay of Gibraltar soon after sunrise and dropped her anchor in waters made dark by the long shadow of the mountainous rock that dominated the little peninsula. The crew then set to work with a will to replenish the frigate's water and food, certain of a run ashore once the task was completed. Barrels and bundles of stores were swayed up from the lighters that rowed out to the frigate from the dockyard, to disappear deep into her hull. By early afternoon, the gratings had been put back in place over her hatchways, the hoists and lifts cleared away, and the deck scrubbed back to a smooth white that satisfied even First Lieutenant Taylor's critical eye. Soon the ship's boats were busy ferrying the hands ashore. Some headed for the delights of the markets, full of exotic Moorish trinkets from North Africa just across the narrow strip of sea. The more adventurous set off to climb the massive rock to admire the view, and to laugh at the antics of the apes that lived up there, but the vast majority got no further than the first convenient grog shop where the prices were low and the serving wenches comely.

At one such establishment, deep in the old town, a group of the *Titan*'s crew took their ease at a trestle table in front of a low building that stood at a busy intersection. They sat with earthenware jugs of wine before them, and watched the world go by in the streets around the grog shop.

'Well, it ain't ale, but sometimes a drop of bishop can make a pleasurable change,' said Rosso, as he sipped at his mug of rough red wine. 'You certain you will not essay any, John?' The *Titan*'s newest recruit shook his head. He was dressed in the same clothes as the other sailors now, but his short hair and big beard still picked him out from the rest, as did the glass of fruit juice that sat before him.

'Thank you, Rosie, but no. My religion forbids it,' he said.

'Remind me never to become a fecking Mohammedan, won't yous,' said O'Malley. 'At least Rosie's new friend here is not shy of a mug of knock-me-down.' Daniel Oates smiled at the Irishman and took a sip from his own cup. He was a small, shy young man, with pale sandy hair and hazel eyes, who had joined the ship at Plymouth as a volunteer. Rosso clapped him on the shoulder.

'He may be new to the sea, but he ain't no Quaker,' he said.

'Bristol born through and through, just like me, ain't you, Dan?'

'That's right, Rosie,' said the volunteer, with a weak smile.

'So does you know each other, like?' asked Trevan. 'I mean from back home, an' all?'

'Not really, Adam,' said Rosso. 'We come from the same side of town, but I don't remember no Daniel Oates.'

'I am the same,' said Oates. 'I thought Rosie's face was familiar when I first came aboard, but I don't recall any Rossos. Dago name, ain't it?'

'Italian,' he answered. 'Mind, Bristol is a big enough place for that not to be strange. Now come, lads, we should be celebrating the return to us of our shipmate. I give you Sean O'Malley, the famous horseman, raised at last from his sick bed.'

His friends gave a mock cheer at this, and the Irishman bowed low to all sides.

'What I don't get is how you came to be on this bleeding nag in the first place,' said Evans. 'Was you trying your hand for a highwayman?'

'Not exactly,' O'Malley began. 'See, I had been caught with this colleen I was after visiting....'

'Aye aye! Ain't that you all over, Sean,' snorted Evans. 'I might have known there'd be a bleeding wench at the bottom of all this! Was her Pa coming after you with his blunderbuss and a set of gelding irons?'

'It was not like that at all,' protested the Irishman. 'Well, the bit about her father sort of was, although it was more clubs and knives, like.' O'Malley waited for the laughter to subside before he continued.

'Anyways, what with him having roused half the county against me, I needed to push off sharp like. So I climb aboard this horse and even though I am no dragoon at all, I'm thinking how

I've seen it done enough times by others. Well, it turns out that getting your actual horse underway is easy enough. You does a deal of shouting and kicking, and the angry mob coming up astern serves to do the rest. The horse shot off up the Ballymore road, which was the wrong fecking way, but any port in a storm, I am after thinking.'

'So how was it that you came to fall off?' asked Trevan.

'Ah, it would seem that getting your horse underway is a deal easier than getting the beast to fecking stop,' said the Irishman. 'We were well clear of trouble, and she's still going along like her tail is on fire. Time for us to heave to, I'm a thinking. I gives a shout of "Avast there! Belay!" and the like, but on she runs like I never said a word. So I leant forward, took hold of her ears and gave them a kind of a tug. Just to bring her to her senses like.'

'Oh! She wouldn't have liked that!' spluttered Rosso.

'No, she didn't,' confirmed the Irishman. 'How was I to know she would take on so? She reared up like one of them stallions, capered around in a circle and sets herself to jump across the ditch, as was next to the road. She cleared it too, but not with me onboard. Back over her arse I goes and down onto my own. She disappears and I am left in the bottom of the ditch, all bust up. It's a fecking miracle I made it back to the barky at all.' His friends all thumped the table with pleasure at the Irishman's story.

'Seems right strange to talk of home when we be out here, a sitting in the sun in the middle of winter, like,' said Trevan, once the laughter had subsided. The Cornishman was basking with his back settled against the wall of the tavern.

'True enough, Adam,' said Rosso. 'I mean, it's not what you'd call hot, but back home it'll be bleak as a Puritan's wake. Is it always like this here, John?'

'Here in the offing of the Barbary coast it is always warm,

yes,' said Grainger, pointing through a gap between two buildings towards the coast of Africa. 'But farther north in the Mediterranean proper, it's cold now. There you will find rain and storms and maybe even a little snow.'

'And fecking prizes galore, what with us being the only British ship in sight,' added O'Malley. 'Here's to a bumper voyage, fellers!' The group of sailors gathered around the table brought their drinks together above the centre with a collective bang and wine sloshed onto the scrubbed tabletop.

'What manner of tattoo is that, mate?' asked Evans. He pointed to Grainger's hand that held his drink. On the back ran a line of shapes. There was a triangle, then some circles and loops, all in smudged blue ink.

'That is right peculiar,' said Trevan, who sat on the other side of him. 'Do it mean anything in foreign, like?' Grainger rubbed his hand, as if to remove the tattoo, and then moved it under the table.

'I am not sure what it means,' he said. 'I was only a young boy when it was done. All the sailors on my ship had it, but what for, I don't know.'

'Well if you wants to see something a bit more regular, like,' said Evans, 'feast your eyes on this!' The big Londoner placed his two huge fists down next to each other on the table. On each knuckle a single blue letter had been freshly tattooed.

'Bloody hell, Sam!' exclaimed Trevan. 'When did you have them done?'

'Just now,' he replied. 'That's why I was a bit behind you all in getting here. I wanted them to set down "Dread Naught" but it seems as how you need a few more fingers for that. Good, ain't it?' His largely illiterate audience looked at the fists in wonder.

'So go on,' urged O'Malley. 'What does it fecking say?'

'Holdfast!' announced Evans. 'Hold on this paw and fast on

that.'

'That be right good, Sam,' enthused Trevan.

'Except that isn't what it says at all,' said Rosso, 'From over here it's set down "fast hold", unless you do this.' He picked up the shocked sailor's hands and crossed his wrists over. 'Now it works.' His friends all roared with laughter, and even Grainger and Oates smiled, while Evans face grew red.

'I am going to kill that little bleeder!' he bellowed. 'He said he had his letters an' all!'

'Talk about the blind leading them as can't fecking see!' laughed O'Malley. 'Why did you not take one of the scholars with you, to see it was set down right? Rosie here, or even Able.'

'Where is Able?' asked Rosso. 'I thought he was going to join us, like.'

'He was after visiting the market first, but if I aren't mistaken that be him now,' said Trevan, waving down the hill. Sedgwick waved back and pushed his way up the crowded street to join the sailors outside the tavern. In his hand he held a book bound in soft brown leather which he placed on the table as he sat down. Grainger glanced across at it, looked again, and then rose from the bench, his face dark with rage.

'My book!' he exclaimed, snatching the volume up. 'Thieving Blackamoor! You have been searching in my kit bag!'

'Easy there,' said Sedgwick, shocked by the fury of Grainger's reaction.

'Hold your tongue, Grainger!' roared Evans, rising to his feet. 'Don't you go talking to my bleeding mate like that.'

'But he is a thief!' spat the newcomer. 'This book is mine.'

'Steady, lads,' said Trevan. 'I am sure there ain't no cause to take on so.'

'That's right,' said Sedgwick, standing up to confront the

furious sailor. 'You're wrong. I just bought this journal in the market.' Grainger tore open the book and saw that all the pages were blank.

'Please forgive me,' he muttered. 'The Moroccan leather, the markings on the cover, it is quite the same as mine. I am sorry.' He returned the book and sat down again.

'Well, glad we got that settled without a mill,' said Trevan. He poured Sedgwick a mug of wine. 'I would say have a drink on it, but John here is dry as a Quaker on the Sabbath.'

'Hey, what do you make of Evans's new tattoo, Able?' said O'Malley, breaking the awkward silence that followed. Evans held out his hands for inspection.

'Fast hold?' queried the coxswain. 'I am not sure I follow, Sam. Is it some manner of prize fighting term?'

'It's a fucking mistake,' growled the Londoner. 'Them words is the wrong way round.'

'Ah, I see,' said Sedgwick. 'Hold fast does make more sense. Is it marked on your hands for good?'

'Aye, it bleeding is. I should have got you or Rosie to check it for me first.'

'That would have been better,' agreed the coxswain. 'Mind you, some might congratulate you on a narrow escape. The man who did this could have set down any manner of word, with you none the wiser. "Sodomite" has eight letters too, you know.' The others all roared with laughter again, while Evans smouldered with rage.

'Ahoy there! Some more grog here!' called O'Malley in the direction of the serving hatch. One of the girls came over with a fresh jug of wine. While the others were busy chuckling at the Londoner's tattoo, Sedgwick sat a little back from the group. He was still puzzled about Grainger's extraordinary outburst earlier over his book, and watched him thoughtfully. The serving girl slipped her way between O'Malley and Trevan to place the jug on the table and reached forward for the empty one. As she did so, she spotted the tattoo on the back of Grainger's hand. The smile slid from her face and she recoiled back from the table, almost dropping the empty jug in her haste. Then she crossed herself and returned to the serving hatch, still looking back over her shoulder.

'What you about then, Able?' asked Rosso. 'Got your eye on that wench, have you? She is a handsome piece, and no mistake.'

'No, Rosie,' said Sedgwick. 'I was just pondering on something. What do think of my new book?' Rosso picked it up from the table and hefted it in one hand.

'Nicely tooled bit of leather, that,' he concluded. 'Are you going to keep some manner of journal then?'

'I mean to set down the story of my time as a slave,' said the coxswain. 'Would you help me with it?'

'Course I will, Able, although you're near as good as me with your letters now. What has brought this desire to write on?'

'Do you remember Mr Linfield back on the *Rush*?'

'The sawbones as saved Pipe's arm?' said Rosso.

'That's right. He was real hot on Abolition, and held that stories like mine would further that cause. He wanted to write my story down, but I said no. But now I got my letters an' all, I thought I would try to do it. Pipe's sister, Miss Clay, she has written books, and she said she would help me to get it turned into something proper. When we return home, like, whenever that shall be.'

'Well I never did,' said Rosso. 'No sooner have you got a fix on your letters, than you're after writing books, eh?'

'I was more thinking of one of them pamphlets, really.'

'Even so, that is mighty impressive, and no mistake.' He held up his mug and knocked it against Sedgwick's. 'Good luck to you, Able.'

Some hours later O'Malley was the first to notice how low the sun was, as it sank towards the western horizon. He pushed himself up from the table.

'Only a scant hour before we're due back onboard, lads,' he announced. 'Who fancies a whore?'

'I thought you were going to stop all of that, Sean?' asked Trevan. 'On account of that wench you was sweet on back in Ireland.'

'And so I shall,' said the Irishman. 'First thing in the morning.'

'Well, I will stay true to my Molly,' said the Cornishman. 'I'll be heading back to the barky.'

'I am with you, Sean,' said Evans. 'It'll take my mind of these bleeding tattoos.'

'Good man,' enthused O'Malley. 'You coming too, John, or ain't it part of your religion either? How about you, Able?'

'I'll stay a little longer and try my luck here,' said the coxswain. O'Malley followed his gaze in the direction of the serving girl.

'Good fecking luck with that!' he said. 'You're a fine looking feller an' all, but when she slaps your face for the second time, come and find us in the bawdy house.' Sedgwick waited till the laughter and oath-edged talk of the sailors had disappeared down the street. Then he finished his drink, picked up his new notebook and rose from the table. He made his way across the terrace to find the girl.

'I am not whore,' she announced, before he could speak, giving her stock reply when approached by a British sailor. 'There are plenty of brothels by the fish market. A few may be willing to accept a black man.'

A Man of No Country

'No, miss, I am not after that,' he said. 'I just wanted to ask you something. The sailor I was with, the tall one with very brown skin and a beard. He had some manner of tattoo on the back of his hand.'

'He is very bad man, to have such a thing,' she spat.

'Do you know what it means?'

'I know the mark of my enemy! Men with these things have plagued this coast for hundreds of years,' she said. 'This is mark of a Barbary slaver.'

'You mean he was a slave?'

'No, not slave,' she corrected him. 'The ones who take innocent people, and make them into slaves. Be very careful of him. They are cruel as the devil.'

Chapter 4
Cartagena

Alexander Clay came on deck just after dawn to find that the *Titan* was sailing in thick fog. He looked towards the forecastle, where the foremast rose like the trunk of a forest tree, wreathed in mist. Beyond it nothing was visible. From above him moisture dripped from the masses of rigging and canvas lost in the gloom over his head. He shrugged his shoulders deeper into his pea jacket and scowled at his officers.

'I had been told that the Mediterranean was warm and clear, Mr Armstrong,' he said. 'This is worse than the Channel.'

'There can be early morning fogs on this coast, when the sea is cold in winter, sir,' replied the master, his wig a pearly mesh of water droplets. 'But it is rare that they persist for very long, once the sun gets to work upon them.'

'So my plan to steal up at dawn and spy on the Spanish fleet at Cartagena before they smoke what we are about will have to wait till that happens, I collect?'

'I fear so, sir.'

'As we have an enforced delay before we can start our observations, may I take the opportunity of inviting you to sup with us in the wardroom tonight, sir?' said the first lieutenant. 'We plan to see in the New Year with some dash.'

'That is very handsome of you, Mr Taylor,' said Clay. 'I accept with pleasure. What revels do you have planned?'

'Tom Macpherson has them in hand, sir,' said Taylor. 'Apparently we English celebrate the New Year in a very indifferent fashion. He has all manner of Caledonian practices he wishes to introduce us to.'

'How intriguing! What do you suspect will be involved?'

'I am not sure, sir. He has secured a pipe of port wine that somehow got removed from the cargo of the *Charlotte*, so there will be no shortage of good cheer. I did overhear him asking the purser for salt, but for what purpose he wants it is a mystery.'

'Has he indeed?' mused Clay. 'Yes, Mr Preston?'

'Sorry to interrupt, sir, but one of the lookouts reports he can hear something on the larboard beam,' said the lieutenant. 'He thought it might be some manner of ship-board noise.' The officers moved across to that side of the deck and listened. Clay placed his head on one side. After a few moments, from somewhere high in the fog came the sound of a slight squeal.

'What was that?' he asked.

'It sounded a little like a line passing through a poorly greased block,' speculated Taylor. 'And I think I can hear voices now, sir.' The three men listened again. After a moment there came another sound.

'That was the flap of a topsail, sir, or I have never heard one,' said Preston.

'It is damned hard to distinguish between the noise of the *Titan* and this newcomer,' said Clay. 'I am almost persuaded that I can hear the sound of a hull passing through the water, but it is quite possible I am just listening to our own progress. Thick mist can play very odd tricks on one.' The officers continued to listen, and a little later a ship's bell sounded clear in the fog.

'That was no trick, sir,' said Preston. 'But I could have sworn it came from the other side of the ship, over there.' The bell had only just stopped when a second bell rang out much farther away, followed by others all around them.

'Christ, it must be a fleet!' exclaimed Taylor. 'We're right in the middle of them, sir.'

'I counted six separate ships, sir,' said Preston.

'Mr Taylor, make sure our own bell is not sounded,' ordered Clay. 'I want the ship to be as silent as possible. Lookouts are to report in person, not by hailing.'

'Aye aye, sir,' replied Taylor.

'Mr Preston, turn up the watch below and man the guns. In absolute silence, if you please.'

'Shall I have the ship cleared for action, sir?' Clay thought about this for a moment.

'No, that would make too much noise,' he replied. 'But do have the galley fire put out. We would not want a stray shot to set us ablaze.'

Clay paced the deck, his hands clasped behind him as he pondered what to do, while all around him the crew crept to their places in silence, like naughty children worried about waking an irritable parent. Keep calm, he urged himself, don't let the people see you are worried. All is well at present; the ship is safe for now. But what had Armstrong said about these fogs, that they barely lasted? He looked up furtively. Was he imagining it, or could he already see a lot more of the ship's upper masts, and did the dome of fog start to have a silvery look as the sun worked on it from above? He stared around him into the mist. On the side that they had heard the first ship a dark shadow seemed to loom up. He looked out on the other beam, but there was no escape in that direction. The first ship's bell had come from that side, and here, too, he could see a shape in the fog. The *Titan* would be caught between the two ships as soon as the fog lifted. What should he do? Think, man think. Then he stopped midstride as the idea came to him.

'Mr Armstrong, how long is it since the lookout first reported hearing noises?' he asked. The ship's master consulted the rough log that hung by the wheel.

'Eight minutes ago, sir,' he replied.

'And yet the ships about us have neither closed nor moved away,' mused Clay. 'So they must be on a similar course and doing much the same speed.'

'That is not so very strange, sir, said Armstrong. 'If they are a squadron bound for Cartagena like us, there is only one line of approach with this wind that will clear St. Anna point at the harbour entrance. We have probably been overhauling them little by little through much of the night.'

'Did you hear all those bells earlier?'

'Yes, sir,' said the master. 'Like Mr Preston, I heard six vessels.'

'Where did you place them?'

'One on either beam, sir, the rest ahead.'

'None astern, then?' asked Clay.

'Not that I heard, sir.' He turned to his other officers.

'Did any of you hear a ship's bell behind us?' he asked. They all shook their heads.

'My thanks, gentlemen,' said the captain. 'That is what I heard too, but this fog can addle the mind. I wanted to have it confirmed.'

'Shall we haul our wind then, sir?' asked Taylor. 'We could let these ships sail on none the wiser that we were ever present.' Clay looked at his first lieutenant, who spotted a well remembered twinkle deep in his pale grey eyes. 'What are you considering, sir?' he sighed.

'I was thinking that we might have a little entertainment first, before we disappear back into the fog,' he said. He turned to his other officers. 'Mr Blake, can I trouble you to have both batteries double shotted and the guns run out? But it must be done as quietly as you are able. There is a ship on either flank, which shall be your targets. When I give the order you are to fire both broadsides together and then secure the guns. Is that clear?'

'Aye aye, sir,' replied the lieutenant.

'Now, Mr Preston, you are to take charge of the sails. Have men posted in the rigging ready to act. The moment the guns fire, I want every sail taken in so the ship will lose her way in a flash. After that we will sit as quiet as possible. Get to your positions, gentlemen.'

'Sir, have you considered that the ships around us might not be enemies?' asked Taylor. Actually this possibility had not occurred to Clay, but he was committed now.

'I had, but I hold it to be most unlikely,' he said, as calmly as he was able. 'We are the only Royal Navy ship that the admiral has sent into the Mediterranean. No, they are Dons for sure, this close to their naval base at Cartagena, or perhaps French. Either way it is our duty to make them uncomfortable.' From the main deck he heard the low rumble of gun carriages as they were eased across the deck, accompanied by a hiss of whispered commands from the gun captains. The two officers moved to one side as a rush of top men flowed past and raced up the shrouds. A curtain of dislodged moisture from the vibrating ropes pattered down on the deck as they disappeared through the ceiling of mist above the quarterdeck.

A Man of No Country

After a while Midshipman Butler came hurrying up the companion ladder.

'Mr Blake's compliments, and the guns are ready to fire, sir,' he muttered.

'Very good, Mr Butler,' he replied. 'That coat looks to fit you rather better now.'

'Yes, sir,' smiled the youngster. 'Hart was very helpful, thank you, sir.'

'Mr Preston,' hissed Clay. 'Are you ready?'

'Aye aye, sir,' came the low reply. Clay returned his attention to the midshipman.

'Give my compliments to Mr Blake, and he may fire when ready.' The young man scampered away, and for a moment the frigate sailed on in its world of silence and fog, with the ships on either side only visible as cliffs of darker shadow. Then Clay heard Blake's quiet voice.

'Gun captains, are you ready?' he asked, and then, 'Both sides, open fire.' With a colossal roar of sound, orange fire engulfed the ship and walls of smoke shot up into the mist on either side. An instant later came the sound of the two broadsides crashing home in the fog. There was a moment of shocked silence, followed by the screams of the wounded and cries of alarm. From the ship on the starboard side came the sound of yelled orders, while on the other side an indignant voice shouted out a challenge. Clay could make out little of what had been said, but the language was Spanish. From down on the main deck Clay heard Blake continue to issue quiet instructions. 'Stop your vent, number three cannon. Make sure those guns are properly secured, larboard side.'

'Now, Mr Preston,' said Clay. A little latter the air above him filled with the sound of whispered orders and the creak of stiff canvas as the sails were gathered in. More curtains of drips pattered down through the fog as the way came off the frigate. Clay walked forwards to the front of the quarterdeck and stared into the fog. The ship on the port side seemed to have recovered from the mass of shot that had appeared out of the mist. He could hear the roar of a drum as the crew went to quarters, the sound advancing ahead of the slowing *Titan*.

'I don't think they can have seen us falling behind, sir,' said Taylor.

'We only have bare poles to show now,' said Clay. 'You would need keen eyes to spot us in this gloom.'

The dark shadows of the two ships dissolved away as they continued to advance ahead of them, but sound still travelled through the damp air. From both ships they could hear the distinctive noise as port lids were banged open, and the rumble of heavy cannon being run out.

'It was hard to tell in the fog, but they looked like ships of the line to me, sir,' said Taylor.

'The one on the larboard side appeared to be the bigger of the two,' added Armstrong, who had joined them at the rail. 'Three-decker, maybe?'

'Ships of the line?' laughed Clay. 'Better and better! What a prodigious mess they will try to make of the enemy who fired on them.'

'Mr Preston's compliments,' said Midshipman Russell, 'and all sail is now off the ship, sir.'

'Thank you, Mr Russell,' said Clay. 'Now, gentlemen, my hope and expectation is that both of our opponents are busily engaged in a search for the enemy that so rudely fired on them. With the fog continuing to clear they should presently catch sight of one another. I have little doubt that if Mr Blake's men shot true, they will be spoiling for a fight.'

A Man of No Country

There was no sign of either Spanish ship now. The frigate was all alone, drifting along at the centre of a disc of green water with a wall of swirling grey all about them. Armstrong looked up.

'The fog starts to break up, sir,' he reported. He pointed towards a small patch of blue that had appeared overhead. At that moment a double line of orange flashes lit up the fog in front of them, followed by a roar of noise. Moments later the other ship responded with a broadside of its own.

'Did you ever see the like!' exclaimed Taylor. 'The Dons battling with each other! Look at them, hammering away like a pair of fighting cocks!'

'A splendid sight, Mr Taylor, I make no doubt, but we must leave them to it I fear,' said Clay. 'With this fog lifting they will soon realise their mistake. I suggest we put some distance between us and them before that should occur.'

It was only later that morning, when Clay was alone at this desk writing his report on the incident, that the full possibilities of the narrow escape the *Titan* had survived occurred to him. He found he was sweating at the extraordinary risk he had run. What if the Spanish ships had been better prepared? Or had spotted his ruse, and reduced sail too? Caught in the crossfire between two ships of the line, his frigate would have been quickly overwhelmed. And what had he achieved of value to set against that risk? At best some minor damage to two of his enemy's ships, which would be quickly repaired, and a few casualties. He glanced across at Lydia, who looked down on him from her portrait, her eyes full of disapproval. Yes, my dear, perhaps I was showing off a trifle, he thought to himself. I will endeavor to be more careful in future.

*****

71

'Will you please do me a kindness and shift them paints, sir!' exclaimed Britton, the *Titan*'s harassed wardroom steward. 'If I don't get these here places set for tonight, Mr Macpherson will be after blood.' Lieutenant Blake let out a sigh, and lay down his brush on the wardroom table.

'Oh very well,' he said. 'I shall stop now, but it is a great shame. I am so very close to achieving a tolerable likeness.' Britton let out a cry and snatched up the paint brush from the polished wood. He glared first at the tiny blob of paint that had been left behind, and then at the frigate's second lieutenant.

'Might you oblige me with some of that spirit of wine, what you uses to clean your brushes, sir?' he asked. 'It may answer to remove this stain, after a deal of scrubbing.'

'Who was your model, John?' asked Charles Faulkner, the *Titan*'s aristocratic purser from the far side of the table. He patted at his auburn curls and twitched at the front of his well tailored coat. 'If it was me, I trust you employed my superior side.'

'No, not you, Charles,' smiled Blake. 'I have been trying to capture the likeness of those members of the crew who possess more interesting features. I started with the boatswain, who makes a fine subject. Every one of his forty years at sea are etched into Mr Hutchinson's face. Then I progressed to our newest recruit. Tell me, what do you think?' He turned his board around, and the purser found himself faced by the startling blue eyes and dark face of John Grainger.

'That is very good,' he said. 'You really have captured him well. That Moorish hue to his skin, those disconcerting eyes... I can almost feel his underlying sense of mystery. Perhaps it is best if you do not paint me. I am not sure I am quite prepared to have my inner being so exposed. What do you think, Jacob?'

Armstrong put his book down and came around the table to

look at the picture.

'Well, I'll be damned,' he exclaimed. 'There certainly is something troubling about that Grainger fellow, and you have it right there in that darn picture. He has a look about him that is, well, not quite civilised.'

'I know what you mean,' said Blake. He turned the picture back towards himself and tilted it first one way and then another to examine it in the light. 'Perhaps it needs just a little more shading around the eyes.' He leant forward to pick up another brush. A cough, close in tone to the bark of an angry dog, stopped him with his hand still in midair. 'I do beg your pardon, Britton. I was about to pack away, was I not?'

'Yes, sir, you was,' said the wardroom steward, his arms folded tight. 'Shall I call for your servant to come and assist with clearing them paints away? That way I may still have some hope of having the table laid this watch.'

'No need,' said Blake. 'I shall behave myself now.' He packed away his painting materials and took them through into his cabin. The picture was left behind on the table. The purser leant forward to examine it more closely.

'What is it that troubles you about the look of our friend Grainger?' he asked the American.

'I am not entirely sure,' said Armstrong. 'I never did wholly buy his curious tale as to how he came to be on that Russian privateer, and we have little notion as to why he should be in the Mediterranean in the first place. I grant you he has some facility with the English tongue, but even my colonial ear can tell what a strange accent he has. Yet it is his manner that truly troubles me. Blake has caught it well in his picture. It is not the first time I have seen that demeanour.'

'Really?' said the purser. 'Where have you encountered it

before?'

'Back in the Americas,' said the ship's master. 'During the revolution I served in a Loyalist militia. Most of the savages were for the King, too, and we fought alongside a large troop of Mohawk Indians for much of one summer.'

'Was that how you came to be scalped, Jacob?' asked the purser, indicating his fellow officer's bald head.

'No, that affected him later,' laughed Blake, as he returned from his cabin to join them. 'Have you not noted that all ship's masters lose their hair in time? It is a consequence of them tearing it out as they puzzle over the indifferent charts the Admiralty supply them.'

'Too true,' smiled Armstrong. 'As it happens the Mohawk do indeed pluck out their hair, tuft by tuft, until all that remains is a square on the back of the head, which they braid and decorate. But it is their gaze, so cold and in want of animation, that put me in mind of our friend Grainger. It is a look that shows their true character, pitiless and stern, and quite without compassion. They fought with us that season, but none of us had any illusion they would just as readily fight against us if the wind should shift to another quarter.'

'I once had a creditor with a countenance like that,' said Faulkner. 'I was in a spot of bother after a wretched run of ill luck at the card tables and the damned cove turned up with his traps every deuced place I went. I have no notion how he knew where I would be, but the first thing I would see when I stepped down from my carriage was him, standing there just looking at me. His face was as solemn as a judge, every bit as savage as one of your Mohawks.'

'Did you ever manage to repay him, Charles?' asked Blake.

'Eventually,' he replied. 'With some help from my people,

which in a curious way is why I am obliged to earn my honest crust as a purser.'

'Now there is a brace of words you seldom encounter together,' laughed Armstrong. 'Honest and purser!'

'My route to becoming a purser is strange, I grant you, Jacob,' said Faulkner. 'But your path must be curious too. How does a militia man find himself navigating a King's ship?'

'By rights, I should have taken over my father's farm in Albany County, if it were not for the damned Yankees,' he explained. 'After the war the government gave us compensation and the chance to buy land in Upper Canada, but my people were done with the Americas, and returned to England. I served as the first the mate and then the master of a trading brig my family owned for a while. My father was always at heart a farmer, and in consequence made a very indifferent ship owner, but I fell quite in love with the sea. I had always had some facility with numbers, and I took to navigation as to the manner born. So when the war came I decided to join the navy, heaven help me.'

'Do you ever feel the urge to return home?' asked the purser. 'To this Albany County you speak of?'

'It was a fine part of the world Charles, but there is little there for me now. Perhaps that is what truly fascinates me about Grainger. Not what is different between us, but what we share. We are both straws in the wind, both men of no country now.'

'Gentlemen, I shall be obliged if you would vacate the wardroom for a wee while,' said Macpherson, as he bustled in through the door. He was resplendent in the full dress scarlet of a marine officer, and over his shoulder could be seen the face of the wardroom's steward. 'You have vexed poor Britton quite long enough. It is a lovely evening out. Will you not take a diverting turn upon the quarterdeck and let the poor man finalise the preparation of the cabin for our Hogmanay feast?'

*****

The lower deck of the *Titan* was a content place later that evening. It was an open space that ran from the officers' quarters abaft the main mast in an uninterrupted sweep of deck a hundred feet long and almost forty feet wide. True, the main deck above the men's heads was uncomfortably low for all but the smallest members of the crew, but once they were seated at the mess tables that ran down both sides of the ship, as they were now, even the enormous Sam Evans could sit comfortably. The lower deck was placed right down on the water line, which meant that only a trickle of natural light reached the men through the gratings from the world above, but on the other hand the glow from the lines of lanterns provided a warm, flattering light. The murmur of the crew's talk mingled pleasingly with the sound of the waves as they surged against the ship's sides a matter of inches from where they sat. A good dinner had been consumed by the men, the quality enhanced by fresh produce taken on board at Gibraltar. All seemed right in their world.

At the third table back from the main mast, port side, was a companionable group of men. They sat facing each other and swayed to and fro on their benches in time with the motion of the ship as they worked at various activities. Sedgwick had his journal out and was copying in fair hand a passage he had scrawled out earlier in pencil on a scrap of paper. O'Malley sat across from him and tuned his fiddle, holding the smooth brown wood to his ear as he thrummed the strings. Trevan was at work with his clasp knife, and was carving a piece of oak, making deft little cuts and then blowing to clear away the dust. Evans was sewing, his thick fingers awkward as a hand of bananas as they gripped the tiny needle. He wanted to add a little more embroidery to his already magnificent shore going shirt. He looked up from his work as the door of the wardroom swung open for a moment, and yet another roar of laughter echoed forward through the ship.

'Them Grunters are celebrating in style, and no mistake,' he said. 'They sound like they're already as pissed as clergy. I mean, I get that it were a neat trick Pipe pulled off on the Dons this morning, but do it really warrant a roister like what they're having?' The other sailors sat around the mess table looked up from their various activities to stare at the Londoner. 'What?' he asked.

'Are you not knowing what fecking day it is?' demanded O'Malley.

'It's Sunday of course,' said Evans. 'I'm hardly likely to have missed that, what with us having a make and mend afternoon.'

'What else about it?' continued the Irishman.

'Eh, it were a bit foggy first thing? Turned out nice later?'

'Have you heard of New Year's fecking Eve at all?' suggested O'Malley, rolling his eyes at the others.

'Really?' said Evans. 'What, today? Are you sure? I could have bleeding sworn it were only last week that we was having plum duff for dinner on account of it being Yuletide.'

'So it was, Sam,' said Trevan. 'The one generally follows t'other fairly sharp like.' The Londoner counted on his tattooed figures, got as far as the 'F' of fast and smiled at his friends.

'You're right,' he announced, and set aside his shirt. 'New Year's Eve, eh? What are we about, all sitting round the table like a bunch of village widows? We should be having a bash ourselves. Why don't you play your fiddle, Sean, and let's have a hornpipe.'

'Well that sounds grand and all, but we're back on watch in less than an hour,' said O'Malley.

'That's plenty of time,' insisted Evans. He turned around on his stool to address the wider deck. 'Hey, lads, it's the last bleeding night of the year. Who fancies a dance?'

'Don't mind if I do,' said Peter Hobbs, a lanky young top man at the next table, known for the unusual grace of his hornpipe. Other figures rose from their seats around the deck and moved towards the open area under the main hatchway where the headroom was a little more generous.

'Will you look at what you've started?' sighed O'Malley. He picked up his fiddle, rose to his feet and called across the deck to a fellow musician as he did so. 'Hoy, Brendan! Have you got your drum to hand, at all?'

Before long several lanterns had been moved to illuminate the open area of deck. To one side sat O'Malley on a mess stool, his violin poised beneath his chin. Opposite him sat Brendan with his small drum clasped between his knees. Both men stamped a foot several times to agree a rhythm, glanced across to one another, and the drummer produced a thunderous beat through which O'Malley stitched a waterfall of rapid notes. Soon the deck was alive with a spinney of graceful bodies, each one twirling and stamping on the spot in the flickering light. Those who watched in the circle of spectators kept the time by clapping their hands, or threw in the odd cry of appreciation as a particularly fine step was successfully executed, while others waited their chance to join the dancing.

Sedgwick watched the dancers too. His head moved in time to the music, but his expression was far away and tinged with sadness. Trevan noticed the look and pushed his way to his side.

'You alright there, Able, lad?' he said. 'You looked proper melancholy just now.'

'I do love a good hornpipe, but when I hear people dancing to the sound of a drum, it is hard for me not to think of home. I have just been writing about those times, and even the noise of bare feet on the deck takes me back.'

'Was it a good place, your village, like?'

'No, not really,' said the coxswain. 'Some huts in the middle of fields, between the forest and the river. Nothing to mark it out.'

'Mind, I always hold as it's the people what makes a place tolerable or no,' said the Cornishman. 'There be no end of villages as is grand enough in the way of stone houses and a fancy church an' all, but if the squire and the parson are right arses it don't signify any. Ships can be the same. Good grunters and decent shipmates is what matter, more than fine paint and fancy scrollwork and the like. Was your home neighbourly, like?'

'In its way it was. Most of the people there were relatives of some degree, uncles and aunts, cousins and the like.'

'You reckon as you will ever go back home?' Sedgwick shook his head.

'What to, Adam?' he said. 'There will be little left. The tribe that attacked my village destroyed everything. The old were all done for, and the young like me were taken away to be sold to the slavers on the beach. There ain't nothing for me there now.'

'That's proper sad, mate,' said Trevan. He patted his friend on the arm. 'When it comes to settle down, once this war is done, you can always come back to the village that me and my Molly hail from. There be always work for a fisherman or a strong pair of hands, although what folks will make of a Negro, I can't rightly say.'

'Thanks, Adam,' smiled Sedgwick. 'You're a proper mate. But you must let me through now. I need the heads.' Sedgwick pushed his way through the crowd that ringed the dancers and headed towards the ladder way that led to the deck above. It was true that he did need to relieve himself, but he also did not want his friend to see the moisture that his memories of home had pricked in his eyes.

On the main deck he made his way forward, ducked under the forecastle and past the galley. The crew's evening meal had been served some time ago, but the firebox of the abandoned stove still glowed orange in the gloom. Beside him the massive cylinder of the bowsprit sloped up and away through the front of the ship. He followed it out of the low door that opened onto the beak head. Above him the long shaft of wood thrust onwards, while hunched beneath it was the bulging carved muscles and swirling cloth of the ship's figurehead. Beyond the bowsprit the empty sea spread away from him, pink and calm in the evening light. Through the open basket of head timbers he could see the bow wave below him, endlessly renewed with a hiss as the frigate sliced through the water. To one side the mountains of Spain were a dark bar on the horizon, while above his head the first stars had appeared. He was alone with the beautiful view, and he felt it calm him as it washed away the memories conjured up by the dancing. He breathed in deep lungfuls of cool evening air as he relieved himself, and then he returned to the main deck, buttoning up his trousers as he came. It was as he returned to the dark of the forecastle that he heard the voices, coming from the other side of the bowsprit.

'I thought you was a bloody mate,' exclaimed the first voice.

'Sure I am,' came the reply, calm and reassuring. 'Which is why I ain't rushing straight to tell the Grunters, an' all. You've got to think of this just as a little bit of trade. No need to get all hot over such matters. I need some money, and you need me to keep my trap shut. All very simple, when you look on it.' The first voice said something low and angry that Sedgwick struggled to catch.

'Well, that's as may be, but I shall not be moved,' said the second man, who was much closer to where the coxswain stood. 'I told you straight how much as will satisfy me. It be your business how you gets it. But surely it is no more than a trifle, compared with what will become of you if I tell what I know? Fact is that you will swing if they should find out what you've done.'

'Damn your bleeding eyes!' snarled the first voice, and Sedgwick heard footsteps as they disappeared along the deck. The second man waited in the dark for a moment, and then began to chuckle to himself. It was that laugh which allowed Sedgwick to place him. It was Daniel Oates, the shy little volunteer from Bristol.

Chapter 5
The Fisherman's Gift

Alexander Clay looked up at the yellow and red flag of Spain that streamed out from the masthead, and then returned his attention to the coast of that country. The fog off Cartagena was several days behind them now, and it was a crisp, clear January morning. The distant shore swung round in a great sweep till it ended in the long finger of Cape de La Nao. Beyond lay the wide gulf of Valencia, and the next naval base on their list to reconnoitre. Lieutenant Taylor stood beside him and eyed the flag with unease.

'Do you hold such a ruse de guerre will be effective, sir?' he asked. 'By rights we should have one of those big wooden crosses hauled up to the peak if we truly wanted to pass off as a Don.'

'They generally do not fool many, I grant you, but given we are the first Royal Navy vessel to be seen in these waters for ten months now, the native shipping may have grown less wary,' he replied. 'If it serves to confuse a possible prize long enough for us to get close, then it will have achieved its object. I had hoped that we might surprise some of the coastal trade as it attempts to round this cape.' Taylor glanced up towards the lookout who stood on the fore royal arm, high above the deck. The sailor was alert as he scanned the horizon with one hand shading his eyes while the other rested on the mast beside him. He fixed on something, and then after a brief moment he turned his head towards them.

'Deck there! Sail ho!' he yelled.

'Where away?' shouted Taylor.

'Full on the bow, sir,' came the reply.

'Let us get the topgallants on her, and see if we can contrive to slip a little closer,' said Clay. 'Mr Russell, kindly take a glass aloft and see what you make of the chase.' The midshipman ran for the main shrouds and bounded up them with the agility of an ape.

'She looks to be a big merchantman, sir,' he reported, once he had regained his breath. 'Might be a snow from the size of her. Spanish colours, and steady on her course.'

'Long may that continue,' said Preston, who was officer of the watch, as he rubbed his hands. 'A heavily laden snow will bring in a bob or two of prize money.'

'Deck there!' yelled Russell. 'She has hauled her wind, sir.'

'Ah, not wholly taken in by our Spanish flag then,' muttered Taylor. 'Please God she should hesitate a while longer.'

'I wonder if she will be carrying any bladders of quicksilver, sir,' said the young lieutenant.

'What a curious cargo to expect, Mr Preston,' said Clay. 'What makes you imagine that she might?'

'I have no certain intelligence, sir,' replied the lieutenant. 'But do you remember Mr Knight, the boatswain on the old *Agrius*? He told me he was once involved in the capture of a Spanish snow bound for the Americas. When they searched the hold they found she was full of these curious bladders, packed in straw. The men thought they might be wine skins and knifed a few to sample the contents. They had the shock of their lives when all this liquid metal poured out, but it proved to be the finest of prizes. The men got paid over thirty guineas a head. Apparently quicksilver is more valuable than treasure, though why I have no notion.'

'That is because it is needed to draw gold dust from pay dirt, Mr Preston,' said Armstrong. 'She will have been bound for the mines of New Granada and Peru.'

'Deck there!' yelled Russell. 'She has gone about now and is busy clapping on more sail, sir.'

'Not a farthing until we catch our prize, Mr Preston,' said Clay. 'Let us get the courses on her, and replace that flag with our own.'

Old Amos, the *Titan*'s impassive quartermaster, stood at his place at the helm while his jaw worked on a piece of tobacco. He eased the wheel first one way and then the other with each wave that battered the frigate's bow as her speed increased, all the time keeping the compass needle steady on the course he had been given. During his many years of service he had developed the ears of a pipistrelle when it came to overhearing officers' conversations. He glanced across at his friend Josiah, the silver-haired captain of the afterguard, and raised a single grey eyebrow, which was sufficient to summon him across. He turned his head and spat his quid into the spittoon by the wheel with long practiced accuracy, and then addressed his friend out of the corner of his mouth.

'Grunters say this chase has some manner of silver aboard,' he muttered. 'Forty guineas a man prize money.' Josiah's eyes widened with greed for a moment, and he sauntered away to rejoin his men.

'Get that mizzen topsail drawing proper,' he growled. 'The ship we're after is stuffed with loot.' It took no more than five minutes for word of mouth to spread the news from the back of the quarterdeck to the top men high up on the foremast.

'Cut the fecking thing if you have too,' urged O'Malley, as he leant over the fore royal yard to remonstrate with his friend. 'That treasure ship is after getting away from us. Haven't you heard? Packed with ingots of gold, so she is, enough to set every man jack of us up for life.'

'I am doing my best, Sean,' muttered Trevan as he worked at the stubborn knot. His long blonde pigtail whipped around his face in the keen breeze.

'What are you doing, Trevan, you Cornish bastard!' yelled Josh Black, the captain of the foretop, and one of the *Titan*'s less patient petty officers. 'Don't you like fucking money?' The rest of the men spread out along the yard growled in agreement, while the whole foremast circled in the air as the frigate raced through the water.

'Got it, Mr Black,' cried Trevan as the knot came free at last.

'Let fall the sail,' roared Black, then turned his head to address the tiny foreshortened figure of Lieutenant Preston a hundred and thirty feet below him. 'Ready to sheet home, sir.'

'About bloody time!' came drifting up from below.

The two sailors had a perfect view of the chase as they caught their breath, perched at the top of the frigate's lofty foremast. The only substantial cable that might have impeded their view was the forestay, but it was below their feet as it dropped down, as steep as a church spire, towards the bowsprit of the ship far below. Five miles of green water away lay the bulky shape of the snow. She had every sail she possessed spread on her twin masts, each of which was almost as tall as those of the *Titan*'s. Together they drove her big hull surging through the water. Her round bow tossed the sea far on either side and she left a churned band of white behind her.

'So do you think we will catch her at all?' asked O'Malley. Trevan judged the distance still to go to the cape of land that now filled the horizon ahead of them with its tall cliffs and sucked in his cheeks.

'I don't rightly know, Sean,' he said. 'We be a good three knots swifter by my reckoning, but that there land is mighty close. Over yonder is where she'll be bound. See that cove there?' O'Malley looked at where his friend was pointing. He saw a small round bay scooped into the headland. The entrance was dominated by the stone walls of a coastal battery built high up on top of the cliffs that formed the sides of the little bay. Above the crenulated parapet the flag of Spain fluttered in the breeze. The two men watched the chase for another few minutes, until an indignant shout from Black ordered them back down on deck. By that time it was clear that the *Titan* would lose the race.

*****

'That is close enough, Mr Preston,' said Clay. 'Bring her up into the wind and get the royals and courses off her.' The last ranging shot from the Spanish battery had skipped across the water, kicking up a chain of splashes as it came. The final one was a bare hundred yards from the frigate's side. Clay saw the dirty white ball of smoke from the cannon that had fired drift away on the sea breeze, while from the middle of the battery he could see a more persistent column of darker smoke that slanted away in a brown feather against the sky.

'They're heating shot up there, sir,' said Taylor. 'Against the prospect of us chancing our arm and going in after that snow.'

'I am afraid so,' said Clay. 'I have only once been subject to such a bombardment, when I was third in the *Minerva* back at the start of the war. Red hot cannon balls make an ill companion for a wooden ship.' He opened his telescope and examined the little bay ahead. The snow had rounded to and dropped anchor now, close under the protection of the battery on the headland above her. As he watched, the last of her sails disappeared, to leave her bare spars and rigging like black pencil strokes against the red cliffs behind her. What a shame, thought Clay. She would be easy enough to cut out with the ship's boats, if only the guns were not there. He examined the battery with care. It was high up and inaccessible on top of its cliff. He could see tiny figures clustered beside the guns. Off to one side stood the lone figure of an officer. The sunlight flashed briefly off him. At first Clay thought it must be the braid of his uniform, but when he looked closer he could see that the Spaniard too had a telescope, and was examining the frigate.

'Mr Macpherson!' he called. 'Kindly bring a glass and give me your opinion of this battery.' The marine examined the little Spanish fortification for a moment.

'I count six large calibre guns, sir,' he said. 'Say ten gunners per piece, an officer, a sergeant and some corporals would make less than eighty men all told. With the element of surprise and the support of a similar number of sailors, my marines could take the place easy enough. What I do not see though is how we might come at them. An ape would struggle to climb those cliffs.'

'You are right,' said his captain. 'I can see little prospect of our attacking the guns, and unless they are taken, that snow is safe. I cannot hazard the ship by exposing it to their fire just for a prize.'

'It is a great pity,' said Taylor. 'Look at those fishermen, slipping into the bay as easy as kiss my hand.' Clay swung his glass towards the little boat that had just appeared around the headland. She was a tiny craft, barely larger than the *Titan*'s launch. Her hull was painted bright blue which contrasted with the single faded brick-red sail that bulged out on her mast.

'Maybe she plans to sell some of her catch to the captain of the snow, sir?' speculated Taylor.

'Perhaps she will come this way next,' added Macpherson. 'A

pan of fish would make a pleasant change from salt pork.'

But Taylor and the marine officer were both wrong. The little boat went past the anchored merchantman, dropped her sail and ran up on to the beach. They watched as two figures jumped out and pulled it through the shallows, while a third stepped ashore carrying several large baskets. Clay felt a prickle of excitement on the back of his neck.

'That catch they have landed is not destined for your stomach, Mr Macpherson,' he said. 'A guinea says it is for the garrison of the battery. Attend closely, gentlemen. How are they going to carry those baskets up the cliff?' While one of the fishermen stayed with the boat, the other two each swung a basket onto their heads, walked across the beach and disappeared out of sight. A little while later the figures appeared again on the skyline as they picked their way upwards, turning first one way and then another amongst the rocks.

'There has to be a wee track of some kind at the back of the beach, sir,' exclaimed Macpherson. 'The start must be out of sight from us here.'

'Do you think you could find your way up it in the dark if we landed you on that beach?' asked Clay.

'I should imagine so, sir,' replied the marine. 'Where a man can go laden with a basket, a marine with a musket can certainly follow.'

'The fishermen are nearly at the top,' commented Taylor. 'It is fortunate that one of them is wearing such a bright green weskit. Otherwise they would be difficult to spot.'

'Mr Armstrong,' asked Clay, 'what manner of moon do we have tonight?'

'In its last quarter and rising at five bells in the first watch, sir,' replied the master.

A Man of No Country

'That will serve handsomely, sir,' said the marine. 'The ship's boats can approach in the dark, slip past the snow and land a storming party on the beach. Find the path and ascend the cliff, and then, once in position at the top, we can attack with the light of the moon to aid us. When we have taken the battery, there will be nothing to prevent the *Titan* from standing into the bay and capturing the prize.'

'A very good plan, Mr Macpherson,' said Clay. 'Mark the layout of the bay well, gentlemen. We shall put back out to sea in a moment, as if we have been confounded by the Dons, but once the sun has set we shall return.'

*****

'Pull steady there!' hissed Taylor in the stern of the longboat as one of the men missed his stroke. His oar foamed through the water, making a faint smear of silver on the calm surface of the sea.

'That was you, Grainger,' breathed Evans from the seat behind him. 'Try not to get us all bleeding killed, eh?' Grainger grunted something unintelligible, and the boat crept on through the velvet dark. Evans pulled on his oar and felt the shaft bend beneath his hands with all the extra weight the boat was carrying. With each stroke his right arm rubbed against the rough serge coat of the marine sat next to him on the bench.

'Can't you shift up any?' he moaned. 'I am packed in closer than a mallard's arse here, and they're watertight.'

'Sorry, mate,' whispered the soldier. 'I am hard up against the corporal on t' other side as it is.'

Evans returned to his rowing and tried to ignore the repeated contact each time he pulled the oar free of the water. He was glad of the chance of some exercise, for it was a clear night, and the air was chill so close to the surface of the sea. Above his head a scatter of stars shone out. Their faint light glimmered off the oily water, giving the men a tiny amount of light to row by. Just behind the longboat he could see a mass of greater darkness in the night, where the launch followed them. He glanced over his shoulder, past O'Malley in the bow, at the approaching loom of the land, a black presence more to be guessed at than seen. Where land met sea he saw a faint line of white appear and vanish as gentle waves lapped against a beach.

'Absolute silence!' warned Taylor. 'We are about to pass the snow now.' Evans glanced to his left and saw the big ship as it soared above him in the dark. A little light spilt out from lanterns below deck, while her rigging and bare spars seemed to net the stars in a mesh of black as they stole past her bow. He could hear the muffled voices of her crew followed by a laugh, sudden and loud in the silence of the night. The sound disappeared behind him as they rowed farther into the bay and entered the blacker darkness close to the land.

'Easy there,' muttered Taylor. 'In oars.' Evans felt sand grate against the underside of the hull and the longboat scraped to a halt. 'Over the side, lads. Pull us up the beach.' The sailors swung their feet over the gunwale and dropped into the shallow water.

'Christ!' hissed the voice of Rosso from the far side of the boat. 'This water's bloody freezing.'

Once everyone was out, the crew ran the longboat up onto the sand. Faint curses in the night, quickly silenced, showed where the crew of the launch too had discovered how cold the water was. Evans leaned over the side and felt for the equipment he had been issued with. He pushed the pistol into his waist band, threw the coiled line and grappling hook over one shoulder and hefted his boarding axe in his hand. Next to him O'Malley checked over his musket by feel.

'Marines to me,' said Macpherson from farther up the beach.

'Larboards to me,' echoed the voice of Preston from off to one side, and Evans and O'Malley went to join the shadowy group gathered around the lieutenant. 'All here?' queried Preston. His extended hand brushed over each member of his party like a blind man in a crowd. 'Good. Make yourselves comfortable on the sand but stay together and stay silent. We shall wait here while Mr Russell reconnoitres the path with a shuttered lantern.'

'Good luck with that,' mouthed Evans. 'It's blacker than a Newgate lockup. How are we meant to bleeding well find the enemy?'

'The moon will rise soon,' said the voice of Grainger from out of the dark. 'That will give us all the light we need.'

'It had bleeding better,' muttered the Londoner as he stretched himself out on the sand.

'Easy with your fecking feet,' cursed O'Malley.

'I said silence!' whispered Preston.

From the wall of cliff at the back of the beach, Evans watched the reconnaissance party work their way up the narrow path. The shuttered lantern gave off a tiny point of light, like an orange firefly in the night, as it danced backwards and forwards up the slope. Occasionally it would pause, and Evans could almost imagine the young midshipman as he peered around him, this way and that, amongst the mass of rocks, wondering which way led up to the battery, and which might end with a sudden plunging fall. Eventually the little spark stopped close to the top, and then began to descend back down. It reached the beach, and a few moments later a figure loomed up out of the dark.

'Mr Preston?' said Taylor.

'Here, sir,' came the low voice of the Yorkshireman.

'You can advance your party up to the top now,' said the first lieutenant. 'Mr Russell will accompany you. He has placed men at most of the less certain points to act as guides. At the top he reports that you shall encounter a sentry who must be silenced. Once that is done, wait for me before attempting anything against the battery. I will be close behind with Mr Macpherson and his marines.'

'Aye aye, sir,' said Preston. 'On your feet, men!'

The little path was steep and treacherous as it picked its way upwards between the rocks. The men were in a single, straggling line that snaked along the path. Each man rested a hand on the figure in front of him so as not to lose his way. Backwards and forwards they went, grinding up the cliff, and with every step they became more aware of the growing drop behind them.

'Christ, that was close,' muttered Evans. He had felt the scree slide beneath one of his feet, and had just grabbed at a rock to steady himself.

'It's not too bad, Sam,' said O'Malley from just ahead of him.

'If you're a bleeding goat perhaps,' muttered Evans. 'Or a top man like you, Sean, which amounts to much the same thing.'

'Be silent there!' hissed Preston. 'We are nearly at the top. There is a shallow slope over on this side. Form up there, but do so quietly!'

Evans crouched down behind a boulder and looked at the final stretch of path. They were halted on a ledge close to the top. He could make out the vague shape of rocks all around him. The ground rose in a gentle slope for twenty yards, and then the night sky resumed beyond that. Silhouetted against the stars was the figure of a soldier. He had his back to them as he stood looking out to sea with a musket slung on his shoulder.

'I need a volunteer to silence that guard,' whispered Preston. Evans was tempted to offer himself, but he knew his huge bulk would be a disadvantage as he crept amongst the rocks in the dark.

'I'll do it, sir,' said a voice next to him.

'I am not sure, Grainger,' said the lieutenant. 'You are very new to the ship. I was thinking of one of the more experienced hands.'

'Please, sir,' said the sailor. 'I have done this before.'

'Really? I thought you were just a merchant seaman?' queried Preston. 'Oh, very well then. Take one of the musket men's bayonets.'

'I prefer to use this, sir,' said Grainger. He slid a long curved knife out of its sheath. Starlight glittered from the edge and then he disappeared into the night.

A few minutes later the moon rose up over the mountain top behind them and bathed the rocks in gentle silver light. Evans saw the sentry turn to look at the moonrise, and he held his breath. Surely the sentry would see the mass of sailors gathered below his feet? He watched the man as he stood surrounded by boulders. Then one of the larger rocks behind him seemed to unfold, and with the speed of a panther it leapt on the soldier. He saw the man's head jerk back, steel flashed in the night, and in the blink of an eye the sentry had vanished. The figure of Grainger stood up and beckoned them forward.

'Mr Butler,' said Preston, 'Go and find Mr Taylor and tell him the coast is now clear. The rest of you follow me.'

'If he's not done that a score of times, I'm a fecking Dutchman,' muttered O'Malley, as they ascended the rest of the path.

'Careful, lads,' said Rosso from ahead. 'Watch your footing. The way here is slick with blood.'

'Bleeding hell, John,' whispered Evans. 'Did you have to cut his throat?'

'Quickest way I know to silence a man, Sam,' said Grainger.

He stooped to wipe his knife on the soldier's tunic, and then slid it back into its sheath.

'Well done, Mr Preston,' said Taylor as he came up the path. Behind him came Macpherson, followed by a long line of marines, the white of their cross belts prominent in the moonlight.

'Thank you, sir,' said the lieutenant. 'I took the liberty of sending Mr Russell forward to reconnoitre the battery. He seems to have some facility at creeping about in the dark. He will be back presently.'

'We can see a tolerable amount from here,' said the marine, pointing a little farther along the cliff top to where the battery stood. Above the wall that surrounded it they could see the pitched roofs of low buildings, while from the front of the structure the barrels of the guns were visible as they poked out into the night.

'Stone built from the look of it,' said Preston. 'The wall that faces the sea looks to be much the most solid.'

'Aye, that makes sense,' agreed Macpherson. 'That is the side they would expect an attack to be made from. It needs to be able to resist bombardment. Now the wall at the back looks appreciably lower to me. Nine, maybe ten foot? Could your boys scale it, Edward?'

'Yes, easily enough,' said Preston. 'Ah, here comes our returning scout. What have you to tell us, Mr Russell?'

'The front of the battery is well guarded, sir,' he said. 'I counted at least three sentries in amongst the guns, but there may be more. On the other hand the rear wall seems to have no one patrolling it.'

'Is there a ditch or fence preventing access to the rear wall?' asked Taylor.

'No, sir,' replied the midshipman. 'A bit of scrub and a few rocks are all that might impede an approach. In the centre of the rear wall is a heavy wooden gate. There is a track that leads from there and winds along the top of the cliff away from us. I could hear guards talking on the far side of the gate, but none on this side.'

'They doubtless rely on the man we killed to warn of any approach up that wee track,' said Macpherson.

'Very well, gentlemen, let us make our plans,' said Taylor. 'We attack the rear of the building, agreed?' The other two officers grunted their assent. 'Mr Preston, your men are to scale the walls and then open the gate. Mr Macpherson, kindly have your marines ready to storm through that gate once it has been captured. Good luck to you both.'

*****

Evans swung his grappling hook twice around his head to gather speed and then flung it upwards. The steel hooks had been wrapped with strips of canvas to deaden the sound, but he still heard a clatter as it struck against the stone of the wall. He held his arms above his head, in case it fell back down on him. When it failed to do so, he looked up again and saw the rope rising above him and disappearing over the wall. He drew the line towards him, till he felt one of the hooks grip on the edge of the parapet and the rope became taut.

'Up you go, Sean,' he said, as he handed the line across to the Irishman.

'Why is it me as has to go fecking first?'

'Coz you're the bleeding top man as scampers up and down ropes all day,' said Evans. 'I doubt if this line will even take my weight, and we're proper screwed if it breaks.'

'What if there should be a dirty great Spaniard a-waiting to stove in my skull as soon as I gets up there?' queried O'Malley.

95

'Tell him you're a fellow papist and see if that answers. Go on, up with you.'

O'Malley scampered up the line, hand over hand till he could reach over and grip the top of the wall. He pulled himself up and over the parapet. On the far side the stone rampart was empty. A second grappling hook caught the top of the wall a little way farther along the wall, followed by a third. He looked across the roof of a long low building towards the row of guns. Off to one side was a smaller structure surrounded with its own thick wall.

'That'll be the magazine,' whispered Rosso as he dropped down next to his friend. 'And the long one in front has the look of a barracks. How many Dons can you see?'

'Just the sentries over by them guns, but there is sure to be more hereabouts.'

'Let's wait for the big man to join us, and then we can head for the gate.' Grainger reached the top of the second line and slid like an eel over the parapet, dropped in a crouch and then came over to join them. The first line began to jerk and the points of the hook squealed against the stone.

'Well give us a bleeding hand then,' puffed Evans, as his head appeared at the top of the wall.

The first four men into the battery stole down a short flight of steps and out onto the cobbled floor. Farther along the wall was an arched opening, from which came the yellow glow of a lantern and the sound of voices. Behind them more dark shapes slipped over the parapet and crept down the steps. The first group worked their way forward until they reached the arch of the gate, expecting to be challenged at any moment. O'Malley was in the lead. He held up his hand and then inched his head forward to peer around the corner of the wall. Suddenly the large figure of a sergeant, backed by two soldiers, marched around the corner and both groups of men froze at the sight of each other. The sergeant was the first to react. He inflated his lungs to yell a warning, but the sound never came. Grainger slid between O'Malley and Evans and plunged his knife into the Spaniard's throat. O'Malley was the next to come to life. He pulled his musket back and thrust at one of the two soldiers with his bayonet. The soldier managed to parry the blow and the two men became locked together in a desperate struggle. Rosso squared up to the other soldier with his cutlass and yelled to Evans.

'Keep going, Sam! Get that gate open.'

Evans ran past the fight and arrived in front of the gate. It consisted of a pair of heavy oak doors, reinforced with beams and peppered with iron studs. A lantern hung on a hook to one side, and in its light he examined the task. From behind him he heard a musket go off, followed by another and a cry of alarm in Spanish.

'Right, open the bleeding gate,' muttered Evans to himself. Across the doors a heavy looking beam rested in metal brackets. He dropped his boarding axe and grabbed it with both hands. It was a colossal piece of timber, obviously designed to be lifted by more than one person. 'Come on,' he urged as it inched upwards. With a final heave it came free and dropped to the ground with a clatter. Evans grabbed the ring in the centre of the door and yanked it hard towards him. Nothing moved. Behind him he could hear the clash and cries as the fight grew in intensity. He glanced over his shoulder. More sailors had come down from the wall, but the garrison were now flooding out of the barracks, many just in their trousers or shirts, but all armed.

'Get a move on, Sam!' he heard Rosso urge.

He turned back to the doors and pulled out his pistol. He searched for a lock that he could shoot, but there didn't seem to be one. In desperation he picked up his axe and hurled it into the wood again and again, but after a few massive blows it was clear the fight would be long over before he could cut through such tough oak. On the far side Macpherson's marines pounded at the gates in desperation.

'Come on, Sam, me boy,' he said out loud. 'Brawn will not answer, try brains. What is it as is holding this door? Think, man, think!' He squeezed his eyes closed for a moment and was a little child once more, back home in London. He saw his mother kneeling down to tend the kitchen fire and his father at the door, locking it for the night. He watched as he turned the key in the lock and then reached first for the top of the door and then stooped towards the bottom and his eyes flew open.

'Bolts, you idiot!' he yelled. It was the work of a moment to find them at the top and bottom of the doors and draw them back. The gates flew open under the pressure of a wave of marines.

'Steady, boys,' roared Macpherson. 'Reorder yourselves there!' The soldiers halted their charge and shuffled back into a solid block. 'Better,' said the Scotsman as he drew his sword. 'Marines will advance! Sergeant, the private three from the left in the second rank is not attending to his duty. Take his name.' The marines swept forwards and the melee in front of them parted before their approach. The defenders dropped back, but then rallied in an untidy group in the centre of the battery under the urging of their officer.

'Marines will halt!' ordered Macpherson. 'Present arms! Single volley, fire!' The night was lit by a line of stabbing flame as the muskets crashed out, and several of the defenders fell to the ground, including the officer. More sailors had surged in behind the marines and they spread out to either side of the scarlet block, fingering their weapons.

'Marines will charge!' yelled the Scot, and with a surge the remorseless line of glittering bayonets swept forwards again. It was too much for the last of the defenders. With a clatter of steel on cobbles, they lay down their weapons and backed away, their hands held aloft.

'Well done, Evans,' said Preston, as he walked through the gate. 'You took your time, but we got there in the end.'

'Aye aye, sir,' replied the Londoner. He wiped sweat from his brow, in spite of the chill air.

'Mr Russell! Go and find Mr Taylor and tell him, with my complements, that the *Titan* can come into the bay and take the prize. Mr Powell has the signal rocket.'

'Aye aye, sir,' said the midshipman, and he dashed off back through the gate.

'You men, follow me,' said Preston. 'Let us see about disabling some of these guns.' He strode into the captured battery, slipped and almost fell, but managed to recover himself.

'Damnation!' he exclaimed. He looked down at the pool of blood he had trodden in and saw the body of the Spanish sergeant.

'Have a care, sir,' said Evans. 'The way is easier on this side of the arch.'

'Was that Grainger again, Evans?' asked Preston. 'What is it with that man and the slashing of throats?'

'I am not entirely sure, sir,' replied the sailor. 'It does answer well to silence a man with speed. That there sergeant was bent on raising the alarm when he was struck down.'

'No matter,' said the lieutenant. 'He did do a tolerable job upon the soldier who guarded the cliff path. I certainly prefer to think of him being on our side of a fight than that of the enemy.'

Chapter 6
Naples

'No treasure at all?' queried O'Malley, his face aghast. 'How can that fecking be? Old Amos said he heard the Grunters speak of it, as plain as plain!'

'I was there when the hold was first broke into, and let me tell'ee, we was that desperate to find the loot, we nearly rolled the ship over,' said Trevan. 'It were like the sack of Rome. Bales and boxes everywhere, but we never found so much as a bent groat in the whole ship. Just bundles of tents and cooking gear, and no shortage of them neither.'

'It will still make a fine prize,' said Rosso. 'Big well founded ship like that, full of military stores. She'll be condemned for sure. It's a shame about the money an' all, but I never quite believed it. Even if Amos heard it right, how would the Grunters have known that this ship they had never so much as clapped eyes on would be full of treasure?'

'Through spies and such like,' insisted the Irishman. 'He's a fecking deep one that Pipe. He had us waiting off that cape just at the moment the snow showed up.' Rosso snorted at this.

'Well that's rot! It was pure chance! There must be any number of merchant ships on this coast. Besides, if he was as deep as all that, with spies an' all, how was it that we wound up capturing a snow with no treasure on board?' O'Malley scratched at his shirt for a moment, but was unable to find a fault in his friend's logic. Instead he rounded on the figure of Evans, who was knelt down on the deck and had pulled all his possessions from out of his kit bag.

'What are you about, Sam?' he asked. 'You've had your head stuck in that fecking bag since we came off watch.' The Londoner sat back on his haunches and glared at his messmates.

'That's because some bastard has been and taken all of me bleeding chink,' he growled. 'I had six crowns in my purse when we left Gibraltar, now I can't find any.'

'Who would have been and done that, Sam?' asked Trevan. 'Are you sure you didn't give it to a whore before we left, like?'

'Nah! We wasn't that pissed,' he said. 'It were only the afternoon, and any road, what kind of doxy costs that bleeding much? I remember paying the one I had, and then I stowed my purse, and it was definitely full of chink. Now look at it.' He held up the small leather bag for inspection.

'No, you're at low tide for sure,' said Trevan peering in. 'Are you certain now? You've not just been an' lost it? Be it in your other jacket?'

'Six whole crowns!' he exclaimed. 'I ain't able to chuck me money around like bleeding Midas, you know.'

'That's a fecking disgrace,' said O'Malley. 'One shipmate stealing from another? I call that as low as it gets.'

'No, that is proper bad,' said Trevan. 'Ain't like we earn that much in the first place. It do seems strange, mind, to have a cutpurse on board all of a sudden like.'

'Or perhaps not so strange,' said Rosso. He indicated where the bearded figure of Grainger sat at a separate mess table.

Philip K Allan

'You all seem very thoughtful,' rumbled a bass voice from behind them. The men turned to find the figure of Sedgwick, his shoulders stooped under the low beams, with his journal tucked under one arm.

'We're after reflecting on lost silver, in all its forms,' sighed O'Malley. 'First there was Amos's fabled treasure as never fecking was, and now Big Sam says he has been robbed of six crowns.'

'Is that so?' said Sedgwick. 'Now that is interesting. Yesterday Stephenson was saying how he had some money taken. Mind, it would be a brave thief that would risk being caught stealing from you, Sam.'

'Too bleeding right,' growled the Londoner. 'Stephenson too, eh? I told you I wasn't making it up. You lads keep your eyes skinned, and a hand on your own purses.'

'Best report it, and let the Grunters sort it out,' said the coxswain. 'Rosie, you ready to help me with my journal now?'

'Sure I am,' said Rosso. 'Let's shove off to a quieter berth.' The two men found an unoccupied mess table towards the stern end of the lower deck, and sat down next to each other. It was early afternoon, and enough daylight came down through the grating above their heads to illuminate the table top. Rosso waited for his friend to open the journal, but instead Sedgwick looked around the deck with care.

'Rosie,' he said, 'before we get back to my writing, I need to ask you something. This lad from Bristol as has joined the ship. How well do you know him?'

'Daniel Oates? I can't say as he is much of an acquaintance at all. He seemed a bit lost when he joined the barky, and kind of latched on to me when he heard my Bristol accent.'

'Does he know anything about your past?' asked Sedgwick. 'About why you changed your name and ran away to sea?' It was

Rosso's turn to look around at this.

'Course not,' he whispered. 'It's only my close mates as knows that: you, Sean, Sam and Adam.'

'Well, just you keep it that way,' urged Sedgwick. 'On New Year's Eve I was on my way back from the heads when I heard that little shit. He was talking to someone, hard by the galley. He was asking them for money in exchange for keeping his mouth shut.'

'Who was it?' gasped Rosso. Sedgwick shook his head.

'I couldn't rightly hear. He spoke that low and angry it was difficult to place, but the other man was definitely Oates. He was proper bullying him, too. He may play the dumb volunteer, but that is so much gammon, I reckon.'

'You have my thanks for the warning, Able,' said Rosso. He sat back from the table and puffed out his cheeks. 'You're right, I do need to be more careful. That's the last time I go drinking with young Oates. You never can tell what may slip when you've had a mug of grog too many. Shall we see how you are getting on with your story?' Sedgwick drew the book towards him and opened the cover.

'I have made a fair start,' he said. 'I thought to first set down where I come from. This part here is about when I was a nipper in Africa, so people will get me better. What do you think?'

'That's a right good way to set about it,' agreed his friend. 'Folk at home have no notion of foreign parts. They'll think of your kind as savages, living a life of dissipation and vice. If you can show it to be more like what they are about, that's all to the good. Let's have a read.' Rosso scanned through the pages of closely spaced lines.

'This is very good, Able,' said Rosso after awhile. 'You and your uncle being fisherman sounds very proper, as does all that about families and houses and the like. Makes it sound like a civilised village anywhere.' He flipped over a page and read on. 'And you have hit the mark with this here wedding of your brother. Good Christian folk will like to hear about you having those. Ah, but they might not be so taken with this bit here, with all that witchcraft. Best not to sail too close to that wind.'

'Do you not think so?' asked Sedgwick, 'You don't reckon I should show how we has religion too?'

'But folk will think your religion is no more than wickedness,' explained Rosso. 'They hold as ours to be the only proper one. I wouldn't go rattling along about any of that, if I were you.'

'Alright,' said Sedgwick. 'I shall take that bit out. Then over here I come to the point when my village was attacked by a rival tribe, and we were captured and taken to the slavers' compound.'

'Hold steady a moment!' said Rosso. 'Are you saying that it was fellow Negros as sold you into slavery?'

'Yes, but from a different tribe,' explained the coxswain. 'One that proper hated my people. It is much like you are always fighting the French. Only they would have done it out of greed, for the trade goods of the slavers.'

'Well, that may be all fine and true I am sure, Able, but you need to be careful,' said Rosso. 'Don't you see how plantation owners and the like will make use of such talk, if you sets it down like that? Why, they shall say as how slavery is quite the norm, amongst Negroes in Africa, cause look'ee here, even the Abolitionists are obliged to say that it's so. And then they might say as how, if slavery be the natural state of your Negro, is us profiting by it such a base thing?'

Able sat back and stared at Rosso. 'I just want to set down the truth. My story is of how a great wrong was done against me. Surely I have only to tell it straight?'

'Is your mark to tell the truth, or are you after bringing an end to slavery?'

'Can I not aim to do both?' said the coxswain.

'You could try, but it may not answer nearly as well. That's how politicking works, mate. Keep the message plain. Nothing too complicated like.'

'So I am not to offend the God-fearing, with talk of religions,' exclaimed Sedgwick, pushing the book away. 'Nor speak the truth about how I was taken. Is that how it should be? I must be fearful in what I says? What manner of freedom is this? I know you are only trying to help, Rosie, but this story won't answer for me unless what I tell is what happened. I am who I am. I took back my freedom from that bastard Haynes, and I want to tell my story. If people choose to use my words against me, or to dislike parts of the tale, so be it. But I must set it down, straight and true, as best I can recall.'

Rosso looked at his friend, and saw the stubborn resolve in his eye. After a moment he stretched his hand across the table and drew back the book till it was in front of them once more.

'Very well, Able,' he said. 'Let it be the truth then, and damn the eyes of the lot of them. So what happened next?'

*****

Even on a blustery afternoon in February, the Bay of Naples looked beautiful. The rain that had fallen since early morning had been pushed aside by the wind, and some watery sunshine had broken through the blanket of cloud to sparkle off the tops of the little green waves. Out at sea, lines of islands had appeared through the murk. Closer at hand the curved sweep of the shore was lined with whitewashed villas, their terracotta roofs polished clean by the last shower. Deeper into the city the tall bell towers of numerous churches rose above the roofs, while farther back still loomed the massive block of San Elmo castle, high on its wooded hill.

'I am afraid you are not able to see the city quite at its best captain,' said a rich voice from behind him. 'When the weather is warm the bay is a tolerable shade of blue, with diverse little boats out on the water. And over there, behind the castle, one can normally see our volcano.' Clay turned from the large window of the villa to see a lady in her early thirties, dressed in a plain white dress that was cut tighter than the current fashion so that the folds of thin muslin clung to the curves of her body. A pair of large dark eyes appraised Clay from beneath a mass of thick, coiling brown hair, a long wisp of which curled down one side of her face.

'Do I have the pleasure of addressing Lady Hamilton?' he asked.

'Please, do call me Emma,' she said, as she came forward and held out a delicate white hand for him to kiss.

'Captain Alexander Clay, at your ladyship's service.' He brushed his lips against the back of her hand, aware all the time of those liquid eyes upon him. His nostrils filled with her perfume, lilac with a hint of something muskier.

'You seem very young to be a post captain,' she said.

'I have been fortunate in the matter of promotion, Lady Emma,' he said. 'I was made post in ninety-six after a successful action with a Spanish ship of the line when I was eight and twenty.'

'How splendidly heroic!' she exclaimed, clasping her hands to her bosom. 'Was it a particularly bloody affair?'

'Eh, I suppose it was,' said Clay. 'I took a bullet in the shoulder, and we had—'

'Did you now?' Lady Hamilton's eyes grew even larger with interest. 'Oh, you poor man! I trust you are quite recovered?'

A Man of No Country

'Yes, I am now. Thank you for your ladyship's concern.'

'Do you know, we had another injured naval captain who came to stay a few years back,' she mused. 'He was a charming little man, but he would talk on and on in the most frightful rural accent, principally about himself. He had been injured in one eye, as I recall. It looked quite black, like that of a fish, but his other eye was rather handsome. A fetching shade of blue, if I am not mistaken.'

'I believe you may refer to Sir Horatio Nelson, Lady Emma. He has lost an arm now too.'

'Goodness, has he really?' she exclaimed. 'Poor man! I wonder what will remain of him when he should next chance to call?'

'Do you make such detailed observations about all your visitors?' smiled Clay. 'If so I must take care in what I say.'

'Only those with which I truly become intimate, Captain,' said Lady Hamilton. 'The question is whether you will permit my acquaintance with you to develop in that fashion?' The pink tip of her tongue flashed for a moment in the corner of her mouth. 'Will you?' she asked, her head held on one side as she looked at him.

'Sir William is ready to see you now, Capitano,' announced the bewigged footman who had marched into the salon. Clay let out a sigh of relief and stood up.

'My apologies, Lady Emma, but I must see your husband.'

'Oh, now I suppose you will be locked away for the rest of the day, talking only of politics and war,' pouted his hostess. 'It is all very vexing. When you are done, I shall insist on you returning to see me, captain. I will trouble you for a proper account of this battle of yours. We get so few visitors since this wretched war has prevented anyone from touring on the continent.'

'If duty permits, it will be a pleasure, your ladyship,' said Clay.

The footman showed him into a large, book-lined study that

was full of tables. They seemed to be randomly dotted around the floor, and every one of them was packed with pieces of either carved stone or shards of pottery. It took him a while to locate His Britannic Majesty's Ambassador to the Kingdom of the Two Sicilies. He was stood in one corner, busy examining a large marble bust. Where Lady Hamilton was all voluptuousness, her husband was anything but. Sir William Hamilton was a spare, bony man in his late sixties. His thin legs barely filled his stockings, and his wiry hands seemed lost within the sleeves of his cavernous olive green coat.

'Over here captain,' he called. 'I was just admiring my latest purchase. Will you favour me with your opinion of it, sir?' Clay threaded his way between the tables, while he tried his best not to knock over anything, and at last arrived beside his host. The bust was cut in creamy white stone and showed the head and shoulders of a stern young man with a thick curly mane that matched his lavish beard. Between the two masses of stone hair, a pair of blank, frowning eyes looked out into the room from either side of a prominent nose.

'It is very fine, Sir William,' he said. 'Pray, whose likeness is it?'

'Marcus Aurelius,' said his host with reverence. He pulled out a silk handkerchief and ran it across the top of the bust's hair. 'In fine condition, is he not, when you consider that he has lain buried in an olive grove for one and a half millennia? I cannot begin to conceive how Senior Bernotti manages to find such treasures for me to buy. I have only to express my desire for something, and it will appear.'

'The condition is indeed remarkable,' said Clay. He examined the clean cut stone. 'Why it looks as if it could have been fashioned yesterday.'

A Man of No Country

'The untrained eye might almost think so,' agreed his host. 'Shall we return to my desk captain?' He indicated a marginally less cluttered piece of furniture on the far side of the room. 'Have a care, I pray you! The tail of your coat so very nearly displaced that priceless Etruscan vase.'

Once the two men were seated, Clay handed across the desk the letter he had brought with him from Admiral St Vincent.

'Thank you, Captain Clay,' Hamilton said. 'Might I offer you some refreshment while I peruse this? Will you assay some Marsala? It is an unctuous wine they make in Sicily. Not quite as fine as a Madeira, but palatable none the less. Giuseppe, a glass for the captain, if you please.' Clay accepted a glass of the wine, while Sir William drew out a pair of little round spectacles, wedged them on his thin nose and broke the seal on the despatch. As he read, he made a little grunting noise to himself at each salient point. Clay tried to ignore the irritating sound in the quiet of the room and instead looked about him at all the various antiquities.

'So the navy is to return to these waters in the spring, I collect?' said the ambassador abruptly, dropping the letter in front of him. 'Upon my word, it is not a moment before time. The French have had matters all their own way for much too long.'

'Yes, Sir William,' said Clay. 'Once the admiral has received his promised reinforcements, he will send a powerful squadron into the Mediterranean.'

'So he says in this dispatch. Do you know who will command it? Admiral Sir Peter Parker, perhaps?'

'I understand that Lord St Vincent is minded to favour Sir Horatio Nelson with the command.'

'Nelson?' queried the ambassador. He greeted this news with a few more of his little grunts. 'He seems very young for such a responsibility. Newly promoted, ain't he?'

'I believe so, Sir William.'

'I suppose Hanging Jack knows what he is about,' mused Hamilton. 'Will they be based on Gibraltar?'

'Only if nowhere better should present itself. The Rock is far from ideal. If a levanter should blow, a fleet based there would be unable to intervene in any mischief the French have planned.'

'At the start of the war we did capture Corsica, which was perfect to guard the French coast from. But then the fleet was withdrawn back to the Channel amid all this talk of invasion, and the French promptly took the island back.' Clay sipped at his drink for a moment.

'I was reflecting earlier how Naples would make an ideal base for a fleet, Sir William,' he said. 'Good sized anchorage in a blow, a decent dockyard, and placed plumb in the centre of the Mediterranean.'

'I daresay it would be most satisfactory,' conceded the ambassador. 'Regrettably the Kingdom is neutral of course, but the King certainly loathes the French, and his wife is poor Marie-Antoinette's sister. I suppose I might be able to arrange for a squadron to receive some support in a quiet way. These things can take time to arrange, especially here in Naples, but let me begin some tentative discussions.' He made a note on a sheet of paper and then looked up. 'What else might I be able to help you with, captain?'

'The principal part of my mission is to reconnoitre these waters to see what the enemy may be planning to do next. I have looked into the Spanish ports, but there was little that seemed amiss. Lord St Vincent suggested that you might be able to offer me some guidance.' The older man looked around him, as if to check that none of the Roman busts were listening, then beckoned his visitor closer.

A Man of No Country

'There is something afoot in southern France,' he said. 'I have it from several sources. The Queen still has contacts there for one, and Lady Hamilton enjoys a close acquaintance with her. The reports I have heard state that some manner of military venture is being prepared.'

'That is interesting,' mused Clay. 'On the way here I was fortunate to capture a ship bound for Marseille with a cargo of military tents and cooking equipment, which might be thought to support such rumours.'

'Very likely,' nodded the ambassador. 'The certain intelligence I have is that an army camp has been constructed at Marseille, and a further smaller camp has been built close to Genoa. I also hear that they are gathering together shipping, and that the French navy have fitted out a number of warships at their naval base at Toulon. Tell me, what is your opinion of this?' Hamilton picked up a newspaper from his desk and passed it across, tapping a short article with his finger. Clay read the name, *L'Echo*, at the top and noticed the date was two weeks ago.

'How have you acquired this?' he asked.

'I have an agent in Genoa who is close to the garrison commander. He forwards me all the French papers, amongst other more choice intelligence.'

'My command of French is a little indifferent,' said Clay, after he had finished reading. 'Am I right in saying that the writer speaks of seamen arriving at Toulon?'

'Precisely so,' said the ambassador. 'Eight hundred marched overland from Brest, with a further five hundred expected shortly from Bordeaux. What do you conclude from that?'

'That our enemy is stripping his Atlantic ports to man his ships here in the Mediterranean,' mused Clay, returning the paper. 'But against what objective will such an expedition be directed, Sir

William?'

'Who can say?' said the ambassador, spreading his arms wide. 'Perhaps here. The French have seized most of Italy from Rome northwards, but they might yet have ambitions to control the whole peninsula. Or they might send their army against the Barbary states, or perhaps the Turks. Their objective may even lie outside the Mediterranean altogether. I am afraid that so far they have managed to keep it secret, from me at least. I do have one further piece of intelligence.'

'What pray is that, Sir William?'

'The Queen has been told that General Bonaparte is to lead the army, principally because the government in Paris fear his popularity and want him off French soil. He is a very dangerous young man. He gave our Austrian allies a most fearful beating last year.'

'It seems that I must head north then, Sir William,' said Clay. 'I shall look into Marseille, Toulon and Genoa and see what I can find out by direct observation.'

'That is where your duty lies, captain,' agreed his host. 'You must try to see what the French are about and report back to St Vincent. Have a care in those waters; they can be very stormy in the winter. If I find out any more through our contacts here, I will send word directly to the admiral. Now, what are the needs of your ship?'

'Chiefly fresh water and firewood, Sir William. I have my purser's indent here.' Hamilton scanned the document for a moment.

'This should all be fine,' he said. 'I will arrange for your ship to be resupplied tomorrow so you can be on your way. As for tonight, are you engaged? Might you do me the honour of joining my wife and me for dinner? We get so few visitors from home in these troubled times. I am sure Emma would be very grateful for company of her own age.'

'I am sure she will,' muttered Clay, under his breath.

'Beg pardon?' said the older man, cupping a hand to his ear.

'I said of course, Sir William. It will be a pleasure.'

The two men went to find Lady Emma, who had moved through to the villa's large orangery. She reclined in a chaselongue beneath a canopy of dense green foliage with a bowl of candied fruit by her side.

'I bring pleasant news, Emma my dear,' said Hamilton. 'I have persuaded Captain Clay to favour us with his company tonight.'

'How very agreeable,' smiled Lady Hamilton. 'I would like that above all things.'

'Oh, and look, captain,' exclaimed her husband, rushing to the window. 'In your honour, the clouds have lifted and you can see Vesuvius in all her glory. She is quite an active volcano you know, although there hasn't been a major eruption for almost four years now.'

'Perhaps there may be one tonight,' said Lady Hamilton. She rolled an appraising eye towards Clay, placed a sweet between her full lips and chewed it with obvious pleasure.

*****

It was unbearably hot on the poorly lit slave deck of the ship. He opened his eyes, and his vision filled with the black hair on the back of a head that lay inches from his face, just as he had for days now. He raised himself a little, and saw that beyond the head were more heads, one after another, disappearing into the gloom. The line of slaves lay on their sides on the hard wood, pressed together like spoons. Against his back he could feel the pressure of the slave behind him. Bony knees against the back of his legs, an arm that

113

jarred against his shoulders as it jerked with cramp, and the man's hot breath on his neck.

The deck he lay on was damp and clammy, sodden with all manner of human fluids. After a week at sea, his sense of smell had been overwhelmed long ago by the acid stench of urine, sweat, vomit and faeces. From the slave deck just above him, more liquid oozed in beads through the gaps in the planking to drip down on those below. With each Atlantic roller the ship pushed through, he felt the deck pitch with a rattle from the row of leg irons that held them in place. All of their ankles had long since been chaffed until they were raw and bleeding.

But it was not the pain in his legs and feet that had brought him to. Nor was it the chorus of groans that accompanied each rolling wave, or the constant sound of weeping that filled the hull of the ship. There was something wrong with the man in front of him. The leg that lay against his was too stiff and the head in front of him lolled and thumped against the deck with each wave in an unnatural way. The dull realisation gripped him that the man was dead, and an involuntary wail rose up out of his mouth.

When Able Sedgwick opened his eyes, there was a moment when he was balanced between the horror of the dream and the real world about him. He could see the planking of a deck just above his head, and he was on a ship that was swaying to the rhythm of the sea, just as the slave ship had done. He stretched up with a trembling hand to touch the solid oak. It was dry.

'Jesus, Able!' exclaimed Trevan from the hammock next to his. 'What manner of nightmare was that? I've never heard a man holler so in his sleep.' Sedgwick looked around him in the gloom of the lower deck. An almost continuous carpet of hammocks stretched away into the dark, all swaying together in time with the rocking of the ship. Those closest to him all had the startled faces of his fellow seamen, looking his way.

'Sorry, lads,' he said. 'Just one of them bad dreams. It has passed. I shall be fine now.'

'I am not sure as you are, mate,' said the Cornishman. 'Why, you're sweating like a sinner in church, and I didn't rightly think your face could turn that pale. What was you a-thinking on?'

'I've been working on my writing with Rosso of late,' he said. 'It must have stirred up some stuff that might have been best left at peace.'

'Ah, that can be right cruel,' said his friend. 'Them phantoms that come and find us out when we sleep. Sea fights can cause them too, you know? A man can behold all manner of grim sights, and think nothing of it at the time. Then years later they can come back to visit you in your dreams. Not rightly sure what you can do about it, mind. Some say that grog helps, but that can be a dangerous road to travel.'

'Well, it has passed now, Adam, and we have no grog to hand,' smiled Sedgwick. 'I am just sorry to have disturbed so many shipmates.'

'Don't you fret on that score, Able, lad,' yawned Trevan. 'What with "All Hands" being called that often night and day, they all knows how to get back to sleep.'

Trevan's prediction proved accurate. With a few grumbles here and the odd sigh there, the lower deck soon drifted back into slumber again. In amongst the snoring men Sedgwick lay still but awake in his hammock. Five bells had sounded some time ago. It would be dawn soon, and he had decided not to sleep again. He had no intention of sliding back into that other world, to relive the death of his brother once more.

*****

Three weeks later, it was dark and bitterly cold when Clay came up the companion ladder and out on to the quarterdeck. Yates, his servant, had warned him of the change as he loaded his captain up with clothes, but even so the chill air came as a shock after the warmth of his cabin. Something crunched under his feet as he made his way over to the group of officers stood around the binnacle. He could see their breath, like smoke in its yellow light.

'Good morning, gentlemen,' said Clay, his words dulled by the scarf that muffled the lower part of his face. The group of men muttered greetings and reluctantly pulled hands from pockets to touch their hats. 'Tell me, what time is sunrise, Mr Armstrong?'

'A little after six bells, sir,' replied the ship's master. 'We will be in position off Marseille in good time for that.'

'It will be a relief to see the sun,' muttered Lieutenant Blake as he flogged his arms against his sides. 'Is it always so damnably cold here, Jacob?'

'It is this wind from the north, Mr Blake,' explained Armstrong. 'The French call it the Mistral. It comes bearing icy air from the continent. But at least it is a dry wind. We shall not have to worry about any snow obscuring our observations.'

'Snow!' exclaimed the lieutenant. 'But it is almost March!'

'They say the Mistral is much favoured by artists, for the clearness of the light that accompanies it,' continued the American. 'I am surprised you do not appreciate it more.'

'Some clear light will be most welcome for our purpose this morning,' said Clay, looking about him. 'When it shall choose to arrive.'

At last the sky began to lighten a little in the east, as a thin line of sulphurous yellow forced its way between dark air and black sea. In the faint light the officers could see that the ship had been covered with frost in the night. It lay like a dusting of sugar on the deck and clung in crystals to the standing rigging.

'Land ho!' yelled the lookout, far up in the foremast. Clay looked towards the figure, gilded by a morning sun that had yet to reach the grey deck.

'Mr Russell! Mr Butler!' he called. 'Up you go with your spy glasses and report on everything you can see in the port. Count with care, if you please.'

'Aye aye, sir,' replied the two midshipmen.

'Take us in closer to the shore, Mr Blake.'

As the frigate approached the dark mass of southern France, Clay could see flecks of light here and there, where the working day had started in the little crofts and cottages ashore. Directly ahead of the ship a denser mass of light shone out, marking where the port of Marseille lay. The frigate crept on, past a number of rocky islands, as it stood in towards the harbour entrance.

'There are a deal of these little islands in the offing, but the water is deep and there are few reefs to trouble us, sir,' explained Armstrong. 'That one there, away to the south, does have some guns sited on it, so we would do well to keep on this line. Ah, see they are awake, in spite of the cold.' He pointed to where a flash of light had appeared in the gloom, as if a furnace door had been briefly opened, and a line of splashes rose up from the cold sea to mark the route of the shot. The last fell a good quarter mile short of them. Clay turned his attention back towards the shore.

'What do you expect we shall find, sir?' asked a muffled Taylor from the rail next to him. 'More of this profusion of shipping, just as we saw at all the other ports?'

'That's right, Mr Taylor,' said Clay. 'What is the tally so far, Mr Armstrong?' The American drew out his note book, licked a finger, and worked his way to the correct place. He held the page down near his waist, where the light of the binnacle could illuminate it.

'Genoa had ninety sail of transports and two frigates, sir,' he reported. 'Toulon had a further hundred and twenty merchantmen, plus sixteen ships of the line, including one very large first rate. Forty-two sail of transporters in the various other minor ports we visited. All told, two hundred and fifty two transporters, and eighteen warships.' He closed his book with a snap. 'Already a considerable armada, sir, and we have yet to see what Marseille has to offer.'

'And still no hint as to where this enormous fleet may be directed,' sighed Clay.

'I believe I can make out a little of the port now, sir,' reported Taylor as he looked through the eye piece of his telescope. 'There is a deal of domes and towers, one of which is very tall.'

'The domes will be the cathedral which lies close to the harbour, and that larger tower to the right is the lighthouse, sir,' said the master. 'During the peace they keep a beacon that burns there all night. The entrance to the harbour lies between the two.'

'Yes, I have it now,' said Clay focusing his telescope. 'Goodness, it is fair rammed with shipping. Why I can see masts as thick as grass.' He tilted his head back and hailed the two figures at the mast head. 'Mr Butler! Can you and Mr Russell see into the harbour?'

'Yes, sir,' replied the midshipman. 'It will take us a while to note all these vessels though.'

'Bring her up into the wind if you please, Mr Blake, and send a couple of hands with glasses to help the young gentlemen.'

While the count of the shipping in Marseille went on, the ship began to come to life. The dark shore had resolved itself into the wooded hills of Provence and the sun had risen above the horizon to bring a little grateful warmth to the officers of the *Titan*. The watch below was turned up, and streamed up the ladder ways to stow their hammocks in the netting, with many a cry of surprise as the bare footed sailors discovered the frost. Clay watched as the men worked away, scrubbing down the decks with mops and holy stones, before they rinsed them off with copious amounts of freezing seawater.

'Tell me, Mr Taylor, is it my imagination or are the hands rather subdued?' he asked. His first lieutenant watched the work of cleaning the deck for a moment.

'Yes, perhaps they are, sir,' he agreed. 'Maybe washing frost from the decks with cold water is not to their taste. I know I would rather not do it on such a morning.'

'On the contrary, I would expect it to have induced much more skylarking than usual. The men should be seeking to splash one another, with exclamations of surprise and the like. Why, they have barely even noted that the coast of France is just over there.'

'It may be because we have had another theft, sir,' replied the first lieutenant. 'During the night. A marine private this time. I was going to inform you once we had completed our observations.'

'Another!' exclaimed Clay, his face growing red. 'How many does that make, four now? Good God, am I in command of a King's ship or a damned prison hulk?'

'We do have a fair number of criminals aboard, in truth, sir,' offered Taylor.

'As did we have last commission, Mr Taylor,' snapped his captain. 'Yet I do not recall such persistent wickedness? Has the master at arms apprehended anyone?'

'He is investigating it, naturally, but with so little to go on he is still no closer to laying a hand on the cutpurse, sir.'

'But he must succeed,' said Clay. 'Surely it cannot be so very difficult to find the culprit. On a ship this size, with so many people living on top of one another? If that is what is causing this unease amongst the crew it must be stopped. Before the efficient working of the ship starts to suffer.'

'Aye aye, sir,' said Taylor. 'I will speak with him again. The young gentlemen have returned from aloft now.' Clay watched Armstrong finish his work with the two midshipmen, a sheath of notes flapping in the breeze. When he was satisfied, he came over and touched the brim of his hat with the two lookouts in tow.

'As we suspected, the chief part of their fleet are here, sir,' he reported. 'A hundred and forty sail of merchantmen, and a further two frigates. When added to the shipping we observed at the other ports, we are a little shy of four hundred transporters, with twenty men-of-war to protect them, sir.'

'Four hundred,' exclaimed Clay. 'God bless my soul! How large an army do the French plan to transport?'

'You could shift fifty thousand men with such a fleet, sir,' said Armstrong, making the calculation. 'And supply them for a good few months.' Clay looked back towards the port. The early morning sunshine shone down on the pale stone of the sea wall now. Behind it he could see the numberless masts poking up.

'Well, now we are at least certain that the rumours of an expedition are true,' he said. 'Mr Armstrong, lay us on a course that will take us back to join the fleet off Cadiz. We need to report all of this to the admiral as soon as possible.'

Chapter 7
Nelson

'Ah, there you are, Captain Clay,' said Lord St Vincent, as his last guest entered the great cabin of the *Ville de Paris*. 'Allow me to introduce you to the others before we sit down to dinner. My flag captain you know already of course.' The elegant Amery shook hands with Clay, and he was then led into the centre of the group to greet the other guests. 'This is Sir James Saumarez, who commands one of my former ships, the old *Orion*. She was among our seventy-fours at my victory over the Dons last year.' Clay found himself facing a tall, haughty looking man with receding brown hair and a prominent nose down which he regarded the new arrival.

'Delighted to make your acquaintance, captain,' he said. 'Are you one of the Jersey Clays, by any chance?'

'No, Sir James,' he said. 'My people come from Hampshire.'

'Pity,' said Saumarez. 'One can never have enough Channel Islanders in a fleet, I find.'

'We cannot all be blessed with your upbringing amongst the reefs and rocks of Guernsey, Sir James,' said the admiral, rolling his eyes a little. He turned towards the captain who stood next in line. He was a shorter man with almost no hair left on his prominent dome of a head. His long, lean face was kindly, and he smiled as he took Clay's hand.

'A pleasure to meet you, captain,' he said. 'I believe we may share the same first name? I am Alexander Ball, and just to make for further confusion my ship too is named *Alexander*. There she lies, directly behind the *Vanguard*.' He pointed out of the stern windows at a bulky looking ship of the line with a black and yellow hull. Clay could just make out that the figurehead was of a man with gold armour and long blond hair crouched over the neck of his white horse.

'I am very pleased to make your acquaintance, Captain Ball,' he replied. 'You have a very fine ship.'

'And now, let me name a very special officer to you,' said St Vincent. 'He has but recently arrived from home, having rushed ahead of my promised reinforcements to get to grips with the enemy all the sooner. Captain Alexander Clay, this is Rear Admiral Sir Horatio Nelson.'

The man who stood before him was tiny, almost a foot shorter than Clay. He had a full head of curly brown hair that he wore long, a prominent nose and a generous, almost feminine mouth. His admiral's uniform was immaculate, complete with the ribbon and star of the Order of the Bath. The right sleeve was empty, and was pinned across his chest. The pupil of his right eye was large and blank, while the other was bright blue and regarded Clay with interest. He opened his mouth to speak and out came a thick Norfolk accent.

'Tell me, captain,' he said, appraising him with his unblinking good eye. 'Does you hate the French?'

'Hate them, Sir Horatio?' queried Clay, unsure for a moment which eye he should look at. He decided at length to fix his gaze on the bridge of the rear admiral's nose.

'Yes, yes,' said Nelson. 'Do you hate them?'

'They are my country's enemy at present, so I naturally fight them whenever occasion serves,' he said. 'And I do hold the manner in which their revolution has degenerated into uncivil terror to be decidedly ill for humanity, but I can't say that I hate them as such.'

'Oh but you must,' insisted Nelson. 'As you would the Devil!'

'What, all of them, Sir Horatio?' asked Clay. 'Even those royalists who have fled the revolution, and now fight with us?'

'Even them, for were they not our foes in the last war? No, no, there is only one way of dealing with your Frenchman and that is to knock him down,' he said. He reached up to tap Clay on the chest with his remaining hand. 'I tell you, captain, my blood fair boils at even the name of one.' Clay was a little unsure what to say next. St Vincent grunted with appreciation at the sentiments that his new rear admiral had expressed, while the other guests looked on without comment.

'I shall... eh, bear that in mind, Sir Horatio,' he said at last, to fill the pause in the conversation.

'I believe that dinner is served now, my lord,' said Captain Amery, coming to his rescue. 'Should we proceed through to the next cabin?' St Vincent looked around and saw the white-gloved steward who waited by the door.

'Capital!' he exclaimed. 'I do declare I am quite famished. I can hold out the prospect of fresh flesh for once tonight, gentlemen. Sir Horatio was good enough to bring a considerable number of live beasts for the fleet out with him. The *Vanguard* must have been like Noah's ark. My cook has selected one of the lambs for our feast this evening. Do please follow me.'

With only six of them, they made an intimate gathering around the dining table. St. Vincent sat at the head with Nelson on one side of him and Saumarez, the most senior of the three captains, on the other. Next came Ball and Clay, who sat opposite each other, and finally Captain Amery took his place at the other end of the table. No sooner had they sat down then the cabin door opened, and in came a line of sailors. Each one carried a steaming dish to place on the table, while the final man brought in a large leg of lamb which he placed in front of the flag captain. Amery promptly stood back up again, picked up a knife, and began to carve while the others watched him.

'I trust I find you in good health, Sir Horatio?' asked Saumarez. 'Are you fully recovered from the loss of your arm?'

'The winter was most vexing, I shall not lie,' said Nelson. 'There were long periods when the pain was so intolerable that I was obliged to take to my bed. But with the turn of the year, the last ligature fell away, and once my surgeon had pulled it free I made a full recovery.'

'Well, let that be our first toast, gentlemen,' said St Vincent. He raised his glass. 'To the happy return.' The guests all drained their glasses with a rumble of approval, and the steward slid forward to replenish them.

'Did I not hear that you too were injured in the arm some years back, Captain Clay?' asked Ball. 'In the Caribbean, was it not?'

'Yes, that is correct,' he said. 'During my action with the *San Felipe* I took a musket ball in the shoulder. I was fortunate that my surgeon was able to extract it quickly and save my arm.'

'Fortunate indeed!' exclaimed Nelson, his lamb skidding around his plate as he tried to cut it with his left hand.

'For God's sake, Amery,' growled St Vincent. 'Can't you cut the damn slices more thinly? Steward! A fresh plate for Sir Horatio, if you please.'

A Man of No Country

'Lady Nelson has had this special device made for me, but I am yet to master its usage.' He held up his fork for them all to see. The bottom tine had been replaced by a thin blade.

'Most ingenious,' said St Vincent. 'That will answer very well, so long as the meat is not indifferently carved.' He shot a venomous look down the table at his flag captain.

'Were you ever injured, Captain Ball?' asked Clay, wanting to move the conversation away from the unfortunate Amery.

'Not yet in the service of my country, no,' he replied. He patted a hand on the polished top of the walnut table. 'But I was almost killed as a boy.'

'Was you now?' said the admiral. 'Could we trouble you for the particulars?'

'It was back when I was at school,' began the captain. 'I would have been no more than ten at the time. A particularly notorious band of robbers were to be hanged in Gloucester, and a group of the boys went to see the event. I recall it drew a considerable crowd, but we succeeded in obtaining a tolerable view by climbing to the top of a cart of hay. We were all much impressed by the manner in which the villains jerked and swung, and could talk of little else all the way back to school.'

'There are few things in life quite as satisfying as a good hanging, I find,' said St Vincent, in a far away voice. After a pause Ball continued with his story.

'When we returned to school, we decided, with the conceit of the very young, that we should play at robbers and hangmen,' he said. 'We found a suitable beam in the stable, and a length of rope. I was nominated as the robber, the rope was placed about my neck and I was hauled aloft.'

'Bess my soul!' exclaimed Saumarez. 'What happened next?'

'I remember I struggled for a while, and my friends delighted at how well my jerks and kicks imitated those of the robbers we had seen hanged earlier. Then all went dark. The next thing I recall was coming to in bed with a poultice about my neck. I couldn't speak for a week, and had a vivid red mark for many months thereafter. I learnt later that I owed my life to the intervention of an older boy. He chanced to be passing, looked in, and observing that my face had turned quite black, he came to my rescue.'

'Pon my soul, if that ain't that the damndest tale I ever did hear!' exclaimed their host. He raised his glass once more. 'That deserves another toast, gentlemen. To the anonymous saviour of young Master Ball, with a bumper, if you please.' The second toast was drunk with as much enthusiasm as before, and the meal moved on to pudding. Once everyone was served Clay saw Amery look across the table towards his admiral and catch his eye. St Vincent waited for a lull in the conversation and then turned towards him.

'Might I trouble you to give the company an account of your recent reconnaissance of the south coast of France, captain?' he asked. Clay put down his spoon, and looked round to see that he had everyone's attention.

'In pursuance of the instructions that your lordship gave me, I visited our ambassador in Naples,' he began. 'Sir William informed me he had intelligence that the French had been massing troops in army camps at Marseille and Genoa, and had spent the winter gathering together a considerable armada of shipping to transport those forces. I visited most of the principal ports on that coast, and found those rumours to be true.'

'What size of force did you discover?' asked Nelson.

'I counted almost four hundred sail of transporters, chiefly at Genoa, Toulon and Marseille, Sir Horatio, supported by sixteen ships of the line, four frigates and a number of inferior craft.'

'Did you say four hundred?' spluttered Ball, spilling his wine.

A Man of No Country

'Upon my word, how big is the army they plan to sail with?'

'That I do not know, but four hundred sail was what I counted some three weeks ago, Captain Ball,' said Clay. 'The size of their fleet may, of course, have grown further since then.'

'Which is why I shall be detaching a squadron from this fleet to return to the Mediterranean and combat this menace,' said St Vincent. 'Sir Horatio shall command it. His acquaintance with that part of the world and his activity and disposition qualify him in a peculiar manner for this service. You gentlemen will form the members of his force.' Saumarez turned his patrician gaze around the room and counted his fellow guests.

'Sir Horatio has his *Vanguard*, I have *Orion*, Ball has *Alexander* and Captain Clay the *Titan*,' he said. 'Three ships of the line and a frigate, to face twenty warships of the enemy?' he said. 'Even under such an able leader as Sir Horatio, those might appear to be troubling odds.'

Nelson smiled at this. 'It was not just the *Vanguard* and fresh lamb that I brought with me from England, James,' he said. 'I also come with news of reinforcements. Sir Roger Curtis will be on his way from Ireland as I speak, with a force of ten ships of the line.'

'Once they have arrived I will release a similar number to join you gentlemen,' explained St Vincent. 'I can do no more till then. I am still obliged to keep sufficient force out here in the Atlantic to blockade the Dons in Cadiz.'

'Were you able to establish what objective this French armada has been gathered for, Captain Clay?' asked Ball.

'Regrettably not, sir,' he replied. 'The French are keeping their cards very close to their chest.'

'Ah, but now you put your finger on the question we would all very much like to know the answer to, Captain Ball,' said St Vincent. 'Where are the French going to attack? Every man seems to have a different notion. You gentlemen may as well pay your guinea and hazard a guess too.'

'The latest copies of *Le Moniteur* from Paris report that Naples will be the objective,' explained Captain Amery. 'Although the government believes that is like to be so much rot. The French often place false reports in that paper, to put their enemies off the scent.'

'Never trust a Frenchman,' offered Nelson.

'The First Sea Lord believes that the French plan to invade Portugal,' said St Vincent. 'But if you attend to the pronouncements of Lord Spencer you will never want for moonshine. What are your opinions, gentlemen?'

'Might their objective be to recapture the sugar islands they have lost in the Caribbean?' said Ball. 'Such a force could certainly achieve that.'

'Most unlikely,' sniffed Saumarez. 'We are their chief foe. They surely mean to strike at our heart, either by landing directly in England, or via Ireland.'

'Oh come now, Sir James!' said the captain of the *Alexander*. 'If the French mean to invade, they can do so with far more convenience by coming across the Channel, not via some force down in Marseille! The Caribbean will be their objective, mark my words.'

'But Captain Ball, they have tried and failed the direct route already, hence a more oblique approach—'

'And what is your opinion, Captain Clay?' said a strong rural accent that cut across the two squabbling officers. Clay looked up to find the bright eye of his new commander looking at him.

'Like the rest of the party, I have no certain intelligence to offer, but if you press me to speculate, it seems to me that the only truth on which we can wholly rely is that the French have chosen to gather their forces in the Mediterranean,' he said, in the quiet around the table. 'Captain Ball and Captain Saumarez's objectives lie outside that sea, as does Lord Spencer's Portugal, for that matter. If any of these were where the French meant to attack, would they not choose to do so from the Atlantic or Channel coasts of France?'

'Very true,' agreed Nelson.

'On that basis, I imagine that whatever the French are after must lie within the Mediterranean.' The rear admiral smiled at his new frigate captain.

'Very ably reasoned, Captain Clay,' he said. 'That is why, when we head back into that sea tomorrow, I shall require that you take your saucy little frigate and press on ahead of our three lumbering seventy-fours. I want you to go back to the southern coast of France once more, and find out for me what those French Devils are about.'

*****

It was mid afternoon, and the *Titan* stood in across the Gulf of Lions towards the French naval base at Toulon. The rugged coast of Provence loomed to the north of them. Dark hills of pine forest combined with rocky cliffs near the coast, while behind them rose a jagged line of patchy, scrub covered mountains. Spring had come at last, to give some warmth to the sun as it shone down on the waters of a Mediterranean that had turned blue in response. The arctic blast that had covered the ship with frost last time they had sailed these waters had been replaced with a gentle zephyr from the south east. The elegant frigate had spread lofty pyramids of snow-white sail to catch what wind there was as she slid through the rolling sea towards the land.

'You seem to be in very good humour, sir,' said Preston as his captain came up the companion way to join him on the quarterdeck. 'I do not recall ever having heard you hum a tune before.'

'Was I doing that aloud?' exclaimed Clay. 'I thought that was only in my head! But why should I not be content? Fine weather at last, an independent commission, and on top of all, the *Vanguard* brought a deal of letters from home, including a considerable correspondence from my wife and sister. I have just passed a very agreeable hour devoted to their study.'

'How are matters at home, sir?' asked the lieutenant.

'In general very well,' said Clay. 'My wife is in good spirits, and my sister Betsy's second novel has been published at last. She tells me that the first reports have given it a warm welcome and inconsequence sales are brisk. It is named *The Bramptons of Linstead Hall* and she has sent me a copy.'

'The wardroom will be pleased,' said Preston. 'We all very much enjoyed her last work, particularly Tom Macpherson.'

'Ah yes, *The Choices of Miss Amelia Grey*. Although I am not sure if I should be wholly pleased at the knowledge that my marine commander finds romantic novels quite so diverting.' The two officers were still chuckling over this when they were joined by a stern-faced first lieutenant.

'You seem discontent, Mr Taylor,' said Clay. 'Does this change in the weather not agree with you?'

'No, sir, the weather is perfectly tolerable. I have just met with the master at arms. I am afraid to say we have had another robbery.'

'Damnation, Taylor!' exclaimed Clay. 'What the bloody hell is going on!'

'Was it money that was taken again, sir?' asked Preston.

'Yes, nearly twenty shillings,' explained Taylor. 'This time the victim was John Waite, Forecastle man in the starboard watch.

A Man of No Country

That makes five such thefts now.'

'I know Waite, he is in my division, sir,' said Preston. 'He can be troublesome when he puts his mind to it. We shall have problems unless we can find the cutpurse.'

'I dare say we will,' said Clay. 'Nothing spreads discontent in a crew like thieving. They start to look upon each other with suspicion. We need to get a grip on this. Has the master at arms made any progress with his investigations?'

'Very little, sir,' said Taylor. 'He suspects that one of the newer hands must be behind it, as we had no such problems before they joined, but he has no conclusive proof.'

'And of course no sailor on the lower deck would ever think of offering information to him,' exclaimed Clay, his hands working with exasperation.

'Why is it always just money, I wonder?' said Taylor. 'An old hand like Waite would have other possessions of value he has accumulated over his time at sea.'

'Because coin can't be traced, I imagine, sir,' said Preston. 'If one of the hands was found with a piece of stolen scrimshaw, it would be easy to identify the criminal.'

'I daresay you are right,' said the captain. 'So what do you gentlemen suggest we do?'

'Might we not attempt something when the hands are all at divisions one Sunday?' said Taylor. 'We could hold everyone on deck and have the marines go through their possessions. Anyone found with an excessive amount of money could be required to give an explanation.'

'When would you propose to do it?' asked Clay.

'Next time we are at anchor in port. That way it would include everyone, idlers as well as the watches.'

'We could try it, sir,' said Preston. 'But I doubt we shall catch this ne'er-do-well so easily. To have robbed five men undetected in a packed lower deck speaks of an uncommon ability. I imagine he will have placed his ill gotten gains somewhere the Lobsters will struggle to find.'

'But isn't that just it?' exclaimed Clay. 'The lower deck is so full of eyes, and more than capable of acts of summary justice for those they catch. What is it that drives a man to run such an awful damned risk for a few shillings?'

'I don't know, sir,' said Taylor. 'Let us try a search of the ship on the next suitable occasion, and see what that reveals.'

'Agreed,' said the captain. 'Breathe no word of this to anyone. It must come as a surprise to the men if it is to have any chance of succeeding.'

'Aye aye, sir,' said the two officers.

'Good. Now let us see what secrets Toulon has to offer up.'

The shore was much closer now. Mount Faron loomed up behind the city, its steep slopes streaked with forest and the summit a dome of bare grey rock. Two headlands extended out towards them, each one with a well constructed fortress on it. Clay looked at their walls and ditches to judge the range. Through his telescope he could see the lines of heavy guns that pointed towards him, and even a few of the crew as they hurried to their posts at his approach. In the bay beyond, he could make out the city walls and bastions that encircled Toulon. The large outer harbour and naval dockyard were out of sight, tucked behind one of the headlands, but they should be visible from the masthead now, he concluded.

'No closer, Mr Preston! Bring her head round and back the foretopsail, if you please,' ordered Clay. 'Mr Russell, Mr Butler! Up you go, gentlemen, and report on what you can see.'

The two youngsters scampered up the main mast shrouds as the ship swung up into the wind and came to a halt. Now the *Titan* was stationary, she rocked in the waves that slopped heavily against her sides, rolling her this way and that with a chorus of protest from her rigging. The officers looked up at the masthead, where the two midshipmen clung on. The gentle motion of the ship at deck level was being amplified by the hundred-and-fifty-foot mast, so that the two young officers swung through a dizzying arc of sky.

'Rather them than me,' said Clay, with a queasy feeling in his stomach from just looking at them. Armstrong came up to join the others.

'I sincerely hope that neither of them has been excessive with their dinner, sir,' said the American, 'with the wind as she presently lies, we shall be directly in the firing line.'

'Well, they do not intend to tarry up there,' said the captain, as he watched first Butler and then Russell swoop down the backstays, risking the skin of their hands with the speed of their descent.

'They have been very quick,' muttered Preston. 'I hope they have not let the ship's motion prevent them from completing a thorough job.'

'Sir, sir!' called Butler, the first to reach the deck. 'They have gone!'

'Now Mr Butler,' growled Taylor, rounding on the excited youth. 'You know better than that. Make your report in proper form to the captain.'

'Sorry Mr Taylor, sir,' replied the midshipman. Both young men pulled their uniform jackets straight and stood at attention in front of Clay.

'Sir, Mr Russell and I examined both the inner and outer harbour. The majority of the French warships we previously observed have departed, as have all the transporters. All we saw was a single ship of the line and two small craft moored in the

133

outer harbour. None of them appear ready for sea.'

'Thank you, Mr Butler,' he said. 'Mr Preston, have the ship put before the wind directly and lay us on a course to rendezvous with the rest of the squadron. We must find Admiral Nelson at once and tell him that the French are out.'

Chapter 8
Storm

The following day, the *Titan* sailed south towards her rendezvous with the rest of the squadron off the west coast of Sardinia. Ahead of her the sky became increasingly threatening. It was still blue overhead, but to the south was a mass of dark cloud that boiled and flickered with the occasional silver thread of lightning. The sea too was becoming wilder, with endless chains of big green waves surging across her path. They broke against her bow with a solid crash that checked her progress and threw columns of white water high into the air to thunder down on to her streaming deck.

'Why is there such a damnable swell running?' asked Blake, who struggled to keep his footing. Armstrong looked about him and sniffed at the freshening wind.

'A sea like this is the harbinger of ill weather in these waters,' he said. 'It is the dog that arrives before his master. The storm that lies ahead of us is the cause. Pray God it is not headed in our direction.'

'We should strike down the top hamper, in case it does,' said Blake, looking up at the masts. He turned to the midshipman of the watch. 'Run along and find the captain, Mr Russell. Give him my compliments, and ask him to come on deck and look at this weather.'

'It does look troublesome, Mr Blake,' said Clay, when he'd come up on deck. He stared at the mass of black clouds to the south, and sniffed at the wind. It was starting to blow with a curious chill to it, like the breath from a tomb. What to do, he wondered to himself. By rights I should be rushing to the rendezvous with our news of the French, yet I have no desire to plunge into the heart of such a storm. He looked back at his officers, and found that Blake and Armstrong were both watching him.

'Ah, hmm....,' he said, while he gathered his thoughts. 'Let us get the top gallant masts off her for now, Mr Blake. As for this storm, let us hope it shall clear from our path presently.'

'Aye aye, sir,' said Blake, picking up a speaking trumpet. 'Mr Hutchinson! Call all hands to strike down the top gallants, if you please!'

'Christ, I am soaked,' moaned O'Malley a little later. 'There are haddock in the fecking sea as is less wet.' He was one of a party of hands on the forecastle, and they were taking the brunt of the waves that crashed against the frigate's bow. Another one thudded home, and a moment later a fresh cascade fell all around him.

'And why are we after sailing towards this fecking storm any ways?' he complained to Rosso, who was stood next to him. 'Shouldn't we be letting it pass?'

'Stow that noise, O'Malley,' said Josh Black, the petty officer in charge of the men. 'If you're dismayed by a little water, why the fuck did you ever come to sea?' The other seamen grinned at this and the muttering Irishman took his place amongst the line of sailors.

With the selective deafness to bad language that all good naval officers possess, Lieutenant Preston continued to watch the party of men that worked high up in the foremast. He too was taking his share of each successive wave. Much of the water poured off his oilskins, but enough had penetrated to ensure that he was now soaked to the skin as well.

'Ready, Mr Hutchinson?' he called through his speaking trumpet. Up in the foretop the grey-haired boatswain waved his hat. 'Very well, Black, have your men haul away.'

'Clap on,' roared the petty officer. The men braced themselves to pull on the line. Josh Black watched the sea with care, waiting for the optimum moment. 'Heave away!' Above their heads the foretop gallant mast jerked free from its cap and swung in the air.

'That will do,' said the lieutenant.

'Easy there!' yelled the captain of the forecastle. 'Lower away. Handsomely now,' he growled as another wave struck the ship's bow and soaked the men afresh. The last of the frigate's upper masts was swayed down, till it settled amongst all the other spars and yards on the skid beams. Another party of men lashed it into place and Preston turned towards the petty officer.

'Well done,' he said. 'Make good here to Mr Hutchinson's satisfaction. I must report to the captain.'

'Aye aye, sir,' said Black, knuckling his forehead in salute. 'Coil that line properly there, Rosso. O'Malley, go aloft and see if the boatswain needs any help to secure the cap.'

'Mr Preston, sir!' shouted Trevan. 'There be something off the starboard bow.' Preston followed where the Cornishman pointed. To one side of the ship was a swirl of white, where the waves broke over a dark curved shape in the water.

'Whale, sir?' queried Black.

'Not one as I have ever hunted, Mr Black,' Trevan said. 'Besides, your whale blows and then dives. He don't hang around on the surface, like.'

'Trevan is right,' replied the lieutenant. 'That looks to me like the hull of an upturned ship. Can anyone observe any sign of life?'

'None, sir,' said Black, shading his eyes. 'Nor like to be with this sea running, poor devils.'

'Yes there is!' exclaimed the Cornishmen. 'On the far side, sir.' Preston looked carefully, and as the hull dropped into a trough he saw a flash of something amongst the foam.

'I believe you are right,' he said.

'Well I'll be buggered!' exclaimed Black. 'There are two of them, sir. Clapped onto a bit of wreckage, like.'

'It must be tethered to the wreck by a cable,' said Preston. 'Keep an eye on them while I go and report it.'

*****

On the quarterdeck the captain was deep in conversation with Taylor and Armstrong. The three men formed a triangle of oilskin-clad figures next to the rail, with the ship's master very animated as he pointed towards the weather ahead.

'This storm is moving to the southwards of us, sir,' Armstrong said. 'It looks uncommon fierce to me. I would urge you to follow on its coat tails for now, rather than plunge into the heart of it.'

'But I need to tell the admiral that the French are at sea!' exclaimed Clay. 'Time is against us, gentlemen.'

'If the squadron are in the centre of that storm, they will have enough to occupy them already, sir,' said Taylor. 'I agree with Mr Armstrong. Even if we make all haste to the rendezvous, I doubt that we shall find the others out at sea. Those high-sided seventy-fours are much less weatherly than we are. They will have run for shelter like smoke and oakum.'

'Sir, sir!' said Preston as he came up to the group. 'Your pardon, but we are passing a wreck of a ship off the starboard bow. I believe there are some survivors.' The group of officers hastened over to the other rail and stared out to sea. 'There, sir,' said Preston, pointing towards the shape amongst the waves.

'Yes, I can see,' said Clay as he focussed his glass on the dome of wood. 'The hull of some small merchantman that has foundered in the storm, I fear. And you say there are signs of life?'

'On the far side. Do you have them?'

'Yes, poor wretches. I mark two of them,' said Clay. 'Mr Blake, bring the ship up into the wind, if you please.'

'What manner of rescue can we affect, sir?' asked Taylor. 'Any boat we launch with this sea running will be swamped in an instant.'

'Let us stand in a little closer,' said the captain. 'And pass the word for my coxswain.' Sedgwick came up onto the quarterdeck and knuckled his forehead towards his captain.

'You wanted to see me, sir,' he said.

'Yes, come to the rail here and direct your gaze at this upturned hull in the water,' said Clay. 'Do you mark the two sailors off on the leeward side?' The coxswain sheltered his eyes with his hand. It had started to rain now, but through the veil of water he could just make out the tiny figures lost amongst the huge waves. One of them waved an arm towards the frigate.

'Aye, sir, I have them.'

'We cannot launch a boat in this gale to pick them up, nor come any closer with the ship for fear of that hull striking ours,' said Clay. 'Yet if we do nothing, they will perish for certain.'

'Do you want me to go and fetched them, sir?'

'I do not ask lightly, Sedgwick, but I have nothing better to propose. It is such a burden that none of your shipmates will think ill of you if you was to choose not to attempt it. But few of them can swim, and none as well as you. I recall how you rescued Evans when he fell overboard in the Caribbean. But that was in calm weather, and this is anything but.'

'Aye, but there will be a deal less sharks here about, sir,' smiled Sedgwick. 'If I can have a line about my waist so I can be pulled back onboard should I founder, I will try it. But I doubt if I will have the strength to make the journey twice.'

'I understand,' said the captain. 'Mr Blake, pass the word for another volunteer swimmer if we have one in the crew. And two lengths of best Manila half inch line, if you please.'

'Aye aye, sir.'

*****

A little later, Sedgwick stood in the main chains with the rain washing down across his naked arms and chest. Around his waist was the line, the knot out of the way behind him. A loop dropped down towards the sea before running back onboard to the group of anxious hands who held the rest of it.

'Good luck there, Able,' called Trevan. 'We be ready when you are.' Sedgwick returned his attention to the sea, holding on to the shrouds and leaning out to peer down. Big green waves surged backwards and forwards against the side of the ship in a foaming melee. The dive he would have to make shrank to a matter of five feet, before growing with the next trough to a dizzy thirty or more. When is the best moment to leap, he wondered?

'Not yet, Able,' said a voice beside him in answer to his thoughts. He looked around to see John Grainger adjust a line around his waist and pull himself up into the chains beside him. 'These waves will dash us to pieces against the ship's side long before we can swim clear. Captain's going to set a scrap of jib to turn the barky across the wind a trifle and give us a bit of shelter.'

'I didn't know you was a swimmer?'

'Nor I you,' said Grainger, the rain soaking his beard. 'I can swim like an eel.' Sedgwick looked at the newcomer's body, long, lean and whipcord.

'I dare say you can,' he said and returned his attention to the sea. The ship had angled round a little now, producing a calmer triangle of water beneath them. Sedgwick drew in a deep breath and tumbled forward in a shallow dive.

He had been braced for the sea to be stinging cold as it rippled across his body, but he was surprised by how warm it was. It was late May now, and in spite of the storm the water was strangely pleasant. Then his head broke the surface, and chaos was all around him. One moment a glass green wave reared over him, next a valley opened up beside him to swallow him whole. Blinding white foam, thick as spittle, was driven by the wind into his eyes. He struck out in a powerful over arm stroke, to impose some control, but every few breaths his head would turn up for air only to draw in a mouth full of choking sea water. Within a few moments he realised he had no idea in which direction the wreck lay.

'Able,' came a voice in the storm. He looked around, and for a brief moment saw Grainger as a wave swept him aloft. 'Take... your mark...ship...,' he heard. He trod water for a moment, rising up and swooping down in the monstrous swell and looked about him. Of course, the *Titan*! There she lay, her normally towering masts oddly shortened with their top third brought down on deck, but the one solid thing in this mad, mad sea. He thought about which direction the wreck had been in when he was on board, and placing the frigate behind his left shoulder, he struck out anew.

Each time he came up for breath, he glanced back towards the ship, adjusting his angle a little. With something certain to reassure him his confidence grew, and swimming became a little easier. He started to gain a feel for the rhythm of the sea. It was not completely random, and if he adjusted the moment that he twisted his head up for air, he could use the tiny lee of a passing wave to draw breath. Occasionally he saw Grainger's head, a blob of dark hair in the white foam, falling behind him as the swam. So much for the eel, he muttered to himself. On and on he swam, fighting through each fresh wave as it tried to suck him back. Now he could feel his arms and legs starting to tire with the demand he was making of them. With every fresh stroke the ship became more and more distant, and the ever lengthening line around his waist grew heavier, drawing him down into the thick green water.

Just at the point when he thought he could go no farther, he caught a glimpse of something dark ahead, a flash of black amongst the waves. He struggled on with renewed vigour against the resistance of the line. Stroke by stroke, he pushed an arm forward, seeming to haul the wreck ever nearer till the black arc of the upturned hull filled his vision. A final surge of the waves brought him crashing up against it. He cried out in pain and desperately tried to grab on. His body urged him to rest, the ache in his limbs becoming overwhelming, but the wreck was covered in slimy green weed. He felt the barnacles and shells that studded the ship's bottom tear at the skin of his hands and arms as he was dragged along by the waves. In desperation he curled his feet around and thrust himself clear, back into the wild sea.

Now swimming was agony. The salt water bit at the fresh wounds in his hands. His limbs were leaden with exhaustion and his right arm had been badly wrenched against the stone-hard wood of the hull. He forced himself to tread water while he took stock, gasping for air as he did so. Then Grainger appeared beside him, his eyes wide and desperate as he struck out for the upturned hull. He swept past Sedgwick.

'No! Not... there!' he choked, but the exhausted swimmer was beyond caring. Grainger's line snaked past his thigh and Sedgwick grabbed it. He pulled him to a halt and then hauled in on the rope till the two men came together in the sea.

'What... fuck... doing?' gasped Grainger, his face twisted with anger, his arm pulled back to strike. Sedgwick briefly broke the surface with one arm, and held a torn and bloody hand to the other man's face.

'Hull... no good,' he yelled. 'No grip. Go... round. Follow... me.' The rage faded from Grainger's eyes and he followed as Sedgwick swam away in a wide circle around the wreck.

When they reached the far side, they saw the piece of broken yard, thick and heavy, as it jerked about in the water beside the hull. Of the two survivors they had seen clinging to it from the ship, one man had vanished. The two rescuers slumped across the curve of wood, barely less exhausted than the sailor they had come to rescue. For the first few minutes they could do little but gasp for breath as they clung on. Then Sedgwick pushed himself up in the water and looked around for the second man, but there was no trace of him in the wild sea all about them. He turned his attention to the first sailor. He was barely conscious at all. His head had a nasty cut were it had struck against the wood, and his fingers were manic claws locked into a knot of cable on the far side of the beam.

'Help get him free,' yelled Sedgwick over the roar of water all around them. He threw a protective arm around the man, and digit by digit they prised him loose. The sailor flopped back off the spa and into the coxswain's arms.

143

'Ready to go back?' he bellowed. Grainger was too tired to answer, but nodded weakly. 'I'll, take him. You signal to the ship.'

Sedgwick braced himself to go, but now the moment had come it was almost impossible to make himself push away from the spa, and let go of the only place of sanctuary in a wild, wild world. He felt more tired than he had ever done, and the *Titan* looked so far away. A wave surged over them, and as they emerged spluttering from the foaming water, he dropped backwards from the yard. His arms were locked around the sailor and his legs kicked frantically to keep them both afloat. He saw Grainger wave towards the ship, and moments later he felt a firm pressure on the line as he was drawn back through the waves.

*****

'How are they?' asked Clay.

'More than half drowned, but alive, sir,' said Taylor. 'Mr Corbett is treating them down in the sick bay, along with the sailor they rescued. Sedgwick is quite cut about the hands and arms, and both men are utterly spent, but the surgeon believes they will recover.' Clay looked at the worsening sea and the waves that surged and roared past them.

'It was uncommon brave of them to hazard all in that fashion,' he said. 'I doubt I would have, even if I were a swimmer.'

'Nor I, sir,' replied Armstrong from his other side. 'And I can swim, after a fashion.'

'I shall take this as a warning not to risk the ship in your storm, Mr Armstrong,' said Clay. 'I daresay our message can wait for it to blow itself out. Do you suppose this gale may have done for the French?' The master shook his head.

'These Mediterranean storms are of short duration, and often very local,' he said. 'The French might be passing down the other side of Sardinia right now under blue skies and a fair wind, with never a hint of the tempest that rages on this side of the island.'

Jacob Armstrong was correct about the storm. They followed it southwards through the night, the sea rough and the wind howling around them, but the worst of the storm was always ahead. The southern horizon flickered with white light to within a few hours of dawn, and then the storm blew itself out as quickly as it had sprung up. The following morning the *Titan* arrived at the squadron rendezvous, under a cloudless sky swept clear by the departing gale. The sea had settled back to a deep blue, flecked with dazzling white as the last of the choppy waves clashed and broke around the frigate.

'Land! Land ho!' yelled the lookout.

'Masthead there!' yelled Taylor. 'Any sign of the squadron?'

'No, sir,' came the lookout's reply. 'Nothing in sight, baring the land off the larboard bow.'

'That will be Cape Pecora, sir,' said Armstrong. 'We are at the rendezvous right enough.'

Clay looked about him. 'Very well, Mr Armstrong. If you were off this point yesterday when that storm struck, where might you have gone for shelter?'

The master stroked his chin for a moment before he replied. 'If it was bad, I might have fled before it, in which case I would be many miles to leeward by now,' he said. 'Or if I had urgent need of relief I might have sought out the shelter of the bay that lies behind the Cape.'

'Let us go there then, and see if the *Vanguard*'s master was of your way of thinking.'

The frigate came round onto her new course, and the coast of Sardinia grew from a faint smudge into a solid bar on the eastern horizon. After a few hours of sailing a fresh hail came from the masthead.

'Deck there!' yelled the lookout. 'I can see the masts of some ships, sir, in a bay three points off the bow. Big ships by my reckoning.'

'Is it the squadron?' yelled Clay.

'Could be, sir, but I only see the two sets of masts, mind.'

'Up you go with a spy glass, Mr Russell. Tell me what you can see.'

Aye aye, sir,' replied the midshipman. A few minutes later there was a fresh hail from the masthead.

'Deck there!' cried Russell. 'It's the squadron alright. The two ships are the *Orion* and the *Alexander*, and I can see the hull of the flagship now, too.' Armstrong and Clay exchanged glances.

'What do you mean, Mr Russell?' called the captain. 'Why can you only see the *Vanguard*'s hull?'

'Because she looks to have been dismasted, sir.'

*****

'Larboard side, sir?' asked Sedgwick from beside him in the stern sheets of the barge. 'They seem to be a mite busy aboard.' Clay looked towards the approaching flagship. Even at this range he could hear the sound of hammering and sawing as the crew worked to repair the damage of the storm. The *Orion* was warped close alongside, and her main yard was being used as the arm of a crane to draw free the stump of the *Vanguard*'s foremast. As he looked it swung free, the top shattered like a broken tusk. Sedgwick was right, the crew would be grateful not to have to gather to perform the naval ceremony that usually accompanied the arrival of a visiting captain.

'Yes, make it so,' he said, and the coxswain pushed the tiller over with one of his injured hands. A slight flicker of pain crossed his face before he settled on the new course.

The bay was wide and sheltered, with a fringe of white sandy beach lining the shore. Farther back the land rose in a series of scrub covered hills. Moored by the entrance to the bay, the *Alexander* sat squat on her reflection in the blue water, her guns guarding against any enemy that might arrive to take the dismasted *Vanguard* at a disadvantage. Clay examined the side of the lofty flagship as they drew closer. A wall of black and yellow loomed up over him, cutting off the light of the sun.

'Easy all,' growled Sedgwick. 'In oars!' The barge slid along the ship's side and came to a halt next to the entry port ladder. 'Hook on in the bow,' said the coxswain. He reached over to steady the stern of the boat, but then stopped himself.

'Here, clap on for me, Abbott,' he said, holding a bandaged hand under the nearest crewman's nose.

'Aye aye, Cox,' said the man, and Clay turned to examine the slats of wood that rose like a ladder above him with care. The bottom few were steep and slippery with weed, but once past those he could see that the pronounced tumble home of the hull would make matters easier. He adjusted his cock hat, checked he still had his report tucked inside his coat, stood up in the boat and jumped across onto the ship's side. A breathless scramble later he was onboard.

'Captain Clay?' said a well dressed midshipman with a shock of bright ginger hair. 'Captain Berry apologises for not being here to greet you himself, but he is otherwise engaged.' He waved a hand forward where a large man was shouting orders. Clay could see lines of men straining at various cables grouped around the forecastle. 'Will you come with me, sir, and I will take you below to the admiral.' The visitor followed the young officer across a deck strewn with wood chips and sawdust, weaving his way past teams of carpenters as they worked away, shaping various new spars.

'I fear you find my flagship in a quite shocking state, Clay,' said Nelson as he rose from behind his desk to greet his visitor. 'Can I offer you a little of this Madeira in consolation?'

'Thank you, Sir Horatio,' he said, turning to accept a small crystal glass from the steward beside him. 'We were fortunate only to catch the tail end of the storm on our way here, but we did come across a wrecked Genoese merchantman. From the state of the swell it appeared to have been uncommon savage.'

'I have been through hurricanes in the Caribbean that were less troublesome!' exclaimed the admiral. 'We were very nearly wrecked ourselves. It descended on us so directly that poor Berry had little time to prepare for the onslaught. Then a squall almost had us on our beam ends. The main and mizzen topmasts went by the board, and we were obliged to cut free our whole foremast just to right the ship. After that we found ourselves being driven towards the lee shore, and were quite certain to be lost.'

'Good lord!' exclaimed Clay. 'How did you survive, Sir Horatio?'

'Captain Ball very handsomely closed with us and took us in tow, right at the height of the storm,' he explained. 'It was the damnedest piece of seamanship I ever saw. Then, at considerable risk to the *Alexander,* he dragged us free of the approaching land. It was touch and go for some time, I can tell you. At one stage I ordered him to cut us loose, as I thought both ships were certain to perish on the rocks, but he ignored me and carried on. The wind backed half a point and by that miracle we were saved.' The admiral turned his good eye on his visitor. 'It is strange how frequently I have felt our Maker's influence in my affairs. Are you a religious man, Captain Clay?' he asked.

'I do believe in God, naturally, but I cannot claim to be especially fervent on matters of faith, sir.'

'How many times have you fought the French?' Clay thought about this for a moment.

'Including on shore and various cutting out expeditions, perhaps twenty occasions, Sir Horatio.'

'And how many times were you beat?'

'I can't say that I ever was.'

'Then you should feel obliged to be a deal more religious than you are,' snorted Nelson. 'Twenty victories without so much as a single defeat? Do you truly perceive no divine influence in all of this?' The admiral touched his empty sleeve and indicated his blank eye. 'God knows I have paid a price for my triumphs, but strange to say, I still hold that the Divine watches over my affairs. That is why we came through the storm. He knows I still have a duty to perform for my country, and that is a comfort to me. Now, what have you to tell me of those wicked French?'

'That they are out, Sir Horatio,' said Clay. 'We reached Toulon three days ago and found that their fleet had sailed. Warships, transports, every last one of them. I have a full report here.' Clay pulled a sealed envelope out from the inside of his coat and placed it on the desk.

'So soon!' exclaimed Nelson. 'I had hoped that my reinforcements might have arrived first. Do you have any notion where they may have gone?'

'None at all, I am afraid, sir,' he replied. 'Other than that we encountered no French on our way to Toulon, so I doubt that they were bound for the Atlantic.'

'Mind you, even if we knew for certain where they were bound, I could achieve nothing against them at present,' said the admiral. 'I shall be stuck here for several days yet, completing my repairs, and in any event I cannot challenge the French until the other ships should arrive. But what I chiefly need is a base to operate from. This storm has shown how vulnerable we are with only Gibraltar to rely on. I need somewhere central in the Mediterranean where I can resupply and repair my ships.'

'Would Naples serve, Sir Horatio?' asked Clay.

'Naples would answer very well,' replied Nelson. 'But they are currently a neutral. Would their government let me base myself there?'

'They might, Sir Horatio,' said Clay. 'When I was there earlier this year I was resupplied by them. I also understand from Sir William Hamilton that the royal family may hate the French even more then you do. I spoke with him about the possibility of us using Naples when I was last there, and he pledged to make enquiries.'

'I would be most obliged if you could conclude such an arrangement,' said the admiral. 'Do you think you can do it?'

'I can at least try, sir. We shall hardly be worse off if they reject the notion. Send me there with your formal letter of introduction to their government and I will endeavour to accomplish what I can.'

'I like your pluck, Clay,' smiled Nelson. 'You remind me of myself at your age. I will give you your letter, and let us see what you can achieve. Do you think their assistance might extend beyond just the provision of supplies and a port to operate from?'

'What did you have in mind, Sir Horatio?'

'A base is all well and good, but it will serve of little value if we cannot find the French,' said the admiral. 'Could they be persuaded to help me more directly? Say through the loan of some of their smaller craft to make searches for us. At present the *Titan* is the only such vessel I have. I can supply crews if necessary and they could operate under British colours.'

A Man of No Country

'That may prove to be a step too far, sir, but I shall see what can be accomplished.'

'Good man,' enthused Nelson. 'I will have that letter and your orders drawn up directly, and you can proceed to Naples with all despatch. I will complete my repairs here and then hasten to join you. The very best of luck, captain.'

Chapter 9
The Kingdom of the Two Sicilies

'This all took a deal of organising, I can tell you, captain,' grumbled Sir William Hamilton, once they were settled in his carriage. 'I had to exert my influence at court to the upmost to obtain an interview for you at such short notice. By comparison, arranging a passage back to Genoa for that sailor you picked up was easy as kiss my hand.'

'And we are going to meet with the Prime Minister himself tonight?'

'Yes, it is all arranged. His name is General Sir John Acton.' Clay looked around from the carriage window in surprise, the beautiful sunset behind Vesuvius quite forgotten.

'Sir John Acton?' he said. 'Am I to understand that the Prime Minister is an Englishman?'

'Ah, well, that would be to overstate the case,' said the ambassador. 'Our negotiation might be altogether easier if he were. Sir John's father was certainly English, and he is the heir to an English title, but he was born in France, educated in Lombardy, and has spent much of his life in command of the army of the Grand Duke of Tuscany. He left Leghorn when the French invaded last year, and is now Prime Minister here in Naples.'

'Does he at least speak English, Sir William?'

'Tolerably well, with something of a strong accent. His Spanish is better, and his Italian best of all, of course.'

'Goodness, the Mediterranean does seem to be full men of no country,' said Clay.

'I am not sure I follow you, captain.'

'I had in mind a sailor on board my ship,' he replied. 'An Englishman who is also a Mohammedan we found on a Russian ship dressed like a Turk off the coast of Portugal.'

'Ah, I see,' said the ambassador. 'Yes, this part of the world is full of such cases. In a way, I am another one, don't you know? I have lived here in Naples for rather longer than I ever did in my native Scotland.'

The carriage rattled on through the evening light. Soon the road began to rise up a hill and the pace slowed as the horses struggled along the cobbled street. Clay looked out onto a wide boulevard with well dressed pedestrians taking the evening air on the pavements. Along both sides of the road were tall walls relieved by the occasional pair of lamp lit iron gates. Between the bars, Clay had tantalising glimpses of the grand villas that were set back among their trees and gardens. At the top of the hill was an open square with a large fountain in the middle. High railings lined one side of the square. Behind them Clay could see a substantial building in white stone with bright light spilling out from its numerous windows. The carriage swung left and in through a well lit gate guarded by soldiers.

'The royal palace, captain,' explained Hamilton. 'We shall soon be there.' The carriage rolled on towards the building and the crunch of gravel replaced the clatter of cobbles beneath the wheels. They passed under a large arch guarded by yet more soldiers and came to a halt before an entrance. A footman in a powdered wig strode forward to open the door, while a second footman folded down the carriage's steps. The ambassador stepped out first, followed by Clay. He found that they were now in an inner court with open sky above their heads. Doors gave into the courtyard on all sides, and at every one was a pair of armed sentries.

'The palace seems to be very well protected, Sir William,' said Clay, indicating all the guards.

'King Ferdinand, like most of the royal heads of Europe, lives in fear of the spread of the revolution from France,' whispered Hamilton. 'With very good cause in his case. He is not loved by his subjects.'

'Your Excellency,' boomed a deep voice from the top of the steps. The men turned to see the large figure of a palace chamberlain. His plump frame bulged out of a heavily embroidered blue coat, covered in bands of silver lace that sparkled in the lamplight. One pink hand rested on the top of his silver-headed walking cane, while with the other he fluttered the air as he bowed. Hamilton returned the bow, and then both men spoke to each other in a flowing river of Italian from which the names Sir John Acton and Sir Horatio Nelson stood out like rocks to the listening Clay.

'May I present Captain Alexander Clay, Visconte?' said the ambassador, switching to English for his benefit. The chamberlain looked towards him, his glance swept over his uniform, taking in the lack of any obvious orders or ribbons, and he gave him a much lesser bow than the one he had given Sir William. He then said something further in Italian to Hamilton and favoured Clay with a slight smile.

'Please to follow,' he said, and waddled off down a marble corridor with his two guests in tow. After several turns they arrived at a pair of double doors with yet more soldiers on guard. The chamberlain rapped on the wood with his cane, then pushed open the doors. He stepped through, bowed low, and bellowed their names into the room before he moved to one side to allow them to enter. Clay followed the ambassador in and heard the doors click closed behind him.

The room was large and square, with a high ceiling, from the centre of which a mass of candles burnt in a spreading chandelier. The light fell on walls that were of green damask and covered with gilt framed oil paintings. Most were either landscapes of Naples bay and Vesuvius, or extraordinarily crowded battles between fleets of Christian and Turkish galleys. The room was dominated at one end by an enormous desk, behind which was a man dressed in a dark blue soldier's uniform with the heavy gold frogging of senior rank. He was a large man in his sixties with a tanned face, which contrasted with the pure white curls of his powdered wig.

'Sir John, may I present to you Captain Alexander Clay of his Britannic Majesty's Royal Navy,' said Hamilton. Clay bowed low, and then gripped the hand that was held out to him across the desk.

'Pleased to make your acquaintance, Captain Clay,' said the Prime Minister in heavily accented but clear English. 'Do please be seated, gentlemen. Can I offer you some refreshment?' He rang a small bell on his desk without waiting for an answer, and two footmen came in through a side door carrying drinks. A silver tray was held next to Clay's elbow and the servant murmured a string of names in Italian. Marsala was the only one that was familiar to him, and he accepted a glass of that.

'So, gentlemen, how may I be of assistance?' said General Acton. He settled back in his chair and made a steeple with his fingers over which he regarded them both. Clay pulled Nelson's letter from his coat and offered it across the desk.

'Here are my credentials, Prime Minister,' he said. 'It is a letter from Rear Admiral Nelson who commands our forces in this area.' Acton accepted the envelope, looked briefly at the seal and placed it to one side on his desk without opening it.

'I am sure it is quite satisfactory,' he said. 'What was the nature of the request you wanted to make on your country's behalf?'

'Admiral Nelson is in need of a harbour to base his fleet, safe from storms, where his ships can be repaired and resupplied,' said Clay. 'He wishes to use Naples in this manner.'

'Naturally his Britannic Majesty's Government will pay a reasonable amount for such services,' added Hamilton.

'Naturally,' agreed Acton. 'How large a fleet does the admiral command?'

'When reinforced, he will have perhaps fourteen ships of the line plus some smaller vessels,' said Clay. 'Certainly less than nine thousand sailors and marines.'

'Nine thousand!' exclaimed Acton. 'But surely you have an excellent naval base in Gibraltar? Why can your admiral not base himself there, captain?'

'It has a number of disadvantages for the nature of operations that Admiral Nelson has in mind, Prime Minister. For one thing it is too far from the centre of the Mediterranean to be of value to combat the threat of the French, and a fleet based there can be held in port by an easterly wind.' The general waved a hand dismissively at this.

'I am sure you understand such professional matters better than I, captain,' he said. 'And your request is an interesting one. Regrettably The Kingdom of the Two Sicilies is a neutral in this conflict you have with France. It would be quite wrong for us to provide support of this character to either side.'

'You extended such facilities to the *Titan* on Captain Clay's last visit to Naples, Prime Minister,' said Hamilton.

A Man of No Country

'Yes, but Sir William, as a seasoned diplomat I am sure you must understand that an offer of water and firewood for a single frigate is one thing. To extend the facilities of Naples to such a large fleet of warships as the captain has proposed is quite another. It would be seen in Paris as a most blatant provocation. Why would we agree to have our neutrality abused in such a way?' Both men looked at Clay for an answer. He set down his glass on the table next to him and leant forward.

'Sir William was telling me earlier that you were once commander-in-chief of the army of the Grand Duke of Tuscany,' he said.

'I had that honour,' conceded Acton.

'I understand that Tuscany was neutral,' said Clay. 'Did that stop the French army from marching in to annex the Grand Duchy the moment they wanted to? My ship was off Genoa earlier this year. It too was a neutral state. Yet it too has been conquered by France.'

'As has also happened to Modena, Piedmont and the Papal states,' added, Sir William.

'The day that Paris decides to add the Kingdom of the Two Sicilies to their growing empire, what protection will your neutrality offer your King?' asked Clay.

'None at all, you are quite right, captain,' said the Prime Minister. 'But why would we hasten that day by letting the Royal Navy abuse our neutrality?'

'Because the navy will protect you,' said Clay. There was a long silence in the room while Acton considered this. Clay became conscious of a large case clock somewhere behind him, its regular beat was loud in the quiet of the room.

'Go on, captain.'

'Have you read the latest copies of *Le Moniteur* from Paris,

157

Prime Minister?' asked Clay.

'We receive the papers from most of the major powers,' replied Acton. 'The small nations of the world need to understand what our more dangerous neighbours are about.'

'Then you will be aware that an armada has been in preparation this winter in southern France, and that Naples is openly spoken of in that paper as its objective. I have come from Toulon. Those ships are now at sea, with an army onboard them. The only thing that will answer to defeat a fleet is another fleet. Do you have one?'

'Only a collection of small vessels, sufficient to patrol our coasts,' said the Prime Minister. 'You are right. It would certainly not be able to defeat the French.' Acton looked up at the chandelier for a moment and Clay held his breath. After a pause he returned his gaze to his visitors. 'You are a very persuasive young man, captain,' he said. 'I will put your proposal before His Majesty and give you his answer in the morning.'

'Thank you, Sir John,' said Hamilton, rising to his feet. Clay remained in his chair.

'Might we wait for an answer tonight, Prime Minister?' he asked. 'I know it is late, but as I have said the French are already at sea. Every moment is precious.'

'Well, this is most irregular,' frowned Acton. He glanced over Clay's shoulder at the clock. 'But the King should still be up at this hour. He is rather fond of his wine, but may yet be in a position to make a decision. Perhaps you gentlemen would wait here?'

'Of course, Prime Minister,' smiled Hamilton.

'Although there was one other matter I wished to discuss,' interjected Clay.

'What a singularly demanding fellow you are, captain,' declared Acton. 'What is this further request?'

A Man of No Country

'Admiral Nelson's fleet is very short of smaller vessels to act as scouts for the main body. Might ships of your fleet be put at his disposal? The admiral would supply crews, and they could operate under British colours.'

'No, sir, they may not,' said Acton. 'That would constitute a virtual declaration of war on France. I have no intention of placing such a request before the King.'

'I understand, Prime Minister,' said Clay. The general rose from his chair and made his way towards the door. Just as his hand reached for the gilt knob another thought occurred to Clay.

'Of course, if your ships were to be despatched out as Neapolitan vessels, and should chance to encounter the French, they would naturally report what they had seen back to your government.'

'They would,' said Acton. 'What is your point, sir?'

'I was just imagining that perhaps such reports might be shared in a discreet way with Sir William?' The Prime Minister considered matters for a moment.

'If the King agrees to your fleet being based here, then I suppose that might be acceptable,' he conceded.

'Upon my soul, Clay, but you're damned persistent!' exclaimed Hamilton as they left the palace later that night. 'You were like terrier on the scent of a rat. It ain't the way we diplomats are meant to proceed, you know, not at all. If you are half this firm in your regular profession, I hope to God I never have to face you in a sea fight.' Clay laughed aloud at this.

'Surely it answered well enough, Sir William?' he said. 'The fleet has its base, and their navy will scout for us. All that we require now is some intelligence of the French.'

'Perhaps I am getting too old for this,' said the diplomat. 'I would never have bullied Acton as you did, but I have to confess we made more progress in a single evening that I normally do in a whole year.' He pulled out his fob watch and angled it towards the carriage lamp. 'It is a half after midnight now, whatever that is in those damned bells you naval coves use.'

'One bell in the mid watch, Sir William.'

'If you say so. In any event, too late for you to return to your ship. Why not come back to my residence for a bite of supper and a glass of something? I can gladly offer you a bed for the night'

'My thanks, Sir William,' said Clay. 'I must confess to being famished after all our exertions this evening.'

*****

After many years at sea, sleeping to the sounds of a ship as it creaked and worked all around him, Clay never slept very soundly when he was first ashore. The bed felt too inert, the room too vast and the walls too silent. So when the lock of his bedroom door clicked open, he was instantly awake. He sat up in bed and looked around him.

'Who is there?' he asked.

'Hush!' said the ghostly figure that slipped through the opening and slid the door closed again.

'Lady Emma?' queried Clay. 'Is that you?'

'Who else would it be?' she giggled. 'Sir William perhaps, come to show you another of his broken pots?'

'Whatever can the matter be?' he asked, as he swung his feet out of bed and stood up. 'Are the French in the offing?'

'No, it is only little me, come in search of company,' she said. 'My, how very tall you are, captain. And rather fetching in a night shirt.'

'Now Lady Emma,' he said. 'If I have been guilty of leading you on, or giving you a false impression I do apologise, but I must inform you that my affections lie elsewhere.'

'It isn't your affections I am interested in,' she said as she advanced on him. 'My objective is all together more carnal in nature.'

'But Lady Emma,' he exclaimed, 'I am but newly married.'

'So am I, you handsome devil,' she purred. She placed both hands on his chest and pushed him towards the bed. 'What of it? I don't want to marry you, just share your bed.'

'What of your husband?' he asked, side stepping her advance.

'He is very accommodating with me,' she said. 'We married because he had need of a hostess for his salon, and I had need of a protector. He knows he can never satisfy my wants at his age, and is quite content to play the cuckold. His real passion is to have beautiful objects in his house, and I am just another one of those. And I am beautiful, aren't I, Alex?'

She drew open the front of her nightshirt, and allowed the thin cloth to slide off her shoulders and down her slender arms. The garment hesitated at her hips, and then dropped to the floor, leaving her long, curvaceous body white in the faint moonlight that came through the window. With one hand she reached behind her neck and tugged at her hair, which cascaded down around her shoulders. A single, curling lock lay over one breast.

'Yes, you are beautiful, Lady Emma,' he said. 'Very beautiful. I give you joy of your liberal marriage. But I fear that I view my own nuptial vows to have been of a rather more binding character.'

'Come come,' she urged. 'Your little wife need never know. Besides, are you quite sure that she too will be as resistant to temptation as you claim to be? How long have you been absent from her?

'It has been seven months now,' he said.

'Seven months apart!' she repeated. 'And no real prospect of your return to her bed in the near future? Can you truly believe that she will be able to remain faithful? You men really know so little of the appetites we ladies need to have satisfied.'

'I am quite certain of her, Lady Emma,' he said. He stooped down in front of her and took hold of the discarded nightdress that still lay in a hoop about her feet. He felt her fingers slide into his hair and smelt the perfume on her skin, so close were her legs to his nose. For a moment he hesitated, still squatting at her feet as temptation swept over him in a wave. Her cool fingers against his neck and scalp sent a shiver through him, and he felt a warm glow deep in his stomach. He tried to fix the image of Lydia in his mind, but found that he struggled to remember her face. He was on the very edge of a pool and only had to let himself slide forward to enter it. Then he pulled his head free of her hand and rose to his feet, drawing the night dress up as he did so. He slipped it over her shoulders and stepped back from her.

'You really must leave now, Lady Emma,' he said quietly, his voice harsh with lust. 'I bid you a good night.'

But she showed no signs of going and instead continued to stand in front of him. Her shoulders trembled a little and then began to shake. The moon slid from behind a cloud and glistened on the tears that ran down her cheeks. He took a step forward, drawn to comfort her, but then he stopped, frightened as to where any close contact between their bodies might lead.

'Does she love you a great deal?' she sobbed.

'My wife?' he said. 'Yes, Lady Emma, I believe that she does. She waited a long time for me when we were apart, and she went against the opposition of her family to marry me.'

'And how does that feel?' she asked. 'To love and be loved in return?'

'Oh, Lady Emma, it is quite the most wonderful thing, which is why I cannot place it in hazard. You really should go, before you are discovered.' His hand took her arm and he tried to ease her towards the door, but she shook him off.

'Do you know that I have been the plaything of men since I was little more than a child?' she sobbed. 'An artist's model, then an actress and finally a mistress. Handed from man to man to be used and then discarded. But all I have ever wanted is to be loved and cherished. Is that so much to ask?'

'No, it is not, but surely it is to your husband that you must look for such affection?'

'Sweet, old Sir William?' she scoffed. 'Really? Do you know that he arranged to take me off the hands of my last lover, the so called Honourable Charles Grenville, without any prior discussion with me? I thought that Charles loved me, but when his fortune ran low, he needed a lucrative match. My presence threatened that, so I was tossed across to Sir William as if I were a discarded coat.'

'I have seen how he looks at you, Lady Emma. In his own way I believe he does admire you.'

'Doubtless he does, as a master is fond of a favoured hound. I need so much more!'

'Then you will need to find it elsewhere,' said Clay. 'I will gladly offer you my friendship and what protection I can, but as for my love I must reserve that for Lydia.'

'Friendship!' she exclaimed. 'What possible use is that to me?' She turned on her heels and stormed out of the room.

*****

Sunday morning in Naples, and the bells of her numberless churches clanged out over the terracotta roofs as they summoned the faithful to mass. At the altar of one of the city's more popular churches, the Basilica of San Lorenzo Maggiore, Father Massimo looked up from his preparations to peer through the wisps of incense that trailed like gun smoke across the body of the church. In the lines of pews there were perhaps a dozen elderly widows, black as crows, but of his normal congregation he could see little sign. He walked towards the church entrance, a puzzled frown on his forehead. The doors stood open, wide and inviting, just as they did every Sunday. He peered outside as he searched for his missing parishioners. The sky above his head was blue and cloudless, the empty square already warm in the sunshine. From high above his head the clamour of the bells rang out across the district. All was as it should be, he thought. He turned in frustration and waved over one of his assistants.

'Andrea!' he called. 'Has the plague returned, or are the Turks attacking the city?'

'I don't believe so, Father, not that I have heard,' said the altar boy.

'Well, where is everyone then?' asked the priest. 'The church is almost empty!'

Father Massimo's congregation, along with those of most of Naples' other churches, had taken to the water. The more well-to-do had found places on the decks of the moored merchantmen that chanced to be in the bay that Sunday. The rest were packed into fishing boats, rowing boats, leisure craft, skiffs and little vessels of every kind. Their brightly painted hulls contrasted with the blue water of the bay beneath the cloudless sky. Every boat was packed with sightseers, eager for a closer look at the huge warships that had appeared during the night.

There were fifteen of them in total, moored in a long, evenly spaced line out in the deeper water. At one end was the *Titan*, a familiar sight now to the locals. Yesterday morning she had been comfortably the largest ship in the bay, but that was no longer true.

A Man of No Country

She had been joined by the newly restored *Vanguard*, the *Orion* and the *Alexander*, and a further eleven seventy-fours. It was the largest fleet that had been seen in Naples in living memory, and no one wanted to miss the sight. The little boats with their chattering cargos sailed between and around the huge ships, like birds amongst a herd of bison.

On board the *Titan*, the call had gone up for all hands to muster for divisions. Throughout the lower deck men sat in front of their tie mates to have their wild, uncut hair plaited into respectable pigtails and secured with coloured ribbon. Elsewhere, others sailors struggled into their best clothes, urged on by the shouts of the boatswain's mates. Farther aft, in the wardroom, the officers pulled on full dress uniform coats and buckled on swords, while their servants gave their best cocked hats a final brush. Macpherson wound his scarlet officer's sash around his waist, and tied a knot by his side. He glanced up and caught Taylor looking at him. He gave the tiniest of nods, in response to the first lieutenant's raised eye brow.

On the quarter deck the marines were being inspected by their sergeant in the bright sunshine. He marched along the ranks, while his eyes darted from side to side and up and down each man he came to. He paused from time to time as he flicked at some imagined dust here, or frowned at a poorly polished button there. A deck below where the marines stood, Clay settled his best china silk neck cloth into place, before turning to slip on the heavy broadcloth coat that his servant Yates held out for him. He pulled it straight, picked up his copy of the Articles of War, and accepted his best cocked hat from the boy, who had now moved to stand by the door. He ducked out of the cabin and walked onto the main deck. He could see that the crew were already assembled in the blocks of their various divisions, out on the deck in front of him. He looked briefly over their massed ranks to check that all was well, and then quickly ran up the companion ladder and onto the quarterdeck. Around him were his officers, touching their hats at his appearance, while the marines at the back of the deck presented arms with a sound of hands slapping against muskets.

'Are all the men present and correct, Mr Taylor?' asked Clay.

'Eh, actually no, sir,' replied the first lieutenant. 'We are deficient by one man. Daniel Oates, landsman in the larboard watch, cannot be found.'

'Oates?' asked the captain. 'Was he not one of the new volunteers that joined the ship at the start of the voyage?'

'Yes, that's right, sir,' said Taylor. 'He was a rather indifferent hand. Altogether too scrawny for much to be made of him, so he is no great loss to the ship. I imagine he must have deserted in one of these wretched shore boats that are all around us. I have done my best to keep them away, but they will persist in returning.' Clay glanced over the rail, straight down into a large skiff that had come alongside. A family of chattering Italians enjoyed a picnic in the centre of the boat. The man at the tiller raised his hat to the two officers.

'Shall I drop an eighteen-pounder ball into her, sir?' growled the lieutenant. 'From this height it should go clean through. That might answer to make the others keep their distance.'

'Best not,' smiled his captain. 'We have need of Neapolitan goodwill if we are to use their city as a base. Are all the arrangements in place?'

'Yes, sir. Mr Macpherson and his men are ready to conduct the search when you give the order.' Clay looked towards the *Titan*'s Scottish marine officer, who touched his hat in response.

'Very well, Mr Taylor, let me first address the men.' Clay strode forward to the quarterdeck rail and looked down on the crew. A sea of faces looked back at him. He paused for a moment to gather his thoughts, and then began to speak.

'Men, this morning there will be no divine service,' he began. 'Nor shall I read through the entirety of the Articles of War to remind you of your duty to this ship.' Faces turned towards each other in surprise and a few mutters of talk swept the deck, quickly silenced by the petty officers. 'Instead I want to read a single Article, number twenty-nine, which states that *All robbery committed by any person in the fleet, shall be punished with death, or otherwise, as a court martial, upon consideration of the circumstances, shall find meet*.' In the silence that followed he closed his copy of the Articles of War and returned it to his pocket.

'You all know of what I speak,' he said. 'We have a cutpurse amongst us. A ne'er do well who preys on his own shipmates. I am quite determined to find this despicable man and put a stop to his antics. If any of you know who this person is, I ask you to step forward now.' His eye travelled over the impassive crew. No one moved. 'Very well, then every man is to stay in his place, while Lieutenant Macpherson and his marines conduct a thorough search of the ship. Carry on if you please, Mr Taylor.'

While the marines clumped down the ladder way to begin the search, Clay stood at the rail and watched the crew. He scanned their faces and looked for any clues as to who the thief might be. Did anyone look nervous, he wondered? He picked out Grainger's lean, bearded face, a comfortable half-head taller than those around him, but no flicker of emotion passed across his features. Up through the main grating came the sound of barked orders and booted feet. Clay moved his gaze on, till he came to rest for a moment on Murphy in the afterguard. His face flushed red as he realised he was under scrutiny. Was that guilt, thought Clay to himself, before he remembered that the young Irishman always blushed at the slightest attention. He moved on to look at some of the other faces. From deep under his feet more noises drifted up as the search progressed.

It was half an hour later that the figure of Taylor appeared at his shoulder. He turned to face the grey-haired lieutenant.

'Well, Mr Taylor, have you found our thief's ill-gotten hoard?' he asked. The first lieutenant shook his head.

'Sorry, sir,' he said. 'The marines have found no accumulations of money of a suspicious nature. But they have found Daniel Oates. I am afraid that he is dead.'

'Dead!' exclaimed Clay. 'Where did they find him?'

'His body was hidden in the gap behind the boatswain's store on the orlop deck.'

'Was it an accident?'

'I very much doubt it, sir,' said Taylor. 'His throat has been cut from one ear to the other.'

Chapter 10
Malta

Lieutenant Thomas Macpherson of the Royal Marines had managed to spread himself across all of the chairs that lined the starboard side of the wardroom table. His body was in his usual seat, close to the back of the cabin, with a second beneath his knees and a third positioned under his feet. His uniform jacket was hung up in his nearby cabin, his neck cloth had been unwound and his white linen shirt had its top two buttons undone to reveal a few curls of black chest hair. By his elbow, on the table was a large glass of watered wine. With a sigh of contentment he picked up the slim leather bound volume, flipped open the cover and began to read. A few moments later a shadow fell on the page.

'*The Bramptons of Linstead Hall. A novel in three volumes by a Lady,*' read Lieutenant Blake as he leant across the Scotsman's shoulder. 'Would the lady in question be Miss Clay, the captain's younger sister, by any chance, Tom?'

'Aye, that is correct,' he said, moving the page back into the light. 'Although that is not known to society in general, which is the chief point of an anonymous work.'

'An anonymous publication,' marveled the young lieutenant. 'I have heard of such things, but only by reputation. Is it of a particularly salacious character then?'

'That is not immediately apparent from the title page, which is as far as I have been permitted to read uninterrupted,' said the marine. He turned in his chair to favour the younger man with a withering glance. Instead his dark eye brows shot up in surprise. 'Good gracious, John, what are you wearing? You look as if you are about to go forth and thresh corn.'

Blake was indeed a curious sight. His normal lieutenant's uniform was visible no higher than his knees. Above this he had a voluminous smock of rough linen, spotted with paint of various colours, a bright red kerchief tied about his neck, and a large straw hat whose tattered brim spread wide on both sides. By way of explanation he pointed towards the wardroom door, where he had left his paint box, a folded easel and a large canvas.

'I have been busy painting ashore,' he announced. 'Oh, but what an agreeable subject I have found!'

'So I can see,' said Macpherson. 'You do know that both of your hands are blue?'

'No matter!' said the artist, wiping some of the paint onto the smock. 'I took a boat over to that headland close to the Hamilton's place, first thing this morning. Do you know that from there one can view the whole sweep of the bay with considerable advantage? The blue of the sea and sky, the red roofs of Naples, the volcano that looms over all, and our magnificent fleet laid out in a single rank. I do hope I have been able to do it justice.'

'Might I see the work?' asked Macpherson, putting down the book.

'Heavens, no,' said the artist. 'It is barely started. No, it shall need many more hours of labour before it is fit to be seen. I hope to return to the same spot tomorrow and continue.'

A Man of No Country

'Goodness, John, what on earth are you wearing?' asked Charles Faulkner, the *Titan*'s elegant purser, as he came into the wardroom. 'You could pass for one of the labourers on my father's estate.'

'Almost my very words,' said Macpherson, with satisfaction. 'Young Mr Blake has been capturing the image of our fleet at anchor in the Bay of Naples.'

'Ah, that will account for the wooden device I almost fell over as I came through the door,' said the purser. 'Might I trouble you for a place to sit, Tom?' The marine surrendered one of his three chairs with a sigh, and Faulkner joined him at the table. 'Tell me, John, while you sweated away like Michelangelo in a passion, did you chance to notice that all the captains in the fleet were being ferried over to a reception, hosted by our ambassador?'

'I believe I may have done,' said Blake. 'There was certainly a deal of boat traffic around a little jetty, close to the spot I had chosen to place my easel.'

'Apparently it was quite an affair,' said Faulkner. 'I chanced to see the admiral's flag lieutenant afterwards, he is an old acquaintance of mine, and he said he had never seen such an amount of gold braid. All our captains were there, the admiral too of course, along with masses of gorgeously attired Neapolitan naval officers. Every man jack of them was either a commodore or an admiral, and this in a navy with nothing larger than a sloop! My friend reports that most of them have never been to sea, and are just on the active list so they can draw a stipend. It was hosted by Sir William and his very handsome young wife.'

'I had heard that Lady Emma can be very, ah...accommodating where naval officers were concerned,' said Macpherson.

'She does have that questionable reputation, don't she?' said Faulkner. 'So you might imagine that our Pipe would be a figure of considerable interest to her? I can't speak for the Dagos, but he is surely favoured with the most agreeable countenance and figure amongst our captains.'

'He is certainly the youngest,' agreed Blake. 'Did she make a play for him then?'

'She did not,' reported the purser. He folded his arms in satisfaction. 'She cut him quite dead, and singled out Admiral Nelson from the whole company for her particular attention. Now what do you make of that?'

'That she isn't partial to tall men with chestnut hair?' suggested Blake.

'Nonsense!' exclaimed Faulkner. 'A lady with her supposed appetites showing a preference for a dwarf with half his limbs missing? What rot! No, our Pipe has spent two nights at the Hamilton's residence over the past few months, and I know how to recognise a lover's quarrel when I see one. There ain't no smoke without a blaze, gentlemen. You mark my words.' He picked up the discarded book from the table top. '*The Bramptons of Linstead Hall*,' he read. 'Is it a tolerable read, Tom?'

'I can confirm that the title page is well composed. Beyond that I have yet to venture.'

'Goodness, but you must have retired down here a good half an hour ago to peruse it. What an indifferent reader you are.'

The wardroom door opened before the marine was able to defend himself, and in came the stooped figure of Richard Corbett, the *Titan*'s surgeon. He was a small man in his late thirties with thin, sandy hair and pale blue eyes.

'And there I was thinking that no officer could have more diverting hands than Lieutenant Blake,' said Macpherson, indicating the surgeon's arms, soiled brown with dried blood up to the elbows. 'What have you been about, Richard? I doubt if Blue

A Man of No Country

Beard himself can have been filthier.'

'Ah, yes,' said Corbett. He paused to examine his hands. 'I have not had occasion to wash them yet.'

'But what have you been doing, man?' demanded Faulkner.

"I have conducted an examination of the cadaver of the unfortunate Daniel Oates, in the hope of discovering some intelligence to offer the master at arms. First all these thefts, and now a killing. The poor man is quite at his wits' end as to who could have committed these crimes.'

'Have you come to any conclusions from the body, Richard?' asked Faulkner. The surgeon wiped his hands on his handkerchief and sat down to join the others.

'I can say with a degree of certainty that the body had lain on the orlop deck for no more than one or two days. On the one hand it was fully stiffened by the rigor mortis, while on the other natural putrefaction had yet to have begun in earnest.'

'So the murder occurred after we arrived here in Naples, then?' said the purser.

'That would make sense,' added Blake. 'The hands' lives are so closely regulated by the needs of the ship at sea, it would be hard to find the leisure to commit such an act unobserved, but at anchor the men have a deal more liberty.'

'How did this Oates meet his end?' asked Blake.

'Oh, that is plain enough,' said Corbett. 'A single slash from a sharp blade, delivered from behind the victim I should say.' The surgeon pantomimed a curved, slicing blow in the air above the table top as he spoke.

'Would that not have generated a prodigious quantity of blood?' asked Faulkner. 'It seems odd that the murder was not detected sooner.'

'Aye, it was a fair way to being a charnel house,' said

Macpherson. 'The perpetrator had chosen his spot with care. It was in a dark, seldom visited part of the ship where we found the poor laddie. Were it not for the flies, my men might have missed him entirely. If the murderer did indeed approach Oates from astern, he might well have barely a spot of gore upon him.'

'So all we are certain of is that we seek a man in possession of a sharp knife?' snorted Faulkner. 'Well that narrows it down! Every seaman aboard owns such a thing. Does anyone have any insights to offer?'

'Perhaps I might,' said the marine officer. 'Watching Mr Corbett's wee demonstration of the how the murder was done just now, has put me in mind of that new hand we took off the Russian pirate ship. The sailor who helped the captain's coxswain during that storm.'

'John Grainger?' said Blake.

'Aye, that's the one. Mr Preston and I saw him dispatch a Spanish sentry in a not dissimilar fashion to that playacted by our good surgeon. He did it during the assault of that battery on the Cape de La Nao.'

'Did he now?' said Corbett. 'That is interesting. I must tell Mr Taylor.'

'Was your search yesterday fruitful in other ways, Tom?' asked Blake. 'Had this Grainger a suspicious lot of money about himself?'

'He did not, and nor did anyone else for that matter,' said the marine. 'We found nothing of note save the discovery of the body. My men did their best, but they are soldiers, not thief-takers. They have a natural disinclination to be overly thorough when required to finger their way through their shipmates' possessions.'

There was a thunder of knocking at the wardroom door. The officers exchanged glances.

A Man of No Country

Someone is in a perishing hurry to tell us something,' said Blake. 'Shall we make him wait awhile to gain a little patience?'

'Come in!' called Macpherson, and an excited midshipman burst into the room.

'Mr Taylor's compliments, and the Blue Peter has just been hoisted in the flagship, sir,' reported Midshipman Butler. 'We shall weigh anchor before nightfall.'

'Do you know what has occasioned this, Mr Butler?' asked Blake.

'I am not sure that it is really my place to say, sir, but I did happen to overhear the captain and Mr Taylor discussing matters on the quarterdeck. Not that I listened to them on purpose, of course.'

'I understand, Mr Butler,' said Macpherson. 'What is it you chanced to learn?'

'One of those Neapolitan navy sloops entered the bay earlier with all sail set, sir. Apparently the Frogs have been seen at last, just off the coast of Malta.'

*****

Even though the line of warships was in close formation, they still stretched across the sea for over a mile. In the centre of the long line was the *Vanguard*. She was easy to distinguish, with her admiral's blue flag flying at the top of her mizzen mast and her distinctive foremast, now a little shorter than the others after the damage of the storm. As for the other seventy-fours, they were as identical as a row of well matched pearls on a string. Each one had a black hull and twin gun decks picked out by long lines of yellow. Every ship had top and topgallant sails set, and every yard was braced around at the same angle. Behind the column of ships the coast of Sicily slid by, brown and rocky close by the sea, rising to pine covered slopes farther inland.

'There is something very pleasing in a well-drilled column of ships,' said Lieutenant Edward Preston as he leant against the quarterdeck rail and admired the view.

'Particularly in this case, when they are all of the same proportion,' added Richard Corbett, who had borrowed Preston's telescope and was moving it along the line. 'So often one has a variety of different ship sizes in a fleet, as was the case with the one we joined off Cadiz. Although it is a little vexing that your spy glass should present such an indifferent image.' Preston leant across and, unnoticed by the surgeon, eased the tube of the telescope in a little. 'Ah, they have suddenly become clearer,' exclaimed Corbett. He continued to examine the ships for a moment, then returned the glass to its owner.

'My thanks, Edward, but there is one thing that I find troubling,' he said. 'Are we not part of the squadron?'

'Indeed we are,' said the lieutenant. He pointed towards the flag that flapped in the breeze over their heads. 'That is why we too fly the blue ensign.'

'Then why, pray, do we not have a part in this magnificent line of ships, and are instead banished to a position out here on the flank?'

'Why, it is a singular honour bestowed on us by Admiral Nelson,' explained Preston. 'We are here so that we may appreciate the magnificent view all the better. But you must make good use of this time, Richard, for soon it will be the *Culloden*'s turn, and we shall be obliged to take her place in the line.'

'Is that so?' said the surgeon. He polished his glasses on his shirt and gazed at the rest of the fleet with renewed interest. Preston turned away from the rail and tried to disguise his laughter in a fit of coughing.

A Man of No Country

'He makes game of you, Richard,' said Blake, who was officer of the watch. 'This is our proper station. When the fleet is at sea, our role is to repeat all the admiral's signals, so that those ships at the ends of the line need only observe us to know what they should be about. It saves them the inconvenience of attempting to read signal flags through a dozen masts and sails. In fact here is a signal now. Mr Russell, have you seen it?'

'Aye aye, sir,' replied the midshipman, who already had his telescope focused on the *Vanguard*. 'General signal, wear ship in succession. Get it hoisted, Jennings.'

'Aye aye, sir,' said one of the sailors who worked with him. He pulled the relevant flags from the locker and handed them to his mate, who attached them to the halliard. The signal rose up to the masthead and broke out to flap in the wind. Corbett looked back towards the line of warships and noticed the same flag had been hoisted aloft in each.

'Mr Russell, signal the flag to say that all ships have acknowledged receipt of the signal,' ordered Blake. 'Mr Hutchinson! Call all hands to wear ship, if you please.'

Down in his cabin, Clay looked up from the letter he was writing to listen to the flow of orders that Blake gave, as they drifted down to him through the open skylight. He heard the squeal of the boatswain's call as the crew was summoned, the thunder of bare feet on oak as the crew responded, and shortly afterwards he felt the ship begin to turn to keep station with the rest of the fleet. All was being done as it should be, he decided, and he returned to the half-written page in front of him.

He was writing to his wife Lydia, which for him was still a relatively new activity. His first few letters had been composed as the *Titan* had beaten her way through the winter storms of northern Europe and had been full of the emotion of their recent parting.

How much he loved her, how he longed to be with her and how much he missed her. But as the months had gone by, he had realised that he could not simply repeat the same formulas, even though, if anything, he missed her more with each passing week. So he had begun to add fresh content to his letters, filling them with glimpses into his world. The places he had seen, the people he had met and the events that surrounded him in the little wooden world of his ship. So far this had worked well, but his frankness to date now presented him with the fresh problem of how honest he should be. He sat back in his chair and looked at the portrait of his wife that his officers had given him. Her smiling blue eyes met his calm grey ones across the space of the cabin.

'Oh, Lydia, my dear,' he said. 'I do so love you, but does that love require me to be wholly honest? On the subject of Lady Emma's nocturnal visit, for example?' Her eyes seemed to twinkle with mischievous encouragement, willing him to tell all. 'And what shall I set down on the subject of poor Oates? How disturbed will you be with the knowledge that my ship has a murderer on the loose?' He looked for an answer in her face for a moment, and then set down his pen in frustration as he thought about the murder. Taylor and the master at arms had made almost no progress with the investigation in the two days since they had left Naples, and he could sense the unease the death had caused among the crew. He rose from his desk and began to pace up and down the line of windows at the back of the cabin, his head tucked down to avoid the low ceiling as it skimmed past.

There were two hundred and fifty souls aboard the *Titan*, he said to himself. No, two hundred and forty nine now. All of them lived in a ship that was a bare hundred and seventy feet long from end to end, and less than forty feet wide. How could it be possible for this to happen, and yet no one have seen anything? His arms jerked in frustration as he paced. Then he stopped at the midpoint of the run of windows, directly above the rudder, and looked down at the sea. A churned mass of ever renewing white bubbled up from under his feet, like a millstream that stretched away behind the ship, straight for a while across the blue sea, before it bent at the point that the frigate had turned. He watched the troubled water for a while and let the constant motion calm him. Of course someone must know something, he told himself. He turned towards the door and called to the marine sentry stationed outside.

'Pass the word for my coxswain!' he ordered. A little later there was a knock at the cabin door.

'Come in,' called Clay. 'Ah, Sedgwick, my thanks for arriving so promptly. How do your hands fare?' The sailor came into the cabin and stood in front of the desk, his legs apart and his powerful body swaying with the motion of the ship. He presented his bandaged fists for inspection.

'Mr Corbett says as how there is no sign of corruption, and that the dressing will be off by the end of the week, sir,' he replied. 'Which shall come as a blessed relief.'

'Excellent,' said his captain. 'You have my gratitude for what you and Grainger did.'

'Thank you, sir, but I would like to think if matters were reversed, some tar might do the same for me.'

'Indeed,' said Clay. 'Well, you may be on the mend, but our poor ship is not. We live in troublesome times, do we not? First all these damned thefts and now matters have progressed to murder. The men have had much to endure. What do you think of their morale?'

'Not good in truth, sir,' said the coxswain. 'They will be game enough come a fight, but some have taken to moving about in the company of others, and they start to shun the newer crew members.'

'Their unease is understandable. Unfortunately, I can hold out very little prospect of us laying hands on the person or persons behind all this,' Clay spread his arms wide. 'The master at arms has no notion who it may be, nor do any of my other officers. Frankly, I have no damned idea where to turn next.'

'I am sorry to hear that, sir.'

'Sorry enough to help me?'

'You knows I will help if I can, sir, but I don't know who has done all this either.'

'I am sure you don't, Sedgwick,' conceded his captain. 'But somebody on the lower deck must. There will be one of your shipmates who knows who the perpetrator is, or at least has some piece of intelligence that will lead us to that person. The men admire you, Sedgwick, and respect you, even more so after your heroic rescue of that poor man. Might you not be in a position to help me to solve these crimes?' The sailor shifted from foot to foot before he replied.

'I mean no disrespect, sir,' he began. 'But if the men do like me, as you suggest, it is in part because they trust me. They know I would never grass on a shipmate, if you understand my meaning, sir.'

'Ah yes,' said Clay, his voice a little bitter. 'The famous solidarity of the lower deck, where no man shall betray a confidence to an officer. But surely this case is different? All the victims have been your fellow shipmates. A man has been killed. Perhaps he shall not be the last. You may be able to prevent that from happening — God knows I can't!'

'But, sir,' pleaded Sedgwick. 'I honestly do not know who has done these things.'

'But could you not find out? Part of your role as coxswain is to supply a link between myself and the lower deck, you know?' Clay watched his coxswain's face, with its sad brown eyes and solid jaw, and willed it to move. It remained immobile, the eyes stared ahead. After a moment Sedgwick began to speak.

'I am sorry, sir,' he said. 'I do not wish to be unhelpful, nor to seem ungrateful for what you have done for me, but I truly have no name to give you.'

'A truly grateful man might seek to repay past kindness,' urged his captain. 'I am asking you to help me, man. You need not even betray the particulars, just give me a name. A member of the crew whom I should discharge from the ship at our next port of call, perhaps, with no more said. I trust you. It would only need a nod on your part, Sedgwick. Mr Taylor has suspicions already about that name, that it might be John Grainger, for example?'

'Please do not press me, sir,' he said. 'You were right in what you said earlier, I can serve you best while the men respect me. No one will trust an officers' lackey.'

Clay pushed his chair back from the desk in exasperation, stood up and glared out of the window once more. The churned wake was still there, now running straight as the fleet headed towards Malta. He let the bubbling water calm him again, and when his breathing had returned to normal, he realised that his coxswain was right.

'Very well, Sedgwick,' he sighed. 'I understand the delicacy of your position, and I will press you no further on this matter. I will not ask you to betray any confidences.'

'Thank you, sir,' said the coxswain, relief evident on his face. He thought for a moment, and then spoke again.

'Captain, sir. May I make a suggestion?'

'Of course. What do you have in mind?'

'If I did find out who had done all this, I could never bring you the name,' said Sedgwick. 'But things might yet be resolved, nevertheless.'

'How might that happen?' asked Clay.

'Do you remember Josh Hawke, ordinary seaman on board the *Rush*?' said Sedgwick.

'Yes, a singularly nasty piece of work,' said Clay. 'I had you and he flogged for fighting with knives as I recall, so perhaps I have not always shown you the kindness you remember.'

'My dozen was fair enough, sir, especially as he got three dozen.'

'And if I remember right, he applied for a transfer out of the ship shortly after,' continued Clay. 'It was much to my relief and I suspect strongly against his inclination. Was that all arranged by the lower deck?'

'Aye, that's right, sir,' said Sedgwick. 'A course of action was suggested to him, and he was obliged to follow it. Would it serve if a similar solution could be found in this case?'

'By all means,' said the captain. 'What did you have in mind?'

'Maybe I can find who's done all this, sir. I could not betray him to you, like I said, but things might be done to solve matters without the need for that. With the mood that the men are in there would be no shortage of people to help. Would that answer at all?'

'Sedgwick, I only desire for this mess to be resolved,' said Clay. 'If you come to me and tell me it has been, without the need for any names, no one will be more delighted than me.'

'I understand, sir. Leave it with me.'

*****

'Would you be so kind as to wait in here, sir,' said Nelson's flag lieutenant as he ushered Clay into the great cabin of the

Vanguard. 'The admiral will join you shortly. Steward, a glass of wine for the captain, if you please.'

'Ah, Clay,' said Captain Saumarez. 'So you have been summoned too?' He rose from the bench seat that ran across the back of the cabin under the stern windows and held out a hand towards him. 'Delighted, I am sure.'

'Likewise, Sir James,' said Clay, shaking the Channel Islander's hand. 'I trust I find you well?'

'Tolerably so, although I should be markedly better if we could find the damned French fleet.' He indicated the view out of the window. It was a bright summer day, the sky was dotted with puffs of white cloud above, and the view below was filled with the massive walls and towers of the fortified entrance to Grand Harbour in Malta. Beyond the walls, Clay could see the domes of churches and the roofs of the buildings. The ship was hove to just out of long cannon shot from the nearest battery, but close enough for him to be able to see the large French tricolour that streamed out from its flag pole, high above the main fortress on Valetta point.

'How did the French come to seize Malta so easily?' he asked. 'I had always thought of it as a place that might require a lengthy siege?'

'Any fortress is only as good as those who garrison it,' said Saumarez. 'If it is defended by poltroons it don't signify how thick the walls might be. Bonaparte turned up a couple of weeks ago with his enormous fleet, and the Knights of St John surrendered without firing a shot, the blackguards.'

'What happened then, Sir James?' asked Clay

'Why, he annexed the place for France. Then he toured the island like a damned Prince, changing everything in sight, from the official language to giving the poor blighters the metric system.

Finally, he confiscated a mass of treasure and has gone on his way, leaving a rather more resolute garrison of French troops behind to keep order.'

'Do we know where he has gone?' asked Clay. 'Surely this huge fleet must have had a greater object in mind then Malta?'

'I dare say they have,' said Saumarez. He waved his drink in agitation. 'They have headed east. That is all we have got out of the local fishermen, which is damned all use. No, we still have no real notion as to where he is bound. But it does, at least, show that I was wrong when I said they must have planned a descent on England or Ireland, and that you were right, sir.' The captain held out his hand to his younger colleague again. 'Well done, Clay. You're a dashed smart cove.'

The two captains sat back down together on the bench seat, with the hot sun shining down through the glass onto their dark blue coats. Clay felt the warmth soak into his injured shoulder and it helped to ease the slight pain. He had slipped on his way up the ship's side, and in grabbing for the hand rope to stop himself from falling backwards, he had jarred the old wound. The thought of his narrow escape from an inglorious plunge down into the sea brought another image to mind.

'Tell me, Sir James, have you ever witnessed the admiral as he comes aboard his flagship?' he asked.

'Can't say as I have,' said Saumarez, running a hand through his thin brown hair. 'Why do you ask?'

'I was wondering how he makes shift to do so with only one arm.'

'I dare say he is obliged to use a boatswain's chair, just like the carpenter's wife,' said Saumarez. He smiled at the thought, and then tilted his head to whisper into Clay's ear. 'On the subject of the Chosen One, what do you notice different about his cabin?'

A Man of No Country

Clay looked around him at the pale grey bulkheads, the red wood of the mahogany furniture and the black and white squares painted on the canvas cover that had been stretched out over the deck. It seemed strangely bare compared with his last visit, he thought, which brought to mind the portrait of his wife that dominated his own cabin.

'Was there not a painting that once hung over there, by the quarter galley?' he said eventually.

'Bravo,' smiled Saumarez. 'It was a rather indifferent likeness of Lady Nelson, painted some time ago. Now I wonder what can have prompted its removal?' He looked at Clay down his patrician nose and slowly winked. 'And how long do you suppose it will be before the image of another man's wife might take her place, eh, what?'

Saumarez chuckled to himself for awhile before turning back towards Clay.

'Mind, you would not want to cross her, you know,' he said. 'She is a comely enough piece, but I understand that she is not a lady to be trifled with.'

'Lady Hamilton?' said Clay, with a gulp. 'Why do you say that, Sir James?'

'She has quite a reputation for getting her revenge, you know,' continued the Channel Islander. 'Back when she was just plain Emma Hart, she was Sir Henry's squeeze for a while. He was a dreadful, lewd old sod. On one occasion, he persuaded her to bathe naked in a hip bath full of Madeira, in front of the members of his local hunt. Then, Sir Henry had the wine rebottled and served up to them that night. His ghastly friends lapped it all up, but it was she that had the last laugh. Apparently when the butler had come to collect the Madeira before dinner, half a pint more came out of the bath than had gone in!'

'I do apologise for the necessity of having to keep you gentlemen waiting,' said Nelson, as he came into the cabin. 'Although from the laughter, you do both seem to be having an agreeable time. We have just fallen in with a neutral merchantman, and I wanted to interview the master to see if he had any knowledge of the enemy.'

'And did he, Sir Horatio?' asked Clay, rising with Saumarez from their place by the window. The good eye that settled on Clay sparkled with excitement.

'I am pleased to say he had,' said Nelson. 'He encountered the French two hundred miles east of here not five days ago, and they were still headed eastwards. It is confirmation of what we learnt from the fishermen. The trail grows warm at last.'

'Then we must hasten to follow them, Sir Horatio,' said Saumarez. He put down his glass. 'A lead of five days! They may be far away now.

'They might be, but only at the risk of becoming impossibly scattered,' said Nelson. 'A fleet of such an enormous size will take a deal of marshaling and will be obliged to sail very slowly. We shall catch them, of that I am certain, but only if we direct our search to the right place.'

'Too true, Sir Horatio,' said Saumarez. 'Where do you hold the right place to be?'

'The main fleet will sail, with all despatch, due east down the centre of the Mediterranean along thirty-five degrees of latitude towards Crete, which we will pass to the south, and if necessary onward till we reach Cyprus. That will cover the possibility that the enemy is bound for the Levant. If so we should be able to overhaul them before they reach their objective and bring them to battle at sea.'

A Man of No Country

'Very well,' said the Channel Islander. 'And what if their objective should lie elsewhere?'

'You gentlemen have command of my two fastest ships, so I shall send you out on either flank of the main body to cover those eventualities. Sir James, I want you to sail to the south. You are to scour the coast of Africa, looking for news of the enemy. Tunis and the Barbary coast and then Egypt.' Saumarez nodded at this, and Nelson turned to Clay.

'You have the swiftest ship of all of us, so I shall require you to be the busiest. Seek for the French towards the Adriatic, and the west coast of Greece. Stop every ship you encounter, neutral or otherwise. Someone will have seen them, or will know to where they are bound. We shall rejoin off the coast of either Crete or Cyprus.'

'So we shall advance eastwards up the Mediterranean rather like a line of beaters, our quarry driven before us, eh?' said Saumarez.

'Very like, Sir James,' said the admiral. 'It will be just like a Norfolk duck shoot. I have your orders here, gentlemen. If there are no further questions, let our hunt commence.'

*****

It was close to sunset, and the fleet had come to the end of another day as it sailed in pursuit of their elusive enemy. A week had passed since the island of Malta had sunk below the horizon. The *Orion* had long since disappeared to search away to the south of the main body, and the *Titan* had vanished away to the north. That left the balance of the Nelson's ships in a line stretched across the empty sea in the dying light of another day, as they sailed ever farther eastwards, and still there was no sign of the French.

187

At the extreme end of the line was the seventy-four *Minotaur*. Her spreading sails cast a long shadow on the sea in front of her bow, like a black slick in the pearl blue water. High up in the foremast her two lookouts sat on the royal yard, one each side of the slender mast. They had been aloft for almost two hours now, and were lit by the last few rays of a sun that had already set for those on deck, a hundred and ninety feet below them.

'Quite a sight, ain't it, George,' said the port side lookout. He indicated the long line of ships that stretched away from him across the sea with the jerk of a thumb.

'That it is, Tobias,' said the starboard side lookout. 'All them warships a-gathered together. Now we just needs some bleeding Frogs to give a knock to. Been days searching for the buggers, without so much as a glimpse.' He looked out to his side of the ship at the semi circle of empty sea, flat and calm seen from above, as it stretched to the lemon sky at the horizon. Then he swung himself around and looked astern of the *Minotaur,* towards the setting sun.

'What you about, a peering over yonder?' asked his colleague. 'We've already searched that there patch of briny when we crossed it. It's up ahead the Frogs will be.' He pointed forward towards the gathering night in the east.

'May be I just likes to see a bit of a sunset of an evening.'

He continued to stare into the west for a while. The sky was ablaze with crimson and magenta as the sun sank below the horizon. Suddenly he stiffened for a moment, then stood upright on the yard and shaded his eyes with one hand.

'George, clap an eye on this,' he said. 'Due astern, right in the eye of the sun. You see anything?' George stood up on his side of the mast and looked where the sailor had indicated. The sun had almost disappeared now. Only a slither of molten gold still showed above the horizon for a moment, and then it was gone.

'Can't say as I clocked nothing, mate,' he said. 'What was it you reckon you saw?'

'Perhaps the ghost of a topgallant sail,' said Tobias. 'A little square of pink, but I can't see it no more. Should we report it?'

'What! Turn the whole fleet around, cause you reckon you might have seen a slip of pink? That sod Wilson will have us swabbing out the heads for the rest of the bleeding week.' George sat back down on his side of the mast and resumed his search of the sea in front of them. His fellow lookout continued to gaze into the west for a while, but nothing further appeared. After a few minutes he too resumed his place on the yard and the long line of British warships sailed on into the purple dusk.

Behind the *Minotaur*, the sky grew progressively darker. The big warships had gone now. Their churned wakes had faded into the dark water, leaving the empty sea to the gathering summer night. No one was left to see the little point of light that appeared, at the very spot where Tobias thought he had seen his topsail. It was no bigger than a grain of silver dust in the night. A few moments later a second spec joined the first, as if a pair of tiny eyes was peering over the horizon. For a moment they burnt next to each other, before a third light appeared to one side of the first two, then a fourth. Soon more little lights joined them, the number swelling like stars in a darkening sky, till the horizon was ablaze with numberless tiny points as the huge French fleet slipped across the wake of Nelson's ships and disappeared again into the dark.

Chapter 11

Vanished

'Shift up there, Sean,' grumbled Evans. 'I need a bit more bleeding room on the bench than that.'

'Will that be on account of the size of your fat arse?' said O'Malley. He slid a fraction to one side and a tiny strip of elm opened up between the Irishman and Rosso. Evans took his chance and sat down in it, allowing gravity and his considerable weight to slide the two sailors further apart.

'A bit snug, but it'll do.' He smiled in response to his two friends' mutters of protest.

'What's with all that smiling, anyways?' moaned the Irishman. 'Haven't you heard about the killer on the loose, at all? Anyone of us could be next to have his throat laid open.'

'Quit yer bleating and tell me what you all reckon on this, then?' Evans held out the fist that had "HOLD" tattooed on it over the mess table, and waited till he had everyone's attention. Then he opened his hand, and a cascade of silver coins rang and clattered down onto the wood. Trevan stirred the pile of money with a finger from the far side of the table.

'What is to be seen with all these coins, then?' he said.

190

A Man of No Country

'It's my bleeding chink!' he exclaimed. 'Only also, it isn't my chink as well, in a manner of speaking.' The other messmates exchanged glances.

'I am not sure I quite follow...' began Sedgwick.

'I ain't said it straight,' conceded Evans. 'Look, this here is six crowns. You know, as was stolen from me. I have just now found them again. They've been put back in my purse.'

'So after all that ballyhoo, are you saying your money was never fecking taken in the first place?' exclaimed O'Malley. 'Where did you have them stowed, then?'

'No, Sean, you aren't getting it,' said Evans. 'My money was definitely taken. I bleeding showed you all my empty purse. And now it's come back.'

'Don't be daft, Sam!' exclaimed the Irishman. 'What manner of fecking cutpurse returns what he's taken? Do you think he's been after finding himself a conscience an' all? No, it must have been there the whole time.'

'Then how does you explain this?' said Evans. He sat back and folded his arms. 'This ain't my money.'

'You just said it fecking was,' exclaimed O'Malley.

'No, it's the right amount, sure enough,' said the Londoner. 'It just ain't the same bleeding coins as them as was taken. See, one of mine had been clipped. The edge was proper flat, yet none of these is like that. And my chink was all shiny, like. Look at the state of that coin there.' He pointed to one that was brown and stained. 'I tell you, them ain't the same ones as was nicked.'

'Does it really matter, Sam?' asked Rosso. 'At least you got your money back.'

'An' I'm right happy for that, Rosie, don't get me wrong. But don't it seem strange to you?'

Sedgwick picked up the dirty coin and examined it. He scraped at the staining with his thumb nail and brown flakes dropped down onto the table. Then he moistened a finger and picked a little of the dirt up. He rubbed his finger tip against his thumb, and sniffed at the result.

'I shouldn't worry about this stain, Sam,' he said, handing back the coin. 'It will come off easy enough with a bit of spit. Dried blood always does.'

'Dried blood!' exclaimed Evans, He rubbed the coin on his sleeve. 'How did that get there, then?'

'I don't know for certain, Sam,' said Sedgwick. 'But I can think of one way.' The sailors gathered around the table looked uncomfortable as the same image came to all of them.

'Might it be something to do with that mate of yours, Rosie?' said O'Malley. 'The poor fecker as had his throat slit an' all?'

'He wasn't really a friend, Sean,' said Rosso. 'Just another hand from Bristol. I reckon you should just be grateful you got your money back, Sam. Have any of the others had their money back?'

'Well that's where it gets proper weird, Rosie,' said Evans. 'Same thing has happened to Stevenson as to me. He can't remember what his coins was like, so he ain't so sure if they are his or no. He's just happy to have his chink back.'

'As should you be, Sam,' said Rosso. 'I wouldn't examine this given horse over closely.' He turned his attention towards the coxswain.

'Any news from back aft, Able?' he asked. 'Are we hot on the heels of them Frenchies yet?'

'Afraid not, Rosie,' said Sedgwick, still looking at the coins. 'We've stopped no end of trading ships this last two weeks without so much as a sniff of the enemy. Whatever way they have gone, you may be sure it is not towards the Adriatic. Pipe has ordered the ship to head for the rendezvous with the rest of the fleet now.'

'I could have told him that, fecking weeks ago,' exclaimed the Irishman. 'See, that Bonaparte he's a right deep feller by all accounts. He will have shaped to head east from Malta just to throw us off the scent like, while he has been doubling backed on us. Mark my words, your man's after slipping past Gibraltar as we speak. He will be headed for Ireland as quick as quick.'

'But how is he planning to get past Hanging Jack and the fleet as is before Cadiz then?' asked Rosso. 'They're still in his way.'

'With the help of the Dons,' said O'Malley. 'They'll all come a-rushing out as easy as kiss my hand.'

'I am not sure that can be quite right, mate,' said Trevan.

'Then you answer me this,' said the Irishman, drumming the table top with one of Evans's coins. 'Where the fecking hell are they?'

*****

John Grainger came off duty, and made his way down to the lower deck with the rest of the larboard watch. When he reached his mess table he flopped down on a stool and stretched out his long legs with a sigh of contentment. Then he eased his shoulders under his shirt and leant back against the side of the ship. The waves that rushed past on the far side of the oak skin made the wood thrum and vibrate on his tired muscles in a pleasing way. At the other end of the table sat Davis, one of the *Titan*'s older sailors. He had taken a piece of wood out of his kit bag and now worked on it, conjuring the shape of a whale from the twisted branch with a succession of tiny strokes from his clasp knife.

'You looks right weary there, John,' said the older man. He stopped carving and polished the cut wood on the sleeve of his shirt for a moment.

'I am that,' Grainger replied. 'Pipe is in a perishing hurry to find those French, and he's after driving the barky hard. I must have reefed and shaken out the foretopsail a dozen times this watch. How is that carving of yours coming along?' Davis pushed the piece of wood across the table for him to inspect.

'It's going to be a bull sperm whale, diving and a twisting,' he explained. 'Them two bits that stick out there will be the flukes. I don't know what manner of lumber that be, with all them kinks and curves and the like, but it put me in mind of a whale when I saw it, washed up on the shore back in Naples.'

'It's an old piece of vine,' said Grainger as he turned the carving in his hands. 'They are often twisted so.' He leant forward to pass it back and as he did so a silver disc on a chain swung out of his open shirt and caught the light.

'What's that you got around your neck, then?' asked Davis, pointing with his knife. 'Is that one of them lockets? You got some sweetheart you're keeping quiet about?'

'No, it's just a little picture I was given as a child,' said Grainger. He tucked the chain away again. 'I shouldn't really wear it by rights. The Koran doesn't hold with images of folk or creatures, but I have had it since as early as I can recall. It might be my mother.

'Don't you remember your Ma, then?'

'Not really. Nor my father, neither. They died that long ago they both seem lost, in a fog like.'

'Maybe that's for the best. I remember my Pa right enough, and a proper evil bastard he was too,' said Davis. 'That'll be why I ran off to sea. I got sick of all his beatings.' He picked up the piece of wood and worked on it a little more. Then he paused as another thought came to him. 'So is all images of life a blasphemy for your Turk?' he asked. 'What about my whale?'

'To a strict Mohammedan, yes,' smiled Grainger. 'But don't

fear, Infidel. I will pray for you tonight and perhaps Allah will forgive you, peace be upon Him.'

'Afternoon, shipmates,' said Sedgwick, as he walked up to the mess table. He gave Grainger a friendly punch on the shoulder. 'Might I join you, Master Eel?'

'By all means, Able,' said Grainger. Davis pulled out a mess stool.

'John here was just telling me how I am headed for the fiery pit on account of my whale,' said the older man.

'Is that so?' said the coxswain. 'How ill is your workmanship, then?' He took the piece of wood from Davis and examined it. 'That does seem a touch harsh. I would say you done a neat job of work, there. You're going to need a proper sharp knife for the mouth and eyes, but John has one of those that he can lend you, haven't you, mate?'

'It's not really made for that,' said Grainger. 'But you can borrow it if you wish. What was it you wanted, Able?'

'It was you I was looking for, John. I was after some advice.'

'Very well, what manner of advice?'

'I heard that you told the Grunters as how you was once on a Neapolitan ship before that Russian privateer captured you,' said the coxswain. 'Navigator, wasn't it?'

'That's right. What of it?'

'So you must know Naples passing well?'

'What is all this about, Able?' he grumbled. 'I am just now come off watch and I am bleeding knackered.'

'See, it's like this,' began Sedgwick. 'Each occasion we have been in Naples these last few months my barge crew have had to ferry the captain ashore, and then to wait upon his return, often for hours. Twice he has sent word that he will spend the night with old man Hamilton.'

'Or with that tasty missus of his, more like,' leered Davis.

'Like enough,' smiled the coxswain. 'But there we are, with hours to wait and no notion where we might go.'

'Very vexing, I am sure,' replied Grainger.

'But then I got to thinking that I should ask you to help us,' continued Sedgwick. 'You must be just the man to know where a thirsty crew might go in Naples. For a mug of grog like, as was not too pricey?'

'My ship was often at sea,' said Grainger. 'Trading in other ports around the Mediterranean.'

'Come, you must have touched at Naples on some occasions?'

'And of course, my religion forbids me to drink.'

'That's right, it does,' said Sedgwick. 'But surely your crew would have still gone on runs ashore. Where might they have gone?'

'How should I know? I told you, I never went with them.' He settled clear blue eyes full of warning on his questioner.

'Alright, steady there,' said the coxswain. 'I am only after a bit of advice. We did try up by that big castle, you know the one, on the hill. Oh, what's its name again?'

'I can't remember it, Able.'

'Really? Well no matter, for it wouldn't answer. All the taverns were full of soldiers who gave us very short shrift. So what about if we wanted to eat? Where would you say we should go?'

'There is no end of eating places in Naples,' said Grainger 'Surely you can just choose one.'

'Aye, but you know the barge crew,' said Sedgwick. 'They can't abide anything too foreign. Where might you go for plain, honest fare?'

'Look, Able, I don't want to be unhelpful, but I have just come off watch and I really want to rest,' said Grainger.

A Man of No Country

'Well shame you couldn't help any,' said Sedgwick. 'I will leave you both, then. Have a good evening.' He rose from the table and walked away down the deck. Grainger sat back and glared around him. He found Davis's watery eyes on him.

'What are you looking at?' he growled.

'If you don't mind me a saying it, John, you be right hopeless at spinning a yarn,' said Davis, returning his attention to his carved whale.

'What do you mean?' demanded Grainger.

'Even an old fool like me can see you ain't spent no time in Naples,' he said. 'And that Able Sedgwick is far from being a fool.'

*****

'Deck there! Sail ho!' yelled the lookout the following day. Lieutenant Preston was officer of the watch that morning, and strode out from his place beside the wheel.

'Where away?' he called, from a clear area of deck where he could see the man at the masthead.

'Three points of the starboard bow, sir,' said the seaman, pointing with his arm. 'Some manner of sailing brig.'

'Mr Butler, can you give the captain my compliments, and tell him that another merchantman is in sight off the starboard bow.'

'Aye aye, sir,' replied the youth, and he dashed for the companion ladder.

'Kindly close with this ship of yours if you please, Mr Preston,' said Clay as he came up on deck, his jaws still working on his last mouthful of breakfast.

'Aye aye, sir,' replied Preston. He gave the new course to the helmsmen and then joined his captain over by the quarterdeck rail.

'What do you make of her, sir?' he asked. Clay continued to stare at the distant ship through his telescope as he replied.

Philip K Allan

'A large looking vessel, ship rigged,' he reported. 'She seems to have altered her course as if she means to try and avoid us, which is a promising sign. I can't make out her colours yet.'

'I dare say she will prove to be yet another neutral ship, sir,' sighed the lieutenant. 'Doubtless with no knowledge of the enemy, just like all of the others.'

'That may be so, Mr Preston,' said Clay. 'You have younger eyes. Take my spy glass and tell me what you make of the chase's colours. I can see a red fly, but little else.'

'Red white and blue for sure, sir,' reported the lieutenant. 'Dutch or French I should say.'

'Both of whom are enemies,' said Clay. 'This is much more promising, and she is on an eastbound course. I have a good feeling about this ship, Mr Preston. Can you kindly set all plain sail to the royals. Let us run them down and see what we have caught.'

As sail after sail blossomed from the masts of the *Titan*, the frigate began to thrust ahead. The press of canvas grew until the deck was pitched at an angle that made it difficult to stand, and white water foamed along the leeside rail. After an hour of pursuit they were almost up with the big French brig, which surged along a few hundred yards off their bow.

'Fire a shot to leeward from the bow chaser, if you please, Mr Preston,' ordered Clay. 'Let her know we are in earnest, and can you have a boarding party told off ready to take possession of her.'

The bang of the gun was menace enough for the ship they chased to heave to, with all her sails flapping. The *Titan* surged up into the wind next to her, and under the threat of her long row of gun ports, the French tricolour made its hesitant way down to the deck, to cheers from the crew of the frigate.

'She is a curious looking craft,' said Taylor, who had come up on deck to join his captain. 'Very broad in the beam for her length, and is that some manner of canvas awning spread out over her main deck? That must make sail handling awkward.' Clay examined the ship as she lay under their lee. He could see a large oblong of canvas that ran all the way from the forecastle to the poop deck, suspended like the roof of a tent above the ship, but for the life of him couldn't think why it was there.

'I have heard of awnings to provide some shelter from the sun, but never to cover a whole ship. What do you suppose it is for?' he asked.

'I cannot begin to imagine, sir,' said Taylor.

'Mr Blake,' called Clay to the leader of the landing party. 'Send back her master with his papers, and try and find out what she is carrying.'

'Aye aye, sir,' replied the lieutenant.

'At last we have netted ourselves a Frenchman,' said Clay, rubbing his hands. 'When the ship's captain should come aboard, I would be obliged if you would take him below to my day cabin, Mr Taylor. Ply him with ardent spirits and question him thoroughly. See if he has any knowledge of General Napoleon's fleet.'

Clay watched as Blake took command of the captured brig. The boarding party swarmed up the ship's side with the lieutenant in the lead, and he then seemed to stop in surprise as he reached the deck After a pause, and what sounded like laughter, the French crew were herded below decks, while a large man in a pale blue coat was sent down into the launch. Clay could see the sailors of the prize crew busy taking in all the profusion of sail that flapped on the brig's yards, where it had been left by the crew when they surrendered. Preston came over to join him.

'Did you hear that, sir?' he asked.

'The laughter of the launch crew?' asked Clay.

'Just after that, sir. It seems strange to say it so far out to sea, but I could have sworn that I heard the neigh of a horse.'

'From the captured ship?'

'Yes, sir. There it is again, only that was more of a whinny.' Clay turned his head a little and heard the sound too.

'I believe you're right, Mr Preston,' he said. 'Do you suppose we have captured some manner of travelling fair?'

'Perhaps, sir,' smiled the lieutenant. 'We shall soon find out, for here comes the launch with Mr Blake and the ship's master.'

'She is called the *Fleur de Provence,* sir,' reported Blake. 'French, of course, three weeks out from Toulon, with a cargo of cavalry remounts. I have never seen the like. The hold could be mistaken for a barn, all full of hay, straw, sacks of oats and prodigious amounts of water. Above that the main deck has been divided into row after row of wooden stalls, hence that canvas awning to keep them shaded. You can't tell from here, being upwind, but the whole ship stinks of horses. There are piles of dung and straw everywhere.'

'Cavalry remounts,' said Clay. 'Now that is progress, gentlemen. There surely can be only one possible destination for such a particular cargo?'

'The French army for sure, sir,' said Preston. Clay looked across at the brig once more.

'That ship is part of their expedition, you mark my words,' he said. 'Perhaps they have got separated from the rest of the fleet, or have been sent later to join them. Whichever it is, we can be certain of one thing. Wherever she is bound is where we shall find our enemy, gentlemen, you may wager your commissions on it. I had best go and join Mr Taylor below and see what he has gleaned from interviewing the French captain.'

*****

A Man of No Country

Clay entered his day cabin to find the master of the French brig seated in shirt sleeves at the table with a glass of service rum at his elbow, and an open bottle close at hand. He was a large man with an ample belly and a florid face, and he seemed to fill the little cabin like a bear in a closet. He dwarfed the figure of Lieutenant Taylor, who sat opposite him at the table with a second glass of rum. The British officer was clearly struggling, judging by the way he was running a hand through his grey hair.

'I am simply asking you where your ship was bound, captain,' he urged. 'Surely you can tell me that?'

'I give you all the papers of my ship, sir,' replied the Frenchman. He spread his arms wide. 'What more you want I say?'

'But they only tell me your port of origin. Where is it that you were going, captain?'

'Why is such a thing so important?' asked the French master. He drank deeply from his glass and then reached across the table to give Taylor a friendly punch on the arm. 'I not going there anymore, eh!' He chuckled to himself, and the first lieutenant looked around in despair. Clay approached the table and held out his hand with a smile of welcome.

'Alexander Clay, captain of this ship,' he said. 'I am pleased to make your acqua—'

'You see!' exclaimed the Frenchman. He rounded on Taylor and jabbed a finger towards Clay. 'Why you ask me all these stupid questions, when he already knows it.' The two British officers exchanged glances.

'Sorry, captain, I am not sure I follow you,' said the lieutenant. 'What is it that Captain Clay already knows?' The French captain sat back with a surprised look and glanced from one officer to the other. He seemed about to say something more, but then shrugged his shoulders.

'I sorry,' he muttered. 'My English very bad. I make mistake. I say no more now.' He pushed away the rum, folded his arms and sat back from the table.

'No, captain,' persisted Taylor. 'What was it that you believe was just said?'

'No more,' the Frenchman said with decision. He stared past the men towards the far bulkhead. 'I say no more.' After a short silence Taylor called over his shoulder towards the door.

'Corporal Edwards!' The door swung open and a marine marched into the room and came to attention.

'Sir!' he bellowed.

'Can you escort this gentleman away, if you please.'

'Aye aye, sir,' said Edwards. 'Come on, you. Alley, alley!'

When they were alone, Clay sat down opposite his first lieutenant in the place where the Frenchman had been and stroked one of his sideburns.

'What on earth did you make of that, George?' he asked.

'I have absolutely no notion, sir,' said Taylor. 'Before you arrived he had been as tight as a clam. Even a second glass of grog was not answering. Then you came in and he made that extraordinary outburst. What was it you said to him?'

'I simply introduced myself in a friendly fashion. I hoped that he might feel inclined to be more open if treated civilly.'

'Yet his change in demeanor followed hard on the heels of you saying your name,' said Taylor. 'Why would that be?'

'I don't really see, George,' said the captain. 'What can there be about my name? Alexander Clay? Can it mean something in French, perhaps?'

'I am no scholar of the language, but I would not have thought so, sir. Alexander is classical in origin, is it not? While Clay is very

English.' Clay felt a prickle of excitement as an idea began to come to him.

'When I came in, you were pressing him about his destination, were you not?'

'I had been for some time, sir, without any success,' sighed the lieutenant. 'You should have heard him a little earlier. All he cared about was how we proposed to care for his damned horses.'

'Then I said my name, and he reacted as though I already knew where his ship was bound.'

'That's right, sir,' confirmed Taylor. 'You said "Alexander Clay, captain of this ship," followed by some manner of greeting.'

'Alexander Clay, Alexander Clay,' muttered the captain, then he stopped and exchanged glances with Taylor. 'Alexandria! In Egypt! That is what he thought I said! His English was a little deficient. He naturally will have known where he was headed, and probably had the location in his mind when I spoke.'

'That must be it, sir!' exclaimed the lieutenant. 'That would explain his peculiar reaction. Then when he realised his error, he attempted to draw back. But is Alexandria a suitable destination?'

'Let us ask our expert,' said Clay, turning towards the cabin door. 'Pass the word for Mr Armstrong there!' They heard the sentry repeat the order and the echo disappeared into the ship. A few minutes later there was a knock, and the American came in.

'You called for me, sir?'

'I did indeed, Mr Armstrong,' said Clay. 'Come and join us. Now, are you acquainted with the port of Alexandria?'

'Why yes, sir,' replied the master. 'I have traded there a handful of times.'

'And would it be a probable destination for the French fleet?' asked Taylor.

'Very likely, sir,' he replied. 'There are plenty of sheltered beaches to land their army there abouts. Once taken, the port could shelter their transport ships, although the entrance would be difficult for large warships. If the French have that huge three-decker, the *L'Orient* with them, Aboukir bay, close to one of the mouths of the Nile River, would make more sense as an anchorage. It is close by, sheltered, with good holding ground.'

'Gentlemen, that must be the answer,' said Clay as he rose to his feet. 'The enemy is bound for Egypt. We must find Sir Horatio and tell him.'

Chapter 12
Searching

For two days after the capture of the *Fleur de Provence*, the *Titan* rushed eastwards in pursuit of the rest of the fleet. Then, just when she had most need for haste, the north westerly that had pushed her across the sea from Malta died on her. It grew weaker and weaker, her sails drooped till they hung limp from the yards and the sea flattened into a mirror of deep polished blue. A fierce sun beat down on the frigate as she turned round in gradual circles on the spot, her rudder unable to make any purchase on the motionless water. Clay looked at the dome of sky above them and noted a few wispy clouds away to the east.

'Do those little clouds portend any return of the wind, Mr Armstrong?' he asked.

'They do, sir,' said the American. 'But I fear that it will not be the wind that we desire. They are the outriders of an easterly for certain. It will often blow at this time of year, and vexingly comes from the very direction in which we wish to sail. We shall have the wind in our faces for several days, perhaps all the way up the Mediterranean.'

'The *Titan* is a weatherly enough ship, sir,' said Preston, from

205

his captain's other side. 'It will not be the first time we have had to beat our way, tack after tack, against the wind.'

'And at least our modest progress will be superior to the admiral's great lumbering ships of the line,' said the captain. 'We should be able to overhaul them in time. When do you suppose this easterly wind of yours will blow?' Armstrong looked up at the cloud, and then at the rest of the sky.

'Sometime in the afternoon watch, sir,' he concluded.

'It will come as a mighty relief, if only from this heat,' said Preston.

'I would not be so certain of that,' said the American as he pulled his wig from his head and mopped his bald crown with a coloured handkerchief. 'An easterly in these parts will have crossed the deserts of the Levant before reaching us here. Cool it will not be.'

'Do you not find your periwig to be an inconvenience when it is so intolerably hot, Mr Armstrong?' asked Clay.

'Not at all, sir,' he replied. He folded his wig with care before he stuffed the prickly mass deep into his coat pocket. 'When my head is excessively warm, as it is now, I have the convenience of being able to remove my hair altogether. It is a pleasure that you two gentlemen, with your fine heads of curls are denied without recourse to a barber's razor.'

'I dare say that is true,' smiled Clay. He ran a hand through his damp hair. 'Perhaps when my locks begin to fail I shall avail myself of one.'

'Are you wholly resolved that the French intend a descent on Egypt, sir?' asked Preston. 'The intelligence you gathered from the master of the brig seemed rather uncertain.'

'I am, although I do not believe it to be their final objective,' replied Clay. 'They may well mean to use it as a steppingstone from which to advance farther east. I wonder if their true objective is not to strike at our possessions in India.'

'It seems a very bold enterprise, sir, said the lieutenant. 'The French would still have many lands to cross to reach Bengal.'

'From what I hear of this Bonaparte, he is a very bold fellow,' said Armstrong. 'Look how swiftly he conquered most of Italy from the Austrians last year. They say he is much taken by the heroes of the classical world. In Italy he was Hannibal, crossing the Alps with his army. Now he wishes to emulate our captain's name sake. Did Alexander the Great not first conquer Egypt, and then march on India?'

'What an eloquent fellow you are, Jacob,' exclaimed Preston. 'I never had you marked as a scholar. Do you suppose it is the proper regulation of your head temperature that has given you such mental endowments?' Clay laughed at this, before turning back to the American.

'Perceptive as well as eloquent,' he said. 'I believe you have the French plan down pat, Mr Armstrong. Perhaps you would oblige me with your view of how to frustrate such an enterprise?'

'Catch the French at sea,' he said. 'Defeat their warships, and capture all their transports before they ever touch the shores of Egypt.'

'That is undoubtedly what the admiral is intent on doing,' agreed Clay. 'But what if we should fail to intercept them and they reach their destination? They might be landing their troops before the walls of Alexandria even now.' Armstrong ran a hand over the top of his head while he thought of this.

'I would still aim to destroy the French fleet,' he concluded. 'If it were done thoroughly then their army will be cut off both from the supplies and support it will require to press on, and the prospect of any retreat to France. In either instance we defeat their ambition, sir.'

'Bravo, Mr Armstrong,' said Clay. 'You make for an able strategist. Now all we need is this wind of yours to propel us on, and of course, we still need to locate the damn French.'

*****

Thin streaks of cloud, some mere lines of gossamer high above the world, spread across the sky from the east as each hot hour passed. It was not till six bells had rung in the afternoon watch, when half the sky was covered by the little wisps of white, that the first of Armstrong's promised wind came whispering out of the east. The lookouts saw it first. There were lines of ripples on the surface of the sea that spoilt the perfect flat calm that had gone before. The initial few breaths felt deliciously cool to the crew of the frigate, after their day spent sweltering in the heat of the central Mediterranean in midsummer, but the wind quickly grew warmer. It made the sails flap languidly for a moment, but barely moved them through the water. Then it returned again, stronger, hotter and more constant. The sails flapped once more, and then filled, while from the forecastle came the first chatter of a bow wave as it started to form.

'Helm be answering,' said Old Amos at the wheel to Lieutenant Blake. 'What course should I steer, sir?'

'Close hauled on the larboard tack if you please, quartermaster,' he ordered. 'Close to the wind as she will lie.'

'Close hauled it is, sir,' repeated Amos. He spun the wheel over and settled an experienced eye on the leach of the main topsail, as he watched for the flap from the canvas that would tell him he had strayed too close to the wind. Blake walked over to the compass binnacle and looked at the heading that the ship was on. His instincts told him that she could go closer to the wind yet.

'Mr Harrison!' he yelled. 'I'll have that foretopsail yard braced round another turn.'

'Aye aye, sir,' came the reply.

Every few hours the frigate went about, first to the north east, then to the south east. Zig followed zag as she hauled herself forward against the pressure of the wind, clawing her way eastwards for the rest of that day. When the sun finally set at the end of the second dog watch, Clay ordered the ship to stand on one long run to the south east through the night so the crew could get a proper sleep. But the wind had other ideas. An hour after the watch changed at midnight it freshened, and all hands had to be called to reduce sail.

With the crew at work, the lower deck was empty. The air was warm and fetid, still full of the smell of the poorly washed bodies that had abandoned it so recently. The mess tables that lined the sides in the day had been folded away, and the space was given over to a carpet of hammocks that hung a foot beneath the beams above. They had all been abandoned when the men below had been called. They swayed to and fro in time to the motion of the ship, illuminated by occasional discs of orange light from the lanterns.

Sedgwick was the first of the crew to come back down the ladder way. He padded on his bare feet along the free strip that ran like a corridor the length of the ship, with a layer of hammocks on either side, eager to get back to sleep. He was too tall to walk upright. Instead he went with his head bent forward below the beams that supported the deck above. With his eyes forced to look down it was easy for him to catch sight of something off to one side, in spite of the gloom. It was a dark oblong that lay flat on the planking. He paused for a moment. There was something familiar about it. He stooped under the ceiling of empty hammocks and crouched down. Surely it was his journal? The front had that distinctive tooled leather with its Moroccan pattern. A frown of annoyance spread across his face.

'What bugger has been and gone through my things?' he muttered as he picked it up. But as soon as he held it, he realised he was mistaken. The feel of the book was all wrong. The leather beneath his fingers felt smoother than it should, as if polished by much handling. He hefted the book, and noticed how the cover was more flexible than his. Not mine then, he concluded. It must have fallen from one of the hammocks above. He envisaged the unknown sailor, startled from sleep, as he tumbled out of bed under the urgings of a boatswain's mate. Perhaps the leather book had fallen to the deck, unnoticed amidst the roar of noise. He stood back upright and pushed his way between the hammocks to looked at the black numbers painted on the beam that identified whose place this was, but it was not one that he recognised.

More and more sailors flowed down the ladder way now, all eager to get back to sleep. Several looked at him curiously as he stood there wondering what to do. Sedgwick was about to toss the book back onto the nearest hammock when something stopped him. He ducked back down out of sight, as a memory came to him. In his mind's eye he could see the angry face of Grainger, as he snatched Sedgwick's newly purchased journal from the table top outside the tavern in Gibraltar. He must have made the same mistake that I have just made, he thought, in which case this must be Grainger's journal. Sedgwick glanced towards the hatchway. The flow of legs passing by had thickened, and all around him hammocks sagged down as they were occupied once more. He pushed the journal under his shirt and crawled away towards the side of the ship. Once there he stood back up and made his way aft towards his place.

'There you be,' remarked Trevan, as he appeared beside his hammock. 'I had started to wonder where you had got to, like.'

'I just needed the heads, Adam,' said Sedgwick, as he clambered back into his hammock and settled down for sleep. He rolled his back towards his friend, conscious of the square bulge of the journal as it pressed against the front of his shirt. 'See you when the watch changes.'

'Aye, unless we get called back on deck again,' muttered the Cornishman, his voice heavy with the return of sleep. Sedgwick lay still with his eyes closed, and forced his breathing to lengthen. All around him he could hear similar sounds as the watch fell asleep once more. The air began to reverberate with their snores. He made himself slowly count to a hundred twice and then opened his eyes once more. In the dim light he listened to the noises around him. Behind his back Trevan muttered something, the only distinct word of which was Molly, the name of his wife. The sailor in front of him lay on his back with one arm cast across his eyes and his mouth gaping wide. When he was satisfied that all around him were asleep, he dropped lightly onto the deck and crawled under the hammocks once more, until he found a patch of light from one of the lanterns that slanted down past the massed bodies. He lay pushed up on his elbows with the journal in front of him.

'Now then, Grainger my friend,' muttered the coxswain as he opened the book. 'Let us see who you truly are.'

Inside the cover was a title written in a strong flowing script. Sedgwick ran his finger along the line and read "*Journal kept by John Grainger on board the Russian ship* Saint Dmitry." He flipped open the first page and looked at one of the early entries.

Philip K Allan

Sailed from Leghorn as a Merchant Vessel, entering into Porto Ferrajo, in Elba four days later, where we were employed getting Shot and Guns and sundry warlike equipment up from under the ballast, where they had been stowed so as not to arouse suspicion. Pierced the sides for the great guns and took on board 50 Muskets, 70 Cutlasses, 34 Blunderbusses and 80 Pistols. Joined by a further 60 men, every Man jack a thief or a pirate.

'I knew there was something wrong about him,' muttered Sedgwick. 'Navigator on a Neapolitan trader, my arse.' He turned over to the next page and read another entry.

Took a Ragusa Brig from Zante with Passengers, plundered her of a Great Quantity of Silk and Dollars. The Captain called all Hands aft, and explained His purpose, which was for every Man in the ship to make his fortune in a few Months, and the readiest way of doing it would be to make no Distinction, but to burn, sink or Destroy all that came in our way and give no Quarter, for the Dead could tell no tales, and the more we took the more we should have. We gave him Three Cheers when he had done speaking. The Dollars were shared at the Capstan to the amount of 50 per man, but the Captain kept the silk.

Sedgwick flipped through the pages and paused here and there to read entries. As he moved through the journal, the accounts became steadily more gruesome. He stopped at one in particular that caught his eye

In the night, armed all the Boats and boarded two

A Man of No Country

Turkish Vessels at anchor laden with Wine, Silk and Honey, cutting the people's Throats as they lay sleeping as I had shown the men they should do. Plundered them and stood for Milo, having first grappled the ships together and set fire to them. Shared Money in gold and silver to the amount of 430 sequins a Man.

'What is it with that man and throat slitting?' he murmured, before turning over a few dozen pages at once. He stopped and read a fresh entry.

Preceded to Damietta, where we took four ships we found at anchor in a bay. One of the prisoners got loose and tried to throw the Captain overboard, for which he was ordered to have his eyes tore out, his fingers chopped off, and the bones of his Arms and Legs broken. He was then set adrift on a grating, in order that he might expire in the extremist of tortures.

'Murdering bastard,' growled Sedgwick as he snapped shut the journal. The breathing of the seaman above his head paused at the unexpected noise. The coxswain lay quiet on the planking and stared hard at the closed leather cover while he let his anger fade. When he was a little calmer, and the man's heavy breathing had resumed, he crept across the deck to where Grainger's hammock hung. He positioned the book on the deck at the same angle as he had found it earlier and then stole away.

*****

John Grainger ducked through the low door to the forecastle and instantly sensed danger. The area around the galley seemed

213

unusually quiet. It was the only place onboard a wooden ship where the men were permitted to smoke, but the normal crowd of yarning, off duty seamen had vanished. The empty space was lit by a single lantern that cast deep shadows all around. He placed the side of the ship to his back and reached for the hilt of his knife.

'I wouldn't do that if I was you, Turk,' came the voice of Josh Black. Grainger turned to see the bulky figure of the captain of the foretop leaning against the carriage of an eighteen-pounder. 'I am a petty officer. They will hang you if you pull a knife on me, don't you know?'

'Nah, let him do it, Josh,' said a second voice from the other side of him. 'He deserves to swing for what he done to that poor little shit. Grunters are too stupid to see what's under their bleeding noses, if you ask me.' The second man stepped out into the light. It was William Powell, a boatswain's mate who was second only to Evans in size aboard the *Titan*. As if that was not intimidating enough, his face bore a long cutlass scar that lay across one eye, the legacy of a savage boarding action earlier in the war.

'Evening, Mr Powell, Mr Black,' said Grainger, not leaving the safety of the oak wall behind him. 'What is this all about?'

'Don't he sound innocent, Bill?' asked Powell. 'Anyone would think nothing had happened on the barky this commission.'

'Aye,' agreed the boatswain's mate. 'Not a farthing pinched before he turned up, and now a man can barely walk the lower deck without some bastard trying to slit his throat.'

'That was nothing to do with me,' said Grainger. 'I had nothing to do with any of this.'

'Really,' queried Black, walking closer. 'So why you been telling so many lies, then? All that crap about Naples. And whoever heard of a man with no notion of where he bleeding comes from?'

A Man of No Country

'That's the truth!' exclaimed Grainger

'No, I don't reckon it is,' said the captain of the foretop. 'I think how you like to muddy the waters, but Bill and me are simple souls. Perhaps that's why we can see past all your shit.'

Powell pushed off the gun he was leaning against and approached him with his hand held out.

'Hand over that wicked knife of yours,' he said, and when Grainger hesitated, he barked. 'That is an order!' Grainger paused a moment longer, then slid his knife out, flipped it around, and held the handle towards the petty officer. Powell took it and instantly slammed his other fist into the sailor's stomach. Grainger had half expected the blow, and had tensed his abdomen. What he did not expected was the heavy, iron shackle pin that Powell had wrapped his fist around to add weight to the punch, and he doubled up in pain. A moment later Black was beside his colleague, and the two petty officers started to methodically beat the seaman till he slid to the ground, his face a mess of blood. They continued to kick at the prostrate figure, as he writhed on the deck, only stopping when a shout came from farther forward.

'Mr Hutchinson's coming, lads,' called the voice of their lookout. Black bent down and pulled Grainger's battered head up off the deck by the hair.

'Understand this. There is plenty more where that came from. Next port we put into, you fucking run, if you know what's good for you, Turk,' he spat. Powell dropped Grainger's knife beside him, and the two men disappeared down the fore ladder way.

*****

It was mid July now in the eastern Mediterranean, and the sun beat down on the *Titan* with savage intensity, day after day, as she battled her way eastwards against a steady wind that seemed as hot

215

as the breath from an oven. A slow drip of melted tar fell from the standing rigging and down onto the scrubbed decks, to the fury of Hutchinson, the boatswain, who had parties of seamen locked in a constant battle with mops and holystones to keep the frigate's decks clean. Awnings had been spread to provide some shade for her crew, and wind sails had been installed to bring a little welcome air down below decks. But none of this did much to reduce the temperature in the airless wardroom, where four of the ship's officers sat around the table in shirt sleeves.

'We tack to the north, we tack to the south, we tack to the north once more,' moaned Charles Faulkner as he fanned himself with an old copy of the *Gazette*. 'Like the wagging tail of a hound, day after day, in this intolerable heat.'

'What I would like above all things is some ice,' said Armstrong, his periwig abandoned and his bald head shiny in the heat.

'Ice?' exclaimed Tom Macpherson as he looked up from volume three of *The Bramptons of Linstead Hall*. 'And where the deuce do you propose we will obtain that out here?'

'We had it in the summer when I was a child, back in the New York colony,' said the ship's master. 'When the rivers froze in the winter, we would cut blocks of it, and store them packed in straw underground. Much of it would melt, but enough survived to make the summers tolerable. I could certainly do with some ice in my drink now.'

'Surely that must be very injurious to the health,' said Taylor, his grey hair darker than normal with sweat. 'Drinking such cold liquid on a hot day will play Old Nick with one's humours.'

'It may well do, but the notion does have a certain appeal,' said Faulkner holding up his warm glass of watered wine. 'Does one simply add lumps of the stuff directly into a glass?'

A Man of No Country

'That's about the size of it,' said the American.

'Do we at least make some progress with all this endless sailing?' said Macpherson as his attention returned from the heavenly notion of ice in drinks to the reality of the wardroom.

'We are, of a rather indifferent sort,' said Armstrong. 'I have just now completed my noon calculations with Mr Taylor.'

'That is some comfort I suppose,' grumbled the marine. 'So when might we join the rest of the fleet, Jacob?'

'Ah, knowing where *we* might be is one thing. Knowing the admiral's whereabouts is quite another. They will have been forced to beat their way against this wind just as we have, so by rights we should overhaul them presently. Perhaps it will happen in a week, but it may prove to be sooner if this damned wind will shift.'

'A week!' said Faulkner, aghast, 'And what then? We yet have no certain intelligence of the French. Is the captain quite decided that their destination is Egypt?'

'He is,' said Taylor. 'Thanks to the revelation of that French captain.'

'It does seem a little thin,' said Faulkner. 'To place such reliance on a Frenchman with poor English who had just consumed a deal of navy rum. What if he was making sport of us?'

'Aye, that's right,' said Macpherson. 'If the French have played us false, and doubled back towards the west, will the admiral not be furious with the man who sent him on a wild chase towards Egypt?'

'No doubt he will be,' said Taylor. 'But the captain is a deep one who rarely gets such matters wrong. He reminds me of a captain I served with back in the American War, when I had just joined the service. He once used a box of bird skins to track down a Spanish treasure fleet. God, but it is hot down here!' The first lieutenant paused to take a thirsty pull from his drink.

Philip K Allan

'Bird skins to track down treasure!' exclaimed the purser. 'Come now George, pray do not clam up. You have pricked our interest now. Will you not oblige us and share the particulars of this incident?'

'If you insist, gentlemen,' said Taylor. 'I was but a master's mate then, serving on board the frigate *Cerebus*, 28 under Captain Mann. We were sent to patrol off the Azores in very indifferent weather, when we came upon a large Spanish cutter. The *Cerebus* was a fast ship and had been newly coppered, so we overhauled her easy enough and forced her to strike. Captain Mann spoke tolerable Spanish and he was able to ask the young lieutenant in charge of the cutter where he was going. Five days out of Cadiz, bound for Havana, was his reply, which seemed reasonable to us. Like enough they were carrying dispatches, and had thrown them overboard when their capture was certain. And then the midshipman who had been sent to make a search of the cutter came running up with these big lead-lined boxes.'

'What was in them?' asked Macpherson.

'They were well sealed, but when we finally had the lids off, we saw they were packed full of beautiful tropical bird skins with feathers of every colour. Well, Captain Mann took one look at them and smoked what the Dons were about straight away.' Taylor glanced expectantly at his fellow officers, who looked blank in return. Eventually Faulkner cleared his throat.

'I do not have the pleasure of quite following you, George,' he said. 'What was the significance of the feathers?'

'Why would any sane man chose to transport boxes of tropical bird skins from Spain, where they are presumably a rarity, to the tropics where there must be all manner of such creatures?' explained Taylor. 'Don't be disheartened, Charles, I was no sharper than you at the time.'

A Man of No Country

'So this Captain Mann concluded from the skins that the cutter must have been travelling from the Americas to Spain as oppose to the other way round,' said Macpherson. 'Very well, but how would that have altered matters?'

'If the young lieutenant had told his story that way about, all might have been well,' said Taylor. 'But he had tried to dissemble. Which made the captain consider, why was it so important for the Dons to conceal that they were really sailing inbound for Spain?'

'Because they were not simply carrying dispatches,' mused the Scot, 'or exotic feathers for that matter. Something more was afoot.'

'And that was Captain Mann's conclusion,' said Taylor. 'He decided that this single innocent cutter might be part of some larger force. An expendable scout sent ahead to observe if the way was clear for those who followed after.'

'A treasure fleet!' exclaimed Armstrong. 'Did you run them to ground?'

'We did, forty leagues to the west of the cutter, and following in their wake,' said Taylor. 'They were too well protected for us to hazard an attack, so we sent the captured cutter for reinforcements, while we kept them in sight. Once the Dons saw they had been rumbled, they put into Santa Cruz in Tenerife, where they were obliged to remain under blockade till the end of the war.'

'Well, I never,' said Macpherson. 'He must have been quite the accomplished cove, this Captain Mann. Whatever became of him? It is not a name with which I am familiar.'

'He died the following year of the Yellow Jack, in Jamaica, I am afraid,' said the first lieutenant.

'Pity, we could have used his powers of deduction to help the master at arms solve the identity of our murderer,' said Armstrong. 'Are we any nearer to catching the ne'er do well?'

'No, nor are we like to be,' said Taylor.

'If you ask me, this Oates fellow was the cutpurse all along,' said Faulkner. 'He tried one theft too many, got caught, and the lower deck administered their own brand of justice. Swift and thorough retribution. Why else would all this thieving have stopped with his demise?'

'Nothing would please me more than for this matter to be resolved, Charles, but I fear you are incorrect,' said Taylor. 'It is true that the lower deck is quite capable of administering what it thinks of as justice after a fashion. But if matters have been resolved, where is the return of our contented crew? Have you not seen John Grainger of late?'

'Aye, I have,' said Macpherson. 'He would seem to have been very badly beaten.'

'And yet he has clearly not been fighting, for where is the opponent with corresponding injuries?'

'So what do you think may have happened?' asked Faulkner.

'I would say he has been set upon, by those who deem him to be in some way responsible,' said Taylor. 'You may think that the murder of Oates was the end of matters, Charles, but it is plain that the men do not agree.'

Chapter 13
Egypt

The light of the lantern sent the men's shadows flickering across the curved surfaces of hogs heads and barrels that were stacked all around them. The atmosphere was close in the hold, deep below the water line, and the air was full of sound. There was the constant gurgle of water as it rushed along the skin of the ship and the groan of the timber frames as the hull twisted and straightened a little with each fresh wave. Beneath this was the scratch and occasional squeal of the hold's many rats, and over all the sound of the two sailor's breathing.

'What the hell are we about down here in the hold, Able?' said Grainger. His face was full of suspicion, with one eye still partly closed from his beating, and a cut visible on his lip. The look of him was not improved by being lit from below, by the shuttered lantern that Sedgwick had put down on the deck at their feet.

'Easy there, John,' said the coxswain. 'It is only the two of us down here. I don't know where Powell and Black are, but I had nothing to do with what happened to you.'

'So what are we doing down here then?' he repeated. 'I warn you now; I am not going to let anyone catch me that way again.'

'I am not going to hurt you,' said Sedgwick. 'I just want you and I to have a little chat about a few things. In the quiet down here, were we shan't be disturbed any. Come on, take a seat, why don't you?' He indicated the pair of boxes he had placed facing each other to one side of the lantern. He had positioned them earlier, and had done his best to estimate how far Grainger might be able to spring with his murderous curved knife. But now that he was down here with the tall, wiry sailor, the seats looked too close to each other. He sat down on his box, and dragged it a little farther back as he did so. His fellow seaman shrugged his shoulders and sat down too. Sedgwick let his right hand rest close to where he could feel the cold touch of his open clasp knife, pushed into the waistband of his trousers.

'All right, my friend, assuming you are my friend, why don't you tell me what this is all about?' asked Grainger, folding his arms.

'I wanted to ask you how well you knew that man what was killed?' said Sedgwick. 'You know, Daniel Oates, the little skinny runt from Bristol?'

'I hardly knew him at all.'

'Is that so?' queried the coxswain. 'Wasn't he a messmate of yours?'

'He was, but maybe I keep myself to myself.'

'Did you know that he knew his letters? Rosie told me he could read quite well.'

'Can't say as I did know that, but what of it?' said Grainger.

'A man as can read might get to looking in places he shouldn't.'

'He might, and what of that? You reckon that's what got him killed?'

'Aye, I think I do,' said Sedgwick. 'I am starting to think that he may have learnt things about a shipmate that had been set down, in a private place.' Grainger uncoiled his arms and leant forward, his face full of anger.

'What the fuck are you trying to say? At least those two turds who jumped me spoke plain. What shipmate do you mean? If you mean it was me, why don't you have the fucking balls to just say as much?'

'Oates had his throat cut, just in the manner that you seem to favour,' said Sedgwick, his gaze fixed on his fellow seaman. 'Done with a deal of skill, I should say. Just like when you knocked off the sentry, when we was storming that battery.'

'Use your head, Blackamoor!' spat Grainger. 'Dozens of men saw me do that, and all the rest learnt of it soon after. Anyone who wanted to finger me for the killing had only to do for him that way for half the ship to believe it was me. Skill, you say? It takes no skill to kill such a puny man if he be taken unawares. One of the ship's boys could have done it. Do you not think I can kill a man in many different ways?'

'Oh, I am sure you can,' agreed the coxswain. He slipped his hand a little closer to his knife.

'So why then would I choose to do it in a manner that so decidedly points back to me? And besides, why would I wish to kill him at all?'

'Do you remember New Year's Eve?' said Sedgwick. 'The Grunters were all having a right roister in the wardroom and some of the lads had a bit of a dance too. I went to the heads, just about dusk. None of the lanterns had been lit under the forecastle then, so when I came back it was dark by the galley. I heard Oates, clear as I can hear you now. He was threatening someone. He said how that person would swing for what he had done, and how Oates would grass on him to the Grunters unless he paid up. I reckon that other person was you.'

'What are you talking about? What would that little shit have on me?'

'I think that Oates had read your journal.'

Although he was prepared for Grainger to attack him, Sedgwick was stunned by the sheer speed with which the man moved. His hand had only just gripped the handle of his knife before his opponent cannoned into him. He was knocked backwards off his seat and down onto the deck, with Grainger on top of him. The coxswain was a powerful man, stronger than the wiry Grainger, but he was also slower. By the time he had wrenched his knife out, Grainger was lying on his chest, his curved blade pressed against the skin of his throat and his battered face, contorted with fury, was close above him.

'Breathe and I shall kill you,' he hissed, through clenched teeth. 'I warned you I would not be taken unawares again. Now drop your knife.' Sedgwick let it fall from his hand and then lay still on the deck.

'When did you find my journal?' Grainger breathed.

'A few weeks ago, when all hands were called on deck to reduce sail in the mid watch. It must have tumbled from out of your hammock. I picked it up because I thought it was mine. The one I bought in Gibraltar.'

'And what have you read there?'

'Enough to see you hanged as a pirate.'

'Well, if you are right, and I murdered that little shit Oates for having such knowledge, what will stop me from killing you in your turn, eh?' Out of the corner of his eye he saw the knuckles of Grainger's hand whiten on the handle of his knife, and felt the razor sharp edge press against his throat. He closed his eyes and tensed for one final effort to save himself, but instead he felt the weight lift from his chest. When he opened them again, Grainger had gone. He pushed himself up onto his elbows, and saw him sat back on his box, his knife returned to its sheath.

'Did you learn nothing about me, when we were in the sea together, then?' he said, his face angry and his eyes glaring at the coxswain. 'I thought you were smarter than Powell and Black, but I was wrong. You're just as stupid as them.' He turned his gaze on the flickering lantern. 'Fortunately for you, Able, I am not the murderer you seek. Oh, I have committed no end of murders in my past, as you now know only too well, but Oates ain't amongst them. When the crew of the *Saint Dmitry* ran off into the woods, on that beach in Portugal, I crossed a line. I decided to stop running, and wait instead for your marines to come ashore. I am weary of all the wickedness I have done. So I decided I would leave that life behind. Since I joined the barky, I swear on all I hold sacred I have committed no more crimes.' Sedgwick picked himself back up and sat down on the other box. He felt his neck, as if surprised it was unharmed.

'How true an account is the one in your journal?' he asked.

'It's as true as I can recall it,' said Grainger, still looking at the lamp. 'Most of it I set down as hard upon the events as I was able.'

'Did you really hack up that poor man for attacking your captain and then set him adrift on a grating?' asked Sedgwick. 'Because I was seven years a field slave in Barbados, and I saw no end of dreadful things done, but none are the match of that.'

'Our captain was a savage man, and not to be trifled with. If I had refused to do what he had ordered, a grating would quickly have been found for me too.'

'But why do you keep such a journal?' asked Sedgwick. 'Do you not care about the risk you run in setting down such things? There is enough to condemn you a hundred times over, all in your own hand.'

'Because it helps me to survive,' said Grainger, his voice choked. 'I have followed this life since I was no older than one of the ship's boys. A Barbary captain named Ali Hamadu took my father's ship. I joined his crew to avoid slavery, and so I became a slave of another kind. They forced me to do such terrible things, so many times that I lost all notion of what was right and what was wrong. But that is not the worst of it. No, that comes later, after many years, when you find that you have come to take pleasure in such base work. I liked to kill. I enjoyed it when I stalked and killed that poor Spanish guard up on the cliff. His was a young throat, tight against my hand, firm against my blade. He was no more than seventeen, I should say. But when I shut my eyes to sleep, the spirits of those I have killed seek me out in dreams. So now I set it all down, every one of my killings. I confess all to my journal. On the page I can control them. It serves to stop them from leaving my book and seeking me out in the night.'

Sedgwick looked at Grainger in the pool of orange light as he tried to decide what he should do. He had been sure that this man was behind the murder, and the thefts too, but he seemed so convincing now, as he spoke from the heart. He could sense the deep ocean of pain and suffering that lay behind the sailor's gruff words.

'Of course none of this is new to you, Able,' Grainger said at last.

'What do you mean? I have never been a pirate.'

'No, but you have been a slave. You must have witnessed some cruel things in the middle passage aboard the ship that took you from Africa. What terrible punishments were done to you on the plantation? Does the recollection not haunt your dreams? Does what has happened to you not plague you? You cope with it just as I do.'

'I am not sure I follow you.'

'I have seen you, with your mate Rosso, as you scribble away in that journal that looks just like mine,' he explained. 'Why do you write all that stuff down? Is it not for the same reason? Do you not try and clap on to a past that you had no grip over at the time?'

'What? No, no, that is not my purpose,' said Sedgwick, his voice confused. 'It is true, I do feel better once I have set matters down, but I have always been clear. I write for the pamphlet I will publish one day, to help the cause of Abolition.'

'Maybe what you do serves both purposes,' said Grainger.

'Maybe,' conceded Sedgwick.

'You and I are not so very different, you know, Able. The men call me a man of no country, but where is yours?' Sedgwick stared in his turn into the lamp. After a while he looked back at Grainger.

'So was all that talk of you being on a Neapolitan ship so much gammon?' he asked. 'It was plain enough you had never spent much time in Naples.' Grainger shrugged.

'I needed to spin some yarn that would convince the Grunters as to how I came to be on the Russian ship. Parts of it were true. I do know my navigation, and I did serve on Barbary ships since I was a boy, but every one of them was a corsair. My last ship was wrecked in a storm off Sicily. I did have a journal that covered those years too, but I lost all my possessions when the ship foundered. The few survivors that made it to the beach that night were all killed by villagers, eager for revenge after years of attacks by slavers like us, but I managed to convince them that I had been a slave too. My blue eyes helped me there. I made my way to Leghorn, and then took up with a Russian privateer. They were happy to recruit any sailor who looked like he had seen some action.'

'There is still something I don't get,' said Sedgwick. 'Your journal is full of killing prisoners and talk of the dead telling no tales. Why was the master and crew of that English trader we recaptured spared?'

'Oh, we didn't do such things to English ships,' said Grainger. 'Partly it was through fear that the Navy would come and hunt us down, but mainly because the crew wouldn't wear it.'

'Why so?'

'Because a good third of them were ex-navy man-of-war's men, deserters and the like. They might do such things to foreigners, but would not have it done to their own.'

'Royal Navy sailors did what you set down in your journal?' said Sedgwick in disbelief.

'You have little notion of what extremes a man may go to,' replied Grainger, his face bleak. 'Believe me, I know only too well.'

'You may be right,' mused Sedgwick. 'Perhaps I have failed to see what a desperate man might do in this case, too.'

'Do you still hold me to be your murderer?'

Sedgwick thought about this for a moment before he replied. 'No, I believe you to be innocent, of this crime at least,' he said. 'In part because you have convinced me, but also because I have just remembered something of great import. Something that was said, that I should have given much more notice to at the time.'

*****

It took several weeks for the *Titan* to catch up with the rest of the fleet. They had searched for them off the coast of Crete, without success, and then had pressed on eastwards for mile after mile of empty sea. In the last few days, the wind had swung round to the northwest, which had brought a welcome drop in temperature, and had allowed the ship to fly along with the breeze on her quarter and every sail set. The southern coast of Cyprus had been in sight for some hours when the lookout first spotted the distant mastheads. As the frigate grew nearer, the topgallant sails of warships, tiny spots of white like the summits of distant snow capped mountains, appeared just proud of the horizon. The ship surged up in the wake of her more massive fellows to rejoin Nelson's fleet at last.

Some hours later, Clay was ushered into the great cabin of the *Vanguard*. The curtains had been drawn across the windows at the rear of the ship, making the cabin very dim. He had just been rowed across a brilliant blue sea in bright sunshine by Sedgwick and his barge crew, and his eyes took a little while to adjust to the gloom. When they did, he saw the small figure of Nelson as he came from behind his desk and held out his left hand.

'I am delighted to see you again, Captain Clay,' he said in his Norfolk accent. Clay returned his right hand to his side and shook hands awkwardly with his left. 'Apologies for the rather indifferent lighting, but I find bright sun sometimes troubling for my eye. I did have a patch that my surgeon had fashioned for me, but I'll be damned if I shall wear such an absurd thing. I am a King's officer, not a damned pirate! May I offer you some refreshment?'

'Thank you, Sir Horatio,' he replied. He picked up the glass that a steward held out on a tray. 'How was it that you came by your injury?'

'Oh, it was no great matter,' said the admiral. He waved him towards a chair on the far side of his desk with his hand. 'I was involved in the capture of Corsica, in the first year of the war. During the siege of Calvi, I was stood altogether too close to a parapet when it was struck by a canon ball from the enemy. A deal of sand and grit was driven into my face and I was rather knocked about. The sawbones who treated me thought I should lose my eye, but they were wrong as usual. I have it yet, although it serves only to distinguish night from day. But I find I can manage well enough with the eye I have been left with. It is certainly good enough for me to study these.'

Nelson picked up a large sheaf of papers, each one containing a diagram of some kind with lines and arrows, annotated in his shaky script. He let them flutter back down on to the desk.

'What is the nature of the documents you have there, Sir Horatio?' asked Clay.

'They are the many and various ways that I plan to defeat the enemy,' said Nelson. 'On every occasion, when weather has permitted, I have had my captains onboard to develop and rehearse projects of attack to cover all eventualities.' He picked up a few sheets at random and peered at them. 'Attacking the enemy fleet in company with the transporters, attacking the warships alone, in open water, close to land, from the windward side, from the leeward side, in the day, at night, at anchor, plans, plans, plans. I tell you Clay, there never was a fleet half so well prepared for battle as mine. All that is missing is an enemy for them to fight. Pray God you bring me some intelligence of them. Have you found the French?'

'Not exactly, Sir Horatio, but I believe I know where they may be bound.'

'Now, that is good to hear!' exclaimed the admiral. He leant forward in his seat. 'All this damned futile searching is destroying my nerves. Where do you suppose them to be headed?'

A Man of No Country

'We captured a large brig off the west coast of Greece with a cargo of cavalry horses, which we deduced must be intended for Bonaparte's Army,' said Clay.

'Like enough,' said Nelson. 'So where were they bound?'

'The ship's master would not say,' explained Clay. 'His English was poor, and my first lieutenant was struggling to get him to tell us. But when my name was first said to him he misheard it, and said something to the effect that we already knew where he was bound. Do you see, sir? My name is Alexander, but he heard it as Alexandria.' The admiral's face fell at this news.

'Alexandria! Not that place again!' he exclaimed. 'I am sorry to say you have been cruelly deceived. I had also thought it likely that Egypt might be their objective, and I had a very similar tale to yours from Saumarez when he returned from his searching. Which was why I was off Alexandria not eight days ago with the fleet. All was quiet, with the port as empty as a eunuch's britches. Not so much as a sniff of the French. No, I am afraid that will not answer at all.' Nelson ran his hand through his hair and stared down at the desktop. 'This is a cruel disappointment. Oh damn the eyes of every Frenchman! How can they have hidden such a vast armada from me? We have failed to do our duty to our King, Clay. We have failed him.'

'Not necessarily, Sir Horatio,' said Clay. 'Consider how slow the French may have been. With so many ships to marshal, they will have hardly advanced at all while that easterly wind was blowing.'

'I suppose it is possible,' said Nelson.

'I submit more than likely. I am certain that you have simply run ahead of your opponents, and arrived first at their destination.'

'It would not be out of character for the French to have been lubbers in their seamanship,' mused the admiral. 'But what of the risks we run? The sole injunction that Lord St Vincent gave me was not to allow the French to slip past us to the west. What if they are even now pressing towards the Atlantic?'

'Your inclination was for Egypt, and both Sir James's findings and mine point in the same direction, Sir Horatio,' urged Clay. 'It is the only sure intelligence we have. Let us return there, and I am sure the French will appear. They may even be there already.'

Nelson fixed him with a thoughtful look as he considered what he had said. Just as when they had first met, Clay found himself torn over whether to rest his gaze on the animated blue eye or the blank one. After a while Nelson moved his pile of plans to one side, picked up a lock of chestnut hair from the desk and began to toy with it. Clay looked at the hair for a moment as the admiral held it to his nose. Strange, he thought, I could have sworn that Lady Nelson's hair was fair.

'Was you ever in love, Captain Clay?' he asked at last. He placed the strand of hair back on the desk and turned to face his subordinate.

'In love, Sir Horatio?' said Clay, surprised by the turn the conversation had taken. 'Why yes. It is only ten months since I was wed.'

'Ah, but being married, and being in love, are not the same at all, you will own,' said Nelson. 'So much else gets put upon a marriage, station, property, advancement, the need for a suitable match. It is not so very strange that many marriages are formed that leave precious little space for true affection. So was you ever truly in love?'

'Yes, I am now, Sir Horatio' he said. 'Whether through folly or not, I did not allow any other considerations to influence my choice of wife. I love her very much indeed. Most of my short time of marriage has been spent at sea, and I must confess that I miss

A Man of No Country

her terribly.'

'Now that was well said,' smiled Nelson. 'I too am in love, you know? With a lady of singular merit, who I feel in my heart is all goodness and charity. Her character is so animated, and wholly without conceit. She seems to understand me as no woman has done before.'

'Ah, yes,' muttered Clay. 'I give you joy in your, eh, acquaintance. But, Sir Horatio, I am a little unclear as to where this conversation tends? We were discussing the French.'

'My point is that if you have ever enjoyed such a union of spirits, you will know that in love you must trust to your instincts' said Nelson. 'Even if they lead you in a direction that is against the general urgings of society. And what is so for love is doubly so for war. My instinct tells me that you are right. I should have remained true to my initial inclination. We shall sail for Alexandria, as you have urged me to do, and let us pray to God that we shall find the enemy there at long last.'

*****

The fleet was together once more. Nelson's ships were spread in a long, regularly spaced line, with each huge seventy-four following in the wake of the one ahead, with every mast a towering pyramid of snowy white sails. A keen northwest wind drove them southward towards the distant coast of Egypt. Two miles to windward, the *Titan* kept station on the flagship in the centre of the line, and repeated each signal the admiral made.

All was calm aboard the frigate, until six bells in the afternoon watch rang out from the belfry on the forecastle. The last echo of the final bell stroke had hardly faded away across the brilliant blue water before it was replaced by the harsher squeal of boatswain's pipes, echoing along the lower deck, just as it had at the same time

233

on every day of the commission so far, except for Sundays.

'All gun crews!' roared Hutchinson, the boatswain. 'Man the guns there! Look lively now!'

Number seven eighteen-pounder was placed in the middle of one of the lines of cannon that squatted massively along the sides of the main deck. Ten feet or so behind the dull red gun carriage was the coaming of the ship's main hatchway, and behind that, the huge column of the main mast soared up as thick as the trunk of some forest giant. Like all the other great guns aboard the ship she had been allocated a number which, like every other gun aboard, was never used by her proud crew.

'How you doing, Shango, me old cock?' said Evans, as he swept a little rope dust from the top of the barrel where the gun's name had been picked out in swirling white letters on the black metal.

'Shango!' exclaimed one of the crew of Belcher, the eighteen-pounder immediately aft of Evans's cannon. 'What manner of name is that? Sounds right bleeding foreign.'

'Don't listen to him at all, Sam,' said O'Malley, who looked up from rigging the gun tackle to the side of Shango's carriage. He glanced across at their rival's gun. 'Belcher is it? Well that's a grand name. It will have taken you scholars a while to come up with that. Why, there can't be above a hundred Belchers in the fleet.'

'It ain't what you might call unique, I grant you. We was going to call her Dan Mendoza, after the prize fighter like, but the crew of number two cannon had already nabbed him,' explained the rival gun captain. 'Who's this Shango bloke then? Is he another prize fighter?'

'Is he a prize fighter!' said O'Malley with distain. Trevan shook his head in disbelief from his place on the other side of the gun.

'No he bleeding ain't,' said Evans. 'He is only the God of Thunder in Africa. Sedgwick told us about him. Now that's a proper name for a gun.'

'Come on, lads,' urged Rosso, who was Shango's captain. He was fitting a length of slow match to his linstock. 'Get the rammer out, Sam. Adam, go and get a bucket of water. Gun drill will start in a moment; I don't want that git Blake on me arse for being the last gun ready, again.'

Lieutenant John Blake stood by the main mast and waited for his officers to report to him that their division's of guns were ready. As second Lieutenant of the *Titan,* he was responsible for the main deck cannon, and it was a responsibility he enjoyed. He looked with approval, as all along the gun deck the crews stripped to the waist and rolled their neck cloths into the bandanas that would protect their ears from the roar of the firing.

'Larboard side guns ready, sir,' said Midshipman Butler as he came hurrying up and stood to attention.

'Starboard side ready too, sir,' added Midshipman Russell.

'Very well, gentlemen,' said Blake. He pulled out the silver fob watch that he had bought with some of the prize money won on the *Titan*'s last commission. It was his pride and joy. Unlike his previous watch, this one had a minute hand. 'Let us commence with forty-five minutes of dumb show, give the hands five minutes of stand easy, and then we will proceed to live firing.'

'Aye aye, sir,' said the two young officers.

'Live fire will be a little different today,' continued the lieutenant. 'I have prevailed on the cooper to let me have some empty casks for them to aim at. Mr Preston will drop them from the launch as targets later.'

'So they are not to just rattle the guns in and out as usual, to achieve the captain's three broadsides in two minutes, sir?' queried Butler.

'By no means,' said Blake. 'They must still fire briskly, but I have noticed of late the men have taken to only concentrating on speed. Yesterday the fall of shot was very indifferently grouped. I shall expect better today with a mark for them to aim at.'

Although the weather was less hot than it had been, the gun crew's torsos soon ran with sweat as they dashed through the routine of pretending to load and fire their guns. Blake walked up and down the long rows of cannon, watching the gun drill with care, looking for where the next tiny improvement might come from.

'Sponge out!' roared the petty officer next to him to his section of guns. 'Load charge, ram home!' These men are working well, thought Blake. I wonder how they will respond to an unexpected problem?

'Rammer men, you have all been killed or wounded,' he announced. 'Drop your equipment and come and join me here. Carry on with the drill if you please, Jamieson.'

'Aye aye, sir,' said the petty officer. He turned back to his guns and scratched at his chin. After a few seconds of thought, his face cleared. 'Hand spike men, take the place of the rammer men. Load ball!' With the slightest of hesitation while the men traded roles, the gun drill recommenced and went smoothly on, despite the crew's reduced manpower. Blake watched for a little longer, before he gave a grunt of satisfaction.

'Well done, Jamieson,' he said. 'Rammer men resume your places.'

Once he had completed his circuit of the guns, pausing to issue advice here and making a small change there, Lieutenant Blake returned to his place beside the main mast. He glanced at the nearest gun and frowned. The gun captain had just brought his linstock down on the touchhole, yet he had shouted no warning to his crew.

'Rosso!' he bellowed. The offending sailor looked round. 'Why are you not attending to your duty? Where was your call to your crew to stand clear? Trevan's foot was directly behind the gun carriage when you fired. If the gun had been loaded in earnest, it would have been crushed.'

'Sorry, sir,' mumbled Rosso. 'I was a bit distracted, like.'

'I have no place for a gun captain that endangers his crew,' said Blake. 'The enemy will seek to do that well enough, without your assistance. Mr Butler! Kindly watch this gun closely for the remainder of the drill, if you please. Report any further cases of neglect to me.'

*****

In the cool of the evening, the larboard watch took their ease after dinner. The temperature had only recently dropped below thirty degrees, but the men had still been fed on a pound of hot salt pork, accompanied by half a pound of boiled pease. This was the Victualling Board's proscribed ration for a Thursday, whether the warship concerned was on the edge of an Arctic ice shelf or deep in the tropics. Even for some of the older hands aboard the *Titan*, long accustomed to such fare, their evening meal sat heavy upon them. As a result, almost all had quit the stifling lower deck to enjoy the fresh air and cooling breeze that was to be had on the forecastle. In consequence most of the mess tables were empty, but at one Joshua Rosso and Able Sedgwick sat opposite each other with the coxswain's journal between them.

'You must have worked on this with proper diligence, Able, to have finished it already,' said Rosso. 'I barely helped you at all.

Does it come right up to the present day?'

'No, Rosie, I stop the tale just after I escaped from Haynes's plantation in Barbados and joined the navy,' said Sedgwick. 'I wrote that last part a mite vague, so as not to finger them as helped me escape. Apparently, they can yet be prosecuted if I am too open. So I end it like this.

"With the assistance of a number of noble souls, I was able to swim out to a Royal Navy ship at anchor in the roadstead at Bridgetown. Once aboard, I made haste to volunteer to serve King George as a man of war's man. I was read in, and seven long years after my freedom had been so violently seized from me, I was a free man once more."'

'That is handsomely put,' said Rosso. 'Even if it is all so much gammon. A right strange manner of freedom you have won yourself. Confined onboard, only allowed ashore when the Grunters permit it, and flogged when we should stray out of line.'

'That's a bit bleak,' protested Sedgwick.

'Is it?' his friend queried. 'Don't you feel the oak walls about you pressing in sometimes? Surely you have but traded one kind of slavery for another?'

'It ain't like you to be so down, Rosie?' asked his friend, watching him from the far side of the table. 'Is all well with you? Adam did tell me how you made a proper mess of gun drill earlier.' Rosso sighed.

'I am well enough,' he said. 'I just got a lot on my mind, like.'

'Anything you want to tell me about?' said Sedgwick, leaning forwards.

Rosso looked up, aware of a strange tone in his friend's voice. 'Why are you asking?' Sedgwick shrugged.

'I've noticed you not being your regular self, too. I just wondered if the death of young Oates might be distracting you in some manner.'

'What has that got to do with me? Everyone knows that it was Grainger what did for him. His helping you rescue that sailor has fooled no one.'

'Everyone *thinks* they know it was Grainger,' corrected Sedgwick. He glanced around the deserted deck before returning his attention to his friend. 'But you and I both know that it wasn't him.'

'I know nothing of the kind,' protested Rosso. 'What's got into you, Able? Why are you talking like this? That Oates was a filthy cutpurse who stole from his shipmates. When he tried to take from Grainger, he got what he deserved, and when that oaf of a master at arms finally catches up with him, he will doubtless swing for his wickedness.'

'But that won't answer, Rosie. If Oates was the thief, who do you suppose it was that gave Sam back his money?' asked the coxswain. 'It can't have been Oates, for he was long dead.'

'Well, I don't know,' said Rosso. 'Maybe Grainger put the money back?'

'In secret?' said Sedgwick. 'Why would he not do it openly? And besides, how would he have come by money that was so well hid the Lobsters couldn't find it? No, it is only these last few days that I have been able to get it all straight in my head. I know now who killed Oates.'

'What?' said his friend, after a pause. 'How come you have that figured out?'

'Like I said, it has only come to me of late, thinking on stuff. You know it was Sean who touched closest to the truth. You remember, when Sam had just got his money back. He said the like of "What manner of cutpurse returns what he has stolen?" I've pondered on that, and I believe I know the answer. A friend does, who feels the guilt at what he's done. A friend who stole in desperation, but then finds he no longer needs the money.'

'Got anyone in mind?' asked Rosso, folding his arms.

'Aye, it was you,' said Sedgwick. 'I can see the truth of it right now, written on your face.'

'Oh that's a right good one!' exclaimed Rosso, after a shocked pause. 'Why the fuck would I have done that?'

'Because Oates was from the same part of Bristol as you,' the coxswain explained. 'When we were all drinking back in Gibraltar he said he thought he knew you, but the talk moved on. Later he must have worked it all out.' Rosso stared at his friend, transfixed. After a while Sedgwick went on.

'I can almost hear what he would have said. "I know you! You're that shipping clerk that vanished with his master's cash box." And then, being the low bastard he was, he thought to squeeze you a little. I heard you and him talking, at the turn of the year, by the galley. I had just come in from the heads. I never realised it was your voice at the time, but it was you, sure enough. Then all the thieving happened. That was you as well; desperate to find the money to make sure he held his tongue.'

'Come on, Able, you know about my past. So does Adam, Sean and even Sam. What threat was that little shit to me with a secret that all of my friends know?'

'Sure, we are no threat. You know we would never grass on you. But Oates would, as easy as anything. He told you he would send word to Hanging Jack, and you knew what a strict bastard he is. Earl St Vincent would have a thief swinging from the yardarm, as soon as look at you.'

'All this writing has got to you, Able, but I do enjoy a good yarn. So what happened next?'

'Next came the attack on that battery,' continued Sedgwick.

A Man of No Country

'The night when we got up to the body of that poor sentry. Evans asked Grainger why he had cut his throat, and he made some manner of comment about it being the fastest way to silence a man. It passed most of us by, but it found its mark with you. Why should I be a cutpurse that has to prey on my shipmates, you thought, when there is a much easier way to gain a man's silence, forever. You agreed to meet him in the hold when we arrived in Naples, and while he was busy counting his pieces of silver, you slit his throat from behind.'

'You can't prove nothing,' spluttered Rosso.

'No, not to a court marshal, nor to the master at arms,' said the coxswain. 'But like I said, I can see in your eyes plain as plain that I am right, and if I can see it, so too will others. I wouldn't grass on you to the Grunters anyway. But you have broken the code, Rosie. You've stolen from shipmates. How do you think Powell and Black will react? The lower deck can be a cruel place for a Jonas.'

'But I gave it all back,' exclaimed Rosso.

'And you killed a man.'

'He was a blackmailing bastard!'

'Why didn't you just come to your mates?' asked Sedgwick. 'We would have sorted that little shit out for you. Big Sam and I could have shaken him down a bit. He would have been meek as a lamb afterwards.' Rosso shook his head.

'I don't rightly know,' he said. 'That's what I should have done, but I suppose I just panicked.' The two men sat and looked at each other.

'So what you going to do, Able?' asked Rosso at last.

'I don't know,' he replied 'I ain't about to grass on you to the Grunters, if that's what you're afraid of. So don't you go and slit my throat while I sleep. But Pipe wants this sorted. Maybe you could transfer to another ship, then I can spread the word that all is well.'

'Maybe that would be best,' said Rosso. 'Be sad, though. As Oates showed, it's still too hot for me to go home, and you and the others are all the family I have right now.'

'Listen, Rosie, if Pipe has got it right, we've got this battle to fight first. Let's get through that and see where we are. Perhaps I can figure out a better way to end all this.'

Chapter 14
Aboukir Bay

In the great cabin of the *L'Orient*, Vice Admiral Francis Paul, Count de Brueys, raised his glass of champagne and watched the candlelight sparkle off the little columns of bubbles rising through the liquid. The other officers grouped around the dinner table matched the gesture with their own glasses.

'1793 may have been a bad year for Louis XVI, but it was a very good year for champagne,' he remarked. 'Gentlemen, I give you a toast. To the army, and to General Bonaparte's most splendid victory over the Ottomans under the shadow of the Pyramids!'

'The army!' came the reply from those around the table, followed by a pause as the wine was drunk.

'It must have been an inspiring sight, Lieutenant Mallet,' said Captain Casabianca, *L'Orient*'s portly commanding officer, as he turned to the young cavalry subaltern who had brought news of the victory. 'Imagine that, a battle fought next to one of the Seven Wonders of the Ancient World.' Lieutenant Mallet pulled at his thin moustache and cleared his throat before he replied.

'The general may have deployed a little... eh, shall we say licence in the name he chose for his victory, sir,' he said.

Philip K Allan

'Whatever can you mean, lieutenant?' queried the naval captain. 'Was this battle fought beside the Pyramids or not?' The young subaltern shifted in his chair.

'They were certainly visible, sir,' he replied. 'Once the dust of battle had settled, on the horizon.'

'I think I comprehend, Lieutenant Mallet,' said the admiral. 'General Bonaparte does have a reputation for reporting his achievements with as much advantage as possible. I dare say the Battle of the Pyramids will seem of more consequence than a victory won beside a village no one in Paris will have heard of.'

'I believe you have the truth of it, sir,' smiled Lieutenant Mallet.

'Ha!' snorted Casabianca. 'So was it even a victory?'

'Oh indeed yes, sir,' enthused the young cavalry officer. 'The Ottomans came on with great dash, particularly their horse. Fully six thousand of their fearsome Mamluk cavalry charged out of the desert, in wave after wave. They were quite a sight in their silk robes and brandishing their glittering sabres. They came on with great panache to the sound of numberless drums.'

'Goodness,' said the captain of the *L'Orient*, helping himself to a little more of the fish stew. 'How were you able to resist the onslaught?'

'Fortunately, the enemy had little notion of the modern way of warfare,' continued Mallet. 'They dashed themselves against our squares in hordes, some even threw their swords at our men, while we responded with volleys of musket fire and artillery. It was glorious to behold, but our men held firm, and in the end we beat them off. With their much vaunted horsemen defeated, their infantry showed very little fight. Our losses were a few hundred, while the enemy's can be counted in thousands. The survivors fled away to the south, and we marched into Cairo unopposed.'

244

A Man of No Country

'I confess that does sound like a very fine victory,' said Captain Dupetit-Thouars, the stern, grey haired commander of *Le Tonnant* from the far side of the table. 'Whatever name young Bonaparte chooses for it.' A growl of approval came from the other naval officers in the cabin.

'What of the English fleet, gentlemen?' asked Lieutenant Mallet. 'Has anything been heard of them? The general is most anxious that his victory on land should not be compromised by a defeat at sea.'

'What of the English?' scoffed de Brueys. 'I hear that they have at last scraped together some ships to operate in the Mediterranean, under this young puppy Nelson, but I have seen nothing of them.'

'I understand that Sir Horatio has acquired some merit as a fighting captain against the Spanish,' added Captain Casabianca. 'But when he is obliged to fight my mighty *L'Orient,* with a crew of southern Frenchman, he will find matters altogether hotter.'

'Perhaps he will lose more than an arm this time,' said another naval captain, to general laughter.

'My ships are in a formidable position, lieutenant,' explained the admiral. He pointed at the view visible through the stern windows of the cabin. A ship's length away Mallet could see the bow of the next warship in the line, with others beyond it in a gentle curve that stretched across the bay, while off to one side was a sandy shore, dotted with palm trees.

'See how we are anchored in a solid line,' continued de Brueys. 'Just behind us is Captain Dupetit-Thouars's fine ship to guard my stern from attack, just as *L'Orient* in turn serves to guard the stern of the ship ahead of us. The shore over there protects us on one side, and we have shoal water ahead and astern of us. I have thirteen ships of the line and over a thousand cannon. If the

245

English are mad enough to attack us here, it will be much the same as when these Mamluks of yours attacked our army's squares. Brave, but very foolish. Please, do go and look. Satisfy yourself with how strong the position of my fleet is, before you return to report to General Bonaparte.'

Under the urgings of the admiral, the young cavalry officer rose from the table and walked across to the stern windows, his spurs chinking on the deck as he went. After a moment of hesitation, a young flag lieutenant at the other end of the table came to join him, while the senior officers returned to their champagne and boisterous talk. Mallet shaded his eyes against the low sun on the water and peered out through the glass. The shore was much farther from the ship than he had imagined. Why, it must be at least a mile, perhaps more, he thought. He noticed a French frigate moored halfway between the flagship and the beach and frowned for a moment.

'Sir, that ship over there,' he said pointing. 'Is it at anchor in deep water too?'

'*L'Artemise*?' said the flag lieutenant. 'It is moored on the very edge of the shoals.'

'Really?' said the cavalry man. 'Am I to understand that deep water lies between us and them? I thought the admiral said that the fleet was anchored so that the shore would offer some protection on that side. Surely there is plenty of room for an enemy to pass between us here and the edge of the shoal water over there?'

'We must have a little sea room to manoeuvre in, should the occasion arise,' said the lieutenant. 'I can assure you that the admiral himself ordered this disposition for the fleet.'

'Of course,' smiled Mallet. 'I did not mean to imply any criticism.' He looked at the heavily gilded bow of the ship moored behind them in the line. The figurehead was of a helmeted goddess who glared back at him across fifty yards of muddy, brown water. Her outstretched arm sought to pass a fistful of thunder bolts to him. These vessels are anchored a lot farther apart than I would have expected too, he thought to himself.

'Was there anything else you wanted to know, Lieutenant Mallet?' asked his companion.

'Yes,' he said, and then he paused. What do I truly know of the sea, he thought? I am used to the packed ranks and tight formations of the army. Ships must surely deploy themselves in some other fashion, he concluded. 'Eh, I was going to ask why the sea is so brown and dirty here in the bay?'

'If you direct your gaze over there, you will see one of the mouths of the River Nile,' replied the flag lieutenant. 'It is the mud of Africa that makes the water so. Have you seen all you wished to, Lieutenant Mallet? If so, perhaps we might rejoin the party?'

'Your dispositions look excellent, sir,' said Mallet to the admiral as he retook his seat. 'I hope the English do attack you.'

'Well said, young man,' said Captain Casabianca, slapping him on the shoulder. He looked past the cavalry man as the cabin door swung open. 'Ah, is this the cheese, at long last?'

To Casabianca's disappointment, the young midshipman who came through the door carried nothing edible. He came across to speak to the flag lieutenant, who in turn rose from his chair, went to stand beside the admiral and whispered something in his ear. The noise of conversation dropped around the table as all the naval officers tried to hear what was being said.

'Really?' said de Brueys in the silence, before he turned to the others. 'Gentlemen, it would seem that this Admiral Nelson has at last managed to navigate his way here. The English fleet is in sight. They are coming up the coast from the direction of Alexandria.'

'In what numbers?' asked one of the other ship's captains.

'Similar numbers to our own, sir,' said the flag lieutenant.

'Please excuse me, Admiral de Brueys, but I must return to my ship and prepare for battle,' said Captain Dupetit-Thouars. He rose from the table, and all around the cabin other chairs were pushed back and glasses of wine were drained.

'Gentlemen, some calm,' said their host. 'The English are still a considerable way off.'

'Yes, and we haven't had pudding yet,' added Captain Casbianca, ever the committed trencherman. *'On ne vieillit pas à table,* as my grandfather used to say.'

'Besides it will be dark soon,' said the admiral. 'There will be no battle today. Only a madman would choose to launch an attack at night into a bay with so many navigational hazards.'

*****

'The flagship is signalling, sir,' said Midshipman Russell. He leafed through his codebook. 'General signal number fifty three. Oh, sir! That is for all ships to prepare for battle!'

Lieutenant Preston looked around him. For the last few hours the fleet had pushed forwards, as fast as it was able, and it was now spread out in a straggling line across a sea that had turned to pale blue in the evening light. Behind the ship a blood red sun hung a hand's breadth above the horizon.

'Does the admiral mean for us to fight tonight, sir?' he queried. 'It will be darker than the Earl of Hell's hat within two hours.'

'Acknowledge the signal if you please, Mr Russell,' ordered Clay, before turning to his officer of the watch. 'After so many weeks of futile searches the admiral has no intention of letting the French give him the slip in the dark, Mr Preston. What are our general orders for a night action?'

'We are to fly white ensigns in place of our blue ones, and all ships in the fleet are to show four blue lights in a line from the mizzen top yard, sir,' replied the lieutenant.

'Very good,' said the captain. 'Kindly have those executed, and have battle lanterns lit down on the main deck, if you please.' Clay turned away and pulled out his telescope. Off to one side was the shoreline of Egypt, flat and low, marked here and there by the curved trunks and feathery tops of distant palm trees. Farther up the coast Clay could see the square mass of a stone castle, flushed orange in the evening light. It was built at the end of a spit of land. Beyond its crenellated walls he could just make out the black lines of ships' masts rising up into the pale evening sky. Tall, heavy masts, he concluded, such as only large warships would carry.

'That castle marks the start of the bay,' said Armstrong, who had appeared beside him. 'We need to give it a wide birth. There is a long line of shoals and rocks that run from that point a good few cable lengths out to sea. Beyond that is the deep water channel that leads into the bay.'

'General orders for a night action put in place, sir,' reported Preston.

'Very good,' said Clay, still looking through his telescope. 'Kindly beat to quarters and have the ship cleared for action. And send Mr Butler to me, if you please.'

When the young midshipman appeared, Clay handed him a telescope. He had to give his instructions rather louder than normal so they could be heard over the roar of the marine drummer as be pounded his instrument just below their feet on the main deck.

'Up you go, Mr Butler,' he said. 'I want a full description of what you can see in that bay.'

'Aye aye, sir,' replied Butler. He rushed over to the main mast shrouds and bounded up the rigging, past a file of slow moving marine sharpshooters as they headed for the main top. When he was settled on the royal yard he opened his telescope and focused on the bay ahead, his body a dark silhouette against the orange sky.

'Enemy are anchored in a line, sir,' he reported in a steady bellow. 'Bow to stern, starting near to the castle and shaping across the bay away from us. I count thirteen ships of the line, with a big first rate in the centre.'

'Thirteen is it?' muttered Armstrong. 'Let us hope that proves unlucky for them.'

'Four frigates, too,' yelled Butler. 'They are moored closer to the shore.'

'Is seventeen a number of similar ill omen, Jacob?' asked Lieutenant Preston from his other side.

'Perhaps not, but four frigates, mind,' said the American. 'It is good to hear there are some opponents for us to cross swords with.'

'Thank you, Mr Butler,' yelled Clay. 'You may come down now.' He turned to find his first lieutenant in full dress uniform, sword by his side, and the quarterdeck crowded with people. All the carronades that ran down both sides had been manned, and Macpherson was busy positioning his marines in the gaps between them.

'Ship is cleared for action, sir,' reported Taylor. 'I sent Hart down to the wardroom with your full dress uniform and sword, your cabin having been dismantled and stowed away, sir.'

'Very good, Mr Taylor,' said Clay. 'Please take command while I shift my clothes.'

'Aye aye, sir.' Clay touched his hat to the older man, and then ran down the companion ladder to the deck below. On the main deck he saw that his suite of cabins had indeed vanished. The setting sun now shone through the windows at the rear of the main deck into a wide open space that stretched the whole length of the ship, and was devoted almost exclusively to the guns that ran down each side. Beneath his feet he felt the crunch of the sharp sand that had been scattered over the planking to give the men better grip. At every gun stood its crew, many stripped to the waist. The captains were whirling their linstocks into glowing red fireflies in the gloom. He headed across to the ladder way that led down to the deck below, but had to wait as a torrent of excited ship's boys came rushing up, each one carrying a heavy powder charge destined for the cannon that they served.

Down in the gloom of the wardroom, Hart helped him dress. Above his head he heard the bark of orders as the guns were loaded, and then came the deafening rumble as they were run out. He watched as the vibration made his sword scabbard skitter about on the wardroom table.

'Coat now please, Hart,' he said. He held his arms out behind him to receive the garment. His right arm was loose and flexible, the left stiff and awkward from the Spanish musket ball that had wounded him there two years before.

'Sorry, sir,' said his steward, fumbling with the broadcloth. 'Yates is so much better at this, only he will be engaged as the powder monkey for number four gun at the moment.' Between them they managed to shrug the coat on, and Hart knelt down to buckle on the sword.

'You have a loaded pistol in your right pocket, should it be required, sir,' he reported. 'I gave the other one to Sedgwick for him to keep for you.' He stood back from his captain and admired what he saw. Clay's tall, lean frame suited his uniform well, and the gold braid and polished buttons glittered in the lamplight.

'Good luck, sir,' he said. He handed Clay his hat and held open the wardroom door.

'Thank you, Hart,' he replied as he ducked under the low

frame. 'Best of luck to you too.'

When he got back to the quarterdeck the castle at the start of the bay was much closer, as the ships pressed on in the evening light. Clay glanced back over the stern to where the sun had sunk even lower towards the horizon. There was a crimson flush to the sky now.

'What time is it, Mr Taylor?' he asked.

'Three bells has just sounded, sir,' reported the lieutenant. 'We have an hour and a half before sunset and no moon till midnight. The admiral has sent two signals while you were below decks. The first was for all ships to be prepared to anchor by the stern, so I have arranged with Mr Hutchinson for our best bower to be moved to the stern quarter, and a second signal to engage the van and centre of the French feet.' Clay nodded at this.

'It is what he has been planning with the other captains all these months,' he said. 'He means to overwhelm one part of the enemy fleet with the whole of his, before then moving on to attack the rest of them.'

'Flag signalling again, sir,' reported Midshipman Russell. 'Number thirty one. That is form line of battle ahead and astern of the admiral, as convenient.'

'Acknowledge, if you please, Mr Russell,' said Clay. 'We are already in our correct position.'

'Will you look at that?' exclaimed Preston. 'Every ship is clapping on more sail for the honour of being the one to lead the line. Race day at Bartholomew Fair ain't in it.'

'My money is on *Culloden*,' said Taylor. 'Look at her go! Studding sails set now. I happen to know from her first lieutenant she had her copper renewed not six months ago.'

'A guinea says *Goliath*, for sure,' said Preston. 'Captain Foley would trample over his grandmother to get to a fight.'

A Man of No Country

'Sir,' said Armstrong, after a pause. 'I cannot help but feel that this precipitous rush to get into action is ill judged by the admiral. Should one of the ships try and cut short her turn around the shoal that extends out from the castle, they will surely run aground.'

'Do you see such a danger?' asked Clay.

'I believe *Culloden* will, if she carries on as she is.' Clay focussed his telescope on the main ships of the fleet. Most were now formed up in a proper battle line, ahead or astern of the Vanguard, but the *Culloden* and the *Goliath* were still racing to be first into the bay.

'She is going to strike, sir!' warned Armstrong. Clay turned towards the signal midshipman.

'Mr Russell! Signal "*Titan* to *Culloden*. Urgent. Navigational hazard ahead." Accompany it with a gun to windward. Quickly now!'

'Aye aye, sir.'

The signal had no sooner been hoisted aloft when the *Culloden* jerked to a halt. Her hull slewed around and her foretop mast snapped off at the cap, and draped down in a confusion of flapping sails and broken cables. Clay looked on for a moment and chewed at his lip in frustration. Then he turned to the American.

'Mr Armstrong, I want you to answer me with absolute candour,' he said. 'How familiar are you with this bay?'

'I do not know it with perfect certainty, but I know it well enough. In time of peace it serves as an overflow for ships waiting to enter Alexandria.'

'Could you lead the fleet in through all these shoals?' asked his captain. 'Be honest now, I will not think any poorer of you if you tell me it is beyond your knowledge.'

'I understand, sir. I could do what you want. At least while this light lasts.' Clay looked at the sun and then assessed how far the fleet had to go. He pulled out his fob watch and calculated with care.

'There will be light enough gentlemen, just,' he said. 'Mr Russell, another signal if you please. "*Titan* to Flag. Ship's master knows bay well. Submit *Titan* leads fleet into battle.' An excited murmur swept across the packed quarterdeck as the signal was hauled aloft.

'Silence there!' bellowed Taylor. 'What is all this chatter? You're worse than a party of Spanish fish wives!' In silence the crew of the frigate waited for Nelson to respond. After a few minutes a series of flags raced up the *Vanguard*'s mizzen halyard and broke out in the evening breeze. Midshipman Russell read the signal and chalked the words down on his slate. He then marched across the deck to where his captain stood.

'Signal from the *Vanguard,* sir. "Flag to *Titan.* Take station ahead of the fleet."'

*****

'Well, here be a proud moment for the barky!' exclaimed Trevan. 'The old *Titan* leading the whole of this here fleet into battle. It's enough to make a Cornishman renounce cider on the Sabbath.' Evans bent forward and pushed his head through the open gun port to look astern. Behind the frigate loomed the huge bulk of the *Goliath*. Its figurehead was a mass of shaggy brown hair and beard that frowned down at him. Close behind the seventy-four he could see the rest of the fleet, now in a long disciplined line. He ducked his head back inside.

'They're all bleeding following, right enough, and why wouldn't they?' he muttered. 'It's us as will run aground if that Yank makes an arse of things.' He waved a hand towards the stricken hull of the *Culloden* as they swept past her. She had taken all her sail in now, and had launched her ship's boats in an attempt to try and haul herself off the sand bank. They were close enough to see that her rudder was twisted over at an impossible angle, pulled off by the force of the impact.

'She'll be no bloody use for days yet,' observed Rosso from his place at the back of the gun.

'An' if we don't wind up high and dry on a bleeding reef,' continued Evans, 'we'll be first up to get a hammering from the Frogs. It may be the dawn sparrow as gets the worm, but it's the second mouse as gets the cheese.'

'What the fecking hell is that supposed to mean?' said O'Malley.

'It's obvious! If we're the first ship to get up with the Frogs, it will be us who will get a proper seeing to, like the mouse what sets off the trap. He gets done for, while them as follow feast upon cheese.' The other men grouped around the cannon exchanged glances. Trevan rolled his eyes up to the heavens, while O'Malley shook his head.

'Never mind the fecking cheese, are you saying we're in for a hiding?'

'Course we is!' exclaimed Evans. 'We're leading the whole bleeding fleet towards the Frogs.'

'Ah, but in your fleet action, your ship of the line won't fire on a frigate.'

'What rot is that?' demanded Evans. 'Why not?'

'What do you mean "why not"?' said the Irishman. 'They just don't!'

'Aye, but why don't they?' O'Malley open and closed his mouth a few times. 'Tell him, Adam,' he eventually said.

'You be right as how they don't, Sean, but what the reason may be, I can't rightly say,' said the Cornishman. 'It has always been so, saving only if we was to fire on them. You got any notion why that should be, Rosie?'

'I reckon it's Grunters' honour, and all that bollocks,' said Rosso. 'We're too lowly a craft to be considered. But mark my words, they'll be after scrapping like stoats in a sack with them as follows us.'

'That don't make no bleeding sense at all,' said Evans. 'It'd be like me going easy in a mill 'cause the other prize fighter was a runt. Believe me, that don't ever happen.'

'Ah, now that is where you're after going astray, Sam lad,' said O'Malley. 'Trying to see some sense in Grunter's honour. Say you was mad enough to want to kill a man, and you had a pistol in your pocket. Would you be after pacing out ten yards and giving your man an even chance of killing you, like what they do in them duels an' all? Or would you shoot the fecker while he wasn't attending? See how mad they are? There ain't no cause to go looking for sense in what they're about.'

'But don't look too disappointed, Sam,' added Rosso. 'Word is the Frogs have laid on at least four frigates for us to have a dance with.'

'Head sails! Man the braces!' shouted the voice of Armstrong from somewhere close to the wheel. The deck beneath their feet heeled over as they turned around the end of the shoal water and doubled back into the bay. The view slid past the gun port and suddenly the French battle line was in front of them, stretched like a curtain in a gentle curve, each huge hull sat astride its reflection in the calm silver water of evening. As the men watched they saw big French tricolours ripple out, two or three to each ship, to stream in the gentle wind. In the centre of the line was the monstrous *L'Orient*. With her triple layer of gun decks and her immense masts, she was easy to pick out even from the eighty-gun two-deckers either side of her.

'Jesus an' Mary, that's a big fecking ship,' muttered O'Malley.

'They say as how she has a hundred and twenty guns,' said Trevan. 'And the same weight of broadside as any two of ours.'

'Lucky they don't hold with fighting the likes of us, then,' said Evans. 'Bleeding lucky.' O'Malley turned away from the scene and looked at his fellow gun crew.

'Hey fellers, give me your hands for luck,' he said. 'I after feeling that tonight we may fecking need it.'

Chapter 15
Night

Clay ran his telescope over the French fleet and saw a long wall of oak and iron that faced towards the approaching threat. He paused at each ship in turn, searching for some flaw in their dispositions. In the sharp circle of magnification, they all looked well prepared for the coming action. He could pick out individual details as his telescope moved along the line. There was the smoke that rose like steam from all the gun captains' linstocks on the upper decks. The crews that were busy rigging masses of boarding netting, which sagged like drying fishing nets along the ships' sides. The groups of sharpshooters, their white cross belts clear in the gloom, stationed in all the main tops. He saw a cluster of officers in dark blue coats with silver braid, looking back at him from the quarterdeck of *L'Orient*. Where was the weakness, the mistake in their deployment? Where was the chink in this wall that might bring the whole mass tumbling down? He felt certain he had seen something important, but the more he searched for it, the more it seemed to slide away from him.

He lowered his telescope and let his eye rest a while. The *Titan* stood on into the bay, the evening breeze on her quarter as it

258

A Man of No Country

wafted her along towards the French. Off to starboard, the waves lapped against the nearest sand bank. The low hump of brown rose out of the surface like the back of a whale. Clay looked around him at the calm water of the bay and wondered where the more dangerous shoals might be, the ones that were not proud of the water. He glanced across at Armstrong. The American seemed to be conning the ship confidently enough, listening to the regular cry from the leadsman in the bow as he announced each successive depth, and them giving calm instructions to Old Amos at the wheel. Behind the frigate came the long line of the fleet, the first eight ships well into the bay now, while the ninth was making her turn around the end of the shoal.

'What do you think of the enemy's dispositions, Mr Armstrong,' he asked.

'Very strong, sir,' said the ship's master. 'Although the place they have chosen to anchor is passing strange.'

'Really?' said Clay. 'Why so?'

'For one thing, they could have placed their ships a deal closer to the shore than they have, sir,' he explained. 'If we should ever chance to break through the line, there will be plenty of deep water on the far side for us to double up on them.'

'They are also spaced more widely than they could be, sir,' added Taylor as he looked up from his own telescope. 'See the gap that has been left between the *L'Orient* and that big two decker directly astern of her. I suppose that is so as to stretch their ships across all of the deep water, so we cannot round the ends of their fleet.'

'Doubtless that is so,' said Clay. He returned his telescope to his eye and continued to examine the enemy. The frigate had sailed much closer since he last looked. Even in the failing light he could now see the mooring buoys that each vessel had in front of her

259

bows. He looked at the ship at the head of the French line. She was a big seventy-four and he watched as her anchor cable strained and lifted against the wind as she swung a little at her moorings.

As she swung at her moorings, repeated Clay to himself. A sensation of excitement prickled the palms of his hands. He looked at the stern of the first ship and searched for a second anchor cable, but he could find none. He moved his telescope on to the next ship. That, too, seemed to be only anchored at the bow. The same was true of the third ship.

'Mr Taylor,' he said, forcing his voice to be calm. 'Would you oblige me and examine the French ship at the windward end of their fleet. Can you tell me how you believe her to be moored?' Taylor looked for a while through his own telescope.

'Anchored by the head only, I should say, sir,' he replied.

'And the second ship?'

'Same as the first, sir,' he confirmed. 'Anchored by the head. Of course with the wind as she lies, that will serve well enough to hold them in the correct position.'

'And if the wind should change?' asked Clay.

'I make no doubt that the French will have allowed sufficient deep water for their ships to swing in, sir,' said Taylor. 'No officer worth his salt would anchor otherwise.... Why are you looking at me like that, sir?'

'Because, my dear George, of what you have just said.' Clay clapped his first lieutenant on the arm and grinned at him. 'At last I see how we might endeavour to lay the fleet against the French to achieve the admiral's desire to overwhelm their van. If the lead French ships are only anchored by the head, they must have left at least a ship's length of deep water all around them. And where there is room for a ship to swing, there is certainly room for one to pass.'

A Man of No Country

'Upon my word, sir, I do believe you are right,' said Taylor. 'We could lead the fleet around the end. With some ships attacking from the far side whilst others engage from this, the enemy will be caught between them.'

'Let us put it to the test,' said Clay. 'Mr Armstrong, lay us on a course to turn about the head of the French fleet, if you please. You will need to sail very close to the bow of that lead ship.'

'Aye aye, sir,' said the master. 'I shall endeavour to let the tip of her bowsprit pass over our heads.'

The *Titan* turned in a long gentle curve and settled on her new course. The sand banks to starboard grew closer, and the depths reported from the bow after each cast of the lead, became shallower. Clay walked back to the stern rail to see if the fleet were turning too. The sun had set now, and he could no longer see any detail of the ships beyond the one directly behind him. What he could see were the rows of blue lights floating through the dusk, all following his lead. He glanced up at the four blue lanterns that now shone brightly above his head and then felt Preston nudge his arm.

'Some sort of commotion, up on the bow of the *Goliath*, sir,' he reported. He glanced back towards the following ship to see a huge bear of a man stride up to the forecastle rail and level a speaking trumpet towards him. Over the gentle sound of the frigate's wake came a loud bellow, in a pronounced Welsh accent.

'Ahoy there *Titan*!' roared the voice. Clay picked up his own speaking trumpet from its becket.

'Good evening to you, Captain Foley, sir,' he replied.

'Never mind good evening, what the hell are you about, Clay?' said the captain of the *Goliath*. 'Do you propose to run me up on one of these sand bars like that damned fool Troubridge?'

'No, sir,' replied Clay. 'The lead French ships are anchored by the head. There will be sea room enough for us to round their fleet

261

and take them between two fires.'

'Round their line, is it?' mused Foley in a loud rumble. 'Are you quite certain there will be enough water? You know I draw a good six feet more than your ship?'

'Quite sure, sir. My sailing master knows what he is about. Follow me closely, and all shall be well.'

'Assuming I can still bloody well see you, that is,' said the Welshman. He eyed the gathering dusk with suspicion. 'Oh, have it your own way, Clay. I had better go and pass the word down the line. If I don't tell Hood in the *Zealous* what your plan is, he will conclude that your navigation is all to cock and head off on his own. Good luck, boyo.'

'Thank you, sir,' Clay replied. Foley waved his speaking trumpet in the air as he hurried back to his own quarterdeck.

Like a mirage, the French ships were melting into the dusk as the *Titan* approached them. Their bare masts and rigging was still clear, a spider's web of black against the evening sky. By contrast, their hulls were now only visible against the shore, because of the glow of light from within them that seeped out through their open gun ports. The faint orange of battle lanterns brushed the surface of the water. Brighter was the occasional red point from a glowing linstock poised above the touchhole of a cannon. On board the frigate, the quarterdeck was washed by an eerie blue light from the lanterns hung high up on her mizzen mast.

The lead French ship was very close now. Her high curved side rose up above him out of the still water. At each square opening, Clay could see a little cluster of faint white faces as the gun crews peered across the narrow stretch of dark water. Others scrutinised him from the quarterdeck rail. Soldiers, with their coats invisible behind the white of their cross belts, pointed muskets in his direction. Officers aimed their telescopes towards him. The murmur of her crew as they talked came clear to him, contrasting with the silence aboard the *Titan*.

'Will they really not fire on us, sir?' whispered Preston, entranced by the mass of cannon so close to them.

'They know that the first broadside, loaded with care before a battle, is the best they will ever fire in an action,' said Taylor. 'They will not waste it on us, for we are too small to count in the balance between the fleets.' He looked back at the *Goliath*, the huge square of her topsail black against the sky. 'That is their mark, God help them.'

'Head sails!' shouted Armstrong, his voice sudden and loud in the night. 'Ready to go about!' The frigate slid on past the lead French ship till she overlapped her bow.

'Helm hard over!' ordered the American and they wheeled around in front of the enemy. Clay felt his hands grip the quarterdeck rail as he waited for the sound of sand and rock grating against the *Titan*'s keel. What if he had been fooled by the French? Perhaps they had moored by the head just to trick him into this bold manoeuvre? Even now the floor of the bay might be rising up towards him. A loud rumble reverberated up through the timbers of the ship, and Clay rushed to the side. Below him he could just make out the lead ship's mooring buoy as it rattled and scrapped along the frigate. The ship continued to turn and the float was left behind. They had rounded the French line.

'What course now, sir?' asked Armstrong, his triumphant face lit from below by the yellow light of the binnacle. Clay opened his mouth to reply, but what he said was lost in an enormous roar as the lead French ship opened fire. The cannon fire was discharged from her far side, just as the *Goliath* had drawn level. For an instant night fled. Clay saw in a flash of brilliant light the British ships as they tailed back across the bay, and the French ones running in a curve away from him. Ahead he saw a single French frigate, moored on her own, and then it was dark again.

'Run down the line of their fleet, Mr Armstrong, and then lay me off the port quarter of that frigate over there,' he ordered. 'The one that is level with the *L'Orient*.'

*****

Night, then day, then night and then day. With each broadside that crashed out, a fresh image of the battle was caught in a burst of light, and each showed the steady advance of Nelson's fleet. Five British seventy-fours had followed the *Titan* around the head of the French fleet, and each had dropped down to anchor next to a different opponent. Now the other ships were ranged up on the outside of the line, so that most of the French had two opponents. The van of their fleet was caught at the centre of a volcano of flame and smoke, while the rest watched helplessly on. With each fresh flare of light, the *Titan* stole closer to the anchored frigate.

'Do you reckon she's seen us?' asked Evans as he watched the latest view of their opponent vanished back into the dark night.

'Aye, she knows we're a-coming alright,' said Trevan. He patted the barrel of the cannon with the flat of his hand. 'We must show up right well against all that there firing away yonder.'

'So why ain't she having a pop?' said the Londoner. He drummed his fingers on the shaft of the rammer. 'We must be in range.'

'Oh, we're in fecking range, sure enough,' said O'Malley, spitting on his hands. 'He's a right cool bastard, that one. Wants us good and close before he wastes any powder on us.'

'Take in topsails there!' shouted the voice of Clay from the dark of the quarterdeck. 'Mr Hutchinson! Are you ready to drop anchor?'

A Man of No Country

'Ready, sir,' came the boatswain's voice from the stern of the ship.

'Mr Preston! Are you ready at the capstan?'

'Aye aye, sir!'

The frigate drifted onwards, her speed slowing all the time as her sail was gathered in somewhere above the seamen's heads.

'Gun crews, are you ready?' said Lieutenant Blake, quieter and closer. The crew of Shango exchanged glances in the orange glow from the battle lamp, and then crouched down into position beside their gun. Rosso knocked the ash from the loop of slow match held on his linstock and then blew the smouldering tip into fiery brilliance. He held his left hand aloft to show his gun was ready. All along the side of the ship similar arms sprang up.

'Drop anchor!' they heard Clay order, followed by a huge splash from behind the ship.

'Anchors away, sir,' yelled the voice of the boatswain.

'Mr Preston, take up the strain!' With a chorus of creaks and groans, the frigate slowed to a halt and rocked to and fro on the water.

'Anchors holding, sir,' yelled Hutchinson.

'There the bastards are,' breathed Evans. He pointed through the open gun port. Close beside them the ghostly lines of a ship seemed to hover above the water, as if they were seeing a reflection of their own frigate, in a dark pool. A line of faint orange squares floated opposite them, and the dark shadows of the gun crews moved about as they made their final preparations. They heard a sharp order in French and the space between the ships became a canyon of fire. Tongues of flame leapt out of the night, followed an instant later by a series of hammer blows all along the side of the *Titan*. Splinters flew as a cannon ball screeched across the planking behind O'Malley, and one of the crew of Belcher reeled back from his gun with blood gushing from his arm. Moments later, debris pattered down from the cut rigging above their heads. In the silence that followed the impact of the French broadside, a calm, strong voice spoke from up on the quarterdeck.

'Mr Preston!' said Clay. 'Let out a further three fathoms of that anchor cable if you please. We are not yet fully aligned with our adversary. Mr Blake! You may open fire when convenient, as can your marines, Mr Macpherson.'

'Main guns! Fire!' yelled the lieutenant. Rosso ducked down to sight along the barrel. The smoke of the French ship's first broadside was thinning and he could see the shadows of the gun crews as they reloaded. A chatter of excited orders in French sounded in the night.

'Point blank range, lads, no need for aiming. Just rattle the gun in and out as quick as quick,' he said, before he yelled a warning. 'Stand clear!' He dabbed the linstock down onto the touch hole. There was a crimson sparkle in the gloom, and the cannon leapt back inboard with a roar, till it creaked to a halt against the pull of the breaching.

Now all their long months of dull training bore fruit. Before the gun carriage had stopped, Evans had the wet sponge of his rammer thrust down the hot barrel to extinguish any sparks, while O'Malley had taken the powder bag from the hands of Dray, the thirteen-year-old allocated to the gun. The boy scampered off, running down to the magazine for the next one. O'Malley and Evans worked smoothly together as charge, ball and wad disappeared into the muzzle, each stage rammed home by the big Londoner.

'Loaded,' yelled Evans as he stepped aside. The rest of the crew threw their weight onto the gun tackles and the cannon trundled forwards till it thumped up against the ship's side. Rosso leaned over and drove his barbed spike down the touch hole and through the serge wall of the charge. He pushed a quill of fine powder after it and stood back.

'Stand clear!' he yelled, and the gun roared out once more.

Again and again they fired their cannon, every move slick and economical as they pummelled away at the French ship. Now any pretence of firing broadsides had disappeared aboard the frigate, as the faster guns outpaced the slower, but none were fired swifter than Shango. Soon the night was lit by a continuous glow of fire that flickered backwards and forwards, up and down the side of the *Titan*. Under the remorseless torrent of shot, the return fire of their opponent started to falter.

Rosso dashed aside the sweat that poured down his face and crouched low over the top of the cannon. It was the twentieth time that they had fired that night and the barrel radiated heat beneath his bare chest, the metal hot to the touch. When Evans had last swabbed out the muzzle, the wet sponge end of his rammer had spat and hissed with steam.

'Stand clear!' Rosso yelled. The gun crew all ducked away to either side and held their hands over their ears against the deep roar of the cannon. But this time there was an ear splitting shriek instead, a shower of sparks flew off the top of the barrel and the carriage collapsed. Shango slumped down, and the sharp smell of ozone filled the air.

'What the fuck...' said Evans. He stared across the top of the cannon into the wide-eyed face of O'Malley. Then he looked down at the the gun and saw a thick, vivid scar of silver scored in the metal. A French cannon ball had flown in through the gun port and grazed along the top of the barrel. All around him dazed members of the crew picked themselves up. Trevan looked at the scar, and then followed the line of it towards the touch hole.

'Where's Rosie?' he asked.

They found the blood-sodden remains of Rosso several feet back. That was where the cannon ball had let his broken body fall to the deck. His lower half seemed untouched by what had happened. His legs lay on the deck, bent and drawn up, like those of someone asleep. But above his wide leather belt, little of their friend was still recognisable.

*****

'The enemy is making sail!' announced Preston. 'Looks like she may have had her fill, sir.'

'I am not surprised, sir,' growled Taylor. 'The men have fought like tigers. We have hit her very hard. I saw her mizzen fall not ten minutes ago, and I believe much of her main mast may have followed it by the board.' Clay walked across to the ship's side. Several of the *Titan*'s cannon chanced to fire at once and their flash illuminated the wreck of their opponent. Her side was pock-marked with holes, and she was now several feet lower in the water. The wreck of her fallen masts littered the black sea all around her. But her tattered tricolour still fluttered over her quarterdeck from the stump of her mizzen, and muskets flashed and banged along her rail. Over the staccato sound of battle, he heard the thunder of axe strokes. They abruptly ended with a heavy splash.

'There goes her anchor cable, sir,' said the first lieutenant from the rail next to him. 'Should we stop firing?'

'Only when she yields, Mr Taylor,' he said. The quarterdeck carronade next to him crashed back on its slide and the muzzle flash lit up the stern of the French frigate as it turned towards them. On the scarred counter, the name *L'Artemise* could just be made out. Above that not a pane of glass remained intact.

268

A Man of No Country

'Mr Armstrong!' called Clay. 'Can I follow her?'

'Not if you value the ship, sir,' said the master. 'She is heading into shoal water, doubtless to run herself aground before she sinks, or is compelled to surrender.' The guns of the frigate continued to batter their opponent, until she limped her way free of the circle of light created by the *Titan*'s muzzle flashes. Clay watched her for a while, sick at heart at the unequal contest. Once she had vanished, he turned back to Taylor and nodded. The first lieutenant put his whistle to his lips and blew a loud blast, and the guns fell silent.

Clay looked around his quarterdeck. It was still illuminated by the cold blue light from above. Most of those who had started the fight were at their posts. Old Amos at the wheel had a bloody rag tied around one hand, and several of the marines had been taken below. Some of the gun crews had lost a few members, but all the carronades were undamaged. A few of the men exchanged backslaps or handshakes, as they delighted in their victory, but most had slumped down for a grateful rest on the deck. At the nearest gun he saw the tall figure of Grainger, stood apart from those around him. The blue light from above hooded his sharp features and made his eyes pools of dark where no expression could be read. Clay walked forward to the quarterdeck rail and looked down onto the main deck. In the warm glow of the battle lanterns, he could see that the eighteen-pounder immediately below his feet had been dismounted by a direct hit. The crew seemed dazed as they stood around the body of a fallen seaman, but most of the other cannon appeared unharmed.

'What state are we in, Mr Taylor?' he asked.

'Surgeon reports fifteen killed and close to thirty wounded, sir,' reported the first lieutenant. 'As for the ship, we have taken a fair battering, but only four balls between wind and water. There is three feet in the well, but the pumps are holding, and the carpenter says he can get at all of the shot holes to plug them. We have two guns out of action. One eighteen-pounder on the starboard side has been damaged beyond repair, and one of the forecastle carronades has been dismounted. The armourer believes he can get the carronade back in action presently.'

'What of the rigging?' asked Clay.

'Cut about mainly,' said Taylor. 'The foretop yard needs to be fished, but the other spars have survived. Mr Hutchinson and his men are working aloft now. All told I believe we can have most of the repairs completed, ready to be back in action in about an hour.'

'Good, because our night's work is not over yet' said Clay. 'Keep the men at their work.'

'Aye aye, sir.'

Clay walked across to the far side of the quarterdeck, to see how the rest of the battle went. The fighting around the van of the French fleet seemed to be over, with that end of the French line invisible in the dark of the night. British warships had slipped down towards him, bringing the battle with them. Now it was the turn of the French centre to be caught between two fires. A few hundred yards from where he stood was a mass of warships, all ablaze with the thunder of cannon. Clay could feel the concussion of the broadsides as solid blows to the front of his chest. Closest to him was the looming cliff that was the massive *L'Orient*. Every one of her hundred and twenty cannon roared away as she battled with the three British ships that surrounded her, like hounds attacking a stag.

'It is a grand sight, is it not, sir,' said Lieutenant Tom Macpherson. The rich scarlet of his marine officer's uniform appeared black in the dark. 'Wonderful, and yet also terrible at the same time. How many scores of men do you suppose are perishing over there with every blast of those cannon?'

A Man of No Country

'I cannot think upon it and yet do my duty, Tom,' said Clay. 'How could I ever take a ship into action, with such thoughts in my mind?'

'No, you are right, sir,' said the Scotsman. 'We military men should not dwell upon what it is we do. But tell me, why do the French ships at the rear of the line not come to their admiral's assistance?' He pointed towards the right. 'There must be four or five of the enemy that have yet to fire a shot away yonder. Are they so in want of courage that they are shy of battle? I am happy to see my enemies defeated, but I would want it done with some honour.'

'It is not courage they lack, just a suitable wind,' said his captain. 'See how the breeze blows from the head of the line towards the rear? It serves us very well as we move down their fleet, and the French not at all. They cannot advance directly into it, and with all these shoals here about, neither can they use it to manoeuvre with.'

'It is strange how the battle has fallen, sir. I thought their dispositions very formidable when we first came into the bay.'

'So they would have been, had we not been able to turn the flank of their fleet. Once that was achieved, they were doomed,' said the captain.

'What should the unengaged ships do then, sir?' asked the Scot.

'The best they could achieve for their country would be to weigh anchor and escape while they yet can and abandon the hopeless position their admiral has placed them in,' said Clay. 'Fortunately for us they have such reserves of both courage and honour that they stay with him, and await the slow, but remorseless advance of our fleet towards them.' He glanced across at the marine and frowned. 'How curious,' he muttered.

'Sir?' said Macpherson.

'My apologies, Tom, I meant no disrespect. It is just that your tunic appeared black a moment ago, and yet now it is scarlet once more.'

'So it is, sir.' Both men looked around them in surprise. The whole ship was bathed in a warm yellow light, as if the sun of a new day had chanced to rise above the horizon. Then the marine caught hold of his captain's arm.

'Good God, sir, look over there!'

The brilliant light came from *L'Orient*, which was ablaze. The guns of her bottom two decks were still in action. They could hear them as they thumped away at the British ships that harried her, but all along her top deck hungry flames licked out of her gun ports and caught on the timber of her sides. As they watched, the fire spread upwards. Beads of golden light rushed in lines up the tarred rope of her rigging, while her masts turned into so many burning crosses as her sails and yards caught fire. High above her were swirling motes of light that flew up to compete with the dome of stars overhead.

Chapter 16
Day

'What a truly dreadful manner in which to perish,' said Macpherson, as he watched the tiny ant-like figures, some with their clothing alight, as they leapt from the blazing flagship into the ink black sea around it. More and more followed as the flames that roared from the hull grew ever fiercer. Fire and smoke had formed into a twisting pillar that rose up above the stricken ship. The *Titan* was several hundred yards from *L'Orient,* yet even in the warm, sultry air they could feel the furnace heat. The sound of cannon fire had petered out all around her, as if the participants in the battle, friend and foe alike, were mesmerised by what they saw.

'Truly dreadful,' repeated Clay. 'But I have no wish to share their fate. That fire will reach her powder shortly. Mr Russell!'

'Sir!' replied the midshipman.

'Go down to the orlop deck and find the gunner,' he said. 'Tell him to close up the magazines. He is to issue no more charges for the guns till he hears from me. Run now, boy!'

'Aye aye, sir,' he replied, as he fled towards the ladder way. Clay strode over to the front of the quarterdeck rail and called down below him.

'Mr Blake! Have all the guns run back in and secured, if you please, and all the ports shut. Any unused powder charges are to be pitched over the side. Then set your gun crews to work filling all the containers they can find with water.'

'Aye aye, sir.' Clay turned next to his first lieutenant.

'Rig hoses to the pumps, Mr Taylor. I want the deck awash with water. Wet the sides of the ship too, and the sails and rigging. Make haste now.'

Throughout the ship, orders rang out as the frigate prepared for what was to follow. From under his feet he felt the rumble of the guns as they were run inboard, and the thump of port lids being slammed shut.

'Mind your back there, begin' yer pardon, sir,' warned William Powell, his voice pure gravel, as he led a party of men past where his captain stood. They all carried buckets that brimmed with water to soak the quarterdeck. Clay looked up into the rigging, every strand of which had turned bright yellow in the fierce light of the blazing ship. High up in the main top Taylor was directing the hoses as they played their jets over the yards and masts. The excess water cascaded down like molten gold.

Satisfied with what he saw, Clay returned his attention to the burning ship. If anything the fire was even more intense. He could no longer look into the heart of the blaze, which seemed as white as a sun. The shadows of British ships moved across in front of him, as they hastened to get clear. He could see that the big French two-decker closest to the blaze had cut her anchor cables and was adrift in the bay, but still *L'Orient* blazed on.

'How can it still be there?' he muttered. 'Surely the flames must have reached the magazine by now?' The sounds of the stricken ship echoed across the water. Above the roar of the fire was the crack of ship's timbers as they burst free to twist and split in the extraordinary heat. He heard the occasional bang of cannons, as they discharged themselves when the flames licked their way up to the touch holes. There was a sudden whoosh as the burning foremast toppled over. And then, in an instant, everything changed.

For the blink of an eye, night was day. The sea was blue at his feet, the ship's side yellow and black, and then the world became fire. The shock of the explosion hit the frigate side on. It heeled her over as it blasted through the rigging like a gale, tearing away spars and stripping the yards of their furled canvas sails. Clay felt himself plucked up and thrown across the deck in a cascade of humanity. Before he reached the planking, the roar of the explosion swept over him in a deafening boom. He crashed to the deck and the wind was knocked out of his lungs. In front of him was Sedgwick, on his hands and knees. He was trying to yell something, but all Clay could hear was ringing. The coxswain pantomimed putting his hands over his head and crouching down, and his captain followed his lead. Moments later, burning debris rained down on the frigate from out of the dark.

Wreckage of all shapes and sizes fell from the sky. The first to arrive were the biggest pieces. Huge baulks of timber, many of them still on fire, that sent up columns of water all around the ship. A few tumbled down through the rigging, ripping and smashing as they came. One crashed onto the long boat, destroying it in an instant. Another struck the ship's belfry and sent the bell rumbling and clanging across the deck. The worst was the curved remains of one of *L'Orient*'s frames, a savage claw of burning oak, that bowled across the quarterdeck. It crushed the crew of the foremost carronade, killing two men outright and badly injured the rest.

Close behind this first onslaught came the smaller pieces. Lengths of spar, pieces of deck planking that whirled and shrieked through the air. Most of them rebounded from the rigging or slammed against the ship's side and then slid down into the dark sea all around them. The last to arrive was the lightest. Little fragments of burning hemp and cinders of smouldering wood, that fluttered down like moths to plop and fizz on the wet planking. Once the last of these had passed, Clay pulled himself unsteadily to his feet. He stamped out a few glowing points near him, and looked around at his ship.

Unnoticed in all the commotion and chaos, the moon had slipped up above the horizon, and it bathed the scene of battle in a silvery light. No ships were firing now. Those that had been gathered around *L'Orient* were all too busy, as they repaired damage and battled with various small fires. Those farther away seemed too stunned to resume the battle. Over the *Titan,* the moon shone down, mixing with the orange glow of battle lanterns on the gun deck and the single remaining blue lamp that still hung in the mizzen mast. In that mixture of light, Clay saw his crew slowly pick themselves up, as if awakened from sleep. They looked about them in surprise, amazed that they yet lived.

'Mr Taylor!' called Clay, his voice faint and distant against the ringing in his ears. He forced himself to gape and yawn and one ear popped clear.

'Mr Taylor!' he said again. 'Where have you got to?'

'Over here, sir,' said a voice from behind him. He turned to see the first lieutenant sat with his back to the mizzen mast, one arm cradled by the other.

'Sorry, sir,' he said, trying to rise. 'The explosion rather flung me upon the mast. I fear my arm may be broke.'

'No matter, George, I can manage very well for now,' Clay said as he helped the officer to his feet and turned towards the midshipman of the watch. 'Mr Russell, will you kindly help Mr Taylor down to see the surgeon.'

A Man of No Country

'I would prefer to stay here, sir,' grumbled Taylor, but he allowed the youngster to lead him below.

'Now Mr Preston,' said the captain to his third lieutenant. 'If you are unharmed, let us set about restoring our ship to some sort of order. Get the beam that destroyed that carronade tossed over the side, and the wounded down to the surgeon. Then see if the armourer can remount it. Tom, your marines can help.'

'Aye aye, sir,' said the Scotsman. He brushed the last few smouldering fragments from his coat and looked around him for his hat. 'Corporal Evans! Over here with your men.'

Sedgwick was already by the dismounted gun. Lying beside it was Grainger, with most of a leg crushed beneath the barrel.

'Alright mate, we'll soon get that off you,' the coxswain said, cradling his shoulders. The planking all around them was slick with blood and the wounded man lay heavy and inert in his arms. He gently felt his neck, and detected the faintest flutter beneath the skin. Powell loomed up on the far side of the carronade with a block and tackle, the afterguard at his heels.

'Leave him, Able, and come and give us a hand,' he growled.

'No, Bill, he is still alive,' said Sedgwick. 'Soon as you get that shifted, I can pull him free.'

'Alive, is he?' said the boatswain's mate. 'That's a shame. I thought the Frogs had saved the hangman a job of work.'

'It ain't like that! You got it all wrong!'

'Have it your own way,' muttered Powell. 'Come on, lads, get this gun shifted. Able's after playing the good bleeding Samaritan. Lively now.'

With a creak and a groan the barrel slowly shifted up off the deck, and Sedgwick was able to pull Grainger free. Blood flowed freely from his wounded leg, and he cried out in pain as he was moved.

'Who is going to help me get him below?' asked the coxswain. The sailors stood around the gun looked on, stony faced. 'He's a fucking shipmate! He wouldn't have left any of you to die!'

'Brown, O'Neil,' ordered Powell. 'Give him a hand.' Two of the sailors joined Sedgwick and helped pick Grainger up, and together they carried him towards the ladder way.

'I am only doing it 'cause you asked, Able,' said the petty officer. 'I ain't doing it for that piece of shit.'

'When this is done, you and me need to talk, Bill,' said Sedgwick, as he disappeared below.

*****

'How can our Rosie be dead?' asked Trevan, half an hour earlier. 'He were stood that close to me, I only had to stretch out to touch him. Then a heartbeat later he had vanished.'

'It was the last fecking shot of the action an' all,' muttered O'Malley. He wiped his eyes on his bare arm. 'That's what was so cruel. The Frogs was beat. Why could he have not hung on another moment?'

'We really owed him, you know?' said Evans. 'Remember how he smoked what was happening when them French soldiers attacked us in St Lucia? He saved our bleeding bacon that day.'

'Able will take it the hardest,' said Trevan, tears now coursing down his cheeks. 'It were Rosie as first showed him his letters.'

'What's going on here?' demanded Midshipman Butler, coming over to the group. Trevan indicated the body of their friend.

'Our gun was hit, sir, and poor Rosso has been an' got himself killed.' Butler looked down at the remains on the deck.

'I am truly sorry, lads,' he said quietly. 'He was a good shipmate. Down there is no place to leave him. Shift his body over to join the others under the break in the forecastle, and then come

A Man of No Country

back. It's cruel, but the battle is far from over. I need you men to close your port lid and pour water over this section of deck.'

'Water on the deck?' queried O'Malley. 'What would we be after doing that for?'

'Mr Taylor's orders,' replied the midshipman. 'It needs to be done sharp. We've got a blazing Frenchie over there that could explode at any moment.'

They lay what was left of Rosso amongst the row of dead sailors and marines. Trevan muttered a few words over their friend and O'Malley made the sign of the cross. Then they hurried back to join the rest of the crew at work on the main deck. They gathered buckets of sea water from those being filled at the pump and threw them all around the ruins of their gun. As they did so, the last few fragments of their friend were washed off the planking and across towards the scuttle where they cascaded over the side and into the sea. Evans looked up from their work and noticed the strange yellow light in the air for the first time. He was just about to comment on it to the others, when *L'Orient* exploded.

The main deck was six feet lower than the exposed quarterdeck where Clay was standing. The sides of the ship rose up like a wall along both sides and those eight inches of seasoned oak protected them from the worst of the explosion. Although they too were stunned by the blast that swept over the frigate, it was only when the ship heeled over that they lost their footing. But the ship's sides could offer them little protection from the beam of oak that descended like a monstrous hammer from the sky. It struck the long boat on the skid beams above their heads, smashing it into a shower of matchwood, and then came to rest next to them, lying amongst the wreckage.

Trevan was the first to shake off all the fragments of broken planking that had fallen on him. He retched and coughed, pulled himself back upright and sucked at a splinter cut on his hand. The huge block of timber rested beside him with smoke pouring up from the blackened surface. It hissed loudly where it sat on the wet deck, while higher up glowing embers of red winked at the Cornishman in the warm air. Some of the fragments of the destroyed long boat that rested against the hot wood burst into yellow flame.

'Fire!' croaked Trevan to the others and pointed at the beam. O'Malley was next to recover. He squatted on his haunches, blood trickling down the side of his face from a cut in his scalp. The light of the fire flickered in front of his eyes.

'Holy Mary!' he exclaimed and stood upright. He kicked Evans, who still lay on the deck. The Londoner rolled over in response with a groan. 'We need some fecking water,' announced the Irishman.

'Good idea,' said Evans as he ran a tongue over his cracked lips. Then he too saw the flames. 'Bleeding hell, Sean! Fuck having a drink. Let's get some of them tubs from around the main mast. Sharp like.'

The men returned with a pair of buckets each and dashed them onto the flames. A large cloud of steam rose up and the fire went out. Then the steam dispersed. The last of the seawater bubbled and spat for a moment on the wall of glowing wood and then vanished with a final hiss. Serpents of smoke replaced the last of the steam. They coiled up from the surface of the wood and a moment later fresh flames licked up the sides of the beam.

'Shit!' said Evans. He looked around for more water.

'What's going on here?' demanded Lieutenant Blake as he strode over. 'A few buckets will never answer! Can't you feel the heat that emanates from it? You might just as well piss on the damned thing! Trevan, O'Malley! Go and get one of the fire hoses.

A Man of No Country

Quickly now, before the whole deck is alight.' Blake watched them go. He rubbed his temples to try and dislodge the ringing in his ears. Then he turned to Evans.

'We need more men,' he said. 'Ahoy there! Mr Butler! Send six men from your gun crews aft to man the pump. You go with them too, Evans.'

'Aye aye, sir,' he said, and stumbled away.

As he took his place among the row of men turning the long bar handle of the pump, Evans looked across the ship. Everywhere he could see signs that the tide of chaos was being turned back into organisation. Up on the forecastle was Hutchinson, the *Titan*'s boatswain, directing his men as they set up a block and tackle to remove the beam that had destroyed the belfry. His long silver pig tail bobbed and swayed in the moonlight as he urged the men on. Pairs of seamen worked to carry away the wounded, taking them towards the hatchways and down to the waiting surgeon in the cockpit. All across the main deck he could see parties of men with buckets of water as they first doused burning fragments of wood, and then carried them to the nearest gun port to be pitched over the side. From below his feet the steady thump of hammers had resumed, as the carpenter continued to repair the earlier damage caused by their fight with the *L'Artemise*. All that he saw showed that the ship had ridden the colossal blow and was now returning to life. And then he caught sight of the line of inert shapes under the forecastle.

'So what have you buggers been about then?' said the man that stood next to the big Londoner. He nodded towards the flaming wreckage of the longboat. 'All you need is a bleeding Guy. I tell you, November the Fifth ain't in it.'

'Just bloody pump,' growled Evans as the long handle whirled round and round. 'I ain't in the mood for no japes.' The canvas hose jerked and swelled into life and a steady jet of sea water pulsed through to Trevan and O'Malley as they brought the fire under control.

*****

'All the debris has been cleared, sir,' reported Preston, the best part of an hour later.

'Was there much fire damage?' asked the captain.

'We did have a nasty looking blaze on the main deck for a while, but Mr Blake was able to deal with it.'

'Good,' said Clay. He looked up into the rigging. In the gentle moonlight he could see parties of men dotted all over the masts, and hear as they called to each other across the dark spaces between the silver threads of cable.

'I have given the boatswain every top man we have, sir, but he still thinks it will be a while before the rigging is to be relied on.'

'Yes, it took the main force of the blast,' said Clay. 'In the meanwhile, let the other hands catch some sleep on the deck between the guns. They must all be exhausted.'

'Aye aye, sir,' said Preston. He stifled a yawn before he turned away. Clay felt waves of tiredness himself, but was determined not to show it. He grasped his hands behind his back and walked over to the quarterdeck rail, where Armstrong stood in the dark and looked out across the sea. He drew in a deep lungful of air, and tasted the tang of burnt wood overlaying the fainter smell of powder smoke.

'It is vexing to have had our ship's bell dismounted,' he said. 'What time do you suppose it to be, Mr Armstrong?' The American looked up at the moon where it rode high over the bay.

'Five bells in the mid watch, I would say, sir,' he replied. 'The night grows old.'

A Man of No Country

Both men gazed at the ships still clustered together in a ragged line across the bay. As they watched a row of orange tongues stabbed out in the night. Moments later the roar of a broadside echoed across to them. A sparkle of little lights glittered in the dark from the same direction, the flashes reflected in the calm water.

'Small arms fire, sir,' said the master. He focused his night glass on the point. 'I think I can see one of our ships lying across the bow of a French one. Might be the *Majestic*?' Another broadside roared out from a different part of the line, followed by a third, and slowly the sound of gun fire increased until it became a steady roar. In the silver light, Clay could see dark shapes on the move as more and more British ships returned to the action. They pushed on down the French line, searching for fresh opponents. Clay watched for a while, and then turned back towards the wheel. He expected to see Preston there, but his place had been taken by the figure of his first lieutenant, without his coat, and with his splinted left arm strapped across his chest.

'George, what are you doing back on deck?' he exclaimed.

'It's only a small break, sir,' said Taylor. 'Mr Corbett has set all to rights. I heard the sound of gunfire, so I returned to my post.' He looked around him, taking in all the damage the explosion had caused, and the mass of seamen at work aloft. 'It looks as if we may be ready for action again shortly. I had best get another three blue lights swayed aloft to replace those we have lost. Before our own side take us for a low Frenchman, sir.'

Clay thought about ordering his deputy below again, but in the faint light of the binnacle he caught sight of the pleading look in his eye.

'Thank you, Mr Taylor,' he said. 'A timely suggestion. Please make it so.'

'Aye aye, sir.' Clay cupped a hand against the side of his mouth and called up towards the main top.

'Mr Hutchinson! The battle has resumed. When can I make sail again?'

'Another hour, sir,' replied the harassed boatswain. 'These here main shrouds have been wounded something cruel. If we was to set any sail now, I couldn't answer for the consequences.'

'Very well, you shall have your hour, and then we sail. Understood?'

'Aye aye, sir!'

*****

An hour later the first rose hint of dawn was visible on the eastern horizon. Some desultory fighting still went on towards the rear of the French line, but across most of the bay, the dark shapes of warships, both victors and their prizes, swung in clumps at anchor in various states of damage. Tendrils of powder smoke drifted like river mist over the surface of the sea. The still grey water was covered by dark shapes that bobbed and slopped in the gentle current. Clay looked at them in the dim light. He could see shattered pieces of wood and fragments of spars, together with other pieces of flotsam that rolled low in the water. One drifted nearer to the ship and he realised that it was a body. There were hundreds of them, dotted all across the sea.

Towards the shore lay the wreck of the frigate they had fought, *L'Artemise*. She was tipped over to one side on a sand bank, where her crew had abandoned her and taken to their boats. The cutter Clay had sent across to set fire to her had only just returned. He could see a thick column of smoke that rose up over her, and the first orange flames, bright in the grey morning light. A little farther east was the blackened and dismasted hull of the French eighty-gun *Tonnant*, hard aground too. Captain Dupetit-Thouars's ship had been just behind *L'Orient*, and had taken the full brunt of the explosion.

On board the *Titan*, the guns were run out and manned once more, and the capstan clanked round as it drew the frigate sternward towards her anchor. Clay stood at the very back of the ship and watched as the thick, wet anchor cable slithered on board. He was so concentrated on the frigate's progress that Taylor had to tug at his sleeve to get his attention.

'Sir,' he hissed. 'Look over there!' Out of the gloom behind them, three huge elephantine shapes had appeared, drifting down towards them. None of them showed any blue lights. Clay called over his shoulder towards the wheel.

'Easy there at the capstan, Mr Preston!' he ordered, and the ship stopped moving through the water. 'Mr Blake, stand by larboard side guns! Mr Russell, a speaking trumpet if you please.' The midshipman ran over to the captain and handed him the cone of brass. Clay pointed it towards the nearest of the ships.

'Ship ahoy!' he yelled. 'What ship is that?' There was a pause, and the huge vessel loomed closer still. Then the angle changed a little, and he saw a row of blue lights appear from behind the spreading square of its topsail.

'*Goliath*!' came the reply in a deep bass. 'Is that you, boyo?' Clay briefly closed his eyes and sighed with relief. The big seventy-four stood on a little farther, and in the pearly light of dawn he could now recognise the ship. The shaggy-haired figurehead had lost most of its beard, replaced with a white gash of splintered wood, but the angry eyes still glared down at him. The sides of the *Goliath* were blackened with powder smoke, and her topsails were full of holes, but all her guns were run out, and she seemed ready for more action.

'Captain Foley!' said Clay. 'I give you joy of this victory, sir.'

'My thanks, but it is not quite over yet,' replied the Welshman. 'Their van and centre have surrendered to us, or blown up like, but their rear is still game. We're off to conclude matters. What state are you in?'

'Just finished repairs and about to weigh anchor,' he replied.

'Good man!' rumbled Foley. The *Goliath* was now level with the frigate, and the Welshman looked straight down on Clay from his quarterdeck rail. He waved a hand towards the other ships. 'I've got Saumarez in the *Orion* and Ball in the old *Alexander* with me. Why don't you join our happy band?'

'With all my heart, sir,' replied Clay. 'Where is the admiral?'

'God knows in all this confusion. Make haste, or the battle will be over.'

By the time the *Titan* had pulled up her anchor, the three battered seventy-fours were a quarter of a mile ahead of the frigate, and stood in towards the remains of the French fleet. The sun had slipped above the horizon, and Clay could now see where another tentacle of British ships advanced down the outside of the French line, to cut off the enemy's escape.

'Did you ever see such a completed victory, sir?' enthused Taylor. He wanted to thump the quarterdeck rail with his fists, but with only one hand available the effect was rather diminished.

'Surely the last French ships can see their peril as clearly as we can, sir,' said Preston from Clay's other side as he looked up from his telescope. 'They have fought well, but they must fly now unless they are all to perish.'

'They must,' agreed Clay. He looked through his own spy glass. 'And I believe they may well be about to, if you direct your gaze towards the nearest ship in that line.'

'What have you seen, sir?' asked Taylor.

'Yes, I see, sir,' said Preston. 'The same is happening with the one beyond it.'

'What is happening?' demanded Taylor.

'And now on board the others,' supplemented Clay.

'So it is,' said Preston as he swung his telescope in that direction. 'Although two have been so badly damaged that I doubt they will succeed in escaping.'

'Sir! Mr Preston! I beg of you! I cannot operate my spy glass with a single arm. Please, please, tell me what is going on!' exclaimed the first lieutenant, his face flushed.

'Your pardon, George,' said his captain. 'That was unforgivable. With our glasses we were able to observe—'

'There they go, sir!' said Preston. Clay's telescope was half way back to his eye when he caught sight of his first lieutenant. He forced his telescope back down again. '—that the crews of the French ships have all been sent aloft,' he continued. 'See, that nearest frigate is weighing anchor.'

The remaining French frigates that were moored near the shallows blossomed into sail, their canvas pink as shell in the light of the early morning sun. They turned tail at the approach of the battered British ships and fled for open water.

'We have little chance of overhauling them, with our patched up rigging, sir,' moaned Preston. 'Au revoir, till we meet again.' He turned his attention to the last four ships of the line.

'They have cut free their anchors and are making sail too,' said Clay. 'But you need no spy glass to see that now, Mr Taylor.'

The officers all watched as the four ships diverged before the menace of the British fleet's approach. The two undamaged seventy-fours headed for the open sea to join the frigates. The two damaged ones turned the other way and limped towards the shallows. The *Goliath*, *Orion* and *Alexander* bombarded them as they went, till the French ships had run themselves aground.

Philip K Allan

'Get in sail and drop anchor again, if you please, Mr Preston,' ordered Clay. 'There is little more we can do now. Once all is secured we will let the hands sleep.

'Aye aye, sir,' replied the lieutenant.

While the frigate moored, Clay and Taylor looked at the two ships that had run themselves into the shoal water. They had launched their boats now, and the first of them were heading for the shore, full of crewmen anxious to avoid capture.

'A fat lot of good that shall do them,' said Clay. 'Without ships they will be doomed to spend the rest of their days here in Egypt.'

'I wonder what they will make of this victory at home, sir,' said Taylor, after a while.

'How do you mean, George?' asked his captain. His head drooped with tiredness.

'I meant the scale of it, sir. Apart from those four that have got away, we destroyed the whole damned fleet! I can't recall ever hearing of such a triumph. Not even Hawke achieved as much at Quiberon Bay.'

'No, you are right,' said Clay. 'It was terrible at times, but I do believe we have played out part in something extraordinary.' He turned from the rail at the approach of the surgeon. He was dressed in shirt sleeves and a blood-spattered apron, and his arms were stained black to the elbows. In odd contrast his hands looked pink and clean, where he had washed them.

'I fear you have had a very busy night, Mr Corbett,' he said.

'I have indeed, sir, but perhaps the butcher's bill is less than you may have feared. Most of those I treated later in the action had minor burns. They at least should all recover.' He handed the list of names across to his captain. Clay scanned through the paper, his lips moving as he counted.

'Joshua Rosso?' he said looking up. 'That is a sad loss. He has

288

served with me since I was a lieutenant.'

'He was killed outright, sir,' said the surgeon. 'I never had the opportunity to treat him.' Clay continued to read, the names flowing past him unnoticed as he thought about the man from Bristol, until another name caught his attention. He backtracked a few lines and looked up.

'How did John Grainger come to fall?' he asked.

'He was part of the quarterdeck carronade crew that was struck by a piece of debris,' said Corbett. 'Your coxswain brought him down to me, while I was treating Mr Taylor here. I had to remove his leg, but he had such massive trauma to his abdomen that he perished soon afterwards.'

'Twenty-two dead and forty-eight injured, said Clay. 'It could have been considerably worse.'

Chapter 17
Home

Two weeks later, Captain Alexander Clay hurried up the front steps of Sir William Hamilton's villa once more, conscious that he was going to be late. He yanked at the bell pull and then stepped back from the door to better see his reflection in the glossy green paint. He pulled his coat straight and checked that his neck cloth had not become too disordered in his rush up from the landing stage, where he had left Sedgwick and his barge. After what seemed like an eternity to the fretting Clay, the door was swung open by the bewigged footman he remembered from his last visit.

'Good day, capitano,' the man intoned.

'Good day to you,' said Clay. 'Is the admiral here?'

'Of course, signore. Please to follow me.' He glided across the polished wooden floor in the direction of the orangery at a stately, but leisurely pace. Clay followed behind him, trying his best not to hop from one foot to the other. When they entered the room, Nelson was reclined next to Lady Emma on the chaiselongue he remembered from his last visit. He thought he had caught sight of her stroking his hair, but they moved apart when he was announced. The admiral rose with a smile towards him and held out his left hand.

'Captain Clay, a pleasure as always,' he said. There was genuine warmth in the blue eye that peered out from below a large white bandage.

'My apologies for being late, Sir Horatio,' said Clay. 'When I received your note I made haste to find you onboard the *Vanguard*. I had no notion that you would be ashore. How does your injury progress?'

'Well enough, I thank you,' he said, touching a hand to his bandage. 'I tell you, Clay, when I was struck on the head, I thought my end was come. I dropped senseless to the deck with a flap of my forehead the size of prayer book hanging down over my good eye. But once the surgeon had stitched it back in place, all was well.'

'So you missed much of the battle, I collect?' said Clay.

'Quite so,' replied Nelson. 'I felt the shock when *L'Orient* took fire, of course, but little else besides. Perhaps you now comprehend why I insisted on rehearsing every possible eventuality with my captains beforehand? They had such a thorough knowledge of my wishes that my inability to direct matters was of little consequence to the outcome of the battle.'

'And you are quite restored, then, Sir Horatio?'

'I still get the most vexing of pains in my head, but I daresay they shall pass in time. The ministrations of Lady Emma have been most beneficial.' Clay turned towards her.

'Good day to your ladyship,' he said. 'I trust I find you well?'

'Tolerably so, I thank you, captain. As ever it is a joy to see you,' she said. If it was a joy to see him, Lady Emma concealed it well. Her face displayed as much pleasure as one of her husband's marble busts. 'But should you not be addressing the admiral as His Grace?' she continued.

'I am not sure that I follow your ladyship,' said Clay.

'King Ferdinand of the Two Sicilies made me a duke this morning,' explained Nelson with a smirk. 'The whole country is quite enthralled by my victory. I am to be guest of honour at a ball tonight at the palace, in which all the ladies are to come dressed *á l'Egyptien*. Isn't it splendid! Apparently news of my victory is spreading like fire across the courts of Europe.'

'I give you joy of your new rank, Your Grace,' said Clay. Nelson held up a deprecating hand.

'Please, Captain Clay, I shall remain plain Sir Horatio in the service. Well, at least until George of the One Britain confirms my earldom, eh what!' Nelson and Lady Emma laughed together at the prospect, and after a moment Clay joined in.

'Do take a seat,' urged Nelson at last. 'Would you like a drink?'

'A glass of Sir William's Marsala would be pleasant, thank you,' said Clay, and Lady Emma waved the footman forward. Nelson accepted a glass and then regarded his frigate captain over its rim.

'I read the surveyor's report on the state of your ship this morning,' he said. 'It would seem that the *Titan* was decidedly pulled about by that explosion. He states that only a major rebuild of the hull will answer to restore her fully.'

'He is quite correct, Sir Horatio. She has become rather crank since the battle. The large frigate we had just defeated had done a deal of damage, and then we were roughly handled by the blast when the *L'Orient* sunk.'

'That is my one regret,' said Nelson, 'that I missed the explosion. Everyone tells me it was truly spectacular. Do you know, she took an absolute fortune down with her? The French looted Malta most thoroughly, as is their wont, and then left all that treasure aboard. Can you imagine all the wealth accumulated by the Knights of St John over the centuries? The gifts of medieval kings, the loot of crusader armies, all of it gone, in an instant.'

'Goodness!' exclaimed Clay. 'Why was it not landed?'

'Frogs thought it was safer aboard.' The twinkle returned to the single eye. 'It was one of many matters in which Admiral de Brueys was sadly mistaken, what?' Lady Hamilton laughed aloud at this and was rewarded by a pat on her knee from her companion, before he returned his attention to Clay.

'I meant to imply no criticism earlier when I raised the state of your ship,' said the admiral. 'It is every Englishman's duty to annoy the French. You can hardly have taken such a forward role in the battle as you did without incurring some damage. I consider your conduct and zeal in the campaign to have been quite exemplary.'

'Thank you, Sir Horatio.'

'No, my problem is that I have thirteen ships of the line, all of which stand in need of considerable repair, and only the modest resources of the dockyard here in Naples to perform them. The state of poor Darby's *Bellerophon* is truly shocking — he fought *L'Orient* for an hour on his own, and had over two hundred of his people killed or wounded. And that is before I even consider the repairs required to the French ships that we captured. I will send some of them into Gibraltar for a refit, but even so, it will be many months before the *Titan* can be repaired here.'

'I understand,' said Clay. He pointed with his glass towards the glittering waters of the bay of Naples and the pine-covered islands out to sea. 'I can imagine worse places to be laid up, sir.'

'I am sure you can,' said Nelson. 'But you misunderstand me. I have no intention of allowing such an active officer as you to remain idle for so long. The *Titan* can be moved safely enough, I collect?'

'She can sail after a fashion,' said Clay. 'But I would not like to answer for her if she was exposed to the rigors of another battle.'

'Good, because after all my pleading to Lord St Vincent for frigates, I find that he is about to bless me with no fewer than four such vessels. I can certainly use them, although it is a pity that I no longer have an enemy fleet to hunt,' said Nelson. 'All of which permits me to release you to return home, where the *Titan* can receive the attention she needs.'

'Home, Sir Horatio?' repeated Clay. 'God bless my soul, how unexpected. Are you sure that you have no further need for me?'

'I can always make use of an enterprising officer,' said Nelson. 'But that is hardly the point.' He had a twinkle in his eye again, but for the life of him Clay could not think why. After a moment Nelson exchanged a glance with Lady Emma.

'Do you truly not see what this means?'

'Beyond the fact that I am to be sent home, Sir Horatio?'

'Alexander, I am sending you home with my despatch on the battle,' said the admiral. 'I am sensible of the distinction that will come to the bearer of such a document, given the news of the great victory it will contain. You are sure to be rewarded. I imagine you will be presented to the King. It is the principal honour I have to offer to one of my captains, and I want you to have it. Are you not pleased?'

'Excessively so,' smiled Clay. 'Sir Horatio, you quite take my breath away. I am truly delighted, both for the honour that you do me, and in truth also at the prospect that I will see my wife again. We have been apart for almost a year now, and before that we had barely spent more than a few months together.' Lady Emma snorted at this, and the two men broke off to look at her.

'My apologies, I am sure. The pollen in here can be quite overwhelming at times. If you gentlemen will excuse me.' She rose to her feet and swept from the room.

'You seem to have a, eh, devoted admirer there, Sir Horatio,' said Clay with care.

'I do, don't I?' said the admiral. He smiled after the departing figure. 'She is so chaste, so pure of thought, so modest. Oh, my dear sir, has the pollen got to you, too? Giuseppe! A glass of water for the captain, he seems to be choking on his drink.'

'I am sorry,' spluttered Clay. 'I do not know what can have come over me.'

'No matter,' said Nelson. He reached across for a heavy looking, sealed package that rested on a small table next to him. 'You seem to be quite restored now. Here is the despatch. Complete your stores today and sail at first light tomorrow. When you get home, you should ride to London and deliver this into the hands of Lord Spencer himself at the Admiralty. Let no one try and prevent you, for the honour is yours and yours alone. You have earned it.'

*****

Later that day, Clay sat at his desk and completed the indents for all the stores that had been taken onboard. It was tedious work to be doing on a hot afternoon. The windows across the back of the stern cabin were all open, which allowed a welcome breeze to drift in and ruffle the front of his shirt. A stronger breath lifted up the pile of papers on his desk for a moment, to reveal Nelson's despatch underneath. He drew the waxed canvas package towards him and hefted it in his hand. His eyes travelled up from the despatch to the portrait of his wife on the far bulkhead.

'What do you think, Lydia my angel?' he said. He held the package up for the blue painted eyes to view. 'Will this truly deliver us some fame and position at last? Perhaps your family might become a little less condescending to me when they hear that I have met with the King? Nelson started life as the son of a rural parson, just like me, you know, and he will be a peer of the realm after this battle.' The eyes smiled back at him, and he noticed for the first time that one eye brow was arched a little higher than the other.

'You are quite right, my dear, I had forgotten the excellence of his connections. Perhaps if I, too, had been blessed with an uncle who was comptroller of the Navy Board, I might have risen rather more smoothly through the service.'

He turned the despatch over and felt the crinkle of the stiff paper inside. At one end of the package his sensitive fingers found some hard, round shapes. A few musket balls, he concluded, to make it sink in the event of capture. I would dearly love to know what he has written about me, he thought, and then he opened the top drawer of his desk and placed the envelope inside. He closed and locked it. All in good time, he told himself. First there is something else I would like to have settled. He raised his voice and called towards the cabin door.

'Pass the word for my coxswain,' he ordered. The sentry outside sent the word on, and he returned to his paperwork. After a few minutes there was a knock at the door.

'Come in,' said Clay. The marine sentry outside held the door open and a burly figure ducked through it. Clay looked up from his desk and returned his pen to its stand.

'Ah, Sedgwick,' he said. 'I sent for you so that I might express my regret for the death of Joshua Rosso. I know he was a good shipmate of yours. He helped you to learn your letters, did he not?'

'Yes, sir, he did,' said Able. 'Thank you, sir.' Clay picked up a sheet of paper from among those on the desk.

'We lost a number of good shipmates in that battle, but few that we shall miss more than Rosso. Did he ever share with you the particulars of his circumstances when he joined the navy?'

'A little, sir. I know how it was all a bit rushed.'

'Indeed, not unlike yourself,' said Clay. 'Did you know that your friend's name was not Rosso at all but Jones, and that he was a fugitive from justice?'

'I did know that, sir, but I am quite taken aback that you should.' Clay laughed at this.

'You mean you are amazed that Pipe should be so well informed? I found all that out before you came into the service. It was back when I was first lieutenant on the *Agrius*. A Bristol merchant aboard an East Indiaman we were convoying chanced to see Rosso and thought he recognised him. Later, I tricked Rosso into responding to his true name, during a storm. That is how I found out. I wonder what made him choose the name Rosso, for he certainly was not Italian.'

'He told me it was painted over a shop front he happened to pass on his way down to the docks to volunteer, sir,' said Sedgwick. 'He thought that with his dago looks, he might pass for the son of one. It answered well enough, although there were some who wondered why he could no more speak the lingo than they could when we was ashore in Naples.'

'I imagine that might have seemed odd,' said the captain. 'How did he cover for his lack of Italian?'

'By telling any that asked that his father came from a quite different part of the country, where the language was much more refined.'

'Did he now?' chuckled Clay. 'He was a clever man. I did think to turn him in for a while, but then I reflected on what a good seaman he was. I spoke about him with a brother officer, who pointed out to me how few sailors would be left, if we once resolved to purge our ships of all their former criminals, and so I let matters rest.'

'Sir,' said Sedgwick, after a pause. 'May I ask a question?'

'By all means.'

'If by some chance the nature of Rosso's past had been reported to you, by another seaman for example, what might you have done?'

'I doubt I would have taken any particular action. Remember that I already knew much of it. Why do you ask?'

'Eh, no reason, sir.' Clay looked at him for a long moment and waited for more, but his coxswain's face remained impassive.

'I note that the crew seem rather more content of late,' he said. 'Does that indicate that you have succeeded in discovering who was behind all the thefts and the murder of young Oates?'

'Yes, sir, I did,' replied Sedgwick. 'As it turned out, the same person was responsible for both. They are no longer in a position to harm the crew.'

'I see. Is that because the person fell in our recent battle?'

'That's right, sir. You committed his body to the deep the day after we licked the Frogs.' Clay pulled the sheet of casualties across his desk and ran his finger down the list. He stopped at one name and tapped it.

'And the hands know who it was, and are content that he is no longer aboard?'

'Yes, sir. I have spread the word, sir.'

Clay stood up and walked across to the open windows. Outside the bay Naples slumbered in the hot August sun. A small fishing boat, its hull painted pale green, sailed under the stern of the frigate and the man at the tiller glanced up at him from under his straw hat and waved in friendly fashion.

'I always had my doubts about him,' he muttered, still looking out into the bay. 'Perhaps one should never trust a man who is prepared to lie so readily about his past. Mr Taylor tells me that amongst his possessions was found some manner of journal in which he had recorded a long catalogue of revolting acts. I sometimes find myself doubting if he was even truly English. Well, if he did such a wicked thing to young Oates, he deserved his fate.'

Sedgwick frowned at this, and opened his mouth to correct his captain, but then he stopped. He regarded Clay's back for a moment, silhouetted against the bright sunlight outside. Perhaps it was better this way. In that moment he decided he would let matters lie, as the captain had once done, when he was a lieutenant, in a storm. After all, it was the last thing that he would be able to do for his friend.

The End

Note from the Author

Historical fiction is a blend of truth and the made up, and this is certainly the case with *A Man of No Country*, in which I have shamelessly woven my story through the momentous events of 1798. For readers who would like to understand where the boundary between fiction and truth runs, the *Titan* is fictitious, as are all the characters that make up her crew. That said, I have tried my best to ensure that my descriptions of the frigate and the lives of her crew are as accurate as I am able. Where I have failed to achieve this, any errors are my own.

One member of her crew requires special mention. This is the Man of No Country himself, John Grainger. While he is my own creation, the extracts from his journal, discovered by Able Sedgwick, are not. I have taken them from one found amongst the personal effects of William Davidson, an able seaman on board HMS *Niger*. I was first introduced to this remarkable document by an archivist at the National Maritime Museum in Greenwich, London. Davidson claims to have served aboard the *Saint Dinnan*, a Russian privateer turned pirate in 1788. Apart from a few minor alterations to correct spelling and grammar, and to fit the extracts to my story, I have essentially quoted him verbatim.

The *Charlotte* of Bristol, the *San Giovanni Battista*, the *Fleur de Provence,* the *Saint Dmitry* and the Spanish snow captured by the *Titan* are made up. Other than this, all other ships mentioned were present in the locations and times that I place them. With regard to named characters, the rule of thumb is that major ones are historic, while the minor ones are my own creation. So, for example, in the dinner scene aboard *L'Orient* at the start of Chapter 14, Lieutenant Mallet is fictitious, but the other named naval officers are genuine. My decision to include so many historical characters in my book comes with a certain amount of trepidation. Trying to imagine how well-loved historical giants such as Nelson and Emma Hamilton spoke and acted is a dangerous business. I have done my best to portray them as I imagine they might have been. If they are very different from the picture you have of them, I hope this has not have spoilt your enjoyment of my novel.

Nelson's chase of Napoleon's fleet the length of the Mediterranean and his subsequent victory at the Battle of the Nile, make a fine backdrop to any work of fiction. My particular account does come at the cost of taking a few liberties with the historical record. The role of persuading Sir John Acton to allow Nelson to base his fleet at Naples, which I co-opted for Clay, rightfully belongs to Thomas Troubridge. I also inserted Clay and the *Titan* into the battle itself so as to allow them to act as the eyes of the reader. In reality there was no British frigate present that night. The British line was led by Thomas Foley of the *Goliath*, and it is to him that the credit is due for spotting the French were moored by the bow, prompting him to take the British van around the head of the French fleet. The *Culloden* did run aground, but this occurred much later in the battle than shown in my account.

About The Author

Philip K. Allan

Philip K. Allan comes from Watford in the United Kingdom. He still lives in Hertfordshire with his wife and his two teenage daughters. He has spent most of his working life to date as a senior manager in the motor industry. It was only in the last few years that he has given that up to concentrate on his novels full time.

He has a good knowledge of the ships of the 18th century navy, having studied them as part of his history degree at London University, which awoke a lifelong passion for the period. He is a member of the Society for Nautical Research and a keen sailor. He believes the period has unrivalled potential for a writer, stretching from the age of piracy via the voyages of Cook to the battles and campaigns of Nelson.

From a creative point of view he finds it offers him a wonderful platform for his work. On the one hand there is the strange, claustrophobic wooden world of the period's ships; and on the other hand there is the boundless freedom to move those ships around the globe wherever the narrative takes them. All these possibilities are fully exploited in the Alexander Clay series of novels.

His inspiration for the series was to build on the works of novelists like C.S. Forester and in particular Patrick O'Brian. His prose is heavily influenced by O'Brian's immersive style. He too uses meticulously researched period language and authentic nautical detail to draw the reader into a different world. But the Alexander Clay books also bring something fresh to the genre, with a cast of fully formed lower deck characters with their own back histories and plot lines in addition to the officers. Think *Downton Abbey* on a ship, with the lower deck as the below stairs servants.

If You Enjoyed This Book Visit

PENMORE PRESS

www.penmorepress.com

All Penmore Press books are available directly through our website, amazon.com, Barnes and Noble and Nook, Sony Reader, Apple iTunes, Kobo books and via leading bookshops across the United States, Canada, the UK, Australia and Europe.

The Captain's Nephew

by

Philip K.Allan

After a century of war, revolutions, and Imperial conquests, 1790s Europe is still embroiled in a battle for control of the sea and colonies. Tall ships navigate familiar and foreign waters, and ambitious young men without rank or status seek their futures in Naval commands. First Lieutenant Alexander Clay of HMS Agrius is self-made, clever, and ready for the new age. But the old world, dominated by patronage, retains a tight hold on advancement. Though Clay has proven himself many times over, Captain Percy Follett is determined to promote his own nephew.

Before Clay finds a way to receive due credit for his exploits, he'll first need to survive them. Ill-conceived expeditions ashore, hunts for privateers in treacherous fog, and a desperate chase across the Atlantic are only some of the challenges he faces. He must endeavor to bring his ship and crew through a series of adventures stretching from the bleak coast of Flanders to the warm waters of the Caribbean. Only then might high society recognize his achievements —and allow him to ask for the hand of Lydia Browning, the woman who loves him regardless of his station.

PENMORE PRESS
www.penmorepress.com

A Sloop of War

by
Philip K.Allan

This second novel in the series of Lieutenant Alexander Clay novels takes us to the island of Barbados, where the temperature of the politics, prejudices and amorous ambitions within society are only matched by the sweltering heat of the climate. After limping into the harbor of Barbados with his crippled frigate *Agrius* and accompanied by his French prize, Clay meets with Admiral Caldwell, the Commander in Chief of the island. The admiral is impressed enough by Clay's engagement with the French man of war to give him his own command.

The *Rush* is sent first to blockade the French island of St Lucia, then to support a landing by British troops in an attempt to take the island from the French garrison. The crew and officers of the *Rush* are repeatedly threatened along the way by a singular Spanish ship, in a contest that can only end with destruction or capture. And all this time, hanging over Clay is an accusation of murder leveled against him by the nephew of his previous captain.

Philip K Allan has all the ingredients here for a gripping tale of danger, heroism, greed, and sea battles, in a story that is well researched and full of excitement from beginning to end.

PENMORE PRESS
www.penmorepress.com

On the Lee Shore

by

Philip K.Allan

Newly promoted to Post Captain, Alexander Clay returns home from the Caribbean to recover from wounds sustained at the Battle of San Felipe. However, he is soon called upon by the Admiralty to take command of the frigate HMS Titan and join the blockade of the French coast. But the HMS Titan will be no easy command with its troubled crew that had launched a successful mutiny against its previous sadistic captain. Once aboard, Clay realizes he must confront the dangers of a fractious crew, rife with corrupt officers and disgruntled mutineers, if he is to have a united force capable of navigating the treacherous reefs of Brittany's notorious lee shore and successfully combating the French determined to break out of the blockade.

PENMORE PRESS
www.penmorepress.com

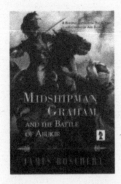

MIDSHIPMAN GRAHAM AND THE
BATTLE OF
ABUKIR
BY
JAMES BOSCHERT

It is midsummer of 1799 and the British Navy in the Mediterranean Theater of operations. Napoleon has brought the best soldiers and scientists from France to claim Egypt and replace the Turkish empire with one of his own making, but the debacle at Acre has caused the brilliant general to retreat to Cairo.

Commodore Sir Sidney Smith and the Turkish army land at the strategically critical fortress of Abukir, on the northern coast of Egypt. Here Smith plans to further the reversal of Napoleon's fortunes. Unfortunately, the Turks badly underestimate the speed, strength, and resolve of the French Army, and the ensuing battle becomes one of the worst defeats in Arab history.

Young Midshipman Duncan Graham is anxious to get ahead in the British Navy, but has many hurdles to overcome. Without any familial privileges to smooth his way, he can only advance through merit. The fires of war prove his mettle, but during an expedition to obtain desperately needed fresh water – and an illegal duel – a French patrol drives off the boats, and Graham is left stranded on shore. It now becomes a question of evasion and survival with the help of a British spy. Graham has to become very adaptable in order to avoid detection by the French police, and he must help the spy facilitate a daring escape by sea in order to get back to the British squadron.

"Midshipman Graham and The Battle of Abukir is both a rousing Napoleonic naval yarn and a convincing coming of age story. The battle scenes are riveting and powerful, the exotic Egyptian locales colorfully rendered." – John Danielski, author of *Capital's Punishment*

PENMORE PRESS
www.penmorepress.com

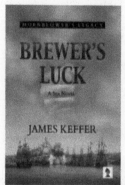

BREWER'S LUCK

BY

JAMES KEFFER

After gaining valuable experience as an aide to Governor Lord Horatio Hornblower, William Brewer is rewarded with a posting as first lieutenant on the frigate HMS *Defiant*, bound for American waters. Early in their travels, it seems as though Brewer's greatest challenge will be evading the wrath of a tyrannical captain who has taken an active dislike to him. But when a hurricane sweeps away the captain, the young lieutenant is forced to assume command of the damaged ship, and a crew suffering from low morale.

Brewer reports their condition to Admiral Hornblower, who orders them into the Caribbean to destroy a nest of pirates hidden among the numerous islands. Luring the pirates out of their coastal lairs will be difficult enough; fighting them at sea could bring disaster to the entire operation. For the *Defiant* to succeed, Brewer must rely on his wits, his training, and his ability to shape a once-ragged crew into a coherent fighting force.

PENMORE PRESS
www.penmorepress.com

Capital's Punishment
by
John Danielski

The White House is in flames, the Capitol a gutted shell. President Madison is in hiding. Organized resistance has collapsed, and British soldiers prowl the streets of Washington.

Two islands of fortitude rise above the sea of chaos—one scarlet, one blue. Royal Marine Captain Thomas Pennywhistle has no wish to see the young American republic destroyed; he must strike a balance between his humanity and his passion for absolute victory. Captain John Tracy of the United States Marines hazards his life on the battlefield, but he must also fight a powerful conspiracy that threatens the country from within.

Pennywhistle and Tracy are forced into an uneasy alliance that will try the resolve of both. Together, they will question the depth of their loyalties as heads and hearts argue for the fate of a nation

PENMORE PRESS
www.penmorepress.com

Penmore Press

Challenging, Intriguing, Adventurous, Historical and Imaginative

www.penmorepress.com

Printed in July 2023
by Rotomail Italia S.p.A., Vignate (MI) - Italy